MW01490456

Even in Death

EVEN IN DEATH

RANDI GARNER

Cover design, map illustration, interior design, and formatting by Rena Violet (Coversbyviolet.com, @violet.book.design)

Interior illustration by Karina Giada (karinagiada.com)

Interior Illustration by Avendell (@avendellart)

Developmental and line edits by Brittany Corley (thisbitchreads.com)

Copy edits and proofreading by Christian Chase Garner (@christianchasegarner)

*To those who **feel deeply and** love fiercely.*
*Don't let the world tell **you that you** are too soft.*

AUTHOR NOTE

Dear Reader,

I am so happy that you are here. From the beginning of this journey, Finnian and Cassian's story has held a special place in my heart. I could fill hundreds of pages with them alone. Parting ways has been difficult, but I am so excited to share their story with you. I hope you fall in love with them as much as I have.

Along with their beautiful, heartfelt moments, their story also has a brutality to it. They are both deeply flawed, morally gray characters. Necromancy and death are also significant parts of the story. Because of that, I want to give you a gentle warning before stepping into this book:

This story contains dark themes and mature content not suitable for readers under the age of 18. On the next page, you will find a list of trigger warnings. I advise looking over them before continuing.

Above all, please do what you need to preserve your peace and protect your mental health. Your happiness is important to me; take care of yourselves.

<3,

Randi

TRIGGER WARNINGS

Dead animal
(does not show the death of the animal on the page)

Sexual abuse
(does not go farther than coercion)

Torture
(physical/mental/emotional)

Abuse
(physical/mental/emotional)

Explicit sexual content

Alcohol consumption

Blood and gore

Swearing

Violence

Bullying

Murder

Suicide

Death

Grief

PTSD

THIRTEENTH YEAR

Finnian

"I will make it better."

Finnian's fingers shook against the damp feathers of the bird. His feet moved faster through the muddy terrain of the jungle. "I will fix it."

With his *boyden's* corpse pressed against his chest, he scanned from tree to tree on the hunt for the lanky papaya that almost reached his waist in height.

Above him, the moonlight pierced through the sea-sky, lapping gently. The light graced him with the view of a baby tree yards ahead.

He was close.

The soles of his feet squished into the sodden soil. His legs trembled as he ran. Alke's body had chilled in his arms. He needed to hurry.

A glint of the water hole came into view, its still surface reflecting like marble. Kapok branches tented over it. Finnian's heart pounded painfully against his chest as he fell to his knees at its bank. Ground cover scraped his skin through the material of his trousers.

He winced, lowering his companion into the starlit water.

Naia, his older sister, had stumbled upon the water hole before his birth, ages ago. She had been bringing him to it since he was old enough to walk. It'd taken him no time at all to sense the magical properties within.

The first time he entered the metallic pool, his skin hummed like currents of lightning trapped beneath tissue and blood. It flooded life into his chest—a magical reservoir.

The silver water washed over Alke, staining his blue feathers and Finnian's hands.

With bated breath, he waited a few moments, arms shaking.

Alke's lifeless head bobbed along in the ripples.

Finnian slammed his eyes shut, pushing the tears to drip down the bridge of his nose. A sob swelled in his throat, but he swallowed it down.

Alke's final moment was pinned at the forefront of his thoughts: majestic and lively, perched atop Mira's arm, his gaze fixed down on Finnian.

After thirteen years of failed punishments, his mother had finally discovered a way to wear him down. He did not miss the cruel curve to her lips as she murdered his beloved companion.

What fate awaited Naia and Father?

Naia had fought back on his behalf. Finnian could hardly believe it when she'd slung Mira across the great hall. Or when the buttress roots smashed through the crystal floor and slammed Mira into the vaulted ceiling—those commanded by Father. Dignified and peaceful, he had gallantly intervened and defended them.

Worry knotted in Finnian's stomach. He had a feeling that Father had held back all these years for a reason.

Silently pleading, Finnian opened his eyes.

Alke remained motionless in his grasp, the feathers of his wings saturated.

Refusal burned in Finnian's muscles, his nostrils flaring and his body tensing.

"I will make it better," he declared. "I will bring you back."

With a breath, he centered his attention on the pool of magic churning in his core, savoring the tidal rush in his veins.

While balancing Alke's waterlogged body in one hand, he used the other to reach into the pocket of his trousers and retrieve the chrysocolla pendant he'd snatched from Naia's neck as they'd run out of the great hall.

Their mother's precious pendant. The item that started this whole mess.

Finnian clenched the jewel in his fist. His horrendous siblings had deceived him by stealing Mira's necklace and then convincing him to give it to their eldest sister as a birthday present. He had not known the necklace was their mother's, a family heirloom.

Finnian would never make the mistake of trusting the triplets ever again. Because of them—because of Mira—Alke was gone.

Dead.

Finnian stared down at the vessel that once held the bird's soul, sparring with how to make sense of it.

Memories played behind his eyes—the company of Alke on his shoulder, flying over his head as they journeyed outside the palace grounds, squawking loudly to assure Finnian of his presence, breaking pieces of licorice to share with the bird. These things would no longer exist. *Never again.*

Finnian would remain and Alke would join the afterlife, because that was what it meant to be a god. Forever outside the realm of death.

Finnian refused to allow those closest to him to slip through the cracks into its Land. Death would not exist in his world.

Finnian's curled fingers stretched open, and he stared down at the pendant. Its omniscient power radiated up his wrist, burning a heatwave in his blood.

He focused on siphoning the energy from its properties. It pricked up his arm and around his nape as the magic flowed down into the hand cradling Alke.

"I will bring you back."

PART I

MAKE IT HURT

ONE

THE YOUNG GOD WHO STEALS SOULS

THE PAST
Cassian

THE BREEZE RUSTLED through the wisteria blossom's long, wispy branches, tickling Cassian's cheeks. Determined to enjoy the stillness, he lay in the lavender stalks, hand propped behind his head.

Focus on the present moment.

Nathaira constantly lectured him to do so, but it was something he could rarely afford due to his ever-growing worklist—meetings with the Council, curse *this* god for whatever line they'd crossed, imprison *that* god for their wrongdoing—and then there were the daily duties that came with running a realm full of souls.

Cassian had lived for over five thousand years, but that length of time had not brought him anything but redundancy. As the Ruler of Death, his days were all the same.

He kept his eyes closed, but his mind continued to work, scribbling a mental list of to-dos: visit the souls in the Paradise of Rest, welcome the new ones at the River and those who arrived with the Errai—deities of Death who shepherded the souls through the gates—and check in on the progress of those wandering the Grove of Mourning. He often worried about those in particular, struggling to heal from the trauma they'd endured in their mortal lives.

"My lord." Mavros's voice appeared behind the *swoosh* of his arrival.

Cassian kept his eyes closed but could sense his attendant's presence awaiting behind him.

Mavros was quiet and reserved, but possessed a dark, prominent aura. The kind fearsome to mortals and apprehensive to deities. One only a god of death possessed.

Mavros had been at Cassian's side for well over three millennia. Their formal relationship turned cordial over the tedious years of operation among the Land of the Dead.

"My lord," he repeated with an exigency in his tone.

Cassian lifted into a sitting position with his elbows on his knees. The wisteria blossoms tangled in his hair and clung to his shoulders.

He inhaled their sweet fragrance before climbing to his feet and sauntering through the lavender at his ankles.

The two made their way down the knoll and into the waist-high stalks, weaving between wandering souls, who minded them no attention as they passed, too occupied with their thoughts and the beauty provided by the Lavender Fields of Healing. These were all souls who had recently arrived in the Land.

Some walked aimlessly, unaware of their surroundings while processing their deaths and the mortal life they'd left behind. Others strolled with luxurious patience, the bloomed lavender catching between their fingertips, pausing to soak in the streams of sunlight parting the frothy-thick clouds.

Mavros's footfalls shuffled behind Cassian, nipping unusually frail nerves within him. A sign of burnout, greatly in need of the *downtime* Nathaira had recommended.

He casually slipped a hand inside his trouser pocket, and amid his next step, he vanished in a black chiffon puff.

The sole of his boot touched down on the bridge overlooking the River of Souls. The hazy lilac current carried the souls forth to the landing bank. From the distance, Cassian could see Nathaira, draped in sparkling green lace, adorned with wildflowers along her sleeves and neckline and sprinkled all over her sandy locks as she offered a hand to the next emerging soul.

She was a middle goddess of nature who greeted those arriving from the River.

"My lord." Mavros appeared at Cassian's side, insistent.

Cassian sighed. "Is there an issue, Mavros?"

He slid his other hand in his pocket, the position forcing his shoulders to relax, and glanced down, surveying the spirits in the stream below the

bridge. Their forms were amorphous, like apparitions trapped below glass. Some clung and writhed against the current, their sorrows wailing like tail-end whispers.

Mavros cleared his throat. "I have news regarding the matter of missing souls."

"Do tell." It came out as a mutter of unenthused petulance as Cassian continued to stare at the souls, admiring the way their mystic glow resembled the luster of spilled paint swirling together.

The second that the High Goddess of Fate cut a soul's thread, it belonged to him. He could feel it floating, waiting for guidance, tethered to him. A feeling all deities of Death were familiar with. The Errai used the sense to find those freshly departed and lead them to the Land.

Daily, they reported corpses with missing souls when they arrived to collect. The river gods occupying the waters in the Land of the Dead protected the souls, and none had disappeared on their watches. Which meant the missing souls weren't making it to the River in the first place.

Then, there were the souls in his Land that disappeared without a trace.

When the issue first arose, it was only a few souls sporadically. Now, it was hundreds, consistently.

"Well, my lord, it is…" Mavros's hesitation only meant it was more severe than he led on, for it was the only occasion when the attendant spoke like a broken instrument. "There is a young god *stealing* these souls."

Cassian turned his head to look at him, eyebrows raised. "You have my attention."

Mavros's waist-length dreadlocks were tied up today. He concealed his joined hands in front of him in the long sleeves of his robe, and his eyes kept blankly fixed ahead, respectfully avoiding Cassian.

It was normal protocol for deities to never look directly at a High God, though Cassian never minded. In fact, he found it more troublesome when they looked away, as if he were conversing with statues.

Cassian rubbed his thumb and forefinger over his flexing jaw muscles, annoyed by the information. "Does this young god have a name?"

"He does." Mavros's stoicism did not alter.

Cassian dragged his hand up over his face and through the longer strands of his hair, swallowing the urge to bite his attendant's head off. "Mavros, spit it out. I may be immortal, but my patience is not."

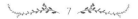

Mavros's gaze snapped to him then. "I believe it will only spoil your rather delightful mood."

Cassian dropped his arm back down to his side, pinning Mavros with an unenthused look. "I do not appreciate your sarcasm. Now tell me before I act on my urge to curse you to Moros."

A beat passed before Mavros said through a stifled breath, "The young god's name is Finnian." His brow pinched, bordering on a look of pain and exasperation. "The High Goddess of the Sea's youngest child."

A breathy, unamused laugh shook out of Cassian.

Of course, her son is the one stealing souls.

He gripped the railing of the bridge and glared down at the River.

It was foolish not to assume Mira was behind the action. Perhaps she goaded her son's power as a threat. Cassian wouldn't put it past her to act out in such a vindictive manner. He was the one who entrapped her beneath the Kaimana Sea in the first place.

Or it could be a spiteful attempt to diverge Cassian's wrath from her onto her offspring. A rather cold action, but there were no limitations to Mira's virulence. She was the type to toss her child to a shark if it brought her gain.

Regardless, the young god was dabbling in death, a realm that did not concern him, stripping souls of their peace in the afterlife. Something Cassian could not let stand.

"What relic is he using? I confiscated the *Rune of Nekromanteía* years ago."

"About that, my lord," Mavros said, "there is something else you should know."

"What?" he grumbled.

"The young god is also a mage."

Cassian turned to his attendant again. Nothing about Mavros's somber expression suggested that he was jesting.

No such deities had been born with the ability to do witchcraft. Deities were born with divine power, never magic. Why hadn't the other Council members mentioned this? Surely, if they were aware, they would have.

"Why am I just now learning of this?" Cassian snapped.

"The god was confined in Kaimana until recently. My presumption is that he kept it a secret. According to my insights, Lady Mira banished him five years ago after learning of his ability to use magic."

It appeared a graver matter took priority atop his never-ending to-do list.

Cassian squeezed the bridge of his nose. Suddenly, he wished the young god had been abusing the power of an ancient relic instead, for the sake of a simpler solution. It was a shame he did not make use of the downtime beneath the wisteria moments ago.

"What shall you have me do?" Mavros asked.

Cassian straightened and peered out along the River's edge where Nathaira stood. She reminded him of a forest fairy in the folktales that he enjoyed reading in his spare time. Grace and tranquility seemed to be inherently passed down in deities of nature—traits Cassian naturally gravitated to in moments of stress. Nathaira's presence provided a sense of grounding.

All too similar to a dear friend of Cassian's, who was now imprisoned in Moros.

Perhaps Cassian would pay the High God of Nature a visit to complain about how much of a nuisance his youngest son was proving to be. Vale would be amused and provide a vexing amount of pride, no doubt.

A pang of guilt caught in his chest. The last thing he wished to do was curse his oldest friend's son.

"I'll take care of it," Cassian said, tone taut. He slipped his hands back inside his trouser pockets, fidgeting with the tips of his fingers. "You are dismissed."

Mavros bowed his head and stepped back into the inky cloud stirring at his backside, disappearing with the sound of a fractured gust.

CASSIAN adjusted the starched, crisp cravat around the neck of his high-collared linen shirt. His hands itched to smooth out the wool material of his waistcoat. He double checked for any lint clinging to the lapels of his velvet tailcoat.

It had been ages since he'd stepped foot on Mortal Land. He'd used minimal glamor and shortened his height to an average male human, dulled the sheen of his divine complexion, and warmed the blond of his hair.

There were no rules amongst deities that said they could not show themselves to mortals, but it was not something one often did. Deities typically morphed themselves to show a completely different appearance.

Mortals tended to better worship what they could not see. The illusion of what they believed to be true about their god or goddess fed their hope and prolonged their commitment to prayers.

Not only that, but Cassian had never crossed paths with the young god, giving no reason to worry about being recognized.

Though, despite his efforts to blend in, a quick sweep around the crowded mortal street where he stood was plenty to notice the passersby gawking. Just as he was doubting his decision not to listen to Nathaira and dress a little less lavishly, the door to the apothecary swung open in front of him.

He side-stepped the mortal exiting the establishment, but the elderly man gave a polite smile and held the door open for him. "Here you are."

Cassian quickly analyzed the man's leathered, wrinkled skin and yellow tint in his eyes, calculating his time until death. Souls growing old in their mortal bodies hardly seemed fair. He wanted to assure the man that death would be a relief, but he was sure that it'd only make the man suspicious.

Taking a step, Cassian grabbed the edge of the door, giving the mortal a slight head bow in a gesture of appreciation.

"Have a good day, Mister." The mortal turned on his heel and hobbled off.

Cassian watched his backside grow smaller in the distance, wondering what sort of illness he had that had led him to an apothecary. Or what sort of intentions the young god stealing souls had with sick mortals to be *working* as an apothecary? Poisoning them, perhaps, simply to revive them for his undead army, or using their hair or blood for some kind of nature-bending ritual.

Cassian gave one last look at the outside of the apothecary—the overgrown ivy, the chipped brown paint of the windowpanes.

He inhaled a breath and relaxed his shoulders on his exhale before stepping through the threshold.

A pungent aroma of herbs greeted him. The inside of the establishment was small, only enough room for a few bodies to stand in front of the large wooden counter. On the wall behind it were rows of metal shelves running up to the ceiling, full of clay and glass jars crammed with an assortment of dried herbs and plants.

"Welcome," a young man said from behind the counter, busy at the workbench stationed against the wall.

Cassian assessed the backside of the man. His apron revealed a tall and lean build, and his long black strands were tied back and hung between his shoulder blades.

"Hello." Cassian positioned himself a few steps to the left to get a better look at what the man was doing with his hands. There was a pestle in his grip, and he seemed to be crushing up something in a matching mortar.

Cassian stood there for a beat, waiting for further acknowledgement.

His unhurried manner bit at Cassian's nerves, and he stepped closer to the counter, eyeing the variety of broken stems and dried greenery spread out around the bowl. "A friend recommended this apothecary to me."

The man placed the blunt tool aside and brushed his hands off on the front of his brown apron. Several silver rings glinted in the midday sunlight that streamed through the windowpanes. "What is it that you seek remedy for?"

Cassian glanced around, pretending to make sure the apothecary was empty before leaning in. "A remedy to raise the dead," he said in a quiet voice. "I heard there is a young man employed by this apothecary who possesses a gift in such areas."

The man lifted his chin slightly, flicking his eyes all over Cassian's face. They were a muted shade of green, similar to a withered leaf that had been under the sun for too long. Clearly glamor, much like the matte complexion of his tan skin.

Cassian was sure of it. This man was the young god. But before Cassian could curse him, he first needed to verify it was, in fact, the *correct* god. Mavros had only provided a location and a physical description—black strands, slender build, and eyes the color of an emerald.

The young god's expression held like a slate of stone, giving none of his thoughts away. He blinked in slow strides, once, twice, leaning back and crossing his arms, scrutinizing Cassian. Perhaps one had to be worthy of his secret talent? Or maybe he, too, could sense Cassian was a deity. Suddenly, he regretted not putting more effort into his glamor. He should've shape-shifted.

To Cassian's surprise, the young god spun around and fished for two ceramic mugs on the second shelf. Nothing about his body language suggested Cassian's request unsettled him. "Was it someone special to you?"

"Yes." Cassian resisted the tugging at his fingers to trace the brass buttons of his waistcoat. He placed his hands inside the pockets of his tailored trousers to cap the urge. "Very much so."

"When did your loved one pass?"

Assuming the answer to the question required a specific timeframe, Cassian was careful with his response. "A few days ago."

The young god moved towards the steaming pot on the corner of his workbench. "Tea?"

Without waiting for a reply, he poured two glasses and placed one in front of Cassian.

He glanced down at the steaming mug in front of him, a pleasant tropical fragrance wafting up his nose, and forced out a grateful smile, perturbed by the god's inability to form full sentences. "Tea sounds refreshing."

The young god tapped his long fingers on the surface of the counter, not touching his tea. "Tell me more about your loved one. Was it a relative or a romantic companion?"

Cassian took a small sip—notes of rose hip and sweet pineapple danced across his tongue. "Family. I do not have a lover. Is that a requirement?"

"I do not believe in the loneliness in which death provides, therefore no. There are no requirements." The look of indifference was an uncanny contradiction to the deep topic he spoke of. "All I request is that you bring me the corpse, and know that I cannot repair the mind of the person you care so deeply for. Their mental state is up to the soul alone."

"You believe loneliness plagues those who step into death?" Cassian blamed his interest in the matter on the calm ambience, the comfort of herbal scents permeating in the air, and the sweet, refreshing flavor of the tea on his tongue.

He had zero motivation to know whatever preposterous reason the god had for resurrecting the dead. At least, that is what he told himself as he awaited the young god's reply.

Finnian leaned in and his upturned eyes shrunk into slits that made the skin on Cassian's cheeks prickle. The dark specks of his glamor spritzed through his emerald irises, glimmering like river stones beneath.

"Why don't you enlighten me on the topic, Lord Cassian?" He tilted his head, an irritating smirk slicing across his mouth. "Do you consider yourself lonely as the Ruler of Death?"

Cassian's jaw pulsed. The young god was dangerously close, and that either made him foolishly arrogant or extremely naïve. Cassian could snatch him in his grip like the jaws of a predator before he even had time to register the act.

The thought lingered steadily as he stared at the young god, studying the features of his face—a pronounced brow-bone, hollow cheeks, somber eyes, pointed like the end of a dagger, framed by chin-length bangs.

Cassian had underestimated the young god's prowess of observation. A mistake he would not make again.

Cassian shed his glamor, revealing his true appearance. His height grew, and he slightly towered over the young god. "Good. We can move past the coy remarks and get to the point. You are violating the dead. I cannot allow that to go on."

Something flashed in the young god's gaze, brazen and defiant. "And if I do not stop?"

His ego was ridiculous.

Cassian held his glare nonchalantly. "Then I shall curse you. Precisely how I cursed your mother and father."

At the mention of Vale, a fissure of emotion struck the young god's face. It flitted away as quickly as it appeared, like a crack sealing up within seconds. If Cassian hadn't been watching closely, he'd have missed it.

"I must say, I've been eager to meet you." Finnian turned and began cleaning his workbench, moving the mortar and pestle aside and sweeping up the pile of crushed leaves and broken stems with his hands.

He tossed the remains in a trash bin beside his foot. "I first heard of you when my sister told me of our uncle Xerxes, and how he was put into confinement due to the insanity you forced upon him. Then I learned how you cursed my mother beneath the sea."

Cassian watched the shifting of muscles in the backs of his shoulders as he reached for a jar from the third shelf.

"From what my sister told me," Finnian continued, "Uncle Xerxes was a moron who never knew how to keep his nose out of places it did not belong, and our mother was most deserving of her imprisonment. I really could not decide if you enjoyed flaunting your superiority, or if they merely had it coming."

Finnian's arms went still.

The silence was loud with the traffic of carriages and trotting horses on the street, muffled chatter from those passing by on the sidewalk. Cassian could feel the air gather with a tension that nipped at his skin. A charge of swelling energy sparking against his pores.

Magic.

"Then you sent your executioners to take my father away, and I had my answer." The contempt in the young god's tone was subtle. He aligned his chin with his shoulder, and his eyes sharply cut to Cassian.

It'd been a few centuries since Cassian had faced a mage. He was never particularly fond of their unpredictable qualities. The explosion of the countertop in front of him was a swift reminder of this.

Shards of wood speared through his arms, cut across his cheeks.

Cassian's divine energy seeped into the air like a puddle of oil, and his form warped into a curling mass of black and gold tendrils as he materialized across the room and out of the line of fire.

The spot where Cassian landed shimmered. Runic symbols glowed around his feet. He stepped to move, but he was bound to the spot, an unnatural gravity keeping his boots glued to the sigil.

Gods, I despise witchcraft.

Finnian stepped around from behind the counter, his hand lifting. "*Colligo.*"

The splinters of wood from around the room gathered in front of him, levitating and aiming their sharpest ends at Cassian.

With a single snap of Finnian's fingers, he sent the barrage of shrapnel forward.

Cassian glowered at the flying objects, not bothering to dodge them.

Speared fragments lodged deeply into his arms and torso.

He reared his arm up and caught a splintered chunk of the wood. Slivers mangled in the palm of his hands and the underside of his fingers.

He sent the sharp piece in his grip flying across the room.

 14

It impaled straight through Finnian's shoulder, and he stumbled backwards into the workbench from the impact.

The commotion settled, but dust still swirled in the air.

"What a little nightmare you are." Cassian plucked the wood from his flesh and then smoothed his palm over the lapels of his tailcoat.

His wounds closed within seconds, but cherry-red stains bled through the material of his tunic beneath his waistcoat.

He clenched his teeth at the uncleanliness, the disorder of his outfit, it being anything but pristine.

Through the rubble of the counter and broken glass and clay stood Finnian, assertive and fearless. Stupidly so. The chunk of debris still jutted out from his shoulder.

"You stole my father, so I steal your souls," he sneered.

"It seems you have inherited your mother's vindictiveness." Cassian glanced down at the markings on the floor, noting how their glow faded.

He inched forward, testing the boundary of the sigil. The magic within it had died.

Lovely.

"I inherited far worse from her." Finnian cocked his head, and the corner of his mouth twitched. "If you wish to curse me, Lord Cassian, then you must catch me first."

Cassian snarled and lunged for him.

A clean slice of distortion ripped through the air. Tendrils of ruby smoke furled around Cassian's fist.

Disturbing laughter bubbled up his throat.

His stomach knotted with a deranged mix of irritation and euphoria.

Smug, little—

He lowered his arm and gripped his hip.

Grounding his jaws, he glared down at the shambles of the apothecary.

He would chase the young god, catch him, and be his reckoning.

TWO

THE KISS OF DELIRIUM

"Who—loathe—most?" Shivani's sultry-pitched voice was the goddess's one and only pleasant attribute.

Finnian blinked a few times, piecing together the words he could not hear from the throbbing of blood in his left ear. His right ear was useless without his hearing aid.

Who do you loathe the most?

It was a taunting question she repeatedly asked him. A tactic to flare his anger. Stir emotions, hoping for a slip-up and desired revelation. Shivani was one of Cassian's loyal servants—a middle goddess of slaughter.

"I haven't—since—High God—Rain—Storm—sixteen-hundreds." She spoke alongside the sound of her sharpening her blade.

I haven't what?

In the mild break of his torture, Finnian assessed himself. Every inch of his skin felt wet. Sticky, warm, and wet.

High God of Rain and Storm?

The lacerations carved down his abdomen were slowly mending. Beneath the tension of stitching skin, he could feel the blossoming of his organs growing back into their rightful places.

Since the sixteen-hundreds?

He gave up attempting to piece together the sentence, assuming it was another snide comment.

The ominous being to Finnian's side, an executioner, tightened the chain bound to his shackles, squeezing his wrists and ankles in a vise grip.

Muscles burned from his limbs being stretched taut as he hung from the stone wall.

It had been months since he'd seen the slate interior walls of his cell, and while he'd rather cut off his own tongue than confess such a thing, he missed it. He assumed it had been months, at least. Time was lost within the dungeon he was currently confined in.

"Though, he—stouter—you," Shivani continued. "Had—meat—bones to carve off."

Finnian got a grip on his panting and ran her words through his mind, slower this time.

Though, he was a bit stouter than you. He had more meat on his bones to carve off.

"And where is this god now?" he asked, his voice hoarse.

"Use—imagination—Moros." Shivani plunged her freshly sharpened blade through Finnian's ribcage.

He ground his jaws to keep from groaning out, but the sound slipped out of his throat. Agony welled up in his chest. The gush of blood coated his insides like ash to fresh paint.

Use your imagination in Moros?

His teeth chattered and his head went light.

He clenched the muscles in his arms and legs to keep his blood pressure from dropping and clung to a focal point in the back of his mind, far away from the wails of pain echoing up his torso.

Use your imagination. You are in Moros.

Shivani ripped the knife free and stepped back.

The release was as painful as it was relieving. A river of warmth consumed his pant legs. Ragged, wheezing breaths escaped him.

He rolled his neck to lift his head. "Enlighten me."

With a casual stroke of her arm, she flung the blood from her blade to the side. It splashed and stained bright crimson along the dark stone of the wall.

Finnian focused on her mouth, watching for her response.

Her lips quirked, as if she found his sudden curiosity towards the subject amusing. "The god is trapped inside his own purgatory. He's no longer a High God. Lost that title decades after he was imprisoned."

A *personalized* hell created by Cassian. If Finnian had to guess, his father would be in a similar place.

"Do enjoy our time together, Finny, because the same brutal fate awaits you." She inched closer. Her tight ponytail pulled back her brunette strands, revealing the glossy bronze skin of her cheeks smudged with his blood. The tip of her blade pressed against the skin of his throat. "Now, be a good boy and tell me where the Himura demigod's blood is?"

The rush of his internal sounds slowly quieted, making it significantly easier for him to hear her out of his left ear against the silent background of the room.

He stared at her, expressionless, keeping the view of her lips in his periphery to avoid mistaking any of her words—with the added benefit of provoking her. "If it's the Himura demigod's blood you seek, why doesn't Lord Cassian simply go steal some from the veins of my darling nephew?"

Naia, with her new title as the High Goddess of Eternity, remained an uncertainty to the Council. They would not risk starting a feud until they learned more about her power.

The executioner snapped forward, baring its barbed teeth, clearly unamused. A deep-chested growl rumbled in the space between it and Finnian.

Shivani retracted the blade from his throat and examined the sharpness of the tip. "I suppose the time has come for me to leave you to the executioners. This one seems rather testy and in need of a meal."

Finnian gauged the beast invading his space—nose absent, two rows of teeth split across its face. Its wrinkled, leathery skin looked as if it had once been the flesh of a human, melted and burned to a crisp, the remains solidified. It was truly a horrendous-looking creature.

Prior to his time in Moros, he'd never actually seen an executioner's face. They were notorious for keeping them hidden in the depths of their hooded cloaks or behind their masks—ashen and made of the bones probably scattered throughout Moros.

Seldomly did Finnian think anything of them. Monsters existed all over, born from divine power or from the wombs of deities. Their intimidating statures, insidiously tall and lanky, and their reputations as devils lurking in the shadows of the Land of the Dead had never frightened Finnian.

That was, until they escorted him into the godsforsaken dungeon he was currently in, bound him in place, and feasted on him for days on end.

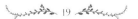

He'd black out and have to crawl out of an abyssal landscape—one of Cassian's illusions. The High God would appear before him, and in a blink, Finnian would descend back into that umbral darkness.

The executioner's reptilian eyes flickered with an edge of excitement that made Finnian's skin writhe. If he were honest, the last thing he wanted was to endure another round of the fiendish creature ripping him apart with their teeth.

Out of the two evils, he preferred the goddess of slaughter.

"How many times are you going to let them feast upon my flesh in the name of your defeat?" Finnian gave an exhausted chuckle, dropping his head to focus on the rosy puddle collecting beneath him. The prickling sensation was already dissolving beneath his skin and numbing the misery. "It is no wonder you are a mere middle goddess."

Shivani forcefully gripped Finnian's long hair and ripped his head back. Pain ruptured across his scalp like pinpricks. A humorous type of pain compared to the horrors she'd inflicted upon him in the passing months.

You have two types of deities, he could recall his father once saying, *those who care about their titles, and those who do not.*

Shivani struck him as one who most certainly did. The hunger for power burned like a torch in her eyes.

"Your skill set is of an amateur's," he continued to taunt her. "If you plan on taking the title from my elder brother, you still have a long journey ahead of you."

"You believe yourself to be in a position to mock me?" She jolted her tight grip on his strands, ripping shreds out in between her fingers.

It was brief, but Finnian cringed.

Shivani drew back slightly, her sneer turning into a narrowed gaze, *noticing.*

A bolt of regret zapped through Finnian's chest. He forced the tension on his face to loosen, his expression to become impassive.

Shivani's lips parted into a gut-churning smile, and she delicately brushed her long nails through Finnian's locks. "My, what beautiful hair you have."

He swallowed hard, watching closely as Shivani plucked a switchblade out of the pocket of her cargo pants. She ran the steel side of the blade down the length of his hair.

His pulse spiked. The knowing of what was to come churned in his not-yet-regrown stomach.

He'd done well to avoid giving away a piece of him that she could break off and devour.

The first time his mother had dropped a hundred sea urchins on him for losing a battle against a middle god in her arena, Finnian thrashed around on the sand with his airways closing. Panic blared through his pulse as he flailed and tore at his throat. It took hours for the poison to leave his system, during which he became accustomed to the burning quench in his lungs. It taught him how nothing could *truly* harm a deity.

Apart from one thing—the blood of his own nephew, a demigod from the Himura clan. A poison to all deities. A poison he possessed a syringe of, hidden away safely.

Shivani twirled a strand of Finnian's hair around the sharp edge of her blade. "Where is it?"

He eyed the dark tuft of his hair between her petite fingers, his anger manifesting with a need to rip forward and crush her windpipe.

She pulled out the slack of his long hair and sliced through it. The severing of the strand reverberated in his skull and echoed in his left ear.

White-hot panic dotted his insides like ink and curdled in his stomach.

Shivani closely tracked every inch of his face, and whatever she noticed in his expression was confirmation she'd *finally* hit a nerve. "It seems you place a high value on being autonomous."

Growing up, he never had allowed the servants to touch his hair, despite his mother's orders to do so. What was his was precisely *his*. No matter the amount of times Mira had threatened him.

Shivani bit her bottom lip back to contain her sickening, gleeful smile and began hacking off layers at a time.

Every forceful tug and purposeful nick of the blade against his scalp constricted the muscles down his neck and arms.

He channeled his concentration to a single point on the wall straight ahead. Beneath the dancing flame of the sconce, there was an unmoving moth with mottled brown wings.

The unwelcome heat bred from Moros's inferno nipped at his nape, making it easy to determine how short his hair was. The ends curled and frayed over his forehead, behind his ears.

Shivani paused and leaned in, nose-to-nose with him, as if to demand his attention. "Tell me, Finnian," she said, slow and tantalizing, "how does it feel?"

She waited until he lowered his eyes onto her before cutting the final lock of his hair.

He swallowed the fire back down his throat. "How does *what* feel?" He forced out through a vacant tone.

"To be powerless."

Her words piled into the pit of his core like stones, uprooting the memory of the day he watched Alke's life end. A sense of helplessness he had spent his whole life trying to avoid jarred through his body.

Before he could react, Shivani cocked her arm out to the side and forcefully thrust her blade into his left ear.

Finnian's body went limp against the support the shackles provided. He chased his breath. Oxygen, though unnecessary, provided a welcome relief to his exasperated synapses. A distraction from the pulsing agony of the blade protruding from his head.

After Shivani had stabbed him, she handed him over to the executioner, and it fed for what felt like hours.

He looked down. Pieces of his pink, sausage-shaped intestines hung from the hole in his gut. Parts of exposed bone shone through the mutilated meat of his thigh. The feel of its claws rummaging through his intestines and tugging was still fresh, and a shudder wracked through him.

There was an absence of sensations and feelings within his body, a failure of functioning: struggling organs, withering arteries, a stinging anguish. It was the same feeling he got the day Mira stole the hearing from his right ear. A feeling he despised more than any form of pain could bring. The absence of something essential.

He lifted his chin off his chest and surveyed the room. Deprived of his hearing, he was forced to rely on sight alone. Silhouettes didn't linger in the shadow-filled corners, nor was there a discomforting presence of power hanging in the air. The room was bare, dreary. A snarling blaze filled the pit

of a large circle cut into the floor. The flames surged at a consistent tempo, the way a vortex constantly swirled.

With that knowledge, Finnian let his head roll back down, allowing his exhaustion to show.

He closed his eyes and curled his fingers around the chains. His folded legs shook underneath him. The throes of his torment crested in aggressive waves, wearing down his mental fortitude with a harrowing persuasion that the agony trapped in his bones would never cease.

By what means had his father lasted so long? After centuries in Moros, what state would Finnian find him in? The horrors in his imagination stabbed through his chest like one of Shivani's blades—his father, once immaculate, beaming with blossoms decorating his dark hair and a gaze as soft as a petal, broken, barely a husk of what he remembered.

Finnian *needed* to find him.

Father, guide me towards you.

He concentrated the small dose of his preserved energy into regenerating his injuries. Ruptured intestines gradually retracted back inside his body, and his skin slithered and stitched itself back together.

High Deities healed rapidly, and over the centuries, Finnian had excelled in regenerating. But because of the power-blocking manacles around his wrists, it was taking much longer than usual.

They were made from the Chains of Confinement. It was what the executioners used the day they escorted Father from Kaimana. A relic to bind a god's divine power—and in this case, Finnian's magic.

Fatigued by blood loss, he leaned the side of his head on the shackle's chain. The handle of the blade lodged in his ear bumped against it, and a painful ache lanced through his skull.

He winced. "Fuck."

The high-pitched ringing in his ear against the silence was louder than the cries trapped in Moros. Loud enough to serve as a blatant reminder of his weakness, coiling an unease in his mending gut.

Finnian lifted his head and did another sweep of the room, searching, thinking. His first priority for escaping and finding Father was to eliminate the shackles binding his power.

His eyes caught on the fuzzy, lush green moss trailing between the creases of the stone wall. It was odd for life to grow beneath the earth

in such a sinister place, and those nonsensical patches of nature were not there earlier. Finnian had scoped out the room many times. The walls were nothing but dull gray slates of packed stone.

The vein of greenery stopped at the wall-floor junction, as if coming from beneath.

A smile curled his lips.

Thank you, Father.

A daunting sensation nipped up Finnian's spine. A foreboding warning. He stiffened.

Across the room, threadlike, golden tendrils snaked around an onyx cloud, and Cassian stepped out of its billowing form.

Amidst the white noise in his ear, Finnian could feel the vibration of his frazzled heartbeat.

Cassian waded through the pool of blood on the floor, the viscous liquid sticking to the soles of his suede shoes. He stowed one hand away in the pocket of his tailored suit. The light from the steady flames cast an otherworldly glow to his face—striking features, all angles and chiseled cuts, and pale skin, as smooth as an opal gem.

He stopped in front of Finnian and looked down at him.

Finnian met Cassian's lethal, topaz gaze head on with tenacity, his ego consuming all common sense to keep his head down.

You will not break me.

Cassian undid the button to his suit jacket and crouched down, eye-level. "Why hello, Little Nightmare." He enunciated the words for Finnian to read on his lips.

The nickname pinched at Finnian's nerves unexpectedly. The first time Cassian ever called him that, it brought a sense of pride knowing he had disheveled the High God's pristine little world. Now, though, it felt stale in his stomach.

"You don't look too good," Cassian said.

Finnian did not try to respond. Talking without his hearing was like attempting to drive with his eyes closed. Therefore, he maintained a dead expression, hoping Cassian would get to the point of his visit sooner rather than later.

Cassian reached out and brushed the wavy strands sticking to Finnian's forehead away.

The tender gesture baffled Finnian for a moment, giving him little time to register Cassian gripping the blade's handle and wrenching it out of his ear.

Finnian groaned, slumping forward and grimacing from the rush of blood purging behind his eyeballs. A blinding jolt split like an ax through his skull and his vision shook.

His eyes darted over the ruby red liquid at Cassian's feet, up the blurred blob of his crouching shape. The instability of control spiked Finnian's pulse. He blinked rapidly.

Warm liquid gushed down his jawline, but the violent shrill gave way to the reprieve as his ear drum mended.

Cassian tossed the blade across the room.

"Now," he said, the single syllable leaving his tongue smoothly, "would you be kind enough to inform me of the whereabouts of the blood?"

A shower of relief watered down Finnian's frenzy. He had never been more grateful to hear Cassian's low-pitched, resonant voice than he was now. Behind it was the sound of the hushed roar of the fire, the trickling of his own blood oozing from wounds against the stone.

Finnian gave a tired chuckle and looked up at the High God. "Kindness is not a thing I grant to those who are meaningless to me."

A flash of something glinted in Cassian's eyes, an emotion Finnian could not decipher fast enough before oiled-bodied serpents slithered out from around the High God's shoes.

They coiled around Finnian's legs, up the line of his spine, settling their spade-shaped heads on his arms and shoulders.

His body went rigid.

Next to his unimpaired ear, he heard the hissing of their tongues.

Suppressing a shudder, he pushed his tongue against the roof of his mouth, determined to withhold any trepidation from slipping free on his face.

"What you endured from Shivani and my executioners is nothing compared to the agony I will bring upon you," Cassian warned.

A serpent slipped up Finnian's nape and into his hair. A wave of goose-flesh sprouted up his neck. "Your arrogance makes me nauseous," Finnian spat back.

"I'll be sure to inform Shivani your stomach has grown back then."

Finnian's eye twitched as he tightened his glare around him. "Let us strike a deal. I know how much you enjoy a good bargain."

Cassian propped his elbow on one of his bent knees and cupped his cheek. He tilted his head, amusement shining in his golden gaze. "Oh, do tell."

One serpent coiled around Finnian's throat. Its thin, forked tongue tickled his Adam's apple as it caressed over his chin.

Finnian swallowed, the motion stifled against the constricting hold of the serpent. "Free my father and the blood is yours."

Cassian's head fell back and a glissando of laughter sang out.

A retching pulled at Finnian's belly as the sound hummed through him. His cheeks warmed, and he felt repulsed at finding any inkling of pleasure in it. He blamed it on the fact that it had been ages since he heard music. He missed it. That was all.

Glowering at Cassian, he said, "That is my deal. Take it or leave it."

Cassian ran a hand through his wavy strands. A singular curl sprang free over his forehead. "Your father committed a grave crime long ago. Unfortunately, he is still paying the price, therefore he cannot go free." His smile stretched further. "What else do you have?"

Saving Father was *always* a possibility, and hearing Cassian clip the end of that thread provoked a frantic rage to light in Finnian.

"The blood will never be yours," he sneered. "I will find my father and escape your awful land."

The serpent wrapped around his throat like a cool scarf gave a harsh hiss. Its scaly body hugged his neck in a warning.

"Unfortunately, you cannot leave, seeing as how your soul belongs to *me* now. It was what you agreed upon when trading places with Naia." Cassian's forearm lifted straight up, his long fingers curling in his palm. The large veins underneath his skin pulsed like black, poisoned worms up his wrist, staining the tips of his fingers as if he had dipped them in tar. "Now, I do recommend you cooperate. Otherwise, you know what comes next."

A curse.

Finnian's throat tightened.

It was impossible to determine the number of curses the High God possessed during his long lifespan. Certain ones stood out more and gained notoriety. Mira and Levina had received the Curse of Eternity. Naia's first

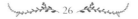

curse was the same. Her second curse was the Mercurial Exchange. The Curse of Weeping, The Call of the Void—all clever and unoriginal names, but worthy of the fear they bestowed in deities.

Finnian had great confidence in his problem-solving skills, resilience, and ability to overcome challenges. If he were a mortal, surviving would be a talent of his. However, uneasiness beat in the stride of his pulse, flickering with doubt.

"Which one?" he asked.

"The Kiss of Delirium."

Finnian's expression fell, making the mistake of showcasing the dread submerging through him.

"It starts as a quiet hum." Cassian spoke slowly, as if to make sure Finnian could interpret each word without mistake. "Darkness the size of a pinprick. A parasite that nuzzles its way into the most precious parts of your mind. With time, it learns your weaknesses, what you fear most, and without realizing it, your mind plays tricks on you. Until it slowly leads you into madness."

Finnian steeled his jaw, sick at the thought. The disturbing sensation of the serpents licking at his neck, up his pant leg, over his arms—it was too much. He wished to burn them to powder. More than that, he resented Cassian and his intoxicatingly powerful aura and patient disposition, as if he had all the time in the world to sit and watch Finnian decide his fate.

"You are a prideful god swathed in power." The charcoal veins in Cassian's forearm darkened, surging like ink through his palms and up into his fingers. "Power that took you centuries to hone and perfect. A deity of magic, of sorcery. Your biggest strength is your mind and all the knowledge it holds."

Knowledge was his most prized possession. Planning, plotting five steps ahead. Memorizing hundreds of incantations and potion recipes. Centuries of lessons and techniques that had carved him into the god he was today. Losing self-control, his mind becoming corrupted, was his worst nightmare.

A nightmare he fully accounted for back when he came up with the idea to switch places with Naia.

He'd planned out his agenda ahead of time. From the moment his darling sister arranged to meet with him at the Kahale residence on Nohealani

Island, pregnant and furious with him for summoning the triplets when she'd located him at Alke Hall. He knew the price of breaking Cassian's curse, and he'd purposely hidden the truth from her. Although, he wasn't foolish enough to believe Naia wouldn't figure it out in the end. She was smarter than she believed herself to be.

Which was precisely why he'd shown up, concealed his aura, and watched Naia and Ronin take on Cassian from afar. Until the opportune moment. When the syringe of Ash's poisonous blood fell from their hands, he swooped in and obtained his leverage to trade places with Naia.

The ticket to right his wrongs.

There were three things he must do. One of which was to free Father. The other two had been set in motion long before he became a prisoner.

He'd considered the chance of becoming cursed during the pursuit of rescuing their father in the Land. Should that occur, he would swiftly carry out his plan, enduring as much as he could. When he made it out, he would concoct a potion and break the curse himself—*without* sacrificing anything of importance. He knew there was always a way.

Looking back now, his faith in his resilience and strength might've been a conceited mistake on his part. Preparing to be cursed did nothing to lessen the reality of it, and now that he approached the threshold, hesitation froze his nerves to stand grounded and wrestle with such fate.

"And what will you do when your curse drives me to insanity?" Finnian narrowed his eyes at the High God. "I may end my life with the very thing you seek. What will you do then?"

Cassian moved closer, wafting a rush of citrus and mint up Finnian's nose. "Even in death, you belong to me."

Finnian's mouth clamped into a tight line. A grim image appeared in his mind—down on his knees, pleading for death to free himself from the curse's torment. He loathed the idea of death and its infinite void too much. Ceasing to exist, without a choice, a reason. He'd gladly wrestle with the torment of a curse over becoming Cassian's prisoner in the Land.

A sharp anger burned through him, and he lifted on his knees, pushing into Cassian's space. The serpents at his feet scattered. "I will not let your curse be my ruin. Death will not touch me. *Ever.*"

Cassian stared at him for a moment, intently. Something about it bristled warmth in the creases of Finnian's bitterness. A distant, unfamiliar longing awakening inside of him. He could not make sense of it.

The snake around Finnian's neck slowly retreated, slithering down his shoulder and onto the floor. It joined the others at the room's center near the blazing pit of flames.

The soft tips of Cassian's forefinger met Finnian's exposed collarbone; the fabric had torn from Shivani's torture.

Finnian's breath hitched from the sudden touch.

Cassian grazed up the ridges of his throat, slowly cupping the side of his neck.

Finnian's heart accelerated, and the sensation tingled in his bloodstream. He blamed it on his body, starved for any form of pleasure after months of misery.

Cassian's thumb skimmed over the scar running up Finnian's jawline and behind his ear.

A sour taste hit the back of Finnian's throat. He'd forgotten about it. Without his divine power to maintain his glamor, it was on display for all to see, like a scroll pronouncing his weakness.

Finnian recoiled from his touch, but Cassian caught him by the throat. His grasp locked, applying enough pressure to bring discomfort.

Finnian sucked in a sharp breath, preparing for the snap of his vertebrae.

"Death cannot touch you?" Cassian's eyes flashed up from Finnian's scar, their golden hue shining fervently. "I *am* Death."

Animosity surged viciously in Finnian's pulse, heating the tips of his ears.

Circumstances would never become him. He had trudged through several hells in his lifetime. He would right the wrongs he'd made the day he allowed the triplets to trick him, ultimately leading to the demise of their father, his own banishment, forced to abandon Naia in Kaimana.

Nothing could hinder him, curse or not.

A heinous smile stretched across his face, revealing his blood-stained teeth. "Do your worst."

Cassian's fingers twitched around his throat, the muscles in his jaws flexing. "I loathe you."

As the words left Cassian's mouth, his large palm met Finnian's pec. The contact was a collision ringing violently through his bones, a shrill scream blaring in his head.

Finnian cried out. The curse mixed with his blood, infesting every molecule, every crease of his brain, like the scouring of tiny insects burrowing and scratching their way into muscle and tissue, settling deep, deep, until a heaviness latched onto his soul.

He felt the mark brand his skin and crawl up his collarbone and over his neck—a boiling, mind-numbing agony. The muscles in his arms spasmed, and he slumped forward, his weight supported by the chains and Cassian's hand against his pec.

That familiar illusory abyss clipped the edges of his vision.

Who do you loathe most?

"You—" Pain jolted through his temples. He winced. Like a spreading blight, he felt the clear sharpness, the proud methodical structure of his mind's web under its force. Another whimper left him.

Cassian leaned in, his lips hovering at the shell of Finnian's left ear. "What was that?"

"*You.*" Finnian jerked his chin up, looking over Cassian's shoulder, his eyes set on the moss growing in the arteries of the wall. "You are the one I loathe the most."

THREE

THE TEMPLE

THE PAST
Cassian

ASSIAN TELEPORTED TO the front platform of one of his temples in the Mortal Land. The basalt columns were flanked by trellises of black roses. Firelight flickered in the basin beside the arched iron doors. An idyllic, overblown statue of what the mortals thought Cassian's appearance was—scowling and cloaked—guarded the entrance of the temple.

He looked over his shoulder through the dusky haze and into the streets of the town. A few carriages dallied by. The footfalls of the travelers padded along the pathway. Trails of smoke weaved into the sky, crawling up from chimneys. The faint smell of firewood and seasoned meats drifted through the air.

Since the young god's departure in the apothecary a few days ago, Cassian had done well to keep track of his whereabouts. It appeared Finnian did not have a place to call home. He wandered from one small town to the next. Just as Cassian sniffed him out, he'd create an annoying distance between them once again.

Cassian blew out a sigh as he faced the temple's doors. He did not find it a coincidence that the young god had brought him here. Inside its walls, he could sense Finnian's aura—bold and bright and thrumming with magic.

He stepped inside and found the young god, to no surprise, standing atop the altar where his worshipers gave offerings. All were strewn off and scattered over the stone floor—wooden bowls, spilled fruits, incense snuffed giving a delightful aroma of frankincense, cracked jars of seeping honey, spilled pots holding plants and flowers, and the burned remains of what appeared to be several chickens.

Cassian stopped at the entrance and took in the young god. His hair was cut shorter than Cassian had last seen it. The strands were now streaked with light brown and met the underside of his jaw.

"Why hello, Little Nightmare."

Finnian's gaze constricted, sharpening the shape of his eyes, and he held his chin up. "Stop chasing me, or I will send all your temples to the same fate."

Cassian ran a thumb over his bottom lip, scrutinizing the audacious young god standing on his altar. "All you have to do is stop reviving my souls and I will gladly leave you be."

It was embarrassing, really, that days had gone by and Cassian still hadn't dealt with the situation. He made the mistake of underestimating Finnian at the apothecary. And after an assortment of challenges to keep on his trail, Cassian was growing irritated by the young god's ability to evade him.

Finnian smirked, a vicious cut splitting apart his mouth. "What fun would that be?"

His snide manner crawled through Cassian's skin, pulsing his jaw as he slid his hand inside his pocket. "Very well."

In a blink's time, Cassian teleported in front of Finnian, slamming the young god's back into the temple wall. The old, mortal-crafted architecture shuddered under the blow, too fragile for a deity's raw power.

Struggling under Cassian's hold, Finnian flicked both sets of fingers in a sharp motion towards his core. "*Skýfa.*"

A thin, gleaming arc of magic launched from the ceiling and cut off both of Cassian's wrists like a guillotine. The pain was comparable to a nip from a needle. Cassian's tolerance to such injuries had exceeded during the long walk of his life.

Finnian struck Cassian's chest with his palm, pushing off the wall and materializing a few feet away, putting distance between them once more.

Cassian's divine power rushed up to his wrists. He flexed the muscles in his arms, quickly regenerating his hands completely.

He eyed the young god like a stalking hunter and gave a low laugh. "It seems you are made of a thousand little tricks. Let me show you one of my own."

He stretched out a hand and a ripple of onyx smoke pulsed across the mosaic floor, swallowing everything it touched. The fruit soured. The chicken carcasses withered until nothing but the bones remained. The plants closed inward and turned to dust. Everything the wave touched was eaten by death itself.

Seeing that the wave was guided by Cassian's hand, Finnian shot his right arm outward and then directly up.

The various bones of the chickens flew towards Cassian and then mimicked the motion, piercing his hand and forcing it towards the ceiling.

The wave of rot followed suit and halted before it could touch its target.

Finnian reached into a small pocket of his trousers, pulled out a vial containing a milky, blue substance, and lightly flung it towards the ground between him and Cassian. As soon as the glass shattered and the substance oxidized, the liquid formed into a dense smog and filled the room. It smelled of the ocean's salt.

Unable to see more than an inch ahead of him, Cassian prepared for a blow from anywhere. He vaguely caught a muffled word exit from Finnian's mouth, and as soon as it was uttered, an ellipse fabricated around Cassian's feet and a claw of spectral vines enveloped his legs, up his waist, pinning his arms behind his back.

Cassian pushed against the strain of the magic ensnaring him. The edge of his shoulder hit an invisible barrier, and the rune of the sigil flashed underneath him.

He growled under his breath.

The smoke cleared. Finnian sat on the edge of the altar, giving a mischievously nonchalant stretch, holding an apple in his hand. A purple crystal inside his ear refracted the light of the sconce.

"Best of luck freeing yourself." The smug playfulness in Finnian's tone swirled and burned in Cassian as hot as an inferno. He felt the muscles in his neck cord like taut ropes.

"Take this as your opportunity to run as far away from me as you can, because when I free myself, you will not escape my growing rage again."

Finnian took a large bite from the apple and stared at Cassian, confidence gleaming in his gaze. "Oh, but I will. You see, I knew this was the outcome that awaited you from the moment you followed me inside your dreary temple."

In an underhand toss, the apple rolled into the magical trap and bumped into the toe of Cassian's shoe.

He kept his glare fixed on the young god, though, as thin wisps of his divine power bled from his pores. "I *will* curse you."

A gathering of black mass grew around him, picking away at the magic keeping him bound.

The smug hues shaded across Finnian's expression disappeared. A set blankness returned. "Such a pathetic threat coming from the one trapped in my magic." He leaned forward, inches from the barrier of the sigil. His fearlessness was the stupidest thing Cassian had ever seen. "*I* will escape you each time you find me, while continuing to raise your souls. And there is nothing you can do to stop me, *Lord Cassian*."

A humorless laugh scuffed out of Cassian. He squeezed his hands into fists at his sides.

There was so much of Mira in him. A ruthless arrogance Cassian wished to snatch ahold of and tear out.

"I have been alive longer than any deity in the world. You do realize that, yes?" Cassian pushed forward as much as the constrictions would allow, his eyes prodding into Finnian's. "When I catch you, I intend to make it hurt."

Finnian's lips twitched, forming a brief sighting of a small smirk. "Until then, I suppose."

Cassian's divine power thrashed against the vines as Finnian's form dispersed like a wraith, leaving only frosty-red wisps and silence.

FOUR

MOROS

THE PRESENT
Finnian

HE EXECUTIONER LED Finnian down the corridor by the end of his chains with Shivani in front, her long ponytail swaying between her shoulders. Withered ivy painted the stone walls without a remnant of green life amongst its perished vines. Smothered by the atmosphere of Moros, no doubt. Smoke hung thickly in the air. The smoldering heat stuck to his skin, damp and crusted with blood.

The pain of Cassian's mark did not last. It traveled as quickly as a fork of lightning and then the pain vanished—suspiciously so.

Afterwards, Cassian left, and an hour passed with Finnian refusing to acknowledge the obsidian brush strokes poking through the torn fabric of his shirt collar. In the end, he could not resist.

Dark tendrils ran over his pec and onto his collarbone and coiled at the base of his neck, like one of the tails of Cassian's serpents. Finnian wanted to peel the engraving of the curse from his skin before it could sink deeper beneath the surface, but it was much too late for that.

A dull pain prodded behind his eyes—what mortals often referred to as a *headache*. A pain he was familiar with. His head had throbbed for months after losing his hearing in his right ear. Once his brain had adjusted to the loss, the pain would find him after long periods of time wearing his hearing aid.

He assumed the symptom was from the curse excavating into his brain.

Since, he'd been hyper-analyzing the reflex of his wit, the storage of his memory, the operation of his cognitive abilities. He tested himself by mentally reciting recipes for potions, or by recalling as far back as he could of his and Naia's jungle escapades in Kaimana.

It starts as a quiet hum.

Finnian sighed, exasperated by the anxious tingling underneath his skin.

Focus.

He could worry about breaking the curse later.

Right now, he had to be vigilant.

He analyzed the executioner leading him by the chain. Its folded wings stuck out from the hem of its robe, dragging its curled talons against the stone. Shivani's cargo pants were full of knives, absent from their sheaths.

They traveled beside a row of cells. Every few feet, executioners were stationed—towering figures encased in a layer of dark robes, scarlet blotches on the smooth ashen-bone surface of their masks that glinted in the firelight.

As they passed the inferno, Finnian peered into the velocity of the flames. It was birthed from a dense, bottomless pit of churning lava.

Where was it coming from? Were there souls within it? Prisoners of Moros?

He didn't trust his hearing without his hearing aid to rule out distant cries buried in its blaze.

"Tell me," Finnian said as they rounded a corner. A hot gust blew across his face. The pyre in the mountain's core roared in a vertical whorl at the compound's center. Stone railings boarded it off from the rest of the floor. "Exactly how long have I been in that dungeon?" He angled his head and listened closely with his left ear in preparation for her reply.

Shivani turned to look back at him over her shoulder, the edge of her smirk twisting his insides with annoyance. "Five years."

Finnian's nostrils flared at the information.

She gave a velvety laugh at his silence, looking ahead as she walked. "Time—Land of the Dead."

Finnian's eyes jumped over the new corridor they crossed into, searching for traces of his father. "You don't track time here."

"Correct," she twisted her head, giving Finnian a clear view of her lips. "In Moros, time is altered to amplify the prisoner's suffering. In the Land, time does not exist. The sun rises and may stay that way for days. Nightfall may come after, or you may experience a delightful dawn."

"How creative," he drawled, his eyes jumping back to the walls. The veil of smoke thinned, clearing Finnian's view of the pale gray grout between the creases of stone.

As they rounded another corner, a river of plush moss caught his eye.

His pulse flickered.

He glanced between the executioner's backside, Shivani, and the green trail.

Another turn and the moss disappeared.

Finnian twisted his head to look behind him, fighting against the slight tilt of his equilibrium without his hearing aid. The arteries of moss continued in the opposite direction of the corridor between the stones.

A giddy sensation lit like tinder in his stomach. A hope he often smothered to avoid the detrimental disappointment that accompanied it.

If he followed the moss, he was sure it would lead to Father.

They crossed through an iron-gated threshold to another corridor full of more concrete enclosures. One held a woman rocking back and forth in the far corner. She muttered incoherent words that Finnian couldn't understand. Her nail beds were red, like ripened fruit, with her nails missing.

A weeping man knelt in the adjacent cell, his face buried in his hands. He lifted his head at the sound of their footsteps, his face normal and human. In an instant, it transformed into something grotesque, baring stained, jagged teeth and piss-yellow eyes.

It slammed itself against the bars, reaching through for Finnian. Its rot-black talons scuffed his arm as the cell bars reconstructed into teeth and tore into the beast.

The executioner and Shivani did not spare a glance in its direction. While it was hardly the goriest thing Finnian had seen in his vast lifetime, it still unnerved him.

He refocused his gaze ahead.

They ascended a flight of stairs and entered a curved corridor with iron bars lined parallel on either side. The view at the end was familiar. He recognized the horrid moans of the creature with horns, as he had been forced to listen to them during the first day of his arrival while he was stuck inside his cell.

Their journey from the dungeon differed from when they first escorted him to it. Back then, they'd climbed eight stairways and had walked nowhere near the inferno of Moros' core.

The corridors shift around.

Finnian rolled his eyes.

What a grand fucking inconvenience.

He counted five executioners stationed at each cell, still, stonelike.

Shivani held open the door to the last cell at the end of the corridor.

Finnian stepped up to its entrance. The executioner unlatched the chain connected to the manacles around his wrist and shoved him inside.

Finnian staggered on his feet before steadying himself. His nostrils flared to get a grip on his frustration before turning to meet Shivani as the door to the cell creaked closed.

On the other side, she stared at him, her gaze glittering pompously. The executioner maneuvered behind her, like her personal bodyguard.

Face blank, Finnian stared back. "Do you have something you wish to say, or are you simply marveling at the view?"

She huffed out a laugh. "Your pretty face has seen better days. And with that dreadful haircut, it is a pity you cannot use your glamor to grow it back."

His insides knotted at the reminder of his short hair.

Despite his discomfort, he grinned as he crept closer to the cell bars. He had a few inches over her in height, and while he rarely asserted dominance using his physicality by *hovering*, of all things, he knew it would jab her pride. "I will not be confined in this cell forever."

She maintained an amused expression. "Be a good boy, Finny. I'll return soon. I have a brand-new cleaver that needs dulling."

He noticed how her eyes briefly flickered to the manacles on his wrist before she turned to leave. Almost like she needed reassurance.

Solid and unmoving, the executioner twisted its head at Finnian, as if it had sensed something skeptical. Its mask covered the top region of its face, the end of it arched above its mouth, edges curled and crusted with blood. It had two slits carved into the place of its eyes, and every so often, he caught the flicker of its pupils dilating.

Finnian gave it a cheeky smile.

A low growl sounded from it before turning to follow Shivani.

Across from Finnian's cell, the horned creature lay flat in its cage, motionless. Its silhouette resembled a transfigured monster—naked, indigo body, fingers that trailed to sharp points, meant for ripping apart. Scattered around it were many of its own severed limbs, like logs from a fallen tree.

Finnian sucked in a breath through his nose, inhaling the pungent odor of its blood—metallic and sour, braided with mint and citrus, dripping with one of Cassian's curses.

He was grateful for its determination in trying to free itself, only to be met with the iron bar's ensnaring bite. From day one in this cell, he meticulously observed and documented every instance. Those twenty-four hours had taught him something about the bars. Something that would prove to be useful now.

Finnian curled both fists around the steel bars of his own cell. Their power hummed in his knuckles, accelerating the stride of his pulse.

One.

Despite Finnian's careful silence, the executioner trailing Shivani paused and glanced back.

Two.

Blood surged in Finnian's temples, quelling the sound waves in his left ear. The solid molecules of the bars shifted under his palms into something squishy and smooth.

The executioner's mouth parted in what Finnian could only assume was another growl as it pushed off its feet towards him.

Three.

The bars morphed into large, oily black serpents. Their heads protruded out. Fangs elongated from their open mouths, and they lunged.

Shivani whipped around, her shoes scuffing on the stone. "Why are you—?" Her eyes went round.

The sensation was a sweet, painful one of teeth latching into the meat of his forearms. He waited until their bite secured around bone and ripped backwards off his heels.

Adrenaline numbed the agony of the serpents' teeth fracturing through his bones. The snap echoed up his elbows as both of his wrists detached from his body. Along with his hands, the serpents swallowed up the Chains of Confinement.

Like the bursting of a dam, Finnian's power rushed back into his veins.

Blood gushed from his severed wounds, splattering onto the tops of his shoes. Speckles littered his vision, and his head felt light. The serpents' glossy, scaled bodies solidified back into iron bars.

Finnian raced against his lethargy and channeled all his energy into regenerating his hands.

One.

The executioner's long arm reached for his cell door, but against Finnian's divine speed, it was not fast enough.

Finnian wiggled his newly formed fingers to revive his nerves, smiled, and then latched onto the once-again solid bars and drove them apart. The iron gave way as easy as plastic to the return of his divine strength.

Two.

In perfect timing, Finnian stepped out of the cell and shot his blood-soaked arm out, meeting the executioner with a hand around its throat. He squeezed, crushing its windpipe and the cartilage between his fingers. Its body crashed onto the floor.

Finnian discarded its severed head over his shoulder before pinning his focus on the blurred figures of the other executioners racing down the corridor straight for him.

Shivani snatched her blades from her stocky, beige pants.

Be a good boy, Finny.

He fixed on the beads of energy dwelling in Moros' stones, the mountain clay, and drew it out like a magnet. Using the movement of his fingers, he molded the particles into five thick icicles, each the size of Finnian's arm. They floated, arcing in front of him like a hand of cards. With a forward slice of his hand, he speared them towards Shivani and the charging executioners.

She sent a flash of kunai from both hands. The icicles met their steely points directly, shattering into peppercorn.

Finnian bent his neck sideways to dodge the sailing edge of a knife. It drove into the cement of the stone behind him.

Out of the corner of his eye, he noted an executioner closing in on him. His index finger and middle finger came together, and he took aim like a pistol. "*Mens tua est mea.*" The incantation left his lips swiftly.

Magic tingled the tip of his finger and the hex shot forth, nailing through the executioner's mask. The material shattered into chipped bones.

A hex burnt into the executioner's forehead, a mahogany star with small, runic characters at each point, an ouroboros in its center. The creature immediately came to a stop.

Finnian clenched his hand into a fist and reared it up, ordering the energy in the stone beneath Shivani's feet to heave. Within the pulse of a heartbeat, spikes tore up and plunged into her legs. Their dagger-like ends jutted in a swirling blossom through her.

She cried out as crimson blotched her pants.

Finnian aimed his finger at the four other executioners that zoomed past Shivani for him.

The spell was instant, stopping them in their tracks.

They each twisted their heads in Shivani's direction with a predatory glint glazed in their eyes, watching her squirm and trying to rip her legs free from the magical pikes that fastened her in place.

One by one, they each turned and stalked towards her.

She stiffened and lifted her head.

A sick satisfaction swelled in Finnian as he watched the panic consume her—the subtle parting of her lips, her movements turning frantic and clumsy, pushing and pulling her limbs.

"Seize *him*!" she shouted, an audible tremble underneath the boldness of her tone. Hands wrapped around the crook of her knee, she tugged, flinging her gaze from her trapped leg to the executioners closing in on her. "I said *seize him*!"

An executioner locked onto her arm. Another onto her neck. The others encircled around her, like wolves waiting for their turn. Her shrieks filled the corridor in a deep, cavernous echo.

Finnian hurried past them and turned the corner. The stone beneath his feet thundered, and the surrounding walls flickered.

He skidded to a stop seconds before smashing into a wall that hadn't been there earlier, blinking and examining his new surroundings.

To his left was a narrow staircase. Before the walls could shift again, he jogged down the steps, dragging his fingers along the grout of the stone to feel for the moss. It didn't matter if Moros rearranged itself a hundred times. The moss would show itself and lead the way.

Finnian emerged from the top of the stairs. The heat in the air swelled as he came onto the compounded floor circling the inferno. He barely had enough time to register the eldritch mask appearing before him.

Instinct had his arms ripping up to catch the executioner's talons before it could bury them into his chest. He gripped its wrist and slung it into the inferno. Its wings expanded from its back, black and leathered. With a few powerful slaps, the executioner stunted its speed and avoided a fiery death.

Finnian ducked before another executioner could grip his neck. He speared his fingers through another's chest cavity, shuddering at the lack of bones in the executioner's rib cage. It choked on a wail as Finnian lurched his hand back. Rotted, berry-blue blood stained his fingers.

He spun and swerved, cocking his elbow back to land a hit on one's mask. The solid plate cracked, and the executioner bared its teeth, snapping for Finnian's forearm.

There were too many. He took one out for two to fabricate in its place.

Doubt crept into his mind. What in the world had convinced him he could successfully fight off hundreds of executioners?

In between blows, his eyes searched for a way to escape.

He squeezed the rubbery forearm in his grip, crushing muscle and blood, and kicked the executioner back by its gut. The force sent it barreling, taking out those in its path. It gave Finnian the time he needed to fixate on an open entrance a few yards to the right.

He did a double take at the object sprouted on the threshold.

Blush petals layered beautifully into a fat blossom. A singular peony.

His breath hitched.

Father.

Peonies were his father's favorite.

A set of talons dug into the top of his shoulders. Another set shredded deep inside of his abdomen. The pull of organs shoved bile up his throat. He nearly bit the tip of his tongue off as his teeth clenched.

He stumbled backwards, his tailbone meeting something sturdy.

A strong current of intense heat seared his backside.

The railing of the inferno, contained in its invisible sphere. Would it fight back if he dipped his hands into its power? It had to have a purpose.

A set of jaws locked around Finnian's bicep. He growled through the excruciating tide of pain cresting up his shoulder and into his neck, as if he were caught inside a meat tenderizer.

The executioner ripped away with a mouthful of Finnian's flesh. Pink meat hung in between its inhuman teeth. Blood drizzled its chin.

Finnian's chest went light, and tingles nipped at his cheeks. More executioners swarmed around him, but he honed in on the one with a chunk of his arm in its mouth. Fury burned up his nape and tinted his vision.

He raised his arm overhead. His muscles tensed as he grabbed onto the inferno's energy. Its power comprised a thousand suns, scorching blisters all over Finnian's hand. He wrestled with its force, guiding its current to bend to his will.

A tremor of euphoria zapped down his spine as the windstorm of its divine power rushed in his blood. It beat viciously behind his eyes, pulsed in his fingertips like individual heartbeats. He could taste it on his tongue, throbbing in his gums—sweet and bitter and calamitous.

The flames spewed out on Finnian's command, like a fountain from a dragon's mouth, torching the executioners to dust.

Ripples of the hellish heat stung his eyes. He directed the channel of flames downward, melting the rock to liquid. He believed his father was located in the depths of Moros. If Finnian could not teleport, he would burn his path to Father.

He leaned into the surge of the flames' monstrous strength.

Burn, burn, burn.

An itch scraped in the center of Finnian's skull, cringing the nerves in his jaw.

His head jerked to the side, desperate to relieve the sensation.

You must right your wrongs.

Something tickled the top of his hand.

He dropped his attention to the two brown moths crawling up the side of his wrist. Yellow markings on their thorax depicted a human skull.

The breath died in Finnian's lungs.

Death's-head hawkmoth.

Panic froze in his blood as more floated down and stuck onto the tattered remains of his shirt.

Holding onto the control of the flames, he jostled his shoulders to spook them away. They scurried up his neck and he shivered, his frenzy growing wilder.

The darkening cloud above drowned out the bright glow of the flames. *Fuck.*

Finnian's spine went rigid at the whirlpool of insects swooping down around him. He hauled the inferno upwards, scorching the collective of moths. Embers of their ashes caught in the tailspin of the flames.

Just as the mass of moths separated, they reanimated and banded back together.

Finnian growled, admitting defeat and releasing the inferno. The flames sucked back into the vortex of the mountain.

The moths descended in a swarm, scurrying over his skin, burying in his hair.

He batted and slapped at them. They crawled up his chin and burrowed in the corners of his mouth. He sealed his lips. Their paper-thin wings brushed his eyelashes.

They were everywhere, all at once—his arms, his legs, underneath his clothes, overwhelming his synapses.

The tiny scratching of their legs tunneling into his ear canal, reverberating loudly in his skull. They gouged underneath his eyelids, up the passageways of his nostrils. He pried at his eyes, crushing moths between his fingers. Their fuzzy bodies coated his tongue and cemented down his throat.

He coughed, attempting to force them out of his esophagus. He clawed at his neck, willing to tear apart his flesh to free them.

His knees buckled and his palms bit the hot stone. The prickling of tiny legs on his cheeks numbed. His eyes felt as if they were stuffed with cotton.

Pressure expanded in his chest, up the sides of his neck, building in his skull.

His hands curled into fists against the stone as he clung to the slipping thread of his consciousness.

You must right your wrongs.

Everything went dark. Control over his body gave way, and his side collided with the floor.

You must find Father.

His fingernails scraped against his own skin to rip the moths' dry bodies away. The wound stung as the air hit it. His vision momentarily cleared, revealing someone crouched down, hovering over him—their face masked with a deer skull, horns twisting out of the top.

Finnian's heart submerged into his stomach as the image eclipsed with his fading consciousness.

"Welcome to hell," said the High God of Chaos and Ruin.

FIVE

EVERETT

THE PAST
Cassian

H*E TURNED HIS* *first lover into a ghoul.*

Cassian strolled down the lantern-lit cobblestone, the brassy glow bouncing off the brick establishments of the city known as Augustus. Established two-thousand years ago, Cassian had witnessed many wars between mortals to conquer the urban settlement, as it sat on the border between the Eastern and Western Hemisphere. It had brought many souls into his Land.

The city's population thrived as the century waned on. Though Cassian never had any interest in stepping foot on its speckled cobblestone, here he was—obsessively turning over a soul named Arran in the back of his mind. A demigod born in Kaimana to a lesser goddess, murdered by Malik, Finnian's older brother.

Cassian remembered every soul in his realm. It was his duty. Arran had entered the Land about a year ago with an immense amount of trauma.

He was sent to the Grove of Mourning, a sacred part of the Land where struggling souls roamed. It was a place to go when one needed time to process and recover from their mortal life before setting forth on the path of healing that the Lavender Fields provided.

After Cassian had broken out of Finnian's sigil in the temple, he'd returned to the Land and immediately ordered Mavros to spill every detail of the young god to him. He'd paced the square feet of his sitting room a hundred times over, livid, his hands itching to latch onto Finnian's neck after their encounter.

It was then when Cassian visited the soul, concluding its way of death was to blame for the mental despair burdening him. Mutilated and shredded by Malik's blade. The pain and suffering he'd endured had been horrendous, and he had lasted four years at Finnian's side as an undead creature.

Why did the young god release him? If he were building an army for power, it made no sense. He would need as many souls as he could acquire. Perhaps he pitied his past lover. If that were the case, it gave Cassian a better idea of Finnian's true character beneath his apathetic ruse.

Cassian rubbed his fingertips against the pad of his thumb as he walked. A poor distraction to keep his hands from entering the pockets of his trousers.

Nathaira had advised against expressing any of his usual gestures. The only thing that had come to mind was the occasional hand swiping through the hair, but she quickly pointed out the way he constantly stuffed his hands in his pockets. A habit he was painfully aware of now.

He turned the street corner to a more crowded pathway. Currents of mortals rushed on either side of the cobblestone, loitering outside the businesses. Grease-stained, rugged men, after a long day of manual labor, stood with promiscuous women on their hips.

Shoulders bumped into him. He overheard the lewd remarks they tossed amongst one another. The lanterns lining the sidewalk decreased in number until barely any at all lit his path. Darkness settled like a fog between the buildings.

The tavern came into view up ahead.

It had been two years since he'd faced Finnian in the temple. The young god vanished, and it had taken Mavros time to locate his whereabouts. It appeared Finnian had learned a spell to hide his aura from Cassian. The game infuriated Mavros to a high degree and became a personal priority for him rather than an order.

Approaching the tavern, Cassian's hand lifted for his pocket, but he caught himself mid-movement, pressing his fingertips against the lines of his palm.

There was a slight edge quivering beneath his skin. An unease, as he casually brushed his fingers over features that were not his—a shorter nose, the tip rounded and exposing the divots of his nostrils; low cheekbones framing curved eyes; a set of jaws giving his face a more circular shape.

The whole thing was absurd. Shape-shifting to alter his appearance entirely. Meddling in the Mortal Land to hunt down a young god when he could've easily sent Mavros in his place.

Cassian had many things to tend to. Preparations for the monthly Council meeting was at the top of his list. He dreaded it immensely, mostly for the fact that he was forced to sit at a table and watch the High Goddess of Fate flash her elegant smiles and speak in poetic riddles when a *yes* or *no* would easily suffice. Cassian hated flourishment.

He smoothed the velvet lapels of his tailcoat. Focusing on what was currently in his control helped. The mere thought of Ruelle was suffocating. He could not afford to be distracted.

Cassian stopped in front of the entrance of the tavern, smoothing out his crisp collar. Its frosted windows were slick with condensation. The bell chimed against the door with each arrival and departure. Above the entrance a sign read: RED FOX TAVERN.

People came and went, chatter and laughter spilling from the door. The chaos made him long for his bedchamber. A gentle fire crackling in the hearth. The sip of a warm cup of lemon tea. He could pretend he came and did not find the young god when Mavros inquired about it.

Despite the appeal, it would be irresponsible and only make the situation more troublesome at the upcoming Council meeting. Once learning of it, they would expect Cassian to have handled it. It was unlike him not to do so. Allowing loose ends to spiral gradually out of control and create bigger messes was unacceptable, both for the Council's standards and for his own.

Cassian topped the steps to the tavern and reached for the door. It flew open before he could grab onto the handle and a man staggered out, belligerently singing and swaying as if gravity had abandoned him.

The horrid stench of liquor stung Cassian's nose. He held his breath, leaning a bit to the right to avoid bumping into the drunk mortal, and slipped inside before the door closed.

Cassian sauntered through the cloud of smoke to the bar and sat on a stool at the end, refraining from resting his arms on the bar top. The streaked, amber globs along the glossy surface looked to be quite sticky.

He joined his hands in his lap and observed his surroundings.

"You got your two pints. Now piss off. I've got others to keep," the barkeeper chided two taller gentlemen while drying glasses.

A slender, hairy man with arms the density of toothpicks laughed, downing his beer as he strolled off.

"Nobody fuckin' talks to me like that, ya hear?" The other with short, brunette strands slurred the words, slamming his pint down on the surface of the bar, his outcry barely coherent. The frothy liquid splashed across the bar top, spraying those sitting in its vicinity.

"Oh, fuck off!" someone crooned from the other end of the bar.

Those sitting nearby shot the man glares, while others dismissed him and carried on with their drink and conversation.

The barkeeper stopped drying the glasses and stepped up to the edge of the bar. "You start something, and I'll finish it. Ya hear?"

A wave of tense silence passed between them. The barkeeper's threat seemed to hold some leverage, because the man backed away on his heel, his balance swaying a little.

He lifted his pint up to scowling lips, turning away from the barkeeper.

The barkeeper cocked his eyebrows with a twitch to his lips that said, *smart choice,* and continued to work.

The man joined a table of people in a dark corner. A playful yelp came from a woman sitting on a different gentleman's lap. Another pair relaxed across from them, drinking and smoking rolled paper stuffed with tobacco leaves.

The vices of mortals were often dull and uncreative, and Cassian grew bored—even slightly annoyed—by the stimulation of the noise and smells congregating beneath the small roof of the tavern. The sooner he located Finnian and cursed him, the sooner he could return to his realm and revel in sweet silence.

"Sir," the barkeeper said with a loud clap to it.

Cassian snapped his attention to the mortal in front of him.

"What will it be?" The barkeeper had a stocky frame with a round face and expressive eyes, their color warm and welcoming, but the folded skin around them showcased his exhaustion.

"Bourbon," Cassian answered. "Neat."

The bartender pulled a bottle out from underneath the counter and poured the bronze liquid into a glass. He slid it across the bar top to Cassian and gave a curt nod. "There ya go, mate."

Cassian bowed his chin in gratitude and brought the glass to his nose. The sharp aroma of alcohol was a welcome distraction from the body odor and tobacco stench amalgamating in the air around him.

He sloshed the contents around the glass, subtly glancing at those sitting beside him. Finnian was more than likely under disguise. After Cassian's random visit to the apothecary, Finnian would've been foolish not to—

"*Bitch*. Don't ignore me. *Aye!*"

Cassian spun around in his stool to find the unmannered man from earlier standing in between two tables, his face contorted, gripping a young woman by the wrist.

She gaped up, shocked by his sudden touch, flicking her eyes all over his angry expression. Her mouth opened and closed, but no words came out.

"I gave ya a compliment, and ya just fuckin' ignore me." He jerked her closer towards his face, the force of it jostling her dark hair over her cheek.

She shook her head frantically, eyes wide like a frightened animal.

At the sign of her fear, the tension in the mortal's shoulders loosened, and he laughed, the sound slimy and vile.

"Ya owe me now, don'tcha agree?"

Cassian ground his jaw.

Do not intervene in mortal affairs.

He swiveled in his stool to face straight ahead, glaring at the shelves of liquor, and took a swig.

"Upstairs will do fine. What d'ya say, la—"

A harsh *thud* cut him off.

Cassian turned his head.

A stranger held the man bent over a table, the side of his face pressed against the surface, his arm twisted behind his back. He was trapped by the stranger's hold on his head—fingers decorated with rings.

The woman stood off to the side, her arms hugging her torso, cheeks flushed.

The bar grew silent. All eyes were on them.

Cassian studied the stranger's profile, their raven-black strands, longer now, grown past their shoulders, and resisted the urge to roll his eyes.

There were no signs of anger or excitement on Finnian's face as he stared down at the back of the man's head. "I'd be wise and leave her alone, or else I might think of ways to rid you of *your* hearing."

Of course, *he* would be the one to interfere with mortal squabbles. Although his aloofness was impressive, it provoked a need in Cassian to locate his triggers and draw out emotion.

"Ya right bastard, when I get outta this…." The man spit out, furious, attempting to buck up and out of Finnian's hold.

"I'd advise you to avoid laying your filthy hands on those who do not request it."

"I'll fucking kill ya!" the man snarled.

Finnian slanted forward, resting beside his ear. "Only after I boil your insides with one of my potions."

The man's body stiffened in response, proving he wasn't completely ignorant. Fear swallowed the glaze in his pupils as they flung around, trying to see Finnian's face from the angle he was stuck in. "I-I apologize, mate."

Satisfied, Finnian pushed away from the man, releasing him.

The man straightened, avoiding Finnian's gaze, and quickly left the tavern.

Voices began to mingle. Glasses clinked in the room once more.

Cassian took another drink to blend in, closely watching the young god out of the corner of his eye. Despite not being able to sense his aura, Cassian couldn't decide if Finnian presenting himself with so little glamor was bold or reckless.

Finnian turned his focus onto the woman, and his eyes fell on the bruises blotting her wrists. His hard shell of an expression softened, and he brought his hands between them in swift, practiced motions that were lost on Cassian.

However, Cassian couldn't stop watching the glint of Finnian's rings as his fingers shifted and formed shapes. The backs of his hands were smooth and the shade of a sun-ripened walnut, with a river of veins running beneath his skin. Long, dexterous fingers. Well-manicured fingernails.

He averted his eyes to the woman. Whatever was communicated brought a grin to her face as she signed something back.

Finnian gave a crooked smile in response, along with a light laugh Cassian wouldn't have heard if he hadn't been eavesdropping with his divine hearing.

A low flutter in his belly took him by surprise, and he slightly tilted his head, noting how the sliver of emotion drew lines around the young god's eyes and filled out the hollowness of his cheeks.

Apparently, there was more to him than Cassian had seen in the apothecary. Infuriatingly cocky and a defiant bastard, yes, but evidently he had some admirable traits, like being considerate, valiant even.

Finnian bid farewell to the woman and exited the tavern.

Curiosity was a fickle thing.

Cassian did not want to admit that Finnian had caught his attention, therefore he simply told himself he would only investigate the matter further before cursing him. Observe him a bit longer, maybe tail him back to his lair to find it stocked full of suffering souls, or a following of mages who, too, could bring back the dead.

Cassian paid his bar tab and followed.

He tailed Finnian down an alleyway. As they walked, he casually studied the backside of the young god's lean build, noticing the loose trousers around his hips and legs, suggesting they'd not been properly tailored.

Finnian's pace came to an abrupt stop, forcing Cassian to dip between two buildings.

He watched closely around the corner as Finnian turned his attention towards a metal bin against the brick.

He strolled over to it and lifted the lid, freeing a wave of decay in the air. The stench did not faze him, though.

To Cassian's surprise, Finnian began digging through the bin and tossing rotten food and trash down at his feet. He buried his hands deeper in the rubbish.

Then, his arms stopped moving. A flash of anger struck across his face, curling his lip and pulsing in his jaws. The muscles in his back flexed underneath the thin, white fabric of his linen shirt as he pulled something out of the bin.

Finnian gripped what appeared to be something large, long, and covered in black fur.

A leg.

He hauled the animal out of the bin and carefully kneeled to lay it on the ground.

A knot formed in Cassian's stomach.

It was a deceased dog, its body bloated and attracting a swarm of flies. The dog's fur was damp and bald in some areas, its skin yellowing. Cassian could tell from the twisted angle of one of its back legs that it had been injured.

"Do not fret." The glint of a crystal caught in the lamplight, drawing shapes along the cobblestone as Finnian placed it on the center of the dog's bloated stomach. "*Vivifica.*"

Wispy ribbons curled out from the gemstone, a kaleidoscope of reds and purples and blues twisting and cradling the dog's corpse. Finnian flipped his palm upright and slowly lifted it. A glowing, phantasmal orb levitated through the ground, floating in front of Finnian like a jellyfish wading in the sea. Small, translucent flecks, like dust in sunlight, orbited the soul.

Cassian pushed his tongue against the backs of his front teeth. The departure of one of his souls affected him. He felt the hollow ache take the place of a weight that had once been there. It was momentary, but Cassian was hyper-aware of the totality of souls within his Land. The first time he felt the shift, he had immediately sent Mavros to investigate.

Cassian's muscles constricted in his shoulders as his divine power roused within.

The young god was stealing one of his souls. Right in front of him.

Do not let him get away with this.

With the guidance of his hand, Finnian merged the soul into the dog's solar plexus. A small gust of power pushed his long bangs back from his face, revealing a wicked smirk. Finnian was proud of what he was doing, proud of keeping a soul from healing in the Land.

Cassian's pulse rose as his molars ground against each other.

A whimper sounded and the dog's body convulsed.

Finnian pocketed the crystal and lifted to his feet.

The dog slowly came to life and climbed up.

Tail wagging, it looked up at its savior.

Finnian leaned down to pet the top of its head. "Much better."

The dog's tongue fell out of the side of its mouth, almost as if it were smiling.

This wasn't right. It was cheating the cycle of life. Souls could not be sustained inside broken bodies. What the young god was doing went against Cassian's sole purpose as the High God of Death and Curses. And yet, despite that, Cassian's gut clenched in disagreement with the voice nagging him to step out and punish Finnian for his actions.

The world and its cruelty were hardly fair, but they were necessary. To know pain was to gain the ability to grant compassion. Neither could exist without the other. He'd accepted this philosophy long ago. But before him stood a young, unseasoned god with a terrifying ability to raise the dead. He could create himself an army of souls at his disposal, and there he was, searching through trash to revive an abandoned dog.

"You are free to do as you wish," Finnian said to it. "I'd start with tearing out the throat of the individual who broke your leg and stuffed you in a bin to die." He gave the top of the dog's head one more scrub before straightening and continuing on his way.

The dog twisted its head, watching Finnian stroll down the alley.

Once the shadows of the looming buildings swallowed his silhouette, the dog rose and sauntered in the opposite direction, passing where Cassian hid.

It stopped and regarded him, panting and its tail wagging in a calm rhythm.

Cassian stared down at the visible chunk of bone exposed in its back leg, the hanging piece of skin dangling on the side of its shoulder, the pink meat of its flesh showing. It was a ghoul now. Undead but alive. Incapable of healing but spared from pain.

Creatures of mortality feared death. They saw it as an end. A journey into the cold Land of the Dead where life did not grow, where there were no pleasures like the ones life provided. A terrible myth Cassian was eager to rid from the terrified souls that appeared on his riverbank or at his gate.

An urge expanding in him as he crouched down and patted the dog's head. "Hello, little fellow."

Perhaps this was the reason he hesitated to curse the young god. It was evident Finnian had strong reservations with death, and Cassian wanted to prove to him those reservations were unnecessary.

The dog stepped forward to lick Cassian's face, but he kindly held it back. "I appreciate it, but how about later? Greet me when I return to the Land."

He pressed his palm against the dog's chest, and his divine power pulled. The same spectral sphere Finnian had summoned from the command of his necromancy balanced in Cassian's hand.

The dog's shell of a body laid lifeless once more.

A form transfigured in the shadows. An Errai emerged, cloaked in graphite, face concealed by a mask of white and black marble reflecting off the warm streaks of the lamplight.

"My lord." They bowed their head in greeting before stepping up and holding out their hand.

Cassian transferred the soul to them and quickly spun around, putting one foot in front of the other, determined not to lose track of the young god.

He came out onto a main street. Pansies decorated the cobblestone pathways. White brick establishments with painted windowpanes lined the walk. Ivy crawled across the exterior. Horses trotted down the streets, pulling carriages.

Cassian could feel the faint twinge of magic in the breeze. He could feel the remnants of Finnian's power and followed it like an animal's trail.

He turned off the main street and spotted vermillion wisps trailing like smoke in front of a theater hall. It was a large, several-story-tall brick structure with arched walkways and a columned peak reaching from its rooftop. Horse-drawn carriages lined the west side of the entrance, unloading patrons.

Cassian hid out of sight behind a nearby building before teleporting inside the hall.

He dropped into a grand corridor on the fourth tier lined with thick velvet drapes, individual entrances to reserved boxes. It was a possibility the young god would be on the floor-level where most of the middle class sat, but Finnian didn't seem to be the type to enjoy the proximity of such close company.

The corridor was filled with travelers. Cassian maneuvered his way forward without knocking shoulders with mortals, tailing the magical trace as the strings of an orchestra echoed from within the auditorium.

He came to a stop in front of the entrance of a box at the end of the corridor. His gut tingled with an odd sense of anticipation.

Quietly, he peeled the curtain back and peeked inside.

Finnian sat with a concentrated posture, his elbow propped up on the arm of the chair, intently watching the performance.

Cassian peered out at the orchestra positioned at ground level in front of the stage, their movements possessing an irresistible synergy as they played. Two women in leotards and ballet slippers twirled and soared in dance to the melancholic notes of the music.

He knew little about the arts but could appreciate them when necessary. Though, it seemed the young god appreciated them fervently.

Pinching the bridge of his nose, Cassian assured himself the bump in its bridge was still there.

With the amount of divine power he'd put into shape-shifting, there was no way Finnian would figure out his identity. He'd turned his pale strands black, his alabaster skin the same honey-tan shade as Finnian's, and had thoroughly reconstructed his facial features to rounder lines, rather than their usual sharp, broad strokes. The final touch had been altering the luster gold of his eyes to an indigo blue. It would be impossible for Finnian to recognize him.

With that assurance, he casually made his way to a chair on the other side of the aisle, on Finnian's right side, and took a seat.

The god acknowledged him with a subtle sidelong glance.

Cassian's heart skipped as he waited. To avoid the predicament that he'd found himself in last time, he'd descaled the traces of his powerful presence. All his efforts proved to be working, because the young god did not spare him another look.

His muscles relaxed. He settled into his chair and fixed on the lovely scenes of song and dance before him.

"You were in the Red Fox." Finnian kept his focus on the show, his chin propped on the heel of his hand. Cassian could clearly make out his rings now—silver bands around the base of his index and ring finger and another sitting on top of the knuckle of his pinky.

Perception was clearly a strong suit of the young god.

"I was merely curious." Cassian pushed his words out at a quicker pace, recalling Nathaira's advice to change his mannerisms and not be so *himself*.

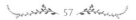

Apparently talking in smooth, slow syllables was another thing he did often. "I found the way you communicated with the woman to be intriguing. The movement with your hands."

"Sign language," Finnian said without looking at him.

"I've never witnessed it before," Cassian lied. He knew what the language was and had seen it a few times in his years. He was well versed in all languages, as he had a variety of souls in his realms from all different backgrounds. However, he never expected a deity to know the language when they themselves had no use for it. Deafness was seen as a flaw, and deities did not have flaws—a concept Cassian believed to be the biggest lie in existence.

"Glad to be of service," Finnian muttered. "Now, if you will, be quiet."

One side of Cassian's mouth tipped up as he refocused his attention on the show. It was easy to become captivated by the row of violins and how they moved their bows in synchrony. The song was full of sorrow, and the ballerinas conveyed tragedy and pain through their heavy movements, reaching towards something they couldn't seem to grab onto, just out of reach.

"Tell me." Finnian turned his head, granting Cassian his full attention—albeit with a blank expression.

Cassian met his look, waiting to hear what else he had to say. A desire to provoke him weighed heavily on Cassian's tongue. To resurface the bold, defiant look Finnian had given him back in the apothecary. Or perhaps, to coax out a smile like he'd seen earlier.

"Are you a stalker, by chance?" Finnian asked.

Cassian couldn't decide if he was genuinely asking or being his usual snide self.

But Cassian could understand why he thought such a thing. If he were being honest, he was exhibiting strange social behaviors—discreetly watching the young god at the tavern, following him to the theater, and inviting himself inside his private box. He hardly understood his own actions. Especially when he'd spent hours daydreaming of all the ways he intended to make the young god pay for their previous encounters.

"No," Cassian said, peering back down at the stage. "I am simply lonely."

He did not know what possessed him to say such a thing, but it was a truth he felt better confessing under the ruse of a stranger's face. He could be whoever he wished to be in this shape-shifted form.

Finnian's response was a single-syllable sound, refocusing on the show. It was difficult to gauge his thoughts—if Cassian unsettled him by over-sharing, or if he simply did not care.

Cassian snuck a glance between him and the stage, noting the lines creasing over his forehead, the swirling look in his eyes, captivated completely.

"You are a fan of music," Cassian said.

"Very much so."

"Have you always been?"

"No." Finnian paused, the muscles in his jaws ticking underneath his extended index finger along his bone. "I grew to appreciate it after it was almost taken from me."

Cassian studied the side of his profile, roving over his sunken cheek to the polished patch of skin along his jawline before meeting his ear. A strong cast of glamor, but not invisible to a deity of Cassian's caliber. A scar of some kind. "I am told loss grants perspective."

Finnian snorted lightly. "Perhaps. Although, I am convinced I would've discovered my love for music without the additional trauma."

Cassian subtly studied the heliotrope crystal lodged inside the young god's ear canal. Its glint reflected under the dim lights of the box. Magic seemed to be laced in its properties. Was it some sort of device to assist with hearing?

There were only two ways a deity could sustain permanent damage—a strike from a more powerful deity, or an effect from one of Cassian's curses.

Finnian had not stepped foot outside of Kaimana until his banishment. If he'd fought with another god, the Council would've heard about it. Which meant there was only one reasonable explanation. The unmerciful High Goddess who Cassian entrapped beneath the sea centuries ago had inflicted permanent damage on him. It made sense to Cassian why Mira had banished Finnian. The Council did not know of his lineage yet, and Cassian wondered if Finnian himself knew he was a High God.

"What is it about this piece you love so?" Cassian asked, slightly am-plifying the volume of which he spoke, in case the young god's right ear was impaired. His eyes swept over the glamor twinkling within Finnian's long strands. Was the young god's hair color truly black? Perhaps he had tampered with the texture of it to appear bone-straight.

Why do you care?

Deities using their glamor to alter or enhance their features was hardly abnormal.

A long somber second passed before Finnian replied with, "It breaks my heart."

Something pinched in Cassian's chest as he stared at the side of Finnian's face. There was a dissonance in his gaze, arched by a tension on his brow. That curiosity in Cassian prodded deeper, interested in following the mixture of Finnian's tranquility and torment to see where it led. What had his life been like until that moment? How did he learn to raise the dead? Why did he do so in the first place?

The theater erupted in applause.

Cassian's breath hitched, slightly startled. He pulled his eyes to the bowing performers on stage and joined in and clapped his hands.

The audience below began rustling and exiting the auditorium, all attempting to be the first out.

Now that the show was over, Cassian scrambled in his thoughts to plan what his next move would be. The box they were currently in was small and hidden, a perfect place to seize Finnian and curse him. Although, after his experience in the apothecary and the temple, he had a feeling the young god wouldn't make things easy. There would certainly be damage and a scene that would alert the mortals in the theater.

And gods forbid there be an invisible sigil mapped out along the floor of the box. If he fell trapped in another one of Finnian's magical antics, he was sure he'd strangle the young god this time.

Cassian let out a light sigh, unsure what to do to dissolve the knot tightening in his stomach.

He stood up in unison with Finnian, smoothing the wrinkles of his tailcoat.

"Which side of the city do you live on?"

Finnian's question prompted Cassian to lift his head, blinking at him in bewilderment.

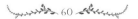

Was he asking out of concern, or purely out of suspicion? Cassian scoured the vacant look on his face for answers, to no avail.

"I am a traveler. Augustus is a mystery to me." Cassian cleared his throat, fidgeting with the buttons of his tailcoat. He had never been any good at lying.

"Very well. I will show you around." Finnian beckoned for him to follow as he started towards the exit of the box.

"Show me around?" Cassian's hand lifted to sail his fingers through his hair, a way to exert some of his nervous energy. Midway, he halted and dropped his arm back down to his side, with Nathaira's warning going off in his mind—*don't act like yourself.*

Finnian waited at the threshold with crossed arms. The stance broadened the contours of his chest, the tan skin of his pecs visible between the unfastened buttons of his shirt. An incomplete outfit without a waistcoat or a tailcoat. It was considered ill-mannered and sloppy to wear nothing but a shirt—unbuttoned nearly down to his diaphragm at that.

"It would be rude of me to abandon my stalker," he quipped.

Cassian's cheeks flushed at the accusation. "I was not stalking you. I—" He pressed his tongue to the roof of his mouth.

Finnian cracked a wide smile. Dimples cut into the grooves of his cheeks. Crinkles drew beneath his eyes, glittering with amusement as he stared at Cassian. "What is your name?"

A flutter caught in Cassian's chest. He replayed the young god's question in his mind. His mouth opened to respond with his real name, but quickly caught himself as he remembered his altered appearance.

He thought quickly, recalling the inventory of souls in the past decade that had journeyed from this region of the Mortal Land for a common name.

"Everett," he supplied.

"Nice to make your acquaintance, Everett. I am Finnian." He pulled the curtain back, gesturing Cassian to step through with a flick of his chin.

Cassian straightened his shoulders and breezed past him. As he took a deep breath, the unmistakable scent of licorice and herbs filled his nostrils. It smelled partially of the beer and smoke from the tavern, but mostly of a garden—lemon balm, yarrow, ginger root.

Traveling down the long stairway lined with velour and golden stitching, he snuck glimpses of the young god at his side, noting how Finnian positioned himself with his left ear, absent of a magical crystal, to face Cassian as they walked.

Cassian could easily do it. Slip his hand underneath the low neckline of Finnian's shirt. Release his divine power and infect the young god's mind. It would be done in less than a second. Another deity cursed, another problem crossed off Cassian's to-do list.

A thought that constricted his gut.

He clenched his jaws, irritated by his own indecisiveness.

Why couldn't he do it?

He rubbed his chin to keep his hand from his hair as they emerged into the street. The cool gust of night whispered across his skin. The moon hung like an ornament in the starry-lit sky, silver and fat and glowing across the town. The streets were less busy. A quietness drifted amongst the distant hooves of traveling carriages.

Cassian couldn't recall the last time he'd strolled in a land that wasn't his own. It felt nice, refreshing even, to be someone else in another's company.

A temporary ruse.

Before the night's end, he bargained with himself. He would curse the young god before the night's end. But not yet. Not right now.

Thousands of years ago, after he earned his title, Cassian vowed to never make irrational decisions. While he did not regret becoming the High God of Death and Curses, he'd decided it on a whim and questioned his sanity for it every day.

It was the same voice of reason chiding in the back of his mind to *wait* as he put one foot in front of another, walking side-by-side with the young god, unsure of his own actions.

This wasn't like him, and worst of all, he was enjoying it.

SIX

THE SERPENTINE FOREST

THE PRESENT
Finnian

INNIAN AWOKE TO a veil of fog melting between the thicket of branches.

His body jolted, and he gasped, his airway free from moths.

Fucking High God of Chaos.

Finnian couldn't ever fathom loathing another person more than he did Cassian, but after his encounter with Chaos—and a newfound fear of moths—he was beginning to believe otherwise.

Slowly, as if not to disturb the eerie silence enveloping him, he rose to a sitting position and did a sweep of his surroundings. Through the monochrome hue and the dense layer of gnarled beech trees, he peered into the hazy shadows as far ahead as his eyes could reach. There was no birdsong, no breeze. Only an unnerving stillness.

The Serpentine Forest.

Something he'd come across during his studies. Geographically, Finnian assumed the forest's placement was close to Moros. It made sense for it to act as a barrier to keep souls from stumbling into the Land's prison, and even more sense to keep those from ever truly leaving Moros. The forest's layout would no doubt be something detesting and fiendish. A labyrinth or maze, or maybe some sort of grotesque illusion.

He climbed up to his feet, eyes flicking around to keep a lookout for jostled movement. His divine power quickly activated in his left ear. The sound waves extended farther out, and with a slow rotation of his head, he managed to grab onto the bubbling of water in the distance.

He followed the direction with his gaze, analyzing the churning darkness and the silhouettes of trees. Through a sliver of prodding gray light between the leaves, he made out the steep incline of ground cover ahead. The sound came from the other side.

He hiked to the top. At the bottom was a hot spring in the clearing, surrounded by bald cypress trees. The anthropomorphic roots protruded from the water, twisting and reaching across the ground cover like skeletal hands. An entanglement of midnight-violet blossoms suffocated the bank. Amid their bell-shaped bodies were fat berries.

Finnian's knowledge of belladonna flowers was extensive due to the amount of grimoires he'd written. He primarily used the poisonous flower as an ingredient in potions to cast temporary illusions or to conjure up a lethal poison of intense paranoia—many of which he had sold in his black market to stir attraction.

Hollow City's prosperity and longevity had been his constant focus.

Only a few years had passed after his banishment when he discovered the belladonna's origin. The flower first blossomed, supposedly, in the very forest Finnian stood in. Where, over five thousand years ago, the High God of Death and Curses bled for seven days and seven nights after becoming one of the first deities in existence.

Envisioning the High God bleeding for days on end was satisfying.

Finnian approached the pool of steaming water. Distant, muffled, animalistic screams caught in his ear.

He stopped with his toes inches from the belladonna, eyeing the gurgling surface of the hot spring.

Interesting.

He lifted a hand, fingers curled. With the command of his magic, he caressed a single droplet from the water, elevating it eye-level with him.

Water held the energy of those it touched.

Finnian twisted his head, angling his ear towards it. The cacophony of hushed sounds amplified and violated his eardrum. He winced, forcing himself to listen carefully to discern the noise.

The spiraling of hurricane wind; a murmuration of deep-toned birds screeching in pulses; a woman's voice echoing an atonal siren song; the rumbling and cracking of earthy crust. It was an uncomfortable, violent ensemble.

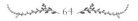

Finnian flexed his fingers, releasing the droplet from his control. It splattered on one of the black petals of the nightshade near his shoe. The substance blackened and frothed, burning a hole straight through the blossom.

Finnian backed away, his eyes jumping to the hot spring. The cloudy water's depth was endless, like a void, all too similar to the inferno in Moros. Where did it lead? Was there more of this dreadful place beneath his feet?

His pulse flickered with dread, blaring his senses into flight.

He spun and started back the way he came. In his periphery, he spotted a fat, blush-toned blossom.

Finnian halted in his step, his breath catching.

Father.

Against the desire to run towards it, Finnian glanced around before slowly making his way through the crunch of twigs and corpse-gray leaves. Wary of his surroundings, he kept the muscles in his arms stiff, ready to call on his magic at the first sign of a threat.

He crouched down and examined its frail layers of petals. Delicate and whimsical, pale pink and stunning.

Paeonia lactiflora. A key ingredient for a calming tincture. Father's favorite flower.

"Where are you?" Finnian murmured.

He waited, hoping his father would hear his plea and give him another sign.

Yards ahead, between two lifeless beech trees, a peony sprouted from the dry soil. Beyond it, the path followed a chasm of darkness.

Finnian's gut spit something foul into the back of his throat as he rose.

The darkness enclosed around him the moment he stepped into its threshold, drowning out the light peeking in through the blanket of branches.

"Belyse." The incantation brazed swiftly off his tongue.

With it, his sight sharpened in shades of gray. Through the spell, he could make out the forest beyond him. A dark pit. In its belly were several hollow tunnels. Dead branches twisted into canopies.

A labyrinth.

Finnian was aware that casting a spell to dissolve the darkness would be futile. A spell he had learned in his younger days to disperse the night

Marina wrought in the halls of their mother's palace. This darkness, Death's shadows, it was something else entirely. Primordial.

If Finnian attempted to burn the trees, they'd only grow back. He could sense the ancient power emanating from them, an energy he was reluctant to siphon out and use.

He turned and studied each path. In the tunnel's mouth to his left, another blossom unfurled, its petals stretching apart and extending in Finnian's direction, as if he were the sun.

He chose the path the peony beckoned him down.

The tunnel moaned in response to his presence. Every flicker in the grainy outline of the twined branches forming the tunnel had his fingers coiling in his palms. One hasty movement and he would strike it down with a sharp cut of his hand.

About three yards from the tunnel's entrance, another peony sprouted.

Finnian swallowed thickly, glancing between it and the crevices of the braided branches above. Eyes, small and piercing, beamed through their creases at him. Proof of life in this ghastly forest.

Shivers pricked down his spine. He felt a presence approaching from behind.

Angling his head slightly towards the left, he held his breath and listened closely through his divine hearing. The grating, wheezing sound drew closer, growing louder than the echo of his heartbeat.

His muscles tensed and he quickly spun with a hand drawn.

A woman crawled towards him, her fingers clinging to the terrain. "Help..." she croaked.

Only her torso remained, no legs. Mutilated flesh and the casings of her intestines dragged behind as her pace picked up, reaching an arm out for Finnian.

"Help me!"

His eyes flitted up into the abyss she'd crawled out of, more concerned by what had torn her in half.

Through the gray outlines of the spell procuring his night vision, he stared deeper into the darkness that spat back a sinister aura.

"Help me," the woman cried, wrapping her fingers around his ankle.

He raised his gaze to the branch-covered canopy, only to find the nocturnal creatures gone. They'd fled.

The woman wept harder.

His nostrils flared with the urge to kick her away. It was clear she was only a soul. Her touch felt like a wet feather, despite the grip she had on his leg. Her fingernails were like pricks of straw against his skin.

Finnian had also used this spell several times, accustomed to the black-and-white filtered view it provided. Within it, bodies were solid, tangible. The same could not be said for the woman. When he looked at her, she appeared grainy and transparent, almost wraith-like.

Her wounds were not real in a physical sense. Whatever had attacked her was not after flesh to sate its hunger. It had intended to devour her *soul* until there was nothing left but a memory. He needed to think fast before it—

A beast on all fours stepped out of the shadows behind her, its spine curled and hunched like a hairless, mutated werewolf. Its thin, elongated legs, and pale gray skin stretched thin over bone, every vertebrae beneath it visible.

Fuck me.

He recognized the creature as an Achlys.

Souls who disturb the realm's peace ended up in the Serpentine Forest, where they would eventually devour one another and become beasts who feasted on more souls—a macabre cycle.

Its small eyes glowed white, and its mouth, shaped like a pear, exposed folds of teeth that reminded Finnian too much of the executioners. In the grasp of its twine-bone fingers was the woman's leg.

It moved at an unreliable speed.

One blink, a step.

Another blink, four steps.

Its form flickered in and out of focus until it was an arm's length away from Finnian.

The woman at his feet screeched, the sound piercing his temporary shock.

He flexed his fingers. The silent command of his magic slung the half-eaten soul a few feet away as he ripped his other arm up, throwing the beast backwards and against a nearby tree trunk.

It let out an ear-piercing cry that quivered the ground beneath Finnian's feet.

His stomach dropped. It was calling the others.

Finnian took off in a sprint. The tunnel of branches did not relent and the further he went, strewn body parts greeted him.

Voices of the souls cried out all around him, muffled and distorted without his hearing aid.

H—l—p m—!

D—leave—e—!

Ta—m—wi—you!

He came to a stop at an intersection of tunnels, spinning to gauge each one, crushingly aware of the malevolent presence behind him.

It chilled his spine. He ducked before the monster could grab him in its clutches.

He brutally flicked his hand, throwing the horrid thing against the tunnel walls. The interwoven limbs moaned against the Achlys's weight as it slunk down onto the ground.

Finnian's breath went shallow. He gave the tunnels another look, casting a double take to the one on his right, quickly noting the peony standing sprightly in its mouth.

An elated sense of relief burst like a blueberry in his chest.

Without looking back, he fled towards it.

"Finny."

It came to him like a whisper caught in a breeze. The soft note of her familiar voice was nearly drowned out by the rushing of blood in his left ear.

The soles of his feet skidded in the dirt, and he whirled around. "Naia?"

An itch burrowed in the center of his skull. A droning, black pang. A tick latching into skin.

The hairs on his nape rose as he took in his sister standing before him in hues of gray. Her silver-coined waves hit her waistline. It was still an odd sight to see her in jeans and a crop-top and not some gaudy gown forced upon her by their mother.

"Finny." Her eyes flicked back and forth on his face, her expression severe. "Make haste. We must leave. *Now.*"

Hope had him lifting his hand to meet hers as a sense of rationality collided with his relief and desire.

He closed his fingers into a fist and squeezed. The itch in his brain quivered the nerves in his jaws. He rolled his shoulders. Something did not feel right.

He pinned his focus on Naia, scrutinizing the feel of her energy. Something he could easily identify in a sea of people. Naia was tranquil, like standing before a morning sunrise, sipping on espresso and gazing out a window during a thunderstorm. An energy he could not pick up on then.

The sister he knew would've thrown herself at him in a bone-crushing hug, crying and smiling like the emotional fool she was.

Finnian glanced behind his shoulder. The beast was gone. Maybe it was never there at all.

"You are not real," he murmured.

A deep rumble of laughter spread goosebumps down his arms.

He jerked his head around to find the tall, curvy figure of his sister being swallowed by an oil-sodden cloud.

Finnian's stomach twisted and he backed up on his heel.

Her silhouette transformed a foot taller, and her shoulders filled out into broad ones hidden beneath a fitted suit.

Cassian's eyes shone like golden jewels through the abyss, turning and swirling around him. "Why hello again, Little Nightmare."

Finnian's eyes jumped from the High God's lips to his eyes. The fear thudding his pulse made his hearing unreliable. It twined like a vine in his ribcage. There was no telling how Cassian would punish him for escaping Moros.

The cage of darkness lifted from around them, an inky mist ascending overhead and dissolving through the creases of the woven canopy of the tunnel.

Metallic light pierced through the branches. It shone across Cassian's profile as he stopped a few feet in front of Finnian, his hands stowed away in his front pockets, suave disposition fully intact.

He tilted his head, the movement dropping that singular, maddening curl into his face. "I must say it is impressive how much destruction you spawned in my prison."

Finnian dug his fingers into his palms, capping the urge to hex the High God. "Come to drag me back?"

"Since Moros wasn't to your liking, I figured the Serpentine Forest with the roaming Achlys would suffice."

Finnian glowered at him. "I'll burn this entire godsforsaken forest to ash before they touch me."

"I do enjoy your fire." Cassian pulled a vial from his pocket filled with a glittering silver substance. He held it up. "Do you know what this is?"

Finnian swallowed, unease tightening in his throat. "A binding potion."

It was strong from the looks of it. Magic glistened in the liquid particles like tiny stars. Whoever ingested it would be bound to the person they received it from. In this case, since it was in Cassian's possession, the victim would be bound to him.

Binding potions were temporary, but they sold for a high price in Hollow City's black market. Finnian would know, given he had been a major supplier in its earlier days when the city's population ran small. It was one of the first potions he ever created—with the help of his apprentices.

Cassian flipped the vial upside down. The viscous liquid oozed along the inside of the glass. "A witch gave it to me a long time ago. I knew it would find its use one day."

Finnian's eyes thinned, his heart pounding like timpani against the cavities of his chest. "If you cannot keep me contained in Moros, your next grand idea is to chain me to you?"

Cassian popped the cork of the vial with his thumb. It rolled across the dirt-laden terrain. "I see no sense in torturing you in Moros when my curse is currently living within you. In time, you will fall to its insanity and tell me where you're keeping Ash's blood. Until then, I cannot give you free rein of my Land."

To be powerless. Shivani's words haunted Finnian.

The cords in his neck went rigid the more he thought about the potion touching his tongue. It grated on his composure. To be confined, stripped of his willpower.

Escape.

Leave Father behind.

Do not link yourself to Cassian.

He could envision his father somewhere in the hellish landscape, filled with hope at the sense of Finnian's presence, only to be overcome with grave disappointment when Finnian turned his back on him once more.

Guilt chiseled down to his marrow.

Don't be a coward.

The alternative was to be a leashed dog.

"Why the hell are you so desperate to get your hands on my nephew's blood?" Finnian snapped, resentment frothing in his tone.

Cassian's eyebrows rose, and he lowered the vial. "What an uncharacteristic outburst. It seems my curse is taking quite nicely to you."

Finnian pressed his lips together, the itch prodding like an ice pick in his skull.

Cassian offered his empty hand. "We can avoid all of this. Simply return the item you stole."

Finnian stared down at his pale fingers, the soft tint of his short fingernails, the blue roadway of veins beneath skin.

The Kiss of Delirium wouldn't break him, but binding himself to Cassian might.

He suddenly yearned to be back in that sweltering hot dungeon with the executioner chewing on his insides and Shivani's bating remarks.

Finnian squared Cassian with a defiant look, grinning, as if he found the whole situation amusing. "After all the years we've played together, it is disappointing you'd assume I would ingest any sort of potion you'd wave in my face voluntarily."

Cassian took a menacing step forward, and the tunnels around them altered.

Their surroundings morphed into a completely different setting. The soil underneath Finnian's feet transitioned into dark, glossy stone. The tunnel hovering over them became a room made of obsidian. Golden basins filled with firelight reflected along the shimmering black walls.

Finnian moved back.

His heel rammed into something solid.

He turned quickly, discovering an altar atop the platform he stood on.

Cassian's temple.

A gust of mint and lemon engulfed him from behind, the mixture stirring nausea in his belly.

He spun and drove his arm up to cast a spell.

Cassian caught his wrist with one hand. The other planted on his chest and shoved him backwards.

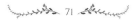

Finnian's back slammed down on the altar. A grunt pressed out of his lungs from the harsh impact.

He shot his free arm upwards, magic gathering in his palm.

Cassian hooked his index finger around Finnian's wrist, locking both of his hands in a steel grip over his head.

Finnian's nostrils flared. He curled his legs up to shove Cassian away. The High God's knee pried in between Finnian's legs and maneuvered in between them.

"I never assumed *voluntarily*." Cassian leaned down, keeping him pinned. "You are far too stubborn to do something when I ask."

Finnian jerked against his hold, cursing his unfathomable strength. He was much older, his divine power more honed. Finnian stood no chance against him in this position.

Worry beat thickly in Finnian's racing pulse. He opened his mouth to cast an incantation.

Cassian's movements were brisk, forcing the vial's spout into Finnian's mouth, drowning his spell. The glass clinked against his teeth. He clamped his throat closed. The potion fizzled on his tongue.

Cassian hooked the thumb of his other hand underneath Finnian's chin, forcing his jaw closed. "If you wish to hex me with that pretty mouth of yours, you'll have to swallow." He smothered his palm over Finnian's lips.

Finnian bucked and squirmed to break his arms free. The potion burned and tingled the inside of his cheeks. The harsh fumes of it tickled his throat. Tears stung his eyes.

He pushed the liquid to the front of his teeth, refusing to swallow. Dribbles leaked from the corners of his mouth, puddling in his ears.

Cassian lifted his hand from Finnian's mouth.

In a fit of coughing, he turned his head and spat out the potion onto the altar. He blinked through the moisture clouding his eyes.

Rage quaked in his limbs.

Cassian tightened his grip on Finnian's wrists, momentarily straightening up.

Finnian locked his thighs around Cassian's waist, lodging his knees in the High God's ribcage to force him back. Anything to prolong the small time he'd been given to clear his mouth.

"*Remotionem—*"

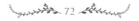

"Don't bother." The High God threw his head back with the vial to his lips and downed the remains.

He tossed the empty vial aside.

The glass shattered.

Cassian's abdomen flexed against Finnian's knees as he bent forward.

He snaked his hand underneath the base of Finnian's skull.

Finnian gasped. *"Remo—"*

Cassian sucked him into a kiss.

His eyes went wide, and he sealed his lips together.

The fight of a dying life force blazed in him, while simultaneously, his body slackened in Cassian's hold. He couldn't make sense of it and had little time to try as Cassian's tongue pried in between his lips to create access for the sterling liquid.

The filmy, bubbling concoction filled the back of his mouth again.

He clenched the sides of his throat and bit down hard on Cassian's bottom lip. The taste of iron infiltrated the potent, bitter taste of the potion.

Cassian tore his lip free from Finnian's teeth and reared up. Crimson ran down the High God's chin.

Before Finnian could spit the potion out, Cassian cupped his face and dug his thumb and index finger into the joint on the sides of his jaw and applied pressure, locking against Finnian's bones. He had no choice but to keep his mouth shut.

Finnian rolled the back of his head over the altar, fighting Cassian's hold. He pushed the potion through his teeth. Trickles of it leaked from his lips.

Cassian planted his palm across Finnian's mouth for the second time. "Quit being so stubborn and just swallow," he growled.

Finnian glared at him.

Cassian cataloged the rebellion in his eyes and responded by settling in closer. He swept down and grazed his lips along the side of Finnian's neck.

Warmth kindled in Finnian's bloodstream.

Cassian's breath fanned over his collarbones, traveling down to his waistband. He pulled the hem of Finnian's shirt up with his teeth, dragging his chin over his abdomen.

Finnian's breath sped up. Tingles scurried up his spine.

He ground his jaw, glowering over Cassian's knuckles plastered over his mouth.

As if he could sense Finnian's eyes on him, he lifted his hooded gaze, a sly determination twinkling within it.

"All—have—swallow," he said against Finnian's stomach.

All you have to do is swallow.

Heat blossomed in his lower belly, nearly forcing him to draw in a breath through his mouth.

Cassian lowered his lips down on the side of Finnian's torso. Gooseflesh spread across his skin. A stroke of Cassian's tongue over the ridges of his ribcage. A wet, staggering kiss, teeth bruising—

A tremor zapped down into Finnian's groin. The tense muscles of his throat gave way and the potion poured down his esophagus.

He gasped and coughed as he gulped it down. Defeat gnawed at his insides—a feeling that never dissolved well. One that would eventually harden into bitterness.

Satisfied, Cassian released his wrists and stepped down from the altar. One hand smoothed back his disheveled strands.

Finnian stared up at the glimmering firelight on the onyx ceiling with the burning of blood beating fiercely in his skull.

A feverish heat surged in his blood. Every nerve ending in his body tingled from Cassian's touch. Desire for *more* flooded his cheeks. The touch of the person he hated the most.

The contents of the potion bubbled in his stomach. A harrowing reminder of how he was now bound to Cassian.

A fresh wave of fury roared through him, the intensity sending quivers down his limbs.

He ripped up and threw his arm out, siphoning the energy residing in the ancient walls of the temple.

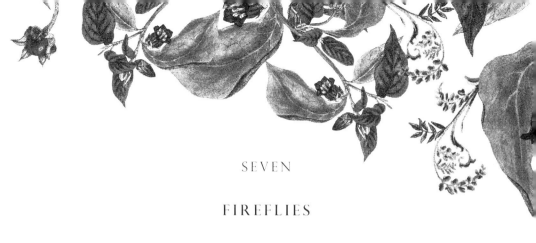

SEVEN

FIREFLIES

THE PAST
Cassian

THEY WALKED UNTIL the lights of the city became speckles masquerading in the night behind them. The stone path at their feet turned to dirt, branching off between small cottages and farmlands on the outskirts of Augustus and leading them into a lush landscape of aged oak trees. Wildflowers decorated the soil between their twisted roots.

"I wouldn't suppose you are leading me out into the middle of nowhere to dispose of me, are you?" Cassian rubbed his thumb and index finger together at his side, a ploy *not* to put his hand inside the confined space of his front pocket.

Finnian gave him a sidelong glance with a hint of a grin playing at the corner of his mouth. "I suppose you will find out soon enough."

Cassian smiled to himself, peering ahead through the streaks of moonlight piercing the branches and glinting off the water. The tranquil lapping of a nearby stream harmonized with the call of frogs and crickets. He inhaled the musky, stale scent of the earth, ravishing in the cool air.

"It is nice," Cassian said without thinking. "To walk and breathe in the fresh air." It was a task he had spent years trying to do, unsuccessfully—even with the graceful guidance of Nathaira, or with the maddening need for release to ease his stress.

"I am happy to provide such pleasures." Finnian pointed ahead. "Do you see?"

Above the stream and scattered amongst the forest were brief flickers of light. Smaller than raindrops. A fleeting glow disappearing and reappearing a few feet from where it previously was.

"Fireflies," Finnian said with a pinch of enthusiasm. "I find them incredibly fascinating. They do not appear in the city, but only in places our light does not touch."

Abruptly, he turned, veering off the dirt pathway and into the over-grown grass around his ankles.

Cassian stalled, hesitant to follow.

Finnian rotated and eyed him. "Are you afraid?"

"Hardly." He dropped his head down to his boots, contemplating what it would do to him if he got his boots muddy.

"Take my hand and step where I step. We'll keep them as clean as we can."

Cassian looked up to Finnian's outstretched hand and onto his playful smile, poking deep dimples on both sides of his mouth.

He staunched the warmth pooling in his chest from the sight.

Take his hand and be done with it.

Curse him and go home.

Cassian grabbed hold of Finnian's hand, measuring the softness of his long fingers as they lightly clasped around him. Gently, he guided Cassian forward.

Pulses of Finnian's power came in tiny surges, traveling up the tendons of Cassian's hand and down his forearm. A side effect of touching a thing of witchcraft. Their magic lived within their bloodstream, often making its presence known without trying, undetectable to an average mortal or a lesser deity. Cassian found an odd pleasure in the sensation.

They made their way down the small slope and closer to the stream. Vines with large, white, trumpet-shaped blossoms decorated the trunks of the oaks, their roots gnarled deeply into the bank and their petals reaching for the waxing moon.

Finnian let go of Cassian's hand and plopped down next to the tree.

He plucked one blossom from its stem and twirled it between his thumb and index finger.

"Moonflowers," he said, staring down at it.

Cassian sat in the space beside him. Their arms grazed, evoking lightning beneath Cassian's skin. A feeling well worth the stain of the damp soil soaking into his trousers. "They are nocturnal flowers, then?"

"Yes. They are my favorite." Finnian looked beyond the flower to the ever-moving current of the stream. "They flourish in darkness, and I find something quite poetic about that."

"Darkness is not as terrible as one would believe." Cassian leaned back on the tree's trunk, its bark rough against the layers of his clothes, mesmerized by the relentless motion of the stream. The sound was a lullaby to him. It had been ages since he gazed into a body of water absent of souls. "Darkness only scares those afraid of the unknown."

Finnian's probing stare tingled along the side of Cassian's cheek. He kept his attention on the water, not confident in the reaction it would whisk awake within him if he met Finnian's eyes.

After a long wave of silence, Finnian said, "Tell me more about yourself, Everett."

Cassian scrambled to think of lies. Anything to make Everett more believable. Too much and not enough came to mind. The effort it would take to sort through it all would be taxing.

"I am tired," he confessed with a sigh.

Finnian spun the blossom pinched between his fingertips, staring down at it. "Tired of?"

"Life."

Finnian glanced over at him. "Do you wish to die?" A question asked out of genuine curiosity, not a threat.

Cassian shook his head, dismissing the ridiculous notion. The High God of Death, longing for death. *What an anomaly that'd be.*

"Nothing like that," he said reassuringly. "I am simply realizing how much I lack enjoyment—*fulfillment.*"

"And what about this moment? Are you enjoying yourself?"

"I am."

"Then do not overthink it." Finnian flicked the moonflower blossom into the current gliding a few feet from where they sat. "Relish in the happiness you so desperately seek, as it is happening before you, and you are missing it."

Cassian blinked at him, mildly baffled by his wisdom. It only pushed his intrigue further, kindling a ridiculous longing to peel back the young god's layers, one at a time.

"Living in the present moment is not a skill I excel in," he said. "But what of you? Tell me something about yourself."

Finnian rested his head back on the tree and he let it roll sideways, facing Cassian. "What if I say that I do not wish to speak any longer?" His hooded gaze drifted from Cassian's eyes to his lips.

The air thickened between them, clotting the oxygen in his lungs.

With Finnian's head tilted back, it exposed the scape of his throat, the bulge of his Adam's apple bobbing up and down as he swallowed. Cassian had this bizarre need to trace it with his tongue, bite down on it to see what sort of reaction it would stir in Finnian.

He was suddenly all too aware of his own breath, of Finnian's flared pupils, and the flutter catching at the bottom of his stomach.

Finnian twisted his torso and leaned in, lifting an arm and sliding a hand around Cassian's nape, guiding him closer.

Cassian slanted forward, utterly confused by the sudden silence in his mind. His mouth went dry as Finnian's lips brushed over his, eliciting a tremor down his spine.

"Are you in this moment with me, Everett?" Finnian murmured, tenderly kissing the corner of his mouth.

Heat simmered and sparked in Cassian's bloodstream. A longing he'd never felt before blossomed in his core, ravaging him piece by piece. The intensity of it caught his breath as Finnian's question resounded in his mind.

You are Everett, not Cassian.

The reality hit Cassian like hailstone in his veins, freezing over his desire.

No matter how much Finnian irritated him, he could not deceive him this way. It felt wrong and too unlike himself.

It served as a sharp reminder of his purpose.

Finnian was still the young god stealing souls; the young god who'd declared time and time again his refusal to give up necromancy; who'd trapped Cassian in sigils and destroyed his altar. Cassian could not afford to sway on his task simply because Finnian's personality, beneath his pompous attitude and infuriating skill of witchcraft, had depth.

Cassian forced his hand to lift from the grass and slip between their chests. "I am." It came out low and gruff as he gripped the base of Finnian's throat.

Cassian felt the upturn of Finnian's lips against his cheek as he smiled. "I must say I am not opposed to choking, but know whatever you do to me, I will do to you tenfold."

Cassian pushed the pads of his fingers into Finnian's throat just enough to make it hurt. "What a fiery god you are." The mellow tone of Everett's voice transitioned into a richer, darker one.

Finnian stiffened beneath his hold and slightly pulled back, his eyes darting over Cassian's face. Not once had Finnian mentioned his divinity.

The lust in his gaze evaporated into a frigid fire as he studied Everett's face. "And who might *you* be?" The friendly ire in his tone reverted to its usual aloofness.

"It's been a while, Little Nightmare." As the words left Cassian's mouth, he shape-shifted into his regular form.

Finnian yanked back.

Cassian shoved the young god firmly against the tree. "Ah, not so fast."

The skin around Finnian's eyes constricted—a visible trace of irritation. Though, his lips twisted into an obnoxious smirk. "Your life must *truly* lack enjoyment if you go through all this trouble to deceive me."

Cassian wanted to reach inside of his twinkling gaze and snatch the smugness right out of it.

"You did trap me in a sigil. Or two." Cassian's fingertips slowly sank deeper into his skin. "And while witnessing you revive a dead dog from a trash bin was endearing, your actions are giving me a rather persistent headache."

"It would've been fun to fuck a High God." Finnian spat back. "You really should have waited ten minutes to reveal yourself."

Cassian's divine power swam through his blood, blackening the skin of his wrist and hand into the fingers hooked around Finnian's throat. "You seem like a kind individual, undeserving of one of my curses. It is not too late to reconsider—"

The chrysocolla pendant around Finnian's neck began glowing fiercely, alluring Cassian's gaze.

His grip around Finnian lessened for a quick second, and the young god struck a palm to Cassian's chest, knocking him backwards. The impact sent a jolt of pain through his body as his back collided with the unforgiving ground.

Finnian's hand went straight for the iridescent stone, and he gripped the pendant between his index and middle finger, tapping into its energy. "*Excitare ex somno!*"

The trees swayed violently as a gust of wind rustled through their branches. A magical force that kept Cassian down on his back.

Glowing globes of milky light shot from Finnian's pendant in all directions, halting in the air around him. Bone, then sinew, then patches of skin wove around the bright spheres.

Souls. He had been keeping them—waiting to turn them into ghouls—in his necklace this entire time.

A rotted hand coiled around Cassian's shin, breaking him from his thought. The bone of his knee snapped.

He grunted through clenched teeth.

The bodies of the ghouls solidified around their spirits, taking an offensive formation around their master. Their dark, brittle bones were reinforced by the young god. Cassian could see the glow around them; it was like an oily flame, yet the color of snow.

Another pair of hands surprised Cassian from behind, swiftly immobilizing him by his shoulders.

Two corpses loomed over him, their decaying flesh clinging to their skeletal frames like a sheet draped over a clothesline.

One drove its bone fingers through Cassian's shoulder.

He chuckled darkly at the twinge of pain twisting in his flesh. The suction of his knee-bone fusing back together reverberated up into his hip, and he lunged up and caught the ghoul's face like a ball in his palm and squeezed.

Its skull shattered and its knees gave in, collapsing as if never coming to life at all. Its soul retreated to the pendant.

Cassian lifted his leg off the ground. The toe of his boot buried into another's chest.

The ghoul flew up in the air and landed in the stream.

Cassian quickly rose to his feet as more ghouls swarmed him. Imbuing his right hand with divine power, he circled his palm above his head, creating a stream of slick shadows around him.

"Rest!" He bellowed the word as he closed his fist, and the ring of ruination shot outwards. It passed through the army of corpses, encircled around the young god's pendant, pulling the souls like a cloud as it touched them.

Cassian's power magnetized the glistening spiritual casings, rightfully releasing them from the husks of meat and marrow, as well as from the dreadful crystal, and holding them in the air.

He scoffed as he patted the dirty smudges from his sleeves. "Do you honestly believe your little ghouls stand a chance against me?"

Charcoal ribbons streaked with gold twisted out from Cassian's back, gathering into a black-tinted mass that swirled and swelled over his head. Twisting left, he fixed his attention on Finnian standing on the other side of the stream.

The abyss flowed down from the tree canopies and the Errai emerged from within it, hidden in cloaks and masks.

"Collect them all," Cassian ordered.

The velocity of their movements painted the forest in a disarray of magenta blue tendrils, wispy fine trails of smoke curling around trees.

Each member of the Errai approached an individual orb and coaxed it into their palms. The luminescence in the forest dimmed as the sea of stolen souls were guided home. When all had been retrieved, the Errai returned as quickly as they entered, trusting in their master's ability to handle himself.

A menacing energy gathered in the atmosphere and nipped at Cassian's skin.

Finnian lifted his hand, and a dazzling burst of magic materialized above his open palm, pulsating and swirling until it took the shape of a vortex. Its power rippled through the leaves on nearby branches. Cassian's hair whipped in every direction.

A roar escaped the young god's mouth as the swiveling nebula burst forth from his palm, ripping up roots and sending stones crashing into the nearby stream.

Cassian's divine power enclosed around him like a shield, pushing back against the devastation.

A thunderous echo reverberated when their powers collided. The impact shuddered through the ground, quaking the forest's foundation.

Cassian's aegis disbanded and lifted like vapor as the magic fizzled into glittering specks.

He raised his chin and met Finnian's fierce glower across the stream.

The young god stood barricaded by the vacant corpses of his ghouls, unafraid, careless, facing Cassian, of all deities.

It was painfully stupid, but Cassian couldn't make sense of the uncertainty clouding his ability to put this young god in his place. Finnian's confidence was infuriating. And yet, a decisive knot clenched in his gut when he thought about cursing him. *Why?*

The moment in the tavern flashed in his mind. Finnian did not hesitate to intervene for the young woman's sake. And in the alleyway when he revived the dog. The young god had a good heart, and for some preposterous reason, Cassian felt compelled to protect it.

"I do not wish to curse you," Cassian said. "Stop hoarding my souls. All you have to do is agree."

"Never." Finnian lowered his chin, shrinking the visibility of his eyes beneath their lids. He stood fearlessly, the moonlight pouring across his dark hair. A remarkable sight.

Cassian yearned to chip away at his bold demeanor and expose his true emotions. "You let go of Arran. He returned to the Land."

Finnian's nostrils flared at the mention of his past lover, another sign of his anger. "Because that is what he wished."

"You are unlike what I had imagined—cruel, hungry for power." Cassian's brow crumbled as he tried to reason with the young god. "You hold on to souls because you do not like endings."

"Is that what you think?" Finnian laughed, the sound harsh, cutting. "That I do not *long* to torment those who have wronged me? My horrid mother and rotten siblings? I dream of all the ways I wish to make them suffer." He inclined his head, bloodlust flashing in the sharp slit of his smirk. "Let me assure you, *Lord Cassian*, my heart is infinitely darker than you believe it to be."

Cassian didn't buy it. After their pleasant evening amongst the fireflies and moonflowers, he'd seen it. There was a softness in Finnian that he hid with apathy.

"And what of the souls you hold on to?" Cassian challenged, taking a step towards the stream. "Are you cruel to them?"

A frown tugged at the corners of Finnian's mouth. *A crack.*

Satisfaction hummed in Cassian as he continued to push. "You care for them. You hang onto them because you are afraid of being alone."

"They live at the hands of Fate, Ruelle and her twisted control, and meet tragic, nonsensical ends." He bared his teeth as he spoke, his face contorting viciously. "Some never experience love or warmth. All because of the bodies they didn't ask to be born into. They crawl through life for no other means than to survive. Some last a few months, others maybe a set number of years. In the end, they die and that is it." A cynical sound scuffed out of him. "Tell me, *Ruler of Death*, what is the point of such despair?"

Cassian swallowed, his heart pinching. He had thousands of years' worth of abhorrent memories. From his own life, from the souls he touched. No one understood life's tragedies better than him. He'd witnessed it time and time again, as he had a landscape of his realm dedicated to the wandering souls, broken and too traumatized to move on from the pain they'd endured in their mortal lives.

The complexities of life, the purpose of balance, neither were his to understand.

"There is peace in my realm." Cassian's tone was gentle, assuring. He was convinced that cursing Finnian would only make his grim outlook on life and death worse. "It is not cold and they do not hurt for what they have lost."

Finnian shook his head. "I do not care what you say. I will continue to hold onto souls." Another foul smirk crossed over his lips. The harshness of it stabbed Cassian in the stomach like a kris. "For no other reason than to spite you for what you have taken from me."

Cassian sensed the finality of his words and materialized across the bank, throwing his arm out to catch him. "Don't!"

Scarlet tufts plumed in the air, their wisps furling around Cassian's empty, clenched fist.

EIGHT

PEONY BLOSSOMS

THE PRESENT
Finnian

HE GLOWING DENSITY of Finnian's magic dispersed throughout the temple, like arrows raining down from the cathedral ceiling. Cassian's form flickered and disappeared. The purple, cracking bolts hit the obsidian walls, deflecting and shattering like glass.

Finnian cursed under his breath and slid off the altar. Reaching his hand out, he latched onto the magical properties of the fire in their basins and jumped from the platform, simultaneously curling his fingers into a fist, holding onto the firelight's energy. The flames lunged from the basins and intertwined in the middle of the temple.

With a sharp thrust of his arm, the firelight swelled and roared across the reflective stone, a vibrant, blood orange cloud billowing smoke, incinerating.

Finnian dashed across the sanctuary towards an entryway flanked with spired columns, their peaks sharp as pikes.

The length he could venture from the person he was bound to depended upon the length they allowed. The first thing Finnian needed to do was to test that length. How far could he go without being forced back to Cassian?

He raced down a wide staircase, assuming it led to the temple's basement.

"Belyse." The incantation warmed up his spine and into his eyes, breaking up the blackness to reveal an empty corridor that seemed to stretch on for miles.

Another labyrinth?

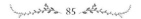

An itch festered inside his head, cracking like a rift in the center of his skull.

His nostrils flared. He picked up his pace, glancing over his shoulder, ready for any shift of energy announcing Cassian's presence.

Something crunched under Finnian's boot.

He stopped and looked down, lifting his leg. Crushed, pale pink petals fell from the bottom of his shoe onto the glossy floor.

A peony.

Finnian snapped his head up and stared deeper into the daunting darkness he was venturing into. *Father.*

From what he'd learned over the years, the Temple of the Dead was located somewhere outside of Moros, near Cassian's castle. For those of his realm to praise him. The basement was secluded. Perfect for isolation.

A precaution in case I ever attempted to break him out.

Finnian set off with haste. The itch in his brain throbbed in pulses. He pressed his teeth together with great force while he ran.

It is nothing.

Don't give it any attention.

Another peony appeared up ahead. Its tip spiraled and birthed a bed of soft, fat petals, striking Finnian's heart with wild anticipation as he jogged past it.

"Father?" he called out.

He listened closely for a reply against the sound of his own footfalls and the *whooshing* of blood in his left ear.

At the far end of the corridor, a glimpse of iron bars caught his eye.

He ran faster. The solid surface of the floor softened, plush-like. He glanced down to see moss, thick and deep-green, overtaking the stone beneath his feet. Along the walls, over the ceiling.

"Finnian." Father's voice was sonorous, gentle, like the sweetest whisper. It was a miracle Finnian had heard it. A voice he'd dreamed of for centuries.

Finnian pushed his legs faster. "Father!"

Approaching a single cell, Finnian slowed to a stop. The cage was constructed with the same iron bars as Moros—sleek, black, crystallized bodies of serpents.

Finnian spotted a body within the cell through his bleary night vision. It wasn't enough. He needed to see him *clearly*.

Finnian swiped his hand up, igniting his magic. A single flame balanced over his palm, the warm light shining brightly across Father's face—one painted with the same tan complexion as his own, eyes the color of freshly budded branches during spring.

Father stood in front of the bars, mouth parted, gaping at Finnian as if he were a ghost. "Son?"

Right your wrongs.

"It's me, Father." Finnian stepped up to the bars, careful to keep from grasping them. A triumphant smile streaked across his face.

Flame in tow, he lifted his hand to get a better look. Father wore a nude, bare-threaded robe. Dirt stains streaked across the front of it. The torn hem brushed over the tops of his bare feet.

Father regarded him with a gaze pooling of adoration, wonderfully stunned, like he couldn't quite believe the god who stood before him was his son.

His features suddenly rearranged with unsettling disbelief. "Finnian, how? You are not supposed to be here." Panic lit in his eyes. "You must leave at once."

"Father, I have come to take you with me. Naia awaits you. She has a child now. Surely, you've seen—"

"You must leave," he demanded, like the words could not exit his mouth quickly enough. "*Now.*"

"You were right. She had a power within her all along. Just as you'd said." Finnian could hardly believe it. Father was before him, and it was as if he were thirteen years old again, spewing knowledge about all the fascinating herbs and plants he'd found in the jungle, near the water hole, and all the fresh teas he could make with them. "From here on, her days will be fruitful. All of ours will be. But first, you must come with me, Father."

"I cannot go. You must understand. I may not leave. You need to go—"

"But you can. I am here to rescue you."

Father turned away as he spoke. "No, you are here to pay for the souls you stole from Cassian."

Finnian blinked, his response stalling. "I realize this is sudden, but we must hurry if we wish to—"

Father spun on him. "I said I will not go. I see all my children from here. I've watched how you've withheld souls within their rotting bones;

how you've murdered innocents with your ghouls in your precious city!" His tone grew boisterous, chiseling the inside of Finnian's chest with his dissent. "Allowing them to feast on mortals to keep them alive. Those they've killed, you turn them into your undead toys, and the horrific cycle continues."

Finnian's mouth opened and closed, his response held hostage in his throat. This is what he'd feared most when he dreamed of their reunion— Father lecturing him over his actions. "Mother banished me."

"You didn't have to threaten Malik after he killed Arran."

"Malik is worse than I. He deserved—"

"You cannot talk about penance when you have done just as much wrong as he!" Father's voice rose.

Finnian grimaced. Regret and humiliation ached in his chest as he glared at his father.

"Malik, High God of Slaughter, who gathered praise from the mortals by murdering those in their prayers. Those who had done them wrong. A bloodlust assassin. That is who you are comparing me to?" Finnian had revived more than he could count of Malik's victims and could attest to the horrors they'd experienced. His brother had been born entirely without compassion.

All his life, Finnian had strived to hang onto a fraction of his humanity. To never sink too far into the abyss, never allowing his disgruntled outlook to truly stick. Each day, he searched for the beauty life held, learning to recognize the affection exchanged between others and appreciate it for what it was. Each day, he struggled to face the light while carrying a lifelong void within. Effort that now felt meaningless. Why had he even bothered?

"Finnian, I said leave me!" Father charged forth, his arm reaching through the bars of his cell. He shoved Finnian back by the chest.

Finnian staggered, his father's strength jarring him. The flame in his palm flared, along with his unclipped irritation. "What did you expect when you and Mother raised us to be this way?" It left his mouth cold and pointed.

The itch in his skull magnified, sending a sharp pang down his neck.

"Do not blame us for your impudence!" Father boomed, fury twisting his expression. "Now, I said leave. I will not go with you."

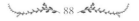

The pain of his dismissal cut deep, splitting Finnian's heart like a knife through fruit.

Any second Cassian will appear. A reminder of his race against time.

"I am getting you out." Determination blazed through the hurt. Finnian's free hand shook as he went to grab hold of the bars. He had three seconds to bend the iron before teeth sunk into his flesh.

"I do not wish to go with you. You are not the boy I raised."

Finnian's hand stopped a few inches from the bars and curled into a fist, the pain of his father's words reverberating in his bones. He wished he hadn't heard it; that his internal sounds had been louder, or that Father hadn't spoken it so legibly.

He jerked his head up, meeting his father's stern gaze. They were eye-level, and his stomach rolled at the stark observation of how much time had passed between them. The last time Finnian was in his presence, he was forced to look up at him by a dramatic height difference. The observation burned white-hot desperation in his limbs, nearly driving him to grab the bars and force them apart.

"Would you rather it be Naia? I can shape-shift myself and turn into her! Or perhaps one of the triplets? Marina? Or have they committed just as many vile acts as I? For fuck's sake, Father, I beg of you, if you love me, come with me!"

"How could I ever love a son like you?" The octave of Father's voice deepened, as if the words were coming out of a devilish being.

Finnian recoiled, the sting of his words branding his insides.

He stepped back, and the end of his heel crunched down on something.

Another ping rattled in his skull. He felt it in his teeth as he dropped his head.

Peonies circled around his feet. One after another, they climbed up from the tiles and unfolded their petals.

But I have already found him—

Finnian looked up, the blood draining from his face.

Father's figure distorted like a glitch. Black circles shadowed around his eyes, sickly and death-like. His head cocked, and his pupils expanded into disks until his gaze was nothing but blackness.

"...Ever love...a son..." Finnian blinked and shook his head. *This is...*

His attention returned to the flowers at his feet.

He crouched and plucked a petal from one of the blossoms and siphoned the magical properties from it between his fingertips.

No magic laced through his skin and dissolved into his blood.

Fear jumped in his pulse, reckoning him with the realization.

"You are not real," he murmured. The petal between his fingers, the flowers at his ankles, they melted away like smoke.

He flashed his eyes up onto his father. "You never were." Gooseflesh crawled down his nape and spread along his back as Father shrank a few feet in height, his face molding into one Finnian recognized well.

He stood in front of a clone of his thirteen-year-old self. Wavy, velvety-dark strands dusted the shoulders of his gray frock coat, brass buttons undone and a burgundy linen tunic sloppily spilling out of the collar. The same outfit he'd worn to Naia and Solaris's birthday celebration many centuries ago—the day Mira murdered Alke.

The thirteen-year-old replica twisted his head to Finnian. "Pathetic." He enunciated the syllables like he'd spat the word on the ground. Narrow eyes sat on a detached expression, judgment beaming from them. "The sight of you makes me ill."

A paralyzing sensation swept through his limbs, coating his palms with a cold sweat. "I will find him."

The younger copy traveled through the iron bars as if they were an apparition. "You are chained to Cassian—*cursed* to go mad. You have already failed."

The muscles in Finnian's chest seized.

You have already failed.

The phrase felt like stones pulling him down.

Failed—again.

The clone stepped into Finnian's space, holding him in his icy stare. "You cannot right a lifetime of wrongs by saving Father. What of Alke and the life he lost? Naia and the torment she endured? Nothing has changed."

"I have a plan," he gritted out. "My plan will work. It will work. I promise it will work."

"You are not strong enough."

"Shut up!" The itch thrummed down his skull, rattling the nerves in his jaws. The urge to reach inside his head and scratch it pleaded on his fingertips.

"You will never be strong enough."

"Shut the fuck up!" Finnian snapped forward and caught his younger self by the throat. He squeezed until he felt the sweet satisfaction of cartilage snapping like elastic. "What would you know in the short thirteen years of your life? I've lived for centuries. I know far more than you ever would."

"I know *you* better than you ever will." Despite Finnian's tight grasp, the clone did not gasp or flail for breath. In a blank, unfazed manner, it continued. "Your impulsive nature is why Father is locked away; why you were banished. You have been down here for five years, and yet, Naia has not tried to come for you once. You are unlovable and that is why everyone eventually abandons you—"

"Stop." Finnian's breath went short. The crescendo in his skull grew louder.

"That's why you are here. You fear loneliness."

"No." Finnian hunkered down, supporting his weight with his elbows on his knees, shaking his head vigorously. "I will make it all better. I will fix it. Right my wrongs."

How could I ever love a son like you?

"You never know when to leave anything alone. If you would've let Alke die, you would've never practiced necromancy. Mother would have never banished you and you could've helped Naia escape Kaimana."

Finny, I did it. I finally found you.

"She is safe now. *Happy.* With a family of her own. A High Goddess."

Don't do this to me, Finnian.

"Father wouldn't be locked away, and you wouldn't have broken the heart of the one person—"

"Stop!" Finnian's hands came up to his head, over his ears.

"You deserve to die for the pain you've caused."

"*Shut your fucking mouth!*" His cry broke through the static screaming inside his head.

The only sound cutting through the thick blanket of silence was his heartbeat thudding loudly in his ear. His chest rose and fell in a rapid rhythm as he regained his senses.

The cool obsidian of the altar was the first thing he registered.

He stared up at the dancing shadows of the firelight along the mosaic tiles of the ceiling.

His eyes jumped over to the flames in their basins and terror welled up in his gut, threatening to push up his throat.

With time, it learns your weaknesses, what you fear most, and without realizing it, your mind plays tricks on you.

When did it begin?

The acrylic taste of the potion lingered on his tongue. It couldn't have been more than five minutes since he'd swallowed it.

Shortly after drinking the potion.

You've already failed.

"Are you ready to depart now?" Cassian's voice was close, near where he'd been before Finnian reared up to strike him with his magic. Or rather, when he thought he had.

Their moment prior to the hallucination rushed through Finnian's mind—the High God pinning him down with their lips connected, forcing the potion into his mouth. His body filled with a mix of pleasure and an unwelcome desire, ignited by Cassian's touch.

A fresh surge of nausea churned in his stomach. He felt a knife to his pride at the thought of sitting up and facing Cassian's steady composure and superiority, waiting for him.

He took his time, unconvinced he could conceal how much the hallucination had frightened him. While he had figured out the peonies weren't real, he detected no suspicions during the journey from the altar to the basement and throughout his encounter with Father. Until he spewed out vicious words. But even then, it was difficult to decide whether Father's feelings were justified and believable.

Little by little, the curse would continue to excavate his sanity. Without the reliance on his mind, what was he to become by the end of this?

Calm down.

It was a future he didn't want to waste energy envisioning, for it would only darken his spirit, ultimately handing over more ammunition to the blight in his head.

The less he believed in himself, the stronger it became.

He drew in an inhale and lifted from the altar.

Cassian waited at the bottom of the platform, hands inside his pockets. His golden gaze was dark, like melted brass. He stood quietly, his disposition casual, but his brow was slightly furrowed, tracking every movement of Finnian's face, as if he were searching for something.

How odd. Finnian expected hostile mockery or a patronizing remark, much like the one sitting on his own tongue. The need to strike and draw blood. All for the joy that came with watching the annoyance and animosity harden Cassian's gaze into gilded stones.

What will your impulsive nature ruin this time?

Finnian swallowed, unsettled by the thirteen-year-old voice trapped inside of his head.

He loosened the tension collected in his neck, disregarded the weariness in his soul pulling at his limbs, and traveled the small distance to Cassian's side.

Finnian fisted his hands to combat the quivering beneath his skin, a sign of the fabric of his sanity fraying. Once he was hidden in the safety of his indifference, he raised his chin and stared ahead at the dark, oak-stained doors across the temple.

Cassian's gaze prickled across his cheek and something about it lulled Finnian to grab ahold of it, but he refused.

Without looking at the High God, he said, "Lead the way."

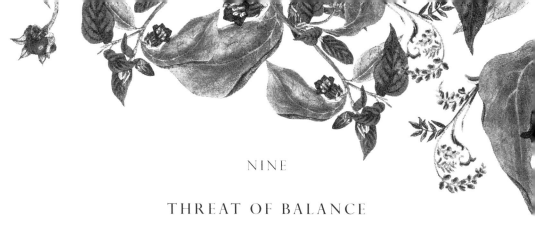

NINE

THREAT OF BALANCE

THE PAST
Cassian

HE LAND OF Entity was far too bright. The white, plush landscape of clouds embraced the High Goddess of Life and Balance's grand temple, forcing Cassian to shield his eyes on arrival.

He stepped out of his shadow, adding much-needed contrast to the heavenly gleam, and ascended the stairs through the open entrance, supported by columns and decorated with cycads and majesty palms.

He strolled down the marble corridor and turned the corner to an entryway, its threshold covered by a veil of ivy permitting only Council members inside.

Encircling a round table made from white jade were five thrones. Each was cut from unique stones, embellished to match the owner.

"It is nice to see you, Brother," Iliana, the High Goddess of Life and Balance, greeted with warm affections.

She sat perched on her rose quartz-cut throne, the sleeves of her chiffon dress flowing around the arms. Long, ivory strands reached her waistline. Her eyes beamed like sandstone topaz underneath the sunlight.

Without her glamor or the glowing orb she often shielded her identity with, anyone could tell she was Cassian and Acacius's sister.

Cassian took a seat on his throne—sleek, Stygian, and unfortunately positioned directly across from the High Goddess of Fate.

"Lord Cassian." Ruelle bowed her head in a formal greeting.

"Lady Ruelle." With a flicker in his eyes, he scanned the alluring fabric of her beige dress, up to her auburn waves, and lingered on the contour of her full lips, aware that her eyes would gleam malevolently if he dared to meet them.

Cassian had done well to suppress his interest in the young god. It existed deep within a chasm inside of him, one he could not completely empty, no matter how much he tried. The twinge in his gut told him Ruelle could sense this.

"Such a familial welcome you give our brother when I barely get a wave, Sister." Acacius lounged back, one elbow resting on the arm of his magnetite throne, his shoulder-length hair pulled back with pieces slipping past his temples. His golden gaze glittered playfully on Iliana. "Are you not fond of my presence like you are of Cassian's?"

Iliana turned her attention to him, scrunching her nose, a sign of annoyance she'd expressed since they were children. "Do not jest with me, Acacius. It will not prompt an honest response from my lips."

Acacius tipped his head back and laughed. "I missed you too, Sister."

"What of the middle god of fire who fell to Solaris?" Azara wasted no time diving into the topics waiting to be discussed. She sat on Cassian's right side, her vibrant red locks adorning her diamond-shaped, freckled face. She held her attention on Cassian, awaiting a reply, expression stern—never one for small talk, a trait Cassian enjoyed.

"He traveled across the Mortal Land to each of the Temples of Fire and threatened the mortals who overturned his statues," Cassian said. "Forty-seven of the souls have emerged from the River."

"What is the state of the god?" Iliana asked.

Cassian did well to block out the incessant tapping of Ruelle's fingernail on the arm of her celestite throne as he replied, "Receiving punishment in Moros."

"How long?" Azara asked.

"Since he has already lost a rank in title, I see a few centuries to be fit."

"You could always send him down to my realm," Acacius chimed in, smirking.

Despite his exasperation, Cassian maintained a neutral expression and refrained from rolling his eyes at his younger brother. Acacius's realm bred chaos and ruin persistently. It tied into Moros and helped fuel the type of misery that was needed in such a prison. Cassian would never send a soul directly to Acacius's realm, no matter how rotten they were.

Ruelle's fingernails ceased their percussion. "And what of the young god stealing souls?"

Cassian's back suddenly became stiff. His sharp gaze flitted over, meeting hers. "What of him?"

Ruelle gave a long blink, as if Cassian's tone momentarily offended her.

"What is she referring to?" Iliana looked between them.

Ruelle shifted her attention onto Iliana. "Finnian, the High God of Witchcraft and Sorcery."

Iliana fell quiet.

Cassian internally cringed. He always found her silences to be unsettling.

"A god and a mage in one. Divine power *and* magic," Acacius said with a disturbing fascination dripping from his tone. "What a frightening combination."

Cassian set his jaw. His hand moved up to rub his chin.

"We must take precautions. The mages and deities have been at odds since the beginning." Azara leaned back in her throne and sighed. "What other pertinent information do we have about this sorcerer?"

"He practices a disturbing ritual that revives the dead. *Necromancy.*" Ruelle shook her head, pursing her lips to express distaste. She twisted to Cassian, pulling everyone's focus onto him. "Lord Cassian, it shocked me to learn that you have not yet punished him. As they are *your* souls he is stealing."

He glared at her with a searing heat crawling up his neck.

"It defiles the cycle of Balance, of Life and Death, Brother," Iliana's soft-spoken voice grew tense. "I cannot have more souls leaving my Land than the souls you have entering yours. It will cause overpopulation."

"I am aware." Cassian kept his tone smooth, composed, clenching his fists in his lap beneath the table. "I assure you it is under control."

"It is crucial that we put an end to this before the other mages learn of it," Azara said.

"You *must* put a stop to this sorcerer." Iliana sat up, bringing her elbows onto the table. Her chiffon sleeves caught in the breeze, ruffling like waves of glittering cornflower. "Tell me you will take care of this."

Cassian could feel Ruelle's cunning stare on his cheek. It nipped at his patience, each tiny cut feeling like a sharp scalpel slicing his skin. His animosity towards her lingered in the back of his throat.

He shifted on his throne and passed Iliana a look of assurance. "Sister, do not fret. Consider the issue taken care of."

Iliana studied his face, her brow furrowing.

There was a twinge of discomfort in Cassian's chest as he locked eyes with her. They'd walked as High Deities for over five thousand years together. Cassian knew Iliana the same as he knew the terrain of his own Land. Every tendril of grass, every root burrowed down in its soil. Just as she knew him. He could feel her concern as she studied him, but he was relieved when she chose not to probe further.

"Very well," she conceded and rose from the table. "Meeting adjourned."

Azara's shape fragmented into countless fiery embers, crackling and popping as they floated in the air.

Iliana bowed her head in parting before exiting through the ivy-curtained doorway.

Without uttering a sound, Cassian stayed firmly seated on his throne, his head swiveling to regard Ruelle with disdain.

In his periphery, he could see Acacius making no effort to move as he warily darted his gaze back and forth between Cassian and Ruelle. A hint of displeasure appeared on his face as his lips turned downward in a subtle frown.

Rising from his reclined position, he held his focus on Cassian. "Brother, perhaps it is time you return to your Land."

"Lord Acacius." Ruelle directed a smile at him. Though Cassian could spot the tension pinched at the corners of her mouth.

Acacius's expression softened at the sound of her acknowledgement. "Yes?"

"Leave us for a moment. We have matters to discuss privately."

Acacius carefully analyzed her. With a look of aversion, his brow knitted, displaying his disagreement with her request.

She held his eyes, unrelenting.

The muscles in his jaws twitched, but he nodded once. "Very well."

He regarded Cassian with a look of unease. "Brother." It left his mouth swiftly, a stiff goodbye.

Cassian kept his eyes trained on Ruelle, minding no effort to return his acknowledgement. Similar to Iliana, Acacius had a knack for deciphering Cassian's thoughts and emotions effortlessly. Cassian was also aware of the sentiments Acacius held towards Ruelle, and he had done well this long without involving his little brother in their feud. Chaos would follow Acacius, like a breeze dipping into an oily flame.

A harsh hiss of his departure resonated in the air, followed by the batting of several small wings. Death's-head hawkmoths fluttered above the table. One landed atop Cassian's shoulder. He brushed it away.

As soon as they were alone, Ruelle's angelic demeanor vanished. The look in her eyes glinted like steel as she inclined her head, the start of a smirk curving across her cherry-stained lips. "I've never seen you neglect a god in need of punishment before."

Cassian licked his own lips, forcing himself to relax against the slab of his throne. Moths drifted between them, slowly following the others towards the dark corner of the room. "What gives you the impression that I have done such a thing?"

"The young god still roams free, performing witchcraft and harboring *your* souls. I find it quite satisfying, yet ironic. Do you not?" She raised her eyebrows.

Heed my warning.

Cassian squeezed his fingers deeper into his palms, resisting the urge to smooth down his lapels and meticulously inspect them for any specks of dust. Something else to focus on, besides the haunting memory that unfolded between them countless centuries ago.

"Is there a purpose to this delightful conversation we are having, Lady Ruelle?"

A light laugh sprung from her, contempt burning in her lustrous gaze. A hideousness hidden away in something beautiful. "You care for the young god, and your feelings for him burden your judgment. Because of it, you have become indecisive, which is why you have yet to curse him."

Whoever yearns in your soul will be just in reach, but never able to fully grasp.

"This is the first deity born with magical abilities," Cassian said in a level-headed manner. "A fact that I assume the young god isn't even aware of. And since you cannot seem to keep your nose out of my business, let me assure you I've been watching him, as well as relinquishing the souls he's taken. Lest you forget, Lady Ruelle, *necromancy* is sorcery. A practiced art. Any mage can replicate it, and before I curse the young god to insanity, I want to be sure I know as much information as necessary to prevent the situation from repeating itself."

Ruelle huffed out another breathy laugh, rising from her throne. The lace material of her dress hugged her hourglass figure as she moved around the table. With every shift of her body, the lace shimmered against the bare skin of her hips.

With a smile of malice, she positioned herself next to Cassian's throne and gracefully leaned down. Her sweet fragrance filled his nose as her auburn hair cascaded over her shoulder, lightly grazing his coat sleeve.

"Forgive my impertinence, Lord Cassian. I was only voicing my concerns because I can see the threads of each mortal and those who, unfortunately, will become tangled in the young god's unhallowed ritual of raising the dead. You see, I do not have control over a soul once their thread is cut, as you are well aware of, therefore the Fate of those mortal souls rests in *your* hands. I do hope you will not take such a thing lightly."

One day, when you know the kiss of love, all you will have left is regret.

A surge of nausea filled his stomach.

He held her eyes, allowing his silence to act as a response.

Ruelle brushed the back of her finger over his cheek, her touch stinging down to his blood.

"Farewell," she hummed, and then she disappeared.

CASSIAN WANDERED through the swaying lavender stalks, massaging his temples with his thumb and index finger. Deities did not get headaches, but his unsettling confrontation with Ruelle remained at the forefront of his thoughts, spurring dreadful anxieties that he had a tendency to turn over relentlessly in his mind.

The High Goddess of Fate wore many faces. To the mortals, she was enchanting and compassionate, the divine being who held their destiny in the palm of her small hands. To deities, she was alluring and gallant, the

divine being who had ascended onto the Council for her reputable status among the Mortal Land.

Neither was the real Ruelle. She concealed her true layers, harboring hatred and a vendetta that she was determined to make Cassian pay for—all because of something that had taken place between them many years ago.

He'd ignored her and her centuries-long grudge. To keep his fate from the crosshairs of her meddling, he attempted to avoid any prospects of love, rendering her scheme for revenge powerless. If he kept his heart closed, she couldn't take anything from him.

A lesson he mercilessly learned after losing someone precious to him because of her meddling.

She'd waited for another round of ammunition. Mentioning the young god had not been an accident. She knew Cassian was not one to delay tasks, and that he still had yet to confront Finnian and his necromancy.

Cassian dropped his arm down to his side and fixed his attention up at the periwinkle sky, the sunrise bursting through it like a budding bulb. The breeze fluttered by, infused with the scent of lavender, causing the wandering souls to pause, lift their heads, and smile. A look of healing that unraveled a bit of the knot in his chest.

"You seem to be in some sort of distress, my lord." Nathaira settled in the spot beside him, overlooking the souls. Her company brought a welcomed stillness.

With hands in pockets, he walked and pondered on how to translate his feelings into words.

Nathaira quietly followed at his side, hands joined in front of her, patiently waiting.

He let out a long breath. "The young god who is stealing souls has thrown off empyrean balance, and now it's my official task to restore said balance."

The breeze shifted and the scent of moss and elm wafted amongst the lavender. Nathaira's fragrance uprooted memories of his mortal life, traipsing in wooded areas, covered in grime and twigs, on a hunt with Iliana, nagging at Acacius to hush. Their expeditions always ended with Cassian growing weary from arguing with them over which direction the deer tracks veered off to in the damp soil.

A simplicity he would kill to have at the moment.

"By cursing him?" Nathaira asked, her voice as tranquil as the murmuring stream.

Cassian's eyes jumped around the myriad of souls in his view, recalling facts about each of them in the back of his mind. "Yes."

"Excuse my straightforwardness, my lord, but it sounds to be that is not something you wish to execute."

Cassian stopped abruptly, turning his full attention towards her.

Her waist-length hair, the shade of chicory, was pulled up, revealing the ivy crawling around her nape and down her collarbones. Green vines curled around her lace sleeves and grew from her dress, adorning the gold accents and flowing material at her feet.

"Since when do you apologize for being straightforward?" He lifted his eyebrow, insinuating a playfulness in his tone.

Nathaira cracked a smile that bunched her almond-shaded cheeks. "I was trying to be delicate with your feelings."

"What feelings?" Shivani materialized in the space on his other side, biting into an apple. "Our lord does not have those."

Cassian continued walking to put distance between him and the crunching of fruit between Shivani's teeth as he recalled the time Finnian entrapped him in his own temple with a sigil. "Are you suggesting that I am devoid of feeling?"

Shivani and Nathaira followed at his side.

"You are a sea of feelings, my lord," Shivani said before biting into her apple. She held it between her teeth and untucked her linen blouse from her baggy trousers.

Cassian stepped onto the planks of the bridge. The river was calm, a steady flow of quiet souls. He rested his elbows on the railing and peered down at the water, glistening like mauve starlight.

Nathaira claimed the spot at Cassian's side, allowing the silence to hum between them for a short while longer.

"Do you, perhaps, have a reason you do not wish to punish the young god?" she finally asked, softly. "It has been years since you last faced him. Since, things have been quiet. No new souls have been reported missing."

Cassian rubbed at his jaw, unsure of the clenching in his chest. "Perhaps."

"You loathe him," Shivani said, casually.

Cassian glanced over his shoulder at her. She settled back on her elbows against the railing across from Cassian. A bite of apple crunched and sloshed around in her mouth.

"Or rather, you are somewhere in between." She swung her apple around in her hand as she spoke. "You despise him *whilst* you enjoy his presence."

Cassian ran a hand through his hair, his jaws pulsing. She wasn't wrong.

It was true that certain qualities of Finnian's made Cassian want to strangle him. However, he felt content in Finnian's presence.

Observing his tense expression, Shivani nonchalantly shrugged, as if she hadn't revealed the harsh reality.

Cassian was grateful each day when Mavros reported no new souls had gone missing. But if he were being honest, it also disappointed him, for he had no reason to seek out the young god.

He'd agonized over it, going back and forth, questioning what kind of retribution Finnian truly deserved—only to be met with that godsforsaken memory of him digging through a trash bin to revive a dead dog. *An inexcusable action.* Tampering with matters that he had no right tampering with.

But then Cassian reminisced on their moment on the bank and the moonflower twirling in his fingers and the glimpse of his smile, all dimples and folds drawn around his eyes.

I want to know that version of him.

Cassian squeezed his hand around his strands and tugged at his scalp, angling his body away from Nathaira and Shivani. The resistance coiling in his gut never gave way when he imagined cursing Finnian.

He peered out at the eldritch, grim tree line of the Serpentine Forest. Nebulous fog bellowed up from its ground and into the branches of the beech trees.

"He steals my souls." The words left his mouth forcefully, full of hostility, hoping he could somehow convince himself of the detestation he wished to feel for the young god. "Forces them to remain in their deteriorating corpses, all because of his personal objection to death. Traps them in a rock and holds them hostage."

"You disagree with his actions," Nathaira said, her calm and composed demeanor only fanning his childish anger. "But you understand them as well."

His gaze fell upon the polished planks of the bridge. Iliana's insistence on balance lingered in his thoughts. "Understanding his actions does not mean I can stand by and allow them to happen." Overall, he agreed with the Council's orders. Imbalance would lead to catastrophe in the Mortal Land.

Nathaira planted a palm on his back, her friendly gesture reaching down inside of him and dissolving some of his frustration. "It is okay to care about him, my lord."

Shivani, thankfully finished with her apple, stepped up to his other side. "I have known you for two millennia and have never seen you this troubled over cursing someone."

Cassian brought his elbows to the railing and hunched over, dropping his face in his hands. The pressure to restore balance clenched his chest, along with the giddy awareness gleaming in Ruelle's eyes.

Nathaira's hand slid up to his shoulder. Shivani rested her cheek on the side of his other arm.

He'd had plenty of opportunities to curse Finnian, but he'd held back each time. A reservation in his body that he didn't comprehend. A guttural feeling that he couldn't help but act on. Perhaps the outcome of cursing Finnian would lead to his own torment.

He shook his head, pressing the heels of his hands into his eye sockets. "I cannot care about him."

"Then what will you do?" Nathaira asked with a wisdom that indicated to Cassian that she already knew the answer.

Cassian pressed his tongue to the roof of his mouth. Before he could respond to her, a sudden, startling *swoosh* interrupted.

"My lord." The sense of urgency in Mavros's tone was disconcerting.

Cassian lowered his hands and rotated to face his attendant. Nathaira and Shivani did the same. "What is it?" he asked.

Distress etched deep lines on Mavros's brow. "You told me to report the young god's movements if they were dire."

Cassian's pulse jumped. "Yes?"

"A situation has come up."

Mavros hesitated for a moment, his gaze shifting to Nathaira and Shivani, before leaping back onto Cassian.

Cassian stepped towards Mavros, fear blowing through his insides. "For gods' sake, Mavros, what—"

"Lady Mira sent Lord Malik, Lord Vex, and Lady Astrid, along with a hired mage, to ambush the young god."

Cassian processed the information at lightning speed, shaking his head. "He is a *god*. He cannot die. What could her outcome possibly be?"

"The goal is to entrap him with a spell cast by the mage."

Cassian's heart sprang up in the base of his throat at the idea of Finnian suffering at the hands of his appalling siblings, entrapped in an ancient relic and the vigorous defiance in his eyes extinguishing entirely. "What is the situation now?"

"It appears they are at the young god's home on the outskirts of a small village known as Elmwood, located in the Western Hemisphere of the Mortal Land. He lives in the cemetery there with two other mages, but they are not holding up well."

The muscles in Cassian's arms and shoulders went rigid as he fisted his hands. "What of his undead creatures? Are they not assisting him?"

Mavros cleared his throat, looking anywhere but directly at Cassian. "You and the Errai relinquished all his souls during your last encounter with him. Since, we have had no reports of any missing souls."

Cassian cursed under his breath.

He knew this. It was a good thing. So why in the hell was he so bothered by it? The young god was agonizingly cunning. Had he not thought ahead?

What will you do?

Cassian rubbed at his forehead, feeling the tension squeeze up his neck. His eyes flitted around the bridge's smooth wood in sync with his racing thoughts, all twisting in his stomach.

What if he's hurt?

What if it is a situation I cannot fix?

What if the mage trapped him already?

Cassian's blood ran cold.

He backed up on his heel, already rearranging his appearance to his shape-shifted form as Everett. His divine power coiled around him like sinuous limbs, with flashes of golden light illuminating the billowy blackness.

He gave each of his most loyal subordinates a look, expressing what he could not say before teleporting away.

I must go to him.

TEN

DEATH

ASSIAN TELEPORTED THEM from the temple into a room made of the same glossy obsidian walls. Velour sofas were arranged under floor-to-ceiling windows, displaying the Land of the Dead's radiant wisteria and achromatic sky.

The Cimmerian stone, smooth and dark as night, brought back memories of the onyx architecture in his beloved city. A sense of homesickness sank heavily in Finnian's stomach.

He had been stuck in the Land of the Dead for five years. A sweeping second in the life of a deity, but to a mortal, it was a long time. If Runa had obeyed his orders, his organizations would now follow Naia. *Only* his sister, not Ronin. Finnian found small joy in antagonizing the leader of the Blood Heretics for his relentless attempts to overthrow his own rule of Hollow City.

Ash would be five years old. Did he favor Naia's personality or Ronin's more? What did he enjoy doing? Did the art of witchcraft excite him?

Finnian's heart constricted, aching in his chest as he imagined the child with Naia's silver hair and Ronin's deep, dark eyes, finding solace in his streets.

Cassian strolled ahead into the room, waving to the frosted-glass door on the back wall. "Clean yourself up through there. You have ten minutes."

Finnian pressed his tongue against the backs of his teeth and started towards the bathroom, eager to isolate himself and unmask his emotions—and try to process everything that had happened in the last few hours.

Without a second thought, he shut the door behind him.

The room was similar to the one on the outside—black walls with smooth edges, a toilet, and a walk-in shower. For whatever reason a High God like Cassian would need such things was beyond Finnian. Perhaps it was similar to how Naia was with food, or maybe he relished the simple pleasure of a hot shower, the warm water spilling over his tired body.

The visual of a nude Cassian filled Finnian's mind, causing his cheeks to prickle.

He forcefully banished the image and shifted his attention to the vanity. Sitting on its buttery-smooth surface was a pile of jewelry, his hearing aid, and a neatly folded stack of clothes.

Before he proceeded in doing anything else, he stepped up to the shower and flipped on the water, letting it run. Cassian's home was too quiet. There were no creaks and moans, the way a typical house sounded. It reminded him too much of the stiff silence within Mira's palace.

He assessed the *bidziil* crystal of his full-shell hearing aid for any signs of damage, running his fingers over its smooth edges, examining its heliotrope body for any cracks or bruises.

The crystal was rare and only produced in a specific area of the Mortal Land. After several years of research and gathering ingredients, he successfully created the device using a spell he'd perfected from scratch.

He slid the device into his ear canal. The transition was immediate, like being stuck inside the eye of a storm before it finally dissipated. The world had opened up once more.

However, the sound of the running water in the shower came to him like he was listening to it on speaker through a cell phone. It wasn't quite right. An issue he'd dealt with once, when he'd created the magical device and wore it in his ear for the first time.

It appeared, after five years, his brain was going to need a moment to process the unnatural translation of his hearing aid. With time, he was confident it would level out.

Finnian exhaled. While it was not the result he'd hoped for, he was grateful to have it in his possession, fully intact. He assumed Cassian would return it to him in pieces.

One less thing to worry about.

He moved onto the clothes.

A merlot, silky, collared shirt and black, slim-fit pants: the casual outfit he often wore when he wasn't acting on city business, as he despised wearing dress vests and slacks when he didn't have to.

Back when he'd first founded Hollow City, it was Isla who bought him his first *proper* outfit. *Befitting for the founder of the city*, she'd said.

Finnian held the shirt up to his nose. The fabric smelled of eucalyptus and rosemary, the charm he cast to clean his clothes, and of the lemongrass and orange blossom incense he burned in his home.

Interesting.

Nausea churned in his stomach at the idea of Cassian inside his home. Not because the High God had invaded his personal space, but because he'd invaded his space and brought back some of his belongings, as what? A kind gesture? He didn't know how to interpret it.

Finnian's attention shifted to the pile of jewelry on the vanity. All his titanium rings, his three necklaces with various jewels hanging from their chains—Mira's pendant, a bloodstone crystal, and an astrophyllite. His favorites. They were all there, unharmed.

A crisp swivel of his wrist and the muck and blood from his time in Moros vanished clean from his skin.

He slipped the rings on his fingers and the necklaces over his head, and replaced the torn rags of his clothes with the fresh ones Cassian provided.

As he fastened the first three bottom buttons of his shirt, he nibbled on his bottom lip, fixated on the absence of the itch boring into the hub of his mind.

The moment he came out of the hallucination and back to his surroundings on the altar, the buzzing of the curse had silenced. It was like a warning that he shouldn't trust himself in those moments.

Dread tightened its grip in his chest as he continued to dwell on it. The itch, resembling a voracious parasite, served as tangible proof of the curse's existence, tormenting his mind without respite. Its fickleness haunted him.

How much of this can I withstand?

Finnian lifted his palms up and stared at the lines mapped out across his skin like tiny roads. He replayed everything in his head to decipher what had been real versus the curse. From the moment Shivani escorted him back into his cell, to now.

The peonies hadn't appeared until *after* Cassian cursed him. He'd noticed the moss on the walls of Moros prior to it, though. A true sign from his father. He had been close after all.

Now that Finnian was no longer in Moros, what was he to do? Without his ability to teleport in this godsforsaken Land, he would have no choice but to trek through the Serpentine Forest—*if* he could find his way back to it. And if he somehow survived traveling through its Achlys-infested territory, he would end up right back where he started—facing executioners and possibly the High God of Chaos and Ruin once more. And that was if Cassian hadn't caught him. All to run around Moros on the reliance of moss alone.

Finnian squeezed his eyes shut and stuck his thumbs into his sockets, rubbing. Time was frail now. No longer a luxury. He needed a better plan.

Finnian turned and planted his palms on the vanity surface, meeting his reflection in the mirror. The sight made him grimace.

Through the open buttons of his shirt, he could make out the vicious curse mark on his pec. The ink-black blight snaked up his collarbone and twisted around his neck several times like a rotted vine.

Finnian huffed out a breath, contemplating buttoning up his shirt fully. He despised how certain fabrics agitated his senses. While he enjoyed stylish outfits, he preferred loose clothes that allowed his skin to breathe.

Fuck it.

There was no use in trying to hide it out of denial.

His eyes flickered up to his awful haircut. He made a face as he ran his fingers through the short, wavy ends of his dark strands. They were choppy and uneven along his forehead, and he suddenly wished he had made Shivani scream a little more after he'd broken out of his cell.

He could easily regrow his hair using glamor, but he hesitated.

You need a better plan.

What was the fastest, easiest solution to find Father?

Cassian.

From their fights and feuds over the years, Finnian *knew* Cassian—his likes, dislikes, his tics, strengths, and weaknesses.

Finnian's eyes jumped to the frosted glass on the door in the mirror. Beyond it, he could make out the silhouette of Cassian across the room, standing in front of a large window, hands in his pockets. Despite his fearsome reputation, Cassian was kind-hearted—and lonely.

Finnian ran his hand over his tousled locks.

Approach him with kindness.

Choosing to keep his hair short was a sign of moral defeat.

Lower your guard.

Proof Cassian had successfully worn his spirit down.

Become someone to him.

Finnian smirked.

And he will tell you all his secrets.

Cassian reserved his emotions through centuries of experience, but something told Finnian that if he were to lower his guard, Cassian could not resist opening up.

Finnian's eyes flitted to the mirror. He took in his poorly cut strands once more and scrunched his nose. They looked horrendous. He'd never cut his hair shorter than his jawline. If he was going to endure it, he'd at least need to clean it up a bit.

With the power of his glamor, the ends of his wavy hair grew into a messy style over his forehead. He didn't bother straightening out any of his curls, and he kept the sides trimmed around his ears and straightened up the line around his neck and sideburns. It sufficed.

He exhaled sharply, turned off the shower, and left the bathroom.

Cassian did not look back as he walked towards the bar cart.

On his way, he observed the shape of Cassian's backside through his suit. The High God was broad-shouldered with a physique that mortals had to spend hours at the gym for each day. Not an unpleasant view for someone so dreadful.

Finnian forced his gaze away from Cassian and uncorked one of the crystal bottles. He sniffed the rim. "I take it that we are in your home." Making a face, he set the bottle of brandy aside.

"Nothing gets past you."

Finnian poured himself a glass of bourbon and tossed it back in one gulp. The smooth liquor glided down his throat, filling his stomach with a comforting warmth. A welcomed distraction from his hearing aid delivering Cassian's words in anything but perfection.

He refilled the glass and moved over onto the sofa, ignoring the urge in his fingertips to snatch the magical device from his ear and tinker with it.

There's nothing wrong.

Cassian turned and scrutinized him, rubbing a thumb over his lips. "You did not fully regrow your hair."

"Nothing gets past you," Finnian remarked, lounging back on the sofa. He lifted his glass in a snide manner to toast the observation and took a swig.

A hint of a smile twitched at Cassian's mouth. "Yes, this is my home."

Finnian glanced around, unimpressed. He was used to the walls of his own home decorated with the artwork he'd collected over the centuries. Oddities and trinkets scattered over the surface of worn furniture he'd scavenged at old markets. The aroma of plants and wet soil mingled with the steam of his four-shot espresso and the licorice he chewed on while he worked on potions or wrote in his grimoire. He preferred the low volume of a vinyl and pretended to be annoyed when interrupted by his ghouls or most trusted friends—interruptions he secretly welcomed.

The home of Cassian was minimalistic and orderly, with surfaces far too clean. The room held only what was necessary—sofas for sitting, the bar cart, and an aroma of lemon-peelings and freshly plucked mint. Such a stiff atmosphere.

"After years of playing a delightful game of cat-and-mouse with you," Finnian said, "I assumed this day would eventually come."

"Years of playing cat-and-mouse?" Despite Cassian's leveled tone, Finnian sensed an edge of enmity beneath it.

Finnian cocked his head with a mocking twist to his lips. "What else would you call our history together? The apothecary, the temple, the grave-yard, my city. All you've ever done is try to curse me."

"Precisely." Cassian's voice went hollow around the words as he strode to the bar cart and poured himself a glass of the same bourbon Finnian drank. "Nothing more."

Finnian noted the tension in his shoulders, unsure what to make of it.

"My souls are in celebration today, as it is the anniversary of when I was granted my title as the Ruler of Death." Cassian downed his drink without turning around. "You will attend the festival in Caius."

The Village of the Souls. Finnian had read about it. Where souls lived in the Land if they did not wish to move onto Paradise of Rest or reincarnate.

"How patriotic," Finnian muttered before taking another sip. "And will you not be joining, *Ruler?*"

Cassian refilled his glass. "I have business to attend to. I assumed you would be happier to reunite with those you transformed into ghouls throughout the centuries."

Before Finnian could come up with a witty response, Cassian turned around and lifted his topped-off drink, returning the snide gesture of a make-believe toast before taking another swig.

It took extra effort for Finnian not to roll his eyes.

Cassian strode back to the sofa and unclasped the center button of his suit jacket before sitting.

All of it grated on Finnian—Cassian's proper posture, the gleam of his watch on his wrist as he swirled the dark brown liquor in his glass, and the perfectly groomed undercut of his hair. He wanted to reach down and yank out all the ugly within Cassian just to prove those parts of him existed.

Approach him with kindness.

Finnian relaxed his grasp around his glass and softened his features, intending to make himself look more approachable. "The origin of the God of Death and Curses is a mystery to me. You were the first of your lineage, as well as one of the first deities in existence."

Cassian's eyebrows raised, his drink hovering in front of his lips. "You are showing interest in me. How fascinating."

"Some things you cannot learn in books." Finnian sat up a little, as if he were genuinely curious. "Tell me the origin story of death. I am *dying* to hear it."

Cassian held his stare for a beat. "Why?"

Approach him with understanding.

Finnian stared back. "It must be tiresome being the Ruler of Death, and it occurred to me earlier that while we've played this game all these years, I do not know how you came to wear the crown."

Something dark flashed in Cassian's brassy gaze before he tossed back his head, emptying his glass.

He rose to his feet and stalked back to the bar cart for another refill. "Death was a personified being created by Existence itself. Just how Fate was. Nature, Night, the Moon." This time, he was careful to avoid clinking the glass, making it easier for Finnian to hear him.

He rested back on the cushion, satisfied that his push to get Cassian to open up had worked. "Death was a *personified being*? Like a skeleton with a scythe? You know, some mortals still paint you in such theatrical ways."

"Yes, something along those lines." With a fresh glass, Cassian walked to the window and peered out into the vastness of his Land. "The Grim Reaper. *San La Muerte. Ankou.*"

"And let me guess, you became one of the first gods in existence by challenging the embodiment of Death?" Finnian stared at the backside of Cassian's solid frame.

"That is precisely what happened." Cassian took a swig of his drink. "I was twenty, my brother Acacius was sixteen, and our elder sister Iliana was twenty-two when an unknown assailant took our lives."

Murdered.

Finnian blinked, trying to picture the High God before him as anything but the divine being he was, fragile, veins pulsing with blood and beating mortal life into his heart. Finnian's sense of victory quickly dissipated, leaving him with a perplexing pain in his chest.

"I refused Death for myself and my siblings," Cassian continued. "Iliana called upon Existence and demanded it to revive us. Acacius called upon Chaos, pleading with it to wreak havoc on the world for what it had done to us. They told us they would grant our wishes and hand over their titles if we won in a duel."

"How? You were mere mortals."

Cassian twisted around to face him. He held his drink in one hand, his other stowed away in his pocket. The light shining through the window entered like a monochromic backdrop weeping around him. "It is amazing what rage and sorrow pushes a person to become. Existence, Death, and Chaos all fell, along with the other personified beings, and the existence of deities were born. My siblings and I were the first to walk out of its mouth. Iliana resides in the Land of Entity. Acacius's realm is beneath mine, and his Chaos brews into Moros."

The spring in the Serpentine Forest.

The siren song, calling him to violent calamity.

Shivers bit up Finnian's spine.

He searched Cassian's face for any traces of the wrath he spoke of. The first time they met in the apothecary, Cassian presented himself cavalier, until Finnian blew the countertop to smithereens and rejected his command to give up necromancy. Rage had left its mark on Cassian's face, distorting its fine contours and leaving behind a hardened expression. Glorious, it was the last thing Finnian saw before teleporting away—a type of fury Finnian did not find threatening, but invigorating.

Lower your guard.

Finnian gulped down the last bit of his drink to numb the discomfort of inquiring about Cassian. "Do you regret it?"

If he would've simply died, deities would have never been born. Finnian and all the others would be nothing but mere mortals at the mercy of another higher power, an insufferable road of thought that he didn't dare to explore. The idea alone was appalling. At least he understood why the Council was formed, and why its members were chosen.

Cassian was slow with his words. "Now that I am aware of what Death truly is, most certainly not. Death is peace. *Rest*—"

"Death is separation." Disgust rose in Finnian's throat. "Ceasing to exist, losing a life of joyous wonders."

"I thought such a thing too once," Cassian replied, his tone composed despite Finnian's disdain. "Before my reign as Death, it may have been so, but that is no longer the case. Death is not so bleak. There is no pain, no hardships. Only peace."

"Save the speech. I've heard it multiple times from you." Finnian stood and stalked back to the bar cart, setting his empty glass aside and glaring down at the elegant drinkware and the long, sparkling necks of the bottles filled to the brim with melted caramel-colored liquor. The urge to flip over the cart ached in his hands. To wreck this pristine room and cause a scene of *some kind*. The silence, stillness, organization—it was suffocating.

"I am surprised you remember."

Finnian turned to find the High God grinning over the rim of his glass, a goading gleam in his gaze. His nostrils flared, longing to choke the look off the bastard.

Approach him with fucking kindness, Finnian.

"All these years of talk and you've never once shown me your Land." Finnian walked around the sofa and rested his tailbone on the back of it, shortening the space between him and Cassian.

The High God tilted his head at the request. "You wish to see my Land?"

"Yes," Finnian said, free of as much sarcasm as he could muster. "Show me around before we attend this festival. Let me see what Death is truly like. For myself."

Cassian analyzed him, his eyes shifting across his face for a long moment.

Finnian's mouth went dry, but he refused to retract his gaze from the golden chasm of Cassian's. No end in sight, no matter how deep he delved. His stomach dipped, as if he were dangling off the edge of a fjord.

Cassian strolled to the space in front of him. He leaned in, bringing his mouth dangerously close to Finnian's unimpaired ear.

The muscles in Finnian's neck pulled taut as Cassian's breathy laugh traveled over his skin. Tingles spread down his set jaw.

"Like you said, we've played our game with one another for years, Little Nightmare. If you desire for me to open up, you'll have to do much better than this."

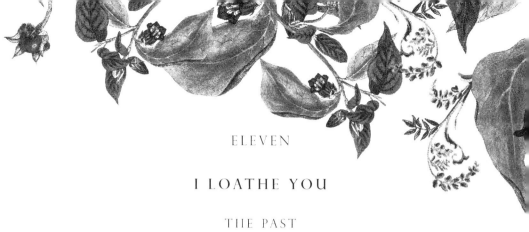

ELEVEN

I LOATHE YOU

THE PAST
Cassian

PINE NEEDLES AND the sharp acrylic of magic dotted the air surrounding Cassian as his feet touched down on dry, butter-colored leaves. Dusk darkened the atmosphere as commotion echoed from the distance.

He rushed to the edge of the tree line, careful to remain hidden while he assessed the situation.

Tombstones encircled a small granite structure just beyond the wooded area. A burial vault. Columns flanked the rusted doors.

Pinned against the vault with his arms severed, Finnian fought against the blades jabbed in each side of his pecs and through both ankles.

Cassian's pulse spiked at the sight.

Finnian shouted out as Malik thrusted the blade deeper into his ribcage. His hair spilled down his shoulders, strands sticking to the rust-colored splatter marring his cheeks and neck. The chalky shade of his olive complexion and the amount of scarlet blotches muddled across his linen tunic had Cassian wondering how long ago the triplets showed up.

Blood spewed like a crimson stream from the wounds of his severed arms. Strewn off the side, Cassian counted four sets of arms tossed about.

A body lay on the pavement behind them, their limp frame engulfed in a cloak.

A few yards away, Astrid lodged her heel against the sternum of a young woman with ginger strands. "Try any more funny business and I'll puncture your frail little heart."

"Isla, run!" Finnian bellowed.

Another woman stood four tombstones away from Vex. She was tall with dark skin and frizzy, brunette curls.

Cassian watched as she arranged her arms to grip a collective of stardust, glittering sunset red, in the shape of a bow and arrow.

She took aim and let the dazzling arrow fly for Vex. His divine speed wasn't enough to evade it as it pierced through his shoulder, the force knocking him back on his feet.

He rolled his neck, the motion ruffling his wavy, silver strands over his forehead and cheeks. A dark smile split apart his lips, revealing a perfect row of white teeth. "My turn now." He started towards her.

Isla's features softened abruptly. She lowered her arms, eyes fixed on Vex in a strange awe. The muscles in her shoulders relaxed. Her lips parted, and she extended her arm to reach for him.

"Isla, look away—" Finnian's roar was cut off by a horrid choking sound as Malik shoved a blade into his mouth.

"Does it hurt, *Finny*?" Malik carved deeper into his throat. Blood gushed like a busted ravine down his chin, over Malik's knuckles, forming long dribbles between the length of his wrists and boots.

Cassian's spine went rigid. Consumed by fury, his mind became a twisted labyrinth, conjuring up the most sinister scenarios to inflict upon the triplets.

Taking a step, his divine power swirled around him. His destination was between Malik and Finnian.

A set of fingers curled around Cassian's bicep and lurched him back before he could teleport.

He recognized the nefarious, nerve-wracking aura that belonged to his brother. "Unhand me, Acacius."

Acacius let go, stepping back with his hand raised as a gesture of peace. "I sensed you were about to do something foolish. Glad to know I was right."

Cassian gave Acacius a once-over in his cloaked frame. At his side, he hung onto his beast skull mask by one of its bony horns. "What are you doing here?"

"I came to pay you a visit as you were departing. Mavros told me of your location." Acacius's brow pinched as he looked at the chaos in the graveyard and then back at Cassian. "Do not intervene, Brother. Let the mage entrap him."

It was the wisest choice. Not only that, but it would be inappropriate for a High God of the Council to intervene in trivial matters, such as a family squabble. It was precisely why Cassian had shape-shifted into the appearance of Everett before arriving.

Standing by and watching Malik gut Finnian was also not an option.

Cassian scowled at his brother. "I did not ask for your advice."

"The Council is counting on you to restore the balance." He said it as a reminder, a form of guilt-stricken persuasion.

Cassian's hand came up to his hair, his insides wrenching. "I am aware," he snapped.

"I can see you care for him," Acacius said in a softer tone. "Leave it be. This way, you do not have to curse him."

Cassian studied the admonishing look Acacius wore. His eyes held a knowing that was almost unbearable.

For a moment, Cassian allowed the future to play out in his head—one where he did nothing. The two young girls would more than likely end up dead. Two individuals who it was clear Finnian cared a great deal for. It was the only explanation for why he was not fighting as recklessly as he typically did.

In the end, the mage, who Cassian presumed was the body lying unconscious, would eventually wake up and entrap him. Things would go back to how they were.

A guttural scream rang out. Tremors rumbled the ground, rattling the tombstones.

Cassian spun to find Finnian's left arm fully regenerated, his flexed hand raised over his head.

A blinding, webbed chasm birthed from his palm and towered over the cemetery. His fingers curled into a fist and the beaming core at its center exploded outward, erupting into the air like blue magma before sinking into the ground around them. "*Vivifica!*"

Hands burst through the earth's surface as if it were made of paper, and corpses emerged from their graves across the cemetery.

"Ah, what a neat little trick." Acacius crossed his arms and leaned against a tree as he observed with intrigue.

In his entire life, Cassian had never experienced such a strong combination of repulsion and pride. It made sense now why Mavros had not reported any missing souls. Finnian had not been hoarding them in his necklace, like in Augustus. Finnian had honed his power since then, about to pull up the souls and imbue them into their corpses during the moments he needed them. The young god hadn't stolen those souls—not yet at least.

What a clever brat.

A corpse made up of mostly bone and rotting patches of skin bit into the side of Vex's neck. He flailed around, trying to sling it off. Nearby, Isla stood idle, gawking at him, stuck under his divine charm.

Another corpse, lodged in the ground mid-torso, caught Astrid by her shin. She puffed in and out of sight, throwing up a vortex of flower petals to surround the other woman lying motionless on the ground. Cassian assumed she, too, had succumbed to a sultry charm. The undead creatures minded the two women with no attention, though.

Malik swiftly cut through Finnian's shoulder with one of his blades.

A deep grunt escaped Finnian, and he hung his head forward.

With a firm grip on Finnian's separated limb, Malik swung it forcefully, using it like a club to crush the jaw of another walking corpse. Simultaneously, he threw his second blade into the skull of a fierce wolf, saving the defenseless mage.

"Protect the mage!" he snarled, reaching for more blades sheathed around his waist.

"Our charms do not work on them!" Vex countered, scooping up a handful of gravel and hurling the stones through the corpses' frail flesh.

"Make him" — Astrid staked her fingertips through a corpse's chest, lodging her arm in elbow-deep — "undo his wretched spell!"

"Such beautiful ruination." Acacius chuckled, patting Cassian on his shoulder. "Leave with me, Brother. They will handle this amongst each other. The situation will be dealt with. You will not have to curse him. The problem will be solved."

It felt wrong to imagine a world without Finnian. Something worse than death, for Finnian would be out of his sight. Somewhere Cassian could not look after him, check in on him. The distance, the unknowing—it would drive him mad. Cassian would be forced to act. He did not know

the lengths he would go to in order to free Finnian from his entrapment; however, he was certain that he would cross every one of the Council's lines.

Malik jabbed his blade through Finnian's gut and twisted. "End the spell or I will carve up your precious apprentices next."

Cassian watched the uneven stride of Finnian's chest rising and falling as the back of his head met the exterior of the vault. He was coughing and spitting up blood through his teeth, lip curled, eyes cut down on Malik. Defiance was sharp inside the emerald darkness of his irises.

Cassian's heart sank into his stomach, knowing whatever Finnian was about to say would only enhance Malik's bloodlust.

All sense of rationality flatlined as he rolled his shoulder, knocking Acacius's hand off.

Acacius was stealthy and just as skilled in speed. Once again, he clasped onto Cassian's arm before he could take another step.

Cassian glared over his shoulder. "Acacius, if you do not unhand me, I will—"

"I know of the quarrel you have with Ruelle."

Cassian's gaze narrowed on him. He did not know what to say. Ruelle was a viper and there was no telling what deception she'd fed to Acacius to twist him in her favor.

Finnian's magic rose back up from the dirt, reforming the magnificent, neon blue mushroom cloud over the cemetery.

Cassian looked up at it, watching the spell reverse. Slowly, its form separated, a miasma gathering in the sky and parting into mist. It coated the crisp leaves on the ground, dampened Cassian's hair, nipped at the skin of his arms.

The swarm of corpses stalled in their steps before crumbling into a carpet of bones and decaying flesh. The cool, white fire of their souls gathered one by one beside their mortal frames, resting.

"It is none of your concern," Cassian said to Acacius, refocusing his gaze on Finnian. The young god buried his chin in his chest again. His surrender unsettled Cassian. Nausea bubbled in his stomach with a need to get to him as quickly as possible.

"Do not give Ruelle someone to hold over you again."

A bitter scoff burned up Cassian's throat as he turned to Acacius, boring into the same golden gaze as his own. "Do not think I am naïve to your feelings of Ruelle. You are only here, begging me to stay within the lines, because you do not wish to stand on the sidelines of our war. Unhand me, Acacius. I will not say it again."

The muscles in his jaw flexed and the look in his eyes grew stale. "Don't say I didn't warn you, Brother."

Releasing Cassian's arm, a midnight blue shadow banded around his backside. He slid the animal skull over his face as its tendrils coiled around his frame.

A disfigured *slice* sounded, and he was gone.

"Good boy." Malik jutted the sharp end of his knife against Finnian's cheek. "Now, wake the mage. You know how to counter whatever spell your nasty little apprentice cast."

"Go…" Finnian croaked, lifting his chin, "fuck yourself."

"Very well." Malik twisted his torso to face Astrid, beckoning her with the jerk of his head. "Bring her to me."

Astrid flicked her chin towards Malik. "Go," she ordered the girl with ginger locks.

The girl lifted from the ground and started forward, expression fully vacant.

Finnian's eyes widened. "Malik," he wheezed. "I'll—do it."

Malik twirled his knife with a disturbing smirk. "I must say, it is a joy to watch you bleed." He cocked his elbow back, the glint of the blade catching on the lampposts stationed at the edge of the mausoleum, aiming it directly for Finnian's face.

Enough of this.

Cassian's form flickered with the taste of vengeance strong on his tongue. It surged within him like a conviction.

He materialized before Malik, the tip of his blade meeting the seam of Cassian's pec.

Cassian caught Malik by his wrist, stopping the blade from piercing through his shirt.

With his backside pressed against Finnian, he did his best to hold his weight on the base of his toes to avoid crushing the young god.

Malik came closer, unknowingly lowering his head into the jaws of a monster. "Unless you have a death wish, I suggest you remove yourself from my sight."

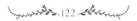

Cassian had never paid the triplets much attention during his visits to Kaimana. Up this close, though, he could pinpoint the similarities between their faces and Finnian's—the hollow cheeks, pronounced brow bone, and the same honey-amber complexion. The *only* resemblance of their kinship. Beyond those few traits, he could see the cat-like eyes of Mira, her superior ego, and her coldness embedded like a web around their souls. Not a trace of their father's kind, empathetic nature.

Cassian would gladly teach them a lesson.

He leaned into the blade, puncturing a hole through the suede material of his tailcoat and through the meat and flesh of his chest. With a chilling curve to his lips, Cassian said, "You and your childish toys do not frighten me."

The rush of his divine power thrummed in his blood as he set it forth onto the god.

Malik staggered away, mouth opening and closing like a fish begging for air. The magnitude of a spiraling illusion ensnared him.

How would a middle god of slaughter feel without satisfaction in his kills?

"Brother!" Astrid charged forth in a flurry of pink rose petals.

Cassian plucked the blade from his skin and tossed it aside, his eyes flashing up on the blur of silver locks charging towards him. "You're next."

A honeysuckle fragrance filled his nostrils. She reappeared with her hand on his shirt, her chest pushing against him, her eyes, two pools of black, reaching into his. A delicate lullaby hummed in his ear, the melody sensual and lighting his bloodstream like a match, lulling lustful urges into his thoughts. How her breasts would feel in his palm, her hand around his—

Cassian cupped her jawline and stuck his thumb in between her lips.

She lightly bit down on his skin and fingernail with a teasing smile.

Ignoring the allurement of her charm, Cassian pressed the pad of his thumb down on her tongue, forcing her mouth open.

His divine power shot like oil down her throat.

She gasped.

Cassian removed his thumb from her tongue and watched as she scraped down his torso and fell to her knees in a strangled mess of breath and trembling limbs.

How would it feel to no longer enthrall the eyes and hearts of those in her presence?

Vex raced forward. One step in and Cassian's divine power coiled around his head from behind, like tiny, blackened mambas prying into his face. It yanked him back and seized through his eyes.

He let out a broken cry.

How would it feel to be alone? Hideous and meaningless to everyone?

Cassian fixed his attention back on Malik. "If you do not get out of *my* sight, I can assure you, death will be something you beg for."

Malik's eyes flitted around with fear, unable to focus on his surroundings. Without muttering another tasteless remark, he vanished in a puff.

Astrid crawled, feeling around the pavement as if she were blind, until she found the arm of the unconscious mage. They both disappeared, leaving behind a tailspin of pink flowers. Vex quickly followed behind them.

Once they left, Cassian whirled around and clenched the knife hilts embedded in Finnian, trapping him against the vault. He removed them one by one. "What were you thinking? Taking on all of them this way? You are only one god!"

Finnian rested his head back on the stone, eyes tracking Cassian's movements. One arm had regenerated to the elbow, while the one Malik had recently severed was still a trunk. "I called on my ghouls. The situation was under control."

Apparently his tongue had grown back just fine.

At the mention of the corpses, slumped and laying across the graveyard, Cassian paused and snapped his fingers.

From the trees, a dark mass descended, swallowing each floating orb in its path.

Finnian watched as the blackness ate away at the corpses, cradling the delicate orbs of the souls, and carrying them away.

"My, what a thorn in my side you have become," he muttered.

Cassian ignored him and tossed the last of the knives aside. "And what would have happened had that mage successfully entrapped you?"

Finnian pushed off the wall and around Cassian. "I would have figured it out."

Cassian followed him. "How? Unless there is a way a mage can perform magic while entrapped that I am unaware of?"

Footfalls sounded from ahead.

The woman with ginger hair threw her arms around Finnian. "I am so relieved you are okay!" She cried into his neck.

Finnian offered her an awkward pat on the back with his forearm, as his hand still hadn't grown back. "Eleanor, please remove yourself at once."

Isla approached, smiling, and lightly prying the woman off. "Eleanor, you know Master Finnian does not enjoy such affection."

"That is the least of my concerns at the moment!" She wiped at her eyes, smearing dirt and blood along her freckled cheeks. "We could have died, but he saved us!" Sniveling, her face twisted as she seethed. "If I ever run into that silver-haired bitch again…"

"Eleanor, you are injured." Finnian brushed forward to inspect the gash on her forehead. "Do you recall the spell I taught you yesterday?"

"Of course!" She beamed and raised her hand. "*Corpus emundare.*" She swiveled her wrist.

The spell cleansed each of their skin of muck and blood, making it much easier for Finnian to examine Eleanor's wound.

Cassian gauged the stained material of Finnian's shirt, observing closely as his stab wounds slowly stitched back up. Then, Cassian's eyes roved up to Finnian's long hair, wondering if Malik had destroyed the magical device in his ear.

Finnian rotated to Isla. His right hand had fully repaired itself. "Go inside. Give her a regenerative potion. Take one yourself." He flicked one of her frizzy curls from her face.

"What about you?" Eleanor interjected, dramatically gesturing to his missing limb. "Your arm is *gone!*"

"My arm will grow back," he drawled. "Now go. The both of you."

Cassian studied Finnian's body language, noting how he did not angle his head a certain way or mistake their words. Surely, without the assistance of his hearing aid, he would be showing a subtle indication.

"Who are you?" Eleanor stepped up to Cassian, her wide hazel eyes probing with curiosity.

His stomach dipped, and he quickly reminded himself of his disguise as Everett. "I—"

Finnian shot him a glare.

Isla eyed him and grabbed Eleanor's hand, tugging her forward. "Eleanor, let's go. Your wound is bleeding again."

As they passed, Isla gave Cassian a smile and dipped her head in parting. They ascended the steps to the arched doorway of the vault.

"You were careless," Cassian continued to chide.

Finnian scoffed out a clipped breath, his expression arranged in an annoyed manner. "Why are you here?"

His indifferent attitude towards the situation infuriated Cassian. Did he not understand the severity? Had he not shown up, what would have happened?

"You are *mine* to chase, to fight with," Cassian snapped. "Nobody else's."

A spiteful smile broke apart his lips, flashing his teeth. "Who knew the High God of Death and Curses to be so possessive?"

Cassian's cheeks kindled. "Stop talking. You are hurt." He swept his eyes over his left arm, not yet fully regrown, dripping blood over the fallen leaves.

Finnian rolled his eyes, not at all fazed by the physical pain. "I am healing. I am fine."

Cassian lifted his hand to tend to the wound of his arm, desperate to staunch it, to halt the bleeding.

Finnian recoiled, his magic pulsing in waves and raising the hair on Cassian's nape.

Cassian's hand stopped midair, studying the flash of fear dilating in his pupils. "After all of that, you still have some fight left in you." He dropped his arm, taking in the rough edges of the young god's features, and grinned. "Impressive, Little Nightmare."

At the use of the nickname, Finnian's nostrils flared. "You swoop in to fight away the predators threatening your prey. Do not take me for a fool. I have no intention of being cursed by you today. That is why you are here, correct?"

It was a question Cassian did not wish to confront yet. "I was simply trying to staunch the bleeding. If you do not wish for me to touch you, then regenerate your wound faster!"

"After Malik cut my arms off for the eighth time, the task became exhausting."

"Why didn't you teleport away?"

"Only someone superior to death would think so frivolously," Finnian said with contempt. "I do not abandon those I care about. Eleanor and Isla

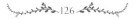

were in danger. My sudden move would have resulted in the triplets killing them without hesitation."

His sense of loyalty truly dumbfounded Cassian, given the dark sorcery he practiced. "If they died, you could have performed your necromancy on them."

"I do not *enjoy* turning things into ghouls!" Finnian came closer, voice raising.

"Then simply *stop* turning things into ghouls!" Cassian shouted back.

Finnian leveled him with an obstinate glare. "Are you going to return my father?"

Exhaustion pulled Cassian's hands up into his hair. He inhaled a sharp breath, squeezing his strands at the roots. "Do you think I wanted to curse my best friend?" He slapped a hand on his own chest. "Your father committed a crime that not even I could save him from. The Council demanded him to be locked away in Moros, but I could not stomach such a twisted fate for a god as good as Vale. You have my apology. I wish I could have done things differently. Please believe me when I tell you that."

A beat of silence passed as Finnian searched his face. Cassian couldn't tell what he was thinking, if he believed his apology to be genuine.

"Give him back then," Finnian said, tone solemn and gratingly stubborn.

Cassian dropped his arms, feeling more haggard than he had in decades. "There are rules even I cannot break."

Something wicked flashed in Finnian's gaze, a recognition or dawning of some kind. He cocked his head, the movement stirring an uneasiness in Cassian as he leaned in. "You follow me, you threaten me, try to curse me, and you save me. You exude a power of the Highest of High Gods, and yet here we are, standing mere inches from one another. You could curse me, you could drag me back to your prison and make me suffer for the crime I have committed amongst Death and your precious souls. Yet, you do not. Something hinders you from doing so."

Cassian turned away with the need to flee. He'd intervened, and now Finnian was safe. He had no other reason to be there.

Finnian caught him by the crisp collar of his waistcoat and shoved him against the wall of the vault.

Cassian's feet fumbled underneath him, too stunned by Finnian's sudden touch to consider fighting him off.

Finnian bound his forearm across Cassian's sternum, clenching the material of his collar. "Your indecisiveness is maddening."

An intense energy sparked in the air between them, and Cassian suddenly became aware of the breath they shared. This close, Finnian's eyes were green like the moss Vale grew along the stones of Moros. *I wish to decorate a place so dreary*, he'd said the first time Cassian brought it up.

Cassian could bridge the small wedge of space keeping them apart if he were to tip forward and...

He licked his lips, feeling his cheeks flush.

Averting his eyes, he said, "Do you think I wish to feel this way?"

Finnian didn't respond right away, prompting Cassian's gaze to return to him.

He stared at Cassian's mouth, his eyes darkening.

Heat dropped low in Cassian's stomach.

"Decide what you want, but stop toying with me." His gaze flitted up to meet Cassian's, sharp and full of intent. "I will never stop raising souls from the dead."

In his declaration, there was loneliness, anguish. All Cassian desired was to unearth the harshest secrets of his soul and merge them with his own.

"Because it is all you have," Cassian finished, voice low, yielding to Finnian's feelings.

He snatched Cassian's chin between his thumb and index finger, and dipped in closer, glowering through hooded eyes. "I loathe you," he said through curled lips.

His breath warmed Cassian's mouth. Desire saturated in his bloodstream, slurring the voice of reason begging him to disappear—to go home and never chase after the young god again. Yet, all he could focus on was Finnian's fingers bruising his skin.

"I loathe you just as much," Cassian whispered.

I long for you, is what he wanted to say instead.

The tension between them surged. Their eyes remained locked. Cassian's stomach flipped from the sensation of tiny currents zapping at his cheeks. *Magic.* Coming from Finnian—

He yanked Cassian forward by his chin and swallowed his gasp with a kiss.

Shock jarred his system, stunting his movements, consumed by the heat pouring down his throat.

Finnian tasted like alkaline, like something sweet and earthy, and Cassian devoured it, guzzled it down deep until he was made of nothing but the taste.

Finnian's tight hold relaxed around his chin, and he spread his palm over Cassian's cheek, hooking his thumb underneath his jawline. A primal instinct awoke in Cassian that razed the strategically structured pillars of his self-control.

He sucked in a breath through his nose and threw an arm around Finnian's waist, pulling him into his chest. Their bodies curved together and burned as one. The strong stride of Finnian's heartbeat thundered against Cassian's ribcage.

The kiss was greedy. Lips fused together. Tongues grazed teeth. An enchantment hummed under Cassian's skin. Sensations fluttered in his stomach.

All the thoughts that plagued him stilled. Silence stretched out across his mind. The never-ending to-do list. Ruelle. Balance. The state of his realm and his souls. Operation and order. All of it shattered into dying white noise, a welcoming static between blood and bone. Nothing before had been able to captivate his full attention the way Finnian so easily did in that moment.

Finnian's tongue danced over his bottom lip. An inferno burned in his abdomen and he locked his fingers around Finnian's nape, drawing him in and kissing him harder.

He slipped his hand beneath the hem of Finnian's shirt and spliced his fingers across the middle of his back, stroking up the side of Finnian's torso, over the ridges of his ribs.

Finnian retracted his tongue from Cassian's mouth and bit down on the cushion of his bottom lip, stretching the skin. Tingles fluttered up Cassian's spine.

He lifted his other hand up into Finnian's long strands and forced his head back. His thumb slightly extended, grazing over the solid crystal still safely inside the canal of Finnian's ear. A confirmation that made Cassian feel better, knowing Malik had not destroyed it.

Finnian scraped his teeth across the nerves and skin of Cassian's lip. A pain mixed with an insatiable pleasure. The sensation made him twitch against the inside of his trousers.

An intense gathering welled up behind his navel. He brought his mouth down onto Finnian's neck, tracing his tongue up the curvature of his throat, nipping and marking his skin to leave proof, if only for a second, before the bruises healed.

Finnian rolled his hips, grinding his hard length against Cassian's pelvis.

Cassian dragged in a breath against the skin of Finnian's neck. A tremor shot deep into his belly as his heart sped up like a butterfly caught in his chest.

He licked up Finnian's throat, ravishing in the sensation of the young god's quickened pulse on his tongue.

Finnian wedged his knee in between Cassian's thighs and softly rubbed against his arousal.

Cassian let out a gruff hiss across the side of his neck.

Finnian froze.

The sound was loud in the silence of their kiss; the transition was sharp and instant.

Cassian's thoughts starkly came rushing back in. From the battleground of feelings waging war in his subconscious to the contentment he felt in this moment with Finnian. What would happen now? What was Finnian thinking?

Finnian forced them apart with a small shove to Cassian's chest.

His brain raced to process the last few minutes through the haze of his lust. The smoothness of Finnian's skin, twisting his fingers through Finnian's hair, and the way Finnian's hunger flourished when Cassian had kissed his throat. Cassian wanted him. More of him. A terrifying expansion of the desire he failed miserably to ignore. Now it had grown tenfold.

The taste of Finnian lingered on his tongue as he stared at the god, tracking every visible sign of emotion his face willingly gave away—bruised lips parted, breathless, creases drawn over his forehead, staring back through glazed eyes.

"Finnian," Cassian said.

A hard look flashed over his features at the sound of his name. "No." He took another step away, his expression sharp. "Do not seek me out again. I mean it. Either curse me now or be done with it."

His hatred, the conflicting resonance in which he spoke, made all the sense in the world. Cassian, the High God, who had taken his father away, showed him affection. After all these years of chasing him, tricking him, and now saving him. Finnian was right. Cassian could no longer go on pretending to be conflicted about the matter.

The truth glared down at him like the sun.

Cassian took a breath. The oxygen traveled deeper than it had in years. He lifted from the side of the vault.

Finnian flinched, but he did not move away, fully prepared to be branded.

Cassian wanted to embrace him. Let his feelings flow freely from his lips. What would Finnian say? Would he feel the same? What would happen then?

Do not give Ruelle someone to hold over you again.

Acacius's warning echoed to the forefront of his mind, extinguishing the warmth in his veins.

He held Finnian's reserved gaze, wishing he could convey a sliver of the adoration he felt towards him. "I do not have it in me to curse you." The confession unraveled the ball of pressure in his chest.

Finnian's eyes flitted around his face, frowning.

An ache spindled in Cassian's heart as he nodded once. "I will not bother you again." He backed away, his limbs growing heavy.

Finnian threw out an arm. "W—"

Before Finnian could reach him, a grueling *crack* reverberated, and Cassian was gone.

TWELVE

THE VILLAGE OF SOULS

THE PRESENT
Finnian

ATHAIRA STROLLED AT Finnian's side as if the wind carried her, in an elegance painfully similar to his father's.

It stirred up memories of their last day together at Naia and Solaris's birthday celebration. Finnian at the dinner table, forced to listen to the tiresome conversation between Vex and Astrid. The fear catching in Naia's breath when a middle goddess called attention to her necklace—the gem Finnian, himself, had gifted to her. Rain splattering along the cobblestone outside the open doors of the palace. Finnian standing in the corridor, trembling and attempting to comprehend the sight of his father in chains. Breath shallow, shaking his head, unable to process the brevity of what was happening.

Afterwards, he slept beside the waterhole with Alke's corpse in his arms. While deities did not grow tired, Finnian had slipped into a state of dreaming, too dissociated from the new reality before him. Sleep was a form of escape, distancing himself from the visceral loss of his beloved companion and father.

He awoke and had forgotten it all. Until he rose and Alke's damp feathers peeled from the inside of his arm.

An ache spiked like an ax through his chest as he recalled those grim days.

"Lord Cassian says you have souls awaiting you at the festival," Nathaira said, her voice like a babbling brook—obnoxiously clement. "They are quite eager to reunite with you."

He swallowed and transitioned his focus outside of the nerves prickling in his stomach.

Instead, he analyzed the sound of her voice coming in through his hearing aid and how it appeared less automated. Which meant his brain was beginning to adjust. Quicker than the long stretch of days it had taken when he first created the device. He despised feeling so... *mortal*.

He pinched at the lavender buds grazing his waist as he walked. Not long after their conversation, Cassian teleported him to Nathaira and disappeared. Finnian was dying to know where.

Nathaira glanced over at him, patient for his reply.

He ignored her, eyeing the passing souls, with no intention of indulging the optimistic goddess in conversation.

The souls appeared like normal people—all young, lively. It seemed ironic to Finnian.

They wandered through the fields with an individual constellation crowning each of their heads. Each aura was unique, a landscape of glittering rainbow gemstones.

"These are the Lavender Fields of Healing," Nathaira told him. "Where we escort the souls when they arrive."

"I didn't ask." He squished the lavender bud between his fingernails, siphoning away its life-force. The crumbled pieces withered.

"This is the River of Eden," she said as they journeyed across the bridge. Their footfalls echoed along the wooden planks.

Finnian turned his head, peering into the forest of elm following along the bank of the river. Was it the Serpentine Forest? He twisted his neck to follow the river engulfing the Lavender Fields and intertwining with the River of Souls. Beyond the ridges of the field, he could not make out what laid behind the river.

"That would be the Grove of Mourning."

Finnian shook his head lightly. "What would be the difference between a field of healing versus mourning? Wouldn't all the souls mourn as they heal?"

She stopped at the end of the bridge and smiled back at him. "The Lavender Fields of Healing are for all souls to process and grieve the life they left behind. The Grove of Mourning is for the deeply scarred souls,

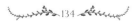

burdened by the trauma they endured in their mortal lives, still unready to begin the healing process."

"If they never move past such trauma, then what happens?"

"They can choose to eat from the Pomegranate Orchard, where the fruit will erase the memories of their previous lives entirely."

He was aware that pomegranates held significance in the Land of the Dead, but he didn't know the reason. "Just like that? They forget all their memories?"

Nathaira nodded. "Yes, but the souls have to receive permission from Lord Cassian in order to do so."

What a fine ingredient the fruit would make for a potion.

Memory-erasing potions existed, but not any strong enough to work on deities. The length and population of their memories were too vast.

Finnian's fingertips itched to get his hands on one of those pomegranates. To craft a potion capable of expelling the memories of gods. Such a rare item would bring in heaps of people and stir all sorts of chaos in his—well, Naia and Ronin's—black market.

Though, he couldn't imagine *choosing* to forget Naia and Father. Their smiles, their laughter, their embrace.

His chest squeezed, and it became difficult to breathe. To distract his body from the sensation, he scratched at the curse mark running up his clavicle, turning his attention over the railing and looking down at the glassy surface of the stream. It languidly swept the wraith-like, half-shaped souls in its current. It reminded him of all the times he sat on the bridge's railing back in Kaimana, Naia at his side. Sometimes they talked, and sometimes they sat in silence, entranced by the River of Souls.

"And what does the River of Eden do?" he asked.

"Those who swim in this river will be reincarnated," Nathaira replied, her patience never wavering to his questions. "It takes them to the Land of Entity to be reborn under Iliana. The High Goddess of Life and Balance removes any memories of their previous life, but when they die, their cumulative memories are given back from all their reincarnations."

He scoffed with the image of Ronin Kahale swimming laps in its waters, annoyingly determined to find Naia in his next lifetime.

They stepped off the bridge into a lush bed of pampas grass rippling in the breeze. Nathaira walked a few paces ahead of him, leading them up a small knoll. Once they made it to the top, she stopped.

He came up beside her, peering out at the land.

"Welcome to Caius." She spread her arms, gesturing to the valley before them.

Nestled between the basalt mountains were winding roads and obsidian stone houses. Wisteria trees lined the stream that was parted down the middle. Marigold and plum wept across the sky between the straw-like branches.

"Come along now." Nathaira waved for him to follow as she started down the hilltop.

Finnian was amazed that Cassian did not name it the *Valley of Celebration*, or something else so simple-minded.

His feet felt heavy as he lagged behind the goddess. Caius was the last place he wished to go. Reuniting with old friends and lovers he'd let go of once already. He did not wish to resurface the ache of loss. To see their faces, hear their laughter, burdened by heartbreak yet again.

They strolled down the dirt road. A knot gripped his stomach with each step.

The souls here were livelier than the ones in the Lavender Fields. They carried themselves lightly and with a calm energy. The passersby appeared just like any other villagers in the Mortal Land, with their baskets resting on the crook of their elbows. Children frolicked in the River, their pants rolled up to their ankles. At the corners of the homes were bloomed irises and poppies.

Mixed in with the souls were deities of Death, known as the Errai. All of Death's lineage worked as a collective beneath their High God. Finnian could sense their chilly auras as they mingled and passed him by. They wore modern clothes rather than their usual ominous cloak and masks—even spoke to the souls in a friendly, acquainted manner. It was strangely refreshing to see them act as if they had a pulse.

Nathaira and Finnian entered a street filled with a bustling market. Ivy decorated the bark of the wisteria. Lanterns were strung between homes and vendors. As they strolled past, Finnian spotted stalls of harvested fruits and vegetables, homemade jams, marmalades, and butters. The aroma of freshly cured meats and baked bread wafted in the air.

His heart warmed, knowing if Naia were here, her cheeks would be filled like a chipmunk, exclaiming how delicious the pastries were.

Around a crackling bonfire, souls gathered at a stall, skillfully weaving and sewing with their hands. They pinned colorful stitched blankets and knitted scarves and socks along a string hanging from one wisteria branch to the next.

The souls acknowledged them with a smile and a wave.

Nathaira waved back, her hand gliding through the warm air.

Centuries of Summer Solace festivals flashed in his mind. Caius was embellished in jewel-toned ornaments, its streets radiating the collective-ness of those occupying it.

Finnian's eyes briefly surfed over the individuals nearby, chatting, laughing, assisting one another in hanging handmade vines of eucalyptus and lavender alongside the lanterns. It was hardly close to the tropical flora and narrow roads of the village of Kaimana, its pastel, opalescent blues and moonstone structures full of villagers cowering to their ruler, but it was still all too similar.

"Am I to follow you around until my master returns?" Finnian drawled as Nathaira paused in the path to examine a stall filled with garlands.

She leaned over and inhaled a bouquet of daisies, unrushed to reply.

Finnian rolled his eyes. If it weren't for the wretched binding spell, he could utilize his time without Cassian to roam the Land for clues.

The length of which Finnian could travel only went as far as Cassian would allow.

Nathaira sauntered a few paces from the flower stall and came to stand in front of a stone cottage. She gazed up at it. "This is where I leave you."

Finnian watched a crowd of souls pile into the threshold, buoyant and singing loudly from inside.

"A tavern?" It came out of him in a deadpan tone.

"Yes." Nathaira giggled.

Before he could respond with a dry remark, a head full of ginger locks caught his eye. The girl shoved her way through the traffic of those entering the tavern. She burst through them and barreled straight for him.

"FINNY!" She threw her arms around his neck. Her body was warm, solid. In his grip. After so many years without her presence, Eleanor was embracing him.

Tears stung the back of his nose as he slowly raised his arms, scared if he moved too fast, the Land would snatch her away from him.

Isla emerged from in between the people flooding through the front of the tavern, her wild curls framing her soft face, grinning at the sight of him.

A stunned laugh scuffed up his throat. Warmth flooded his chest as he beckoned her forward with a wave.

Her face lit up as she leaped and crashed into Eleanor's back, wrapping her short arms around them tightly.

Finnian swallowed them both in a hug, one he'd gone over a century regretting never giving.

Another wrong made right.

THE carbonation of the beer bubbled in his stomach as he sat his pint down on the countertop of the bar. "Hollow City's population was at four-hundred thousand, but that was five years ago."

Eleanor's chin fell. "So many people!"

Mid-swig of her pint, Isla's eyes widened.

Finnian chuckled at their reactions, leaning back on his stool and crossing his arms. "On the contrary. Nowadays, the amount is normal for a successful city."

"The crime rate?" Eleanor leaned sideways, her elbow propped up on the bar counter. He could count every freckle dotting her rosy cheeks as he watched her lips.

The atmosphere was full of loud chatter, and his brain had to naturally work harder to decipher all the sounds through his hearing aid.

"Homeless rate?" Eleanor continued, her knee bumping against the side of his thigh. "Oh gods, Finny, what about hospitals? You must have more than one. What about authorities? How much of the population are mages? You kept the city board running, yes? I will kill you if you say no."

When she was alive, Finnian detested her habit of intensely invading his space, despite her reasoning that she was accommodating his

impairment—regardless of the amount of times he explained that his hearing aid could pick up her words like any other mortal ear—but now he couldn't help but find it soothing.

"Authorities exist, but they stick to the non-magical side of the city," he explained. "I would deal with the magical side or send one of my organizations to do so. There are three hospitals, and they are quite large. Crime rate was down when I left, but there is no telling what happened after my departure. Homeless rate was normal for a city so big. I created a place called the Valley, designated for the homeless community, and often supplied them with food and other necessities. And yes, the board you created still lives on."

"Could you imagine, Isla?" Eleanor craned her neck to look around Finnian, her elbow scooting against his stein. Frothy liquid crested over the sides. "When we were alive, it was a couple thousand."

Isla lightly nudged Finnian's arm on his other side, a cue to look at her before she spoke—something she had regularly done during her lifetime they spent as friends. "I am proud of you, Finny. It seems like you've created a wonderful home."

"*We* created," he corrected her, his voice quiet against the steady talk of the tavern.

Eleanor giggled, playfully bumping her fist into his arm. "Do you remember how we first met?"

Finnian shot her a look. "You mean how you tried to hex a priest and your spell hit a horse instead?"

Isla threw her hands over her mouth, laughing.

"The horse turned psychotic and tried to eat us!" Eleanor exclaimed, her facial expressions just as animated as they were when she had been alive. "Good thing you were there to remove it." She wiggled her brows at him, grinning.

He rolled his eyes at her, unable to resist the pinching of a smile.

"Finny chided me for weeks after I convinced him to allow you to join us." Isla wiped the tears leaking from her eyes, grinning widely. "Shortly after, the triplets nearly ended our lives."

"I h—d nigh—m—s of Astrid f—ears after—ards," Eleanor shuddered, her words drowned out by the sudden squeals and laughter from a nearby table. Without meaning to, his concentration had gone to the louder noise, and he'd missed what she'd said.

Finnian looked at her, replaying the glimpses of her words through his mind.

Discomfort he was painfully familiar with coiled through his chest. A feeling that came with having to decide to halt the conversation and ask the person to repeat the phrase, or pretend like he'd heard what had been said. He usually did the second option, but since it was Eleanor, he didn't mind to sit in the uncomfortable feeling and ask her to repeat herself.

Before he could do so, though, she said, "Thank heavens for Everett."

Everett?

Finnian stared at her, confused. "Who?"

His pulse picked up, nervous that he had misread her lips. A skill he'd spent centuries perfecting.

"Eleanor," Isla hissed.

Eleanor exchanged a terse look with Isla.

Finnian glanced between the two, unable to hide his bewilderment. "Who is Everett?"

Eleanor flitted her gaze to Finnian, slightly raising her chin, too confident with whatever internal decision she'd made. "Everett showed up and saved us."

"What are you talking about? Cassian showed up not long after the triplets. We abandoned the vault. I knew I could not take on them *and* him while protecting the two of you," he said. "We ended up in a small village where I came across the—"

"The hollow cave beneath an elm tree," Isla interrupted, the tone in her voice reminiscent.

"Where we dreamed up Hollow City," Eleanor added.

"A place where deities would not be welcomed," he finished.

A history that felt like lifetimes ago.

Finnian swallowed the bitter taste down his throat that came with thinking about the reality of death. A lifetime he spent with them. He only got one. It wasn't fair.

A moment passed. The seconds pulled, the speed of a cloud in the sky.

He scrutinized their faces, trying to make sense of their hesitant expressions. There was something they weren't saying.

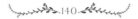

"Forgive us, Finny," Isla said in her soothing tone of voice. She lightly patted him on the top of his shoulder. "Our memory is a bit hazy in the afterlife."

Eleanor grew quiet, staring down and drawing circles in the condensation on her pint with her thumb. She'd always been a terrible liar.

His heart sank, fearful the curse was playing tricks on his memory. Plucking his mind one seam at a time until everything unraveled. He wanted to ask more about it, but he wasn't sure *what*.

"Tell me," Isla continued, changing the subject. "How is my great-great-great-granddaughter?"

Finnian took a drink of his pint and licked his lips, his tongue heavy like lead.

He crossed his arms again and attempted to ground himself back into the conversation. "Runa runs an organization within my ranks. She should be at my sister's side now, helping her grow comfortable in her new role. If her soul is not amongst you, I presume all has gone smoothly."

"As the High Goddess of Eternity," Isla elbowed him proudly. "I imagine your organizations are traveling wide—"

Someone a few tables away barked out another startling laugh. The sound echoed through his hearing aid. He ground his molars at the dull ache grinding on the right side of his head.

Isla glanced over her shoulder at the noisy table and then back to Finnian, noting the agitation on his face with a reassuring curve to her mouth. "I imagine your organizations are traveling wide and fast to spread your beloved sister's name amongst the Mortal Land," she repeated, just as patient in the afterlife.

His lips twitched at the irony of her statement.

"Ah, I know that smirk." Isla leaned into his side, her long brunette curls tickling the skin of his forearm. "I suppose I still have a gift for figuring out your schemes." She lightly pinched at the visible dimple in his cheek.

Finnian gave her a pointed look. "An extremely irritating talent, I'd say."

Isla stole his mug and peered down at the honey-colored liquid in nostalgia. "I am proud of us, Finny. The city we could help you create; the legacies we left behind."

Her words stabbed his heart. A reminder of how they were not real, but souls trapped in the Land of the Dead. And suddenly, he felt foolish sitting amongst them in a tavern in a village of souls. Stuck in a fleeting dream-like fantasy. He could not stay here, nor could he save them.

His stomach churned with a sourness. "Do not speak of the past to me, Isla, as if you no longer exist."

"Do not pretend we are still alive, Finny," Eleanor snapped from his other side.

Her words barely reached him over the overwhelming static of the environment, and the fucking frequency of his hearing aid. The extra effort he was putting in to listen grated on his nerves.

His pulse struck, and his chest grew tight.

On edge, he stood from his stool and stormed out of the tavern.

Out of the corner of his eye, he could see Isla and Eleanor on his heels. They did not speak, and he refused to stop walking until his feet ran out of road to follow.

Solace immediately found him in the silence. The open air, not trapped under a roof of blubbering souls. Who knew they would be just as loud as the living?

The dull ache thrumming behind his ear lessened. He felt relief in his brain, like a muscle that had strained for too long. Without all the other competing sounds, he would not have to work so hard to listen to Isla and Eleanor's voices.

The gravel crunched beneath his feet as he hauled himself out of the busy streets and to a secluded bluff overlooking the valley.

Abruptly, the harsh tugging of what felt like invisible twine constricted around his organs.

His breath caught, and his feet scraped in the gravel as he came to a stop. An excruciating tension hung in his insides. Startled by the pain, he staggered backwards. The pull around his organs released instantly.

"Fuck," he grunted, massaging his diaphragm.

The binding potion.

Apparently, he'd traveled too far from Cassian's approved boundary.

Pulse stammering in his skull and throbbing his eyes, he straightened and glared out at the rolling hills of windswept lavender and the souls caressing it. His nostrils flared with a furious urge building inside of him. He wanted to scream, pour magic from his fingertips, inflict some kind of destruction—anything as an outlet to release it.

I need to find Father and get out of here.

He could feel Isla and Eleanor lingering behind him. There were too many words, too many feelings colliding and thrashing in his chest. He raised his hands to the sides of his head and fisted his hair at the scalp.

I miss you.

I hate this.

I love you both.

Come back to me.

Leave this place.

I don't understand.

He frowned down at the gravel, running his hands over his face. The chilled metal of his rings felt good on his cheeks.

"This is not good enough," he murmured. "I wish for you both to be full of blood and with beating hearts."

They both came closer. On one side, Isla took his hand and rested her cheek on the back of his shoulder, and on the other, Eleanor hooked her arm around his and held it tightly.

"We miss you too, Finny," Eleanor said softly.

As the fight in his muscles subsided, he sank into their embraces, resting his cheek on Isla's hair and raising a hand to cradle the side of Eleanor's head.

"Promise us something," Isla said.

"No."

"You stubborn fool. It's been centuries and you still have no manners." Eleanor gave his arm a firm squeeze.

Finnian cracked a small smile.

"Promise that once you see all your plans through, you'll find happiness. Slow, quiet happiness."

Finnian twisted his head to look at Isla, reading the sincerity of her expression.

There was a spot within his heart dedicated to her and Eleanor alone, and since their passing, it felt like a tender bruise, incapable of healing. Looking at them both now, that spot throbbed in deep agony until it became hard to breathe.

After he burned their bodies and released their ashes into their favorite parts of the city, time slowed. Witnessing a new sunrise each day became meaningless. The silence he claimed to always miss when Eleanor filled it with gabble was unbearable. Coming home to find his workbenches messy and cluttered with potion ingredients, rather than clean and organized and Isla nose-deep in one of his grimoires, kept him from entering the space altogether.

There was no remedy for their absence, and he selfishly regretted not turning them into ghouls against their will.

Death was resolute. Once a person floated in its River and onto its Land, that was it. No matter the peace they found in the afterlife, it did not make up for the years it forced Finnian to walk without them at his side.

"Why should I grant you anything?" The words stung his own tongue as he spit them at Isla. "It is not as if you are alive to watch over me."

Eleanor laughed, the loud and bubbly sound scratching at that tender scar in his heart. "Oh Finny, there is not a day that passes that we do not miss you and our lives together."

His eyes burned as he looked straight ahead.

"The river will continue to flow no matter how much you fight against the current," Isla said in her soft-spoken voice. "The memories we made together were worth every tragic experience we faced in life. Do not mourn us any longer, Finnian, for we are at peace."

"Let me go." He lightly squirmed to break free from their embraces, but they held onto him. He brought his hands up to his face, kneading his eyelids with his fingertips. "Let me be alone."

"Absolutely not." Eleanor delicately took hold of his hands and lowered them from his face. He opened his eyes and met hers, bright and blue as the Kaimana Sea. "Don't you get it, Finny? Even though we are a realm apart, we are always with you."

Finnian hung his head upward, blinking at the sky through his tears. The plum-marigold streaks remained unchanged since his arrival to Caius.

He took a step to remove himself from their hold on him. Otherwise, he wasn't sure if he ever could. They let him be this time.

Hands gripping his hips, he took a deep breath to recollect himself. He scrubbed a palm over his face discreetly to erase any signs of tears and up into his tousled hair before facing them again.

They both stood side by side, watching him carefully.

He took a moment to truly look at these versions of them. Both young, without the wears and tears of mortal life creasing their skin. It was nice to see them this way again, unriddled by the throes of time. That had been the hardest part, watching their bodies grow old and wither away until none of his potions could heal their illnesses.

His eyes sought for familiars—Isla's frizzy curls springing in every direction, her long fingernails painted bright yellow; Eleanor's baggy pants and the pockets spilling with flowers and curative plants.

He stepped up and twirled a finger in one of Isla's ringlets and playfully tugged.

With glistening eyes, she smiled faintly up at him.

Words were never needed between them. It had been this way since the day they'd met and she'd caught him stealing herbs out of her garden.

"I see you still enjoy tea in the afterlife." He reached down and plucked a chamomile blossom from Eleanor's pocket. "You would have enjoyed the twenty-first century. Pants are a thing made for women now, with deep pockets."

"I no longer need the medicinal effects to help me sleep." She raised a hand and ruffled his already disheveled hair, grinning happily. "But I still enjoy drinking it, because the taste reminds me of the nights we all shared in those cramped up holes we used to call our homes."

Memories of them huddled under a flimsy blanket on a dirt floor, steaming, cracked mugs of tea in their laps, Finnian teaching them an incantation to spark a simple fire—they flickered in his mind and his heart constricted.

Pursing his lips to combat the lump forming in his throat, he tucked the flower delicately back into her pocket, and then leveled both of them with a somber look. "Who is Everett?"

They both stared back at him quietly.

"Do you lie to your master in the afterlife?"

Eleanor's expression scrunched. "Do promise when you leave us, you will learn proper etiquette," she huffed.

"Eleanor," he said in all seriousness.

Isla reached for him, giving his hand a tender squeeze. "He was your lover."

The words felt like a punch to his sternum.

He staggered backwards, pulling his arm from Isla, reeling into the deepest folds of his mind for any recollection of this person they spoke of.

Before Arran, there had been Solaris's attendant, Emris. A quick-burning series of nightly hook-ups. Nothing more. A few guards here and there. But Arran had been his first love—and his first ghoul.

Arran taught him much about the ghouls and what they needed to sustain consciousness, but turning him into one had been a mistake. Arran stood by his side afterwards, but he wanted nothing romantic to do with him.

After his banishment, it wasn't long when he released Arran's soul. The years that followed, he sought pleasure from men in a shape-shifted form to avoid tarnishing his reputation among the Mortal Land. For, at the time, most mortals had been too small-minded to accept two men enjoying each other's company, among other things. And he needed their favor to grow stronger as a High God, to make his wrongs right.

Throughout the centuries of his life, he'd had many sexual encounters with others, but certainly never another *lover*.

"It is all going to be alright, Finny," Eleanor said, her eyebrows drawn together.

"I am cursed. You speak of a man I do not recall." His racing heart drummed in his chest, pulling the muscles painfully taut. He pressed his trembling hand on his pec, tracing the snaked spill of his curse mark. "I do not know what is real anymore."

And that terrifies me.

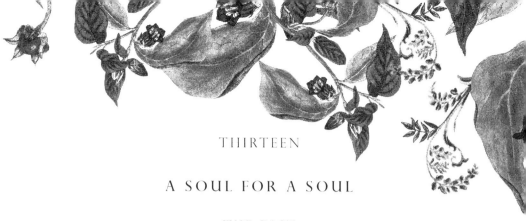

*D*O NOT SEEK *me out again. I mean it.*

Cassian sat on his throne. He brushed his thumb over his bottom lip in a repetitive motion, mind lost in the final moments he'd shared with Finnian a few days prior.

The young god's touch, the taste of his lips—they haunted him. How long could he stay away from Finnian? Was that truly what Finnian wished?

Cassian glided a hand through his hair and sighed.

A light gust brushed across his cheek. In his periphery, Mavros materialized beside him.

"My lord," he greeted, reverently.

"How many souls today?" Cassian asked, continuing to peer through the long stretch of his throne room.

"One. He has come to you several times before."

Cassian rested his head back on the stone. "Bring them in."

"My lord, before we begin, I must inform you, there are over one-hundred souls unaccounted for today. The Errai say it is the young god."

Cassian's jaw set, a stone hardening in his chest. "I will deal with it."

"Iliana has sent her *boyden* with a message requesting an update on the issue."

"Mavros," Cassian turned his head to look over at his attendant.

Mavros's gaze flitted down at him. "Yes, my lord?"

"Please bring in the soul so I can move along with my day."

Mavros gave an exasperated sigh and bowed his chin obediently. "Right away, my lord."

The massive iron doors unfolded at the end of the hall. A soul flanked by two Errai entered down the velvet pathway lining their feet. The hem of the deities' graphite cloaks swayed at their ankles as they strode. Their plated masks glistened like liquid white and black marble under the firelight.

Cassian took in the soul between them. It appeared in its human form, but Cassian could see the beaming orb of red tinges flaring at different capacities, like a ball of berry crimson, levitating in the space of its ribcage.

Once a soul entered the afterlife, they could choose to shed their human forms and scour the Land in the natural forms of their spirit. However, the trend was to do it only at night or deep within shadows of the wisteria. As the dusk fell upon the realm, glowing orbs of light filled Caius and illuminated the trees like vibrant treasures.

Cassian loved to sit and watch them on the balcony of his bedchamber, swirling around the midnight sky.

Like fireflies.

Finnian, feathered in the snowy moonlight, appeared in his thoughts.

He swiftly dismissed the image and refocused, analyzing the soul a bit longer.

Embedded within the fluttering orb's cherry-red outer layer was an intense density. Streaks of red currant and mahogany entwined around its core. The markings of wisdom.

This soul had lived six different lives in the past six centuries, when most souls only reincarnated once every two to three centuries.

The soul yearned for something—or *someone.*

They stopped at the steps of the dais and bowed.

Cassian rose from his throne and descended the steps towards the soul. "You wish to reincarnate again?"

The soul did not look up. "Yes."

Something about it beckoned his full attention. "What do you seek?"

"My other half."

"May I check something?"

The soul lifted its chin and gave a small nod.

Cassian gently pushed his hand through the nebulous form of the soul's abdomen and grasped their spirit. Its human form disfigured into smoke as he held the floating ball of energy in the palm of his hand. It burned brighter, a hauntingly beautiful, blood red globe. Cassian balanced it with ease.

Divine power pulsed down his arm. Dark tendrils splayed like trails of smoke from his fingertips and curled around the soul.

Show me.

Streams of achromatic light burst through the outer shell of the soul. Around it was a web, glistening and reflecting in the heavenly glow like oiled strings.

The threads of Fate.

Cassian could not see the threads of one's Fate outside of his realm. However, in his Land, while they were one of *his* souls, he could glimpse it with a single touch.

Tracking the threads, he pieced together this soul's destiny—how it would be reborn for the seventh time and finally meet its other half. His time with them would be short, and a powerful goddess would tragically end his life. It would require time to recover after such a traumatic death. When they healed, they would reappear before Cassian again and request to be reincarnated once more.

Cassian would grant it, knowing *that* time would be the final one. Its threads were intertwined with a soul he'd met once before. A goddess with no title who would one day bore a demigod from the Himura clan.

"Ha," Cassian breathed out, smiling darkly. A zealous hunger wound through his insides.

He retracted the claws of his divine power and released the soul. It fabricated back into its human form.

Cassian tucked his hands inside his pockets. "You may enter the River of Eden and return to the Land of Entity to be reborn. I hope you find what you are looking for in this lifetime."

The soul lifted its face to meet Cassian's eyes, honed and full of tenacity. "I will find her this time."

Cassian admired its perseverance.

The soul turned and started back down the velvet lining.

The two Errai bowed their chins to Cassian before turning to follow.

"I am counting on it," Cassian murmured, watching the soul step through the doors.

Mavros descended the stairs unhurriedly to Cassian's side. "My lord, you seem disturbingly eager."

When Cassian did not respond, Mavros turned his head and stared at him.

Cassian's cheek prickled from his inquisitive gaze. "No need to fret, Mavros. It appears a solution has fallen right into my lap."

"Do tell, my lord." It came out with dry enthusiasm.

"I do not appreciate your tone." Cassian pinned him with a look.

Mavros maintained passivity as he said, "My sincerest apologies, my lord."

"You can express your apology by delivering a message for me, to the High Goddess of the Sea."

CASSIAN topped his freshly squeezed lemonade with a mint leaf and journeyed through his kitchen onto the balcony overlooking his garden. A canopy of climbing vines led to a series of pointed, arching basalt stone ruins covering the walkway.

He took a sip of his drink and admired the night embers and black pansies encasing the entrance of the arch, dangling with eucalyptus.

Mavros materialized behind him and scooted out a chair tucked underneath the outdoor table.

"Cassian," he greeted, his tone less formal than usual.

While Cassian appreciated Attendant Mavros greatly, he favored Friend Mavros.

"I take it this is an off-duty visit." Cassian sat across from him and offered a drink of his citrusy beverage.

Mavros shook his head and settled back in the chair. He crossed his arms over the dreadlocks resting on his chest and fixed Cassian with a look. "It's not entirely an off-duty visit, but my formalities have run dry for the day. I suppose we could chat as friends would."

Cassian lifted an eyebrow while taking another swig of his drink. The tang and mint washed across his tongue. A delightful combination. "Did you give her the list?"

Mavros reached for Cassian's drink, apparently changing his mind. After taking a sip, his face twisted in a grimace. "Yes." He slid it back across the table and refolded his arms. "That is truly disgusting."

Cassian wiped the lip smudge on the rim of the glass. "And?"

Mavros released a ragged exhale. "Mira agreed to take responsibility for her son's necromancy. Malik will take the list of souls you've given and slaughter them."

The list contained individuals in the Mortal Land who were corrupt and failed to learn empathy and compassion, even after multiple reincarnations. Cassian only gave a soul so many chances before casting them into the Serpentine Forest for the Achlys to feast on.

Cassian took another swig, noting how Mavros purposely avoided his gaze. "Is there more?"

"Balance will be restored in our realm for the souls we are losing because of the young god, but…" Mavros fidgeted with his lip between his teeth.

Cassian folded his hands in his lap, a physical attempt to cling to his patience. "Mavros, I swear on my title if you do not spit it out—"

Distressed, Mavros rubbed at his forehead. "For Lady Mira to oblige, *reciprocity is required*. Her words."

Cassian gave a satisfied smile. "Wonderful."

Mavros looked up and his face fell at the sight of Cassian's approval. "How dare she propose a bargain with *you*?" He sat up straight in his chair, planting the heel of his fist down on the table. "The goddess is absurd if she thinks—"

"Mavros." Cassian lifted a hand to stop him. "Do you honestly believe I sent you to *request* something from Mira without a proper plan in place? The High Goddess is obsessed with power and control. I knew she would use the situation to her advantage, which is why I sent you to her. Now, I assume she requested I curse an individual of her choosing?"

Mavros slouched back in his chair, baffled. "That is exactly what she requested."

"Lovely."

"What plan could you possibly have to involve such a disgraceful excuse of a goddess and her unhinged son? I don't feel an inkling of guilt for the souls Malik will slaughter, but you and I both know whatever he does to them, the souls will come back utterly broken."

Cassian gave a breathy laugh, amused by Mavros's nervous rambling. "Do you recall the soul who came to visit me the other day?"

"The one who reincarnated for the seventh time?" Mavros drawled. "Why yes, Cassian, I was there."

Cassian rolled his eyes at Mavros's sarcasm. "I glimpsed into their Fate, and it appears that I am braided within its threads."

Mavros shook his head. "How so?"

"The soul will find its other half in this life. Shortly after, it will be murdered." He paused and took another quick sip of his drink, let out a satisfying sound, and continued. "When it is reborn for the eighth time, it will be a member of the Himura clan. When it turns twenty-eight, it will find its other half and together, they will have a child."

"Who is its other half?"

Cassian smirked. "Naia."

Mavros's eyes grew in realization. "A demigod child within the Himura clan."

"I presume you are aware of the Himura clan and what demigods in its bloodline can do to us?"

"That means the goddess will leave Kaimana." Mavros rubbed a hand over his face, exasperation tugging at the corners of his eyes.

"When Mira drags her back, that is when I will be summoned to curse her to Kaimana."

Mavros reached over the table again and grabbed his drink. "What do you gain from cursing her?" He took a giant swig and then hissed between his teeth.

"To give her a reason to summon me on her eight-hundredth year and ask me to remove it." Cassian snatched the half-empty glass out of his hand.

"Which you cannot do." He coughed, his eyes watering. "The only way you can null a curse is to replace it with another."

"Exactly."

"The child," Mavros twisted his head at Cassian, suddenly aware. "You want it."

Cassian nodded subtly. "For its blood."

"To use against Ruelle," Mavros finished.

The mention of her name soured the pleasant aftertaste in Cassian's mouth.

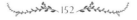

He watched a bead of condensation trace a path down the side of his glass, feeling pressure mount in his chest. A sudden solemness befell his mood. "It is time I deal with Ruelle and the war she decided to wage between us. I refuse to allow her torment to continue any longer."

"What of the young god?" Mavros asked. "I do not think he will take it well when he figures out you intend to curse his sister."

Cassian's gaze flashed up at the mention of Finnian, meeting the concerned look of his attendant.

A dull ache reverberated through his middle. Distance was the last thing he desired, but he would respect Finnian's wishes. To do so, it was best if they remained enemies.

"I do not plan on seeing him again." Jaws flexing, Cassian stared beyond the balcony's ledge at the dark botanicals of his garden. "Therefore, it really doesn't matter. Let him loathe me."

FOURTEEN

ABSOLUTE

 VERETT.

Finnian repeated the name in his mind as an attempt to stir awake buried memories.

He followed the passage outside of the village, through the market, past the homes. The river cutting through the middle of the valley came out into a grove of wisteria. The ends of their blossomed branches swayed with the breeze, kissing the edges of the stream.

After the reunion with Eleanor and Isla, he needed solitude to sort out the emotions gnawing in his chest.

He felt adrift all over again. To see them after missing them for so long, it had slit open the scar of their deaths and the wound throbbed now. Some part of him found peace, while the other refused to acknowledge the feeling. The fact remained that they were still dead, and it was tiring to convince his brain that nothing had really changed, leaving him to sit in the agony of their absence all over again.

Out of habit, Finnian's eyes scoured the bank and the ground cover over the small patches of grass for anything to forage. There was nothing but velvet violet poppies and blue irises. The oils extracted from both flowers were beneficial, but they weren't ingredients for the potion Finnian's fingers were itching to make.

He was no stranger to creating elixirs to awaken long-forgotten memories, having perfected the craft over the course of his days to sell in his black market. Though, he was doubtful any of his current potions would

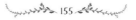

be strong enough to devour the Kiss of Delirium. He would need to craft a new one from scratch to counter its symptoms. But it wasn't as if he could concoct a tonic without a cauldron or ingredients or, worst of all, time.

He walked, the tips of his fingers rubbing against the pad of his thumb, his gaze shifting to the tranquil river running alongside him. The water was transparent and glimmered beneath the lingering golden hour. Souls lapped in the current of the River of Eden, luminescent masses of ghost-like whorls that reminded Finnian of the way an octopus carried themselves across the sea. These souls were migrating to the Land of Entity to reincarnate.

The idea seemed like such a ruthless cycle—to be reborn into an unfair world, forced to go through childhood and adolescence again, if they made it that far. It baffled Finnian by how little time a mortal received to mature when it had taken him no less than a century.

He continued down the path woven between the wisteria. Amongst the weeds sprouting around their trunks he identified hawthorn and goldenseal.

Back in his apothecary days, he'd often use the herbs to create draughts for mortals with high blood pressure and diabetes. For magical use, the blossom, stem, and root made excellent ingredients in many elixirs.

It took a generous amount of self-control for Finnian to silence the instinct within to pluck them.

He missed his freedom and his craft room, full of centuries of books he'd collected, grimoires he'd written with his own quill. His uninterrupted days surrounded by plants he'd spent decades cultivating; the steam billowing from his cauldron and climbing up the walls; a giddy tingle in his fingertips as he chopped and ground the greenery. Creating something from nothing gave him a sense of satisfaction that he was addicted to.

Mid-step, a thrash of pain blanched throughout his insides. He winced. *The binding potion.*

Quickly, he stumbled back on his heels. The splitting agony spasmed in his organs, and he curled over with a hand on his stomach. "Fuck!" he grumbled.

Like a thick fog, the High God's divine power emanated from the ground and coiled itself around his legs. Cassian was about to teleport him away.

A clear sign he'd gone too far outside the proximity Cassian allowed. It meant he was close to something he shouldn't be.

Finnian snapped his head up, searching through the thickening smog. His eyes stretched along the River of Eden as far as they could reach, through lavender stalks, where it merged with the River of Souls.

Beyond it was a forest of bald cypress, beech trees, and evergreens. Smooth, pale branches reached over the deep green like elongated fingers. An opaque fog hovered over the forest like a cloud, monochrome and pale against the vibrancy of the sparkling river and lilac meadow.

The Serpentine Forest.

The gathering of energy dropped his stomach and lifted him from the ground. Cassian's power swallowed him like a vortex and spit him out into a different terrain.

His conviction grew stronger than ever that Moros had to be on the other side of the Serpentine Forest.

Finnian clenched his fist, frustration burning in his blood. The invisible chain locking him to Cassian's side felt tight, suffocating, like a collar. He detested being restrained.

Releasing a terse exhale, he straightened, relieved that the grueling squeeze of his insides had given way, and took in his new surroundings.

Before him was an olive-dusted highland covered in flowing, cornflower blue grass.

In the distance, he could see the basalt bluffs of the valley and the twinkling River wedged in between the village, the sounds of music and voices carrying from Caius.

Cassian's ivory-blond strands caught his eye, glistening like a pale citrine against the backdrop of the champagne horizon.

The High God jogged in a large circle, chased by a pack of dogs at his heels.

He leisurely pulled back his arm, grasping a ball of tightly wound vines in his hand.

The ball flew gracefully through the air and the dogs raced across the field to fetch it.

Cassian stood back and watched, his demeanor more at ease than Finnian had ever seen. That singular curl over his forehead dangled in his eyes. His suit jacket was strewn aside on a branch of a nearby wisteria, and his waistline and toned shoulders were accentuated by the crisp button-up tucked into his tailored pants.

Finnian's eyes floated up to the rosy tint of his cheeks and over the blissful grin spread across his face as the dogs trotted back.

Cassian stooped over slightly and took the ball from a golden retriever. The other dogs crowded around him.

"Good boy!" He petted their heads one by one. "You all did wonderful. But Linus, how about you let another have a chance this time?"

A flutter quivered in Finnian's chest as he observed this version of him.

As if he sensed his presence, Cassian twisted his head towards Finnian. From a few meters away, Cassian's eyes reflected in the honey-glow sunset, two golden gemstones dripping and filling Finnian's ribcage.

Repulsed by the feeling, he squashed it away and started towards Cassian.

The sound of his footfalls shuffling in the grass called the dogs' attention. Heads swiveled in his direction. Tongues hung out of the side of their mouths, tails wagging. They quickly gathered around his legs. Dogs of all sizes, all breeds, left slobbery kisses over his pants.

He wanted to reciprocate their greeting and pet them, but as he assessed each one and the cosmic phantom glows atop each of their heads, a depressing thought met him.

They are all dead.

A copper-haired poodle nudged the ball of vines against the back of his fingers. He dropped his head to regard it, unable to reject its doe-eyed look.

Sighing in defeat, he held out his hand, and the dog plopped it in his palm.

Finnian reared his arm, and the dogs moved as a collective, preparing to run. The excitement of their open mouths and beaming eyes coaxed a weak smile out of him as he threw the ball.

They all sprinted across the clearing.

Cassian came to stand in the space at his side, rolling his sleeves up to his elbows. "Was the village to your liking?"

"Mm." Finnian had no interest in reliving his reunion with Eleanor and Isla for him.

Cassian gave him a squinted sidelong glance from the brassy sunlight hugging the mountaintops. "Eleanor and Isla ask me about you every time I visit."

Finnian kept his gaze fixed on the dogs as they made their way back. "If this festival is in your honor, why aren't you there celebrating?"

"I like to see it as a celebration in the honor of my realm."

"Sounds like an excuse." Finnian raised his eyebrows.

"I don't particularly enjoy the attention."

Before he could make a remark, the dogs bombarded their legs in a frenzy of wet-nosed nudges and eager tail wags.

"Good girl, Maple." Cassian scrubbed the ears of a brown Boykin Spaniel, accepting the ball from its mouth.

Finnian crossed his arms, not looking too long at the glittering, nebulous clouds crowning each of their heads. "These are souls?"

"Dogs of the Land," Cassian said, continuing to give affection to each one in a series of ear massages and relaxed pats. "Most animals reincarnate, but some wish to hold out until they are reunited with their loved ones."

The notion of a dog meeting the soul of their owner at the entrance of the Lavender Fields snagged in his chest. An endearing sentiment, but hardly enough to erase the time forced to spend apart.

"You seem well acquainted with them," Finnian murmured.

Cassian looked up at him, the curl caught in his eyelashes.

Like a reflex, Finnian's hand lifted to push it away. He caught himself quickly and folded his fingers into a fist at his side. The innate reaction took him by surprise.

"I am acquainted with all of my souls," Cassian said, "but yes, I enjoy playing fetch with them. Souls of humans are more complex beings. They require lessons and experiences to learn unconditional love, not take it for granted. Dogs do not."

I do not, he wished to say, but he knew it was a lie. Regret ate away at him each day for failing to appreciate his father during the short thirteen years he'd gotten to spend with him. If he knew their moments would've fallen short, he would've taken the time to really look at Father, appreciate all his kind qualities, and tell him how much he admired him.

"Right there." Cassian pointed to a mixed black Labrador with floppy ears and animated eyes. "Do you recognize that one?"

The stray from Augustus that Finnian had found in a trash bin and brought back to life.

He recalled the day vividly. He'd almost missed the decaying odor. It was thanks to the shift of current that the stench hit his nose. It was what prompted him to stop and pick up on the dwindling energy of a dying soul—like catching the brief flicker of a dying flame.

Finding the deceased dog with a broken leg, abandoned so carelessly, smashed any hope that the Mortal Land and its occupants differed from the barbarity that existed in Kaimana with his mother.

Apathy, unfortunately, bled everywhere.

Finnian crouched down, and the dog came up and sniffed his hand, giving it a few licks.

"He remembers you," Cassian said.

Finnian bore into its eyes. Within them, there was a stillness epitomizing a deep peace. For that, he was glad.

He scratched its furry neck. "I suppose he does."

"Souls do not forget their mortal lives, unless they wish to." Cassian snapped back his arm and sent the ball flying.

Rising at a leisurely pace, the dog trotted after the rest of the group.

"By ingesting one of the pomegranates grown in the Land." Finnian straightened up and looked at the High God.

Cassian's brow quirked, shooting him a bemused glance. "Does my Land interest you?"

Finnian gave a small shrug. "Know thy enemy, they say."

"What else do you know?"

"I know that you have a place called the Paradise of Rest where the souls can choose to go if they seek… Well, *rest*."

Amusement curved at the corners of Cassian's mouth as he peered into the distance of the pack. "I prefer to keep things self-explanatory, to avoid confusion."

Finnian followed his gaze onto the dogs. He held it there to avoid the light-hearted smile on Cassian's face, noting how it softened all the angles of his sculpted features. "Or you simply lack creativity."

A feisty, black Dachshund jumped up and snatched the ball from a Great Dane's mouth. The short-legged furry companion took off through the sea of dogs, its long ears catching in the air like the wings of an airplane as it ran.

"I have a feeling you resented my *creativity* during your time in the Serpentine Forest."

Finnian shot him a deathly look. "The Achlys are despicable creatures."

Cassian laughed and Finnian could feel the sound strumming in his chest, clear and leveled out through his hearing aid. It appeared his brain was finally adjusting to the device.

He rubbed at the curse mark on his pec, the conversation with Isla and Eleanor resurfacing in his mind.

If you do not know what is real or not, try asking Cassian.

He expected such an insane suggestion from Eleanor, but certainly not from Isla, who had been the one to say it.

While she'd always had a way of granting perspective and simplifying matters, Finnian would be an idiot to trust anything that came out of Cassian's mouth. But what other option did he have? Without the ability to create a draught, his memories would gradually disappear without his consent.

It took him a long second to work the confession from his throat. "Your curse is messing with my memories."

The High God rotated, studying his face intently, as if searching for something.

Finnian inclined his head, locking eyes with him. "Can you tell me who Everett is?"

A flicker of affliction crossed his face, and he turned away. "I believe he was your lover."

An emotion that Finnian could not translate saturated in the space between them; a heaviness soaked his skin.

"So I've been told," he said with perfect indifference. "Is his soul here in the Land?" According to Isla and Eleanor, Everett had swooped in and saved them from the triplets and Cassian. Which meant Everett had to have been a deity or a witch.

"Yes."

A witch then. A *dead* one.

"He must've meant a great deal to me for the curse to target my memories of him." As he said it, a thought chilled his blood.

Did I recall Everett prior to being cursed?

He thought back to the days isolated in his cell in Moros. The grim hours spent in the dungeon with Shivani's blade fileting his skin from his flesh. Where had he drifted off to in his head? Who did he hang onto during those moments of misery?

His mind drew blank.

He felt sick.

Finnian couldn't recall thinking of anyone other than Naia and Father.

The vibrational hum started beneath his ear. A reverberating in his jaw irritated the nerves up into his skull.

He ground his teeth.

An itch spread like tiny spiders breaking through their sac and swimming in his blood, scratching and burrowing into the flesh of his brain.

The curse. He'd triggered it. By thinking of Everett. Someone of importance. Just as it had with Naia in the Serpentine Forest.

He dug the heel of his hand into the spot on his chest and swallowed to counter the dryness of his throat.

Calm down.

He removed his hand from the curse mark, curling his fingers into a fist until his knuckles went white. A physical sensation. A distraction from the paralyzing fear flaring through his system.

Anything could be an illusion. A fabrication of his worst nightmares.

The dogs gathered at Cassian's legs. He took the ball and tossed it with less vigor. It traveled half the distance across the field than the other times.

"I suppose so," he finally said. "Though some say you loathed him just as much as you longed for him."

The words made no sense. Finnian stared at the side of his face, watching the muscles of his jaw jump beneath his skin. It was clear this topic was affecting him, and for whatever reason, Finnian was determined to know why.

Approach him with kindness.

"Why lavender?" Finnian jerked his head to the horizon, past the valley of the village to the field. Despite the trembling in his fingers, he did well to speak casually. "Is it because of the calming effect the herb has?"

Cassian did not look at him as he said, "After I became the High God of Death, I was tossed into this realm. Only, back then, it was barren. After I endured seven days and nights of the Bleeding, I was wandering around when—"

"The Bleeding?" Finnian shook his head. "It sounds like a malicious ritual."

"After obtaining my divinity, I bled out every last drop of my mortal blood. The ritual was slow and brutal. The Bleeding took place in what is now the Serpentine Forest."

Cassian took a heavy breath before continuing. "Back then, my emotions were heightened, and I was overcome with sorrow, unable to process the pain and devastation of my death as a mortal. I collapsed in the field and dreamt of my mother's lavender tea. She would crush dried stalks of it with the tips of her fingers, which always left the pleasant fragrance embedded in her hair and clothes. It was a cherished memory that brought me comfort. When I woke, the Land was a lavender meadow."

Finnian imagined Cassian, young and wounded, dropped in a vast realm full of gray nothingness—right after being murdered and forced to duel the personified being of Death. It must've been difficult to bear the weight of such turmoil.

"And the Grove of Mourning?" Finnian crossed his arms, holding his gaze on the side of Cassian's profile, coaxing him to look over.

"It is where I wandered during my time of denial, refusing to accept my new responsibility as the Ruler of Death and leave behind the only life I'd ever known."

Lower your guard.

"That is precisely what led me to the apothecary you first found me in."

Cassian took the ball from one of the dogs and stared down at it in his palm. "Is that so?"

Become someone to him.

"My time of denial was working in that apothecary, refusing to accept that my actions were what led to my father's demise. As well as abandoning my sister to endure our heinous family alone. After many failed attempts trying to sneak back into Kaimana, I learned Mira's word was absolute." Finnian paused, the harsh fact clotting in his throat. "And I was doing alright until you came and disrupted my peace."

Cassian looked over then, eyes shining with a sentiment lost on him. "I—"

Abruptly, his attention shifted as he tilted his head down, dropping his gaze from Finnian to the ground.

Finnian assumed the interruption was a summoning. Not that he had much experience with the unexpected disruption—thanks to Mira wrecking his ear. Apparently, his impairment blocked all connections to hearing summons.

A beat passed.

Cassian twisted around, handing the ball off to a Doberman. "Keep them in line, Lucy."

He disappeared and reappeared a few yards to Finnian's right, beneath a wisteria where his suit jacket hung on a short branch jutting out from the trunk. He dusted off the wool material and slipped it on.

Clasping the center button of the jacket, he took a step and materialized in front of Finnian. A gust of citrus and spice lightly swept across his face. "You are wrong about something."

"I doubt so," Finnian said in a snide manner.

"Mira's word is not absolute." Cassian pushed back his windswept strands, completing his immaculate look. "Mine is."

Finnian's pulse fired at the mention of his mother. "I take it you are going somewhere, then?"

He flashed Finnian a sly look, his lips slanting, as he held out his hand between them. "Come along, Little Nightmare. It seems a middle goddess has challenged your mother for her title."

FIFTEEN

THE SUMMONING

THE PAST
Cassian

IN ALL OF Cassian's eternal life, five years had never felt more like a trek across a desert landscape, agonizing over when the end would come in sight. His thirst felt like the sides of his throat had dried together, parched with a self-doubt of how much further the distance would stretch on.

A year to a deity was as fleeting as a day. And yet, each passing one squeezed Cassian's insides like a fist. An ache tormenting him, each excruciating second.

What was Finnian doing? Did he remain in the cemetery, or had he moved on to another location? Another village perhaps, or a city? Was he well?

Not knowing ate at Cassian little by little. The unknown forced him to bite into his tongue each time Mavros appeared to keep from ordering his attendant to find the answer to these incessant questions.

He'd supplied Mira with a list of souls to match the amount Finnian stole. Five years and that number had climbed up to nearly one thousand.

Over eight hundred souls, so far, had met their end by Malik.

An act of karma for the crimes they'd committed in their mortal lives—killing, raping, raiding homes and lands. Cassian always judged a soul with an open mind. He understood nothing was black and white, but he could not excuse these souls when they had chance after chance at life on Mortal Land.

These tainted souls proved to be ignorant and even disrupted the peace of the Lavender Fields within their first day of arrival.

One fled the Fields and stormed into the Pomegranate Orchard. Their intention was to eat the fruit without Cassian's permission. The serpents guarding the orchard quickly devoured them.

Another dove into the River of Eden and tried to escape Death. The High God of the River caught them and tossed them back onto dry land. The Errai roaming the Fields restrained them and escorted them to Moros.

Within the jagged mountains and desolated territory were a series of tunnels and multi-story labyrinths. All built around the volcanic fire spitting out a relentless surge from Acacius's realm of Chaos. Cassian took pride in his design of the hellscape as he made his routine rounds.

A set of executioners flanked him as he strode down the ever-changing corridors. Smoke and ash rippled at his feet, the particles knowing better than to stick to his suit.

The souls who disobeyed Death's law were sentenced to time in Moros—a grace period Cassian often gave before tossing them into the Serpentine Forest.

He'd relieved Shivani of her duty and took over their torturing. Only a few had a change of heart and graduated from Moros to the Lavender Fields. The executioners distributed the others as meals to the Achlys.

Cassian obeyed Finnian's wishes and stayed away. It was the best, for both of their sakes, regardless of the feelings that Cassian was now aware he had towards the young god.

Until Cassian got his hands on the Himura demigod's blood and took care of Ruelle, it was best not to get involved with Finnian. And if he needed another rational excuse, he reminded himself of how he'd formed a bargain with Mira to curse Naia. Something Finnian would unlikely approve of.

Yet, despite these logical reasons, Cassian coasted through his garden in the late hours of the night. He brushed past the night embers and Black Barlow and burgundy hollyhocks, down the rows of lemon trees and the flourishing mint at their roots. Nuzzled in the back, beyond the blossoms and greenery, was vacant land, surrounded by an iron fence.

Cassian sat on a stone bench at the edge of the emptiness and day-dreamed of the magical plants that could fill it. With little knowledge of plants and herbs for potion ingredients, he instructed Mavros to gather information.

"Sage, mandrakes, rosemary, valerian," Nathaira listed off, her tone inquisitive. "Are you positive about this?"

"Certainly." Cassian stood next to her, looking out at the barren soil. "The basic plants for a mage. And a small stream here." He pointed ahead, drawing a curved outline in the air with his finger.

He stepped back, assessing which tree would fill the space best. "How about making it flow between a coppice of hawthorn? The blossoms will be a lovely addition, don't you think?"

Nathaira's delayed reply made him look back, catching her exchanging a glance with Shivani beside him.

Shivani pursed her lips, which failed to suppress her grin.

"Yes, my lord, right away," Nathaira said.

He fidgeted with his thumb and index finger inside the pocket of his slacks. "Is there anything else you think would provide usefulness?"

Nathaira's arms gently rose and her fingers danced in a fluid movement. Tiny green stems budded from the dirt in a neat row along the fence. "Hemlock and passionflower. I also hear buckthorn and monkshood are common ingredients that mages forage."

Shivani strolled over to the stems curling like fingernails up from the ground and squatted down to ogle at them like a child in awe.

Cassian nodded. "Add that in as well."

"And what shall we call this area of the garden?" Nathaira's arms remained lifted as she looked over at him.

His mouth curved up into half a smile. "Finnian's Grove."

A scowl burdened Cassian's lips as his foot touched down on the solid ground of his realm. While he welcomed any excuse to end a Council meeting early, worry dampened the skin of his palms. Acacius had not shown, and when Iliana informed them of the war, his insides kneaded with dread.

"My lord." Mavros appeared at his side, the gust of his presence rippling through the tall stalks of lavender. He fell into step alongside Cassian.

Fresh spirits backed up along the shallow edge of the River of Souls. They climbed out along the bank, stretching across the field and intertwining with the River of Eden, something that happened when the water's population grew too dense. Cassian rarely witnessed the sight—except during the grim periods of mass killing within the Mortal Land.

The Errai dotted the bank, guiding souls from the water.

Nathaira was kneeling in front of a group of children, all sniveling and weeping. "You are safe now. No need to cry." She wiped their damp faces with the back of her fingers.

"I lost my mommy," a little girl cried, burying her face in her hands. "The *boom* separated us."

"How about we go search for her?" Nathaira tucked a strand of the child's amber hair behind her ear.

She brought her tear-filled eyes up from her palms to the goddess and nodded pitifully.

Nathaira smiled, taking her by the hand. "Let us go."

Cassian surveyed the number of souls. "Mavros," he said in a demanding tone.

"The Mortal Land is at war, as you are probably aware of by now," Mavros explained. "These are all casualties of a recent attack."

In his five-thousand years, war had become familiar to him. Among gods, mortals, mages. He had grown desensitized to it all. Death was tragic and gory within the art of war, but in the end, death was still death. However, when the waves of war claimed innocent lives—especially children—it triggered a pang in his chest.

"Acacius." He cursed his little brother's name. Just as peace was required to exist in the world, so was chaos. Cassian could recall Acacius mentioning at previous Council meetings that Chaos would unfold soon. He now regretted paying little attention when Acacius spoke, too occupied by thoughts of Finnian.

Cassian swallowed the nausea clawing up his throat, his mind already sprinting to problem solve. "I will go assist those at the front gates myself," he told Mavros. "Assist the Errai here."

"Understood, my lord."

Cassian's eyes flickered around the amassing lump of souls flooding the River. He lifted a hand into his hair, his cheeks going numb as worry split down in his stomach.

The Mortal Land is at war.

"Mavros," he called out before his attendant vanished. "What is the war over?" He could hear the distinct edge in his voice, feel the trembling of his fingers against his scalp.

"Land," Mavros said, eyeing him with concern. "Two nations are disputing over land."

"Where?" Cassian's hand lowered from his hair, anxiety flooding his system.

"In the western hemisphere."

Cassian's heart dropped.

Was Finnian safe? Harmed in any way? He needed to lay eyes on him. See for himself that he was okay. While Finnian was a god and a mage, Cassian had witnessed mortals and the ardor of their greed and violence.

"Where is the young god now?" It came out as a demand, his tone frantic and curt.

"I am not sure, my lord." Mavros stepped closer, regarding Cassian with a cautious look, as if one wrong word spoken might spook him away. "It seems he's once again activated some sort of spell, preventing me from locating his whereabouts."

Of course he had. The fact should not have stung Cassian's insides, that after their time in Augustus and in the cemetery in Elmwood, the young god had no interest in being found by him.

As much as the idea pained him, he still needed to make sure Finnian was okay. He would find a way even without seeing the young god. He simply needed to ensure the lives of Finnian's apprentices were not among the souls.

"Eleanor and Isla, the two mages," he said. "Confirm that no souls by those names have entered the Land because of this war."

"Right away, my lord." Mavros nodded once and vanished.

Cassian stared down at the planks of the bridge. Finnian was fine. He had to be. He was meticulous and cunning, always five steps ahead. Surely, he had sensed the war coming and took precautionary measures to protect himself and his apprentices. Worrying was useless until Cassian learned more.

For now, he had no choice but to push Finnian from his thoughts and welcome the horde of new souls to the Land of the Dead.

CASSIAN strolled through the gates of his garden, a solace in him aching to decompress right outside the spired columns and rigid peaks of his obsidian castle.

With one hand in his pocket, his other held a glass filled to the brim with bourbon. The burn of the liquor drowned the cries stuck in his ears, of the souls falling apart, begging for another chance of life, on the bank of the River, at the threshold of the gates.

I do not wish to die.

Please.

I am not ready for death.

Let me go back.

I want to live.

I must see my husband again. Take me back. My children. Let me go. My mother. I must return. My father. They are waiting.

For hours, Cassian greeted souls at the gates until some of the Errai had returned after guiding them from the Mortal Land.

Once the gate was secure, he assisted the Errai in sorting the souls. They had taken over half to the Grove of Mourning, too scarred by their traumatic deaths to heal properly in the Fields.

Cassian had been relieved to learn no young souls by the names of Eleanor or Isla had entered his Land. He questioned whether Finnian would have turned them into ghouls upon death, but then he remembered Finnian's words at the cemetery: he didn't enjoy turning people into ghouls.

Something told Cassian that if his apprentices had died, Finnian would've respected their wishes and let them pass on.

He pinned that thought in the forefront of his mind and let it give him the assurance he needed to believe Finnian was okay—wherever he was currently hiding.

Cassian strolled through his grove of lemon trees. The sharp twang in the air filled his lungs. He took a swig of his drink and claimed a seat on the bench overlooking the thicket of black roses climbing along a trellis. The vines strangled a set of ruins.

He lounged back and propped his elbow on the stone bench. After a minute of massaging his temples, he took another gulp of his drink.

The liquor warmed his belly as he peered through the metallic streaks of moonlight glittering on the surface of the stream that winded through the hawthorn.

Augustus slipped into his thoughts. The dirt path outside the small city. Country cottages and livestock housed within a picket fence. A melody of cicadas and the breeze ruffling the leaves like wind chimes. Finnian at his side, pointing out the twinkling specks of fireflies between the trees.

Cassian slouched his head back, exhaustion fraying his mental state. Over the treetops, the luminous orbs of his souls floated across the sky. The view was serene. If only he was not alone.

He lifted his drink to his mouth—

"Cassian, High God of Death and Curses."

The rim of the glass paused at his lips.

He sat up, his pulse jumping to the sound of the deep, sweet-toned voice. *"Come to me."*

THE summons led him through a veil of magic and dropped him into an alleyway hugged between city buildings. A city he did not recognize. One he had never stepped foot in.

Hooves thudded against the smooth ground, followed by the turning of carriage wheels down the narrow backstreet. And at its dead end, less than a pace away from Cassian, stood Finnian.

It had been five years since he'd last laid eyes on him. Eyes that now devoured the young god, tracking every change to his person. His hair was longer, hitting right above his waist like black silk. His features had lost their roundness. Their edges appeared sharper, more defined than when Cassian had last seen him.

The linen shirt he wore was unbuttoned halfway down his torso. At least his poor fashion sense had not changed.

Cassian's eyes fell to the gleam of gemstones dangling over the carved surface between his pecs. Three necklaces, each a different crystal.

Finnian crossed his arms as he stared at Cassian with a look of indifference. It didn't bother Cassian, though. Reserved as Finnian was with his emotions, *he* had summoned Cassian to him. Proof, regardless of the reason, that he'd been on Finnian's mind, too.

"Little Nightmare," Cassian greeted casually, slipping his hands inside his pockets. It took everything in him to ignore the steady thumping of his accelerated heart, and the puddling excitement in his chest. "Glad to see you've abandoned the graveyard."

"I had no choice. Seeing as you relinquished the souls of the corpses buried beneath it."

"All souls that were living peacefully in my Land until you stole them."

"I do not wish to fight." Finnian blew out a breath and dropped his arms. His shoulders relaxed, and he regarded Cassian with a milder look, turning and beckoning him to follow with a wave. "Come with me."

Cassian stared back at him, skeptical.

Finnian paused in his step, noting Cassian's hesitation, and gestured to the dark-stained door on the side of the building with a flick of his chin. "This is the back entrance of my home."

Cassian gazed up at the several-story-high building and its black brick exterior, pretending to take in the structure when he was actually attempting to gauge the situation. Was Finnian's invite friendly, or a way to lure him into another one of his magical traps?

"There are no *surprise sigils* awaiting you," Finnian said with an amusing lilt to his tone.

Cassian dropped his chin, his expression sullen as he nodded and trailed behind him.

He stepped inside a small room and a waft of earthy, botanic scents traveled up his nose. He closed the door behind him as Finnian swiveled a hand in the air. The scattered candles lit and a glow furnished the small room.

Finnian strode over to the workbench positioned in the back corner. Above it were shelves full of oddities. A thick grimoire with tea-stained pages. The skull of what appeared to be a small animal. A black cast-iron pot. Crystals and jewels of various shapes and colors. Bundles of dried herbs. Vials and jars stocked with odd items—seashells, fuzzy brown spider corpses, roots of some kind, green leaves, mushrooms.

Finnian plucked two orchid-colored crystals from the shelves and aligned them within the sigil drawn on the wood surface of the workbench. "Do you know where we are?"

"I am familiar with this land." Cassian kept his distance across the room, guard up. "However, it seems we are somewhere cloaked with magic. A city that is new to me."

"Hollow City," he said with his back to Cassian as he worked.

Cassian's eyes grazed over Finnian's shoulders and down his waist, noting how his lithe physique had slightly filled out. "Never heard of it."

"Because I created it about three years ago with Eleanor and Isla. I needed to teach them how to activate a sigil properly, and we had nowhere to live, so…"

He created his own city.

He was okay. Safe. Building a home for himself. Cassian was proud to hear this, but equally unsettled. "There is a war going on in the western region within the Rowena continent," he said, unsure of how to go about expressing his worries. "The border is mere miles from here. I do not know how far the ruin will spread."

Finnian paused and glanced at him over his shoulder. "When the war began, I cloaked the city to keep the residents safe as a precautionary."

Not to hide from him. Or perhaps both? Cassian didn't have it in him to ask.

As if he could hear Cassian's thoughts, Finnian held his eyes for a long moment, reassuringly. It was plenty to settle Cassian's doubts.

Finnian continued working.

Cassian inched closer to get a better look over his shoulder, curious. Drawn on the wood surface of the workbench in blood was a runic arc.

Finnian reached up on the shelf and grabbed individual bundles of dried white sage and mugwort twined in string. He placed them in the center of the sigil and snapped his fingers, the glint of his rings catching in the candlelight. The bundle of herbs caught fire.

Finnian held them both up and blew out the flame, though the herbs continued to burn.

Tufts of smoke curled in the air. The pungent odor thickened. Cassian's throat tickled, moisture collecting in his eyes.

He cleared his throat. "Are the citizens of your city human?"

Finnian waved the smoking herbs in a precise circle above the sigil. "Some, yes. It is a safe place from all deities." He let go of the bundle, though it remained fixed in the air. "A significant influx of mages has occurred in the past year. According to Eleanor, I have become something of an inspiration to them."

Or they were mages who favored his necromancy.

Cassian brought a hand up to his hair at the idea of Finnian's necromantic ways being spread amongst others. The thought spiked his stress.

A jar levitated from the shelf and floated down to Finnian's open palm, filled to the brim with dead scarab beetles.

He sighed and returned his hand to his pocket. "Why have you called me to your home?" His kept tone was subdued, purposefully reserved.

Finnian silently placed a few insect carcasses from the jar into the glyph's center. He swiped his hand in a casual dismissal and the jar glided back to its spot on the shelf.

His arms paused in their movement, and he angled his head sideways towards Cassian. "How is my father?"

It came out quiet, uncomfortable. The Finnian he knew would never ask such a personal question. Cassian could deflect it or refuse to answer, which would only pain Finnian. It was a line of fire the young god rarely put himself in the middle of.

Cassian recognized his vulnerability and wanted to do everything in his power to nurture it.

"He is well," Cassian replied delicately.

"Do you visit him regularly? He enjoys company." Finnian's hands did not stop moving.

"I visit him when I can, but he is getting by just fine."

"Naia always worried that he suffered." Finnian rotated to face him, expression terse, bothered by the thought. "Tell me, is he suffering?"

Their last conversation sprang into Cassian's mind—the emotional confession he'd given Finnian, how punishing Vale was something he never wished to do, words that Cassian wasn't sure if they'd cut through Finnian's detached persona and truly reached him.

It seemed, though, they had.

"Unfortunately, suffering is a part of his imprisonment, but I can assure you I do not make his days torturous," Cassian said. "Unable to explore the world or be with his children is more than enough."

Finnian looked down at the broken stem of white sage between his fingers. "I am glad to hear you still care for him."

Cassian studied him for a long moment in search of answers he desperately longed to know. "What am I doing here, Finnian?"

Finnian lifted his chin. A look of mild astonishment passed over his features as Cassian addressed him by his name.

As quick as it appeared, it vanished.

With his usual stoic expression back in place, Finnian said, "It has been years since you last disrupted my peace."

Cassian's eyebrows raised. "That is what you asked of me. Is it not?"

"Yes. It was." More discomfort rattled in the timbre of his voice.

Cassian started across the room, doing the very opposite of what the voice in his mind chided.

As the bridge between them shortened, Cassian could feel the static of Finnian's aura pricking at his skin. Bold, persistent, and warm—colors of magic and fierceness that he hadn't realized how much he longed to be in the presence of until now.

He removed a hand from his pocket and held his fingertips over the hollowness of Finnian's cheek. A silent permission.

Finnian's eyes flickered from Cassian's fingers to his face. A silent approval.

He cradled Finnian's jaw and gently tilted his head sideways, tracing his thumb over the jagged, white puffy patch of skin beneath Finnian's right ear. With the motion of his thumb, the glamor hiding the scar lifted.

Finnian sucked in a breath as Cassian measured the width of it by comparing it to his index finger. It matched the span of a water-woven whip he'd witnessed annihilating the flesh of its victims many times during the duels he was required to attend.

He studied the heliotrope crystal nestled in Finnian's ear canal, lightly pressing his thumb into the base of the scar, wishing he could siphon the horrid memory from its tissue.

You care for him, Ruelle's singsong voice chimed in his head.

"Tell me," he murmured, moving his eyes up to Finnian's. "Why did she do this to you?"

Finnian's nostrils flared, but he did not pull away. "After Malik killed…" He looked sideways. "Killed Arran, I acted impulsively and revealed my necromancy to her. We fought. I lost. She banished me."

Cassian knew about the violent exchange, but never gave it a second thought. Deities harmed one another as easily as blinking. Now, though, simply picturing Finnian lying on the moonstone floor of Mira's great hall, wailing, sent ripples of fury through Cassian's blood. So much so, he had to force the image aside to dilute his taste for vengeance, knowing he would not be satisfied until he inflicted the same amount of pain on the High Goddess.

"Can you hear anything out of your right ear?" he asked.

Finnian grabbed Cassian's hand and lifted it from his face. The scar disappeared. "No. Not without my hearing aid." He twisted his head and tapped on the crystal fitted inside of his ear. "I created it using a rare crystal."

Cassian lowered his hand. "It's powered by its properties and a spell?"

Finnian turned and resumed working on the sigil. "Yes. Though, it took trial and error to perfect. I went through several beforehand that gave me issues—relentless static, volume that was unstable and undecipherable. Once I managed to find the right crystal, the spell worked seamlessly."

Cassian was quiet for a beat, jaws clenching. While his witchcraft and dedication never ceased to amaze Cassian, it did not water down the climbing rage towards Mira for inflicting such injury on Finnian in the first place.

"Do not pity me," Finnian said, voice small. "I am able to hear just as an average person can with it."

"Do not mistake my quiet response as pity."

"Then what shall I take it as?"

"A deep anger towards your mother. She loathes you because of what you are," he said, lip curling in disgust the more he thought about it. "She is afraid of those who hold more power than her. You are the first deity born in existence who is also a mage."

Finnian gave a small chuckle. "I figured that out long ago in Kaimana. The servants talk."

Cassian ran a hand over his squared jaw, suddenly wishing he'd cursed Mira with a punishment far worse than a lifetime trapped beneath the sea. It appeared the High Goddess kept Finnian's title tight-lipped within the sea-dome of her kingdom.

"Your siblings aren't any better," he scowled. "Save for Naia."

Finnian paused in his movements, drawing in a breath. "The last time we met, I was not living in a graveyard for the reason you believe." His confession left his mouth in a murmur. Whether he was intentionally allowing his discomfort or show to not, Cassian was unsure.

He recalled the comment he'd made upon his arrival, swiftly pointing out that Finnian's home was no longer a graveyard. It appeared the slightly judgmental comment had stuck with the young god. "Then why?"

"I prefer the silence of graveyards because, while I've perfected my hearing aid, the fact is, without it, my hearing is broken. In loud, busy environments, my brain must work harder to listen during conversations. It causes me to experience a mental fatigue that no potion or spell can remedy."

"Do you have any other side effects?" he asked, meeting Finnian's vulnerability with empathy.

"Some, yes. When it first happened, I experienced a persistent ringing in my ear and vertigo until my brain adjusted to the loss. Now, those things have settled. Though, it does take my brain a moment to adjust if I go a certain length of time without wearing the crystal. The noise coming in does not sound… *natural.*"

Cassian cataloged all of this information in the back of his mind, appreciating every small, intricate detail Finnian shared with him.

Finnian lined a white powder alongside the symbol of blood. "Back at the graveyard, what did you make the triplets see?"

"Illusions of their worst fears."

Finnian glanced back at him, intrigued. "Illusions are your niche, I presume?"

Cassian smirked, sliding his hand back inside his front pocket. "My talents go much further than ruling the Land of the Dead."

Finnian stared at him, somber, almost as if he understood something Cassian was afraid to admit to himself. That a part of him had always held back on the young god. Whether it was intentional or because he had

underestimated Finnian in the beginning, there had always been a part of him that never desired to curse him.

"What are you working on?" Cassian turned his attention to the sigil.

The question snapped Finnian out of his thoughts, and he raised a hand. "*Ignis.*" He matched the incantation with a languid wrist motion.

Mystic red flames devoured the bundle of white sage and mugwort in its center. Embers rippled up in the charcoal caps of smoke. The frail pieces transformed into tangible specks of light.

Cassian tilted his head back and took them all in, painting the room.

Finnian swiped his hand in a backward motion and the candlelight snuffed out. Darkness engulfed the room and filled with a swarm of harmonious, medallion-like orbs buzzing around them.

Fireflies.

"Do you recall that night in Augustus?" Finnian asked.

Cassian peeked over at him, peering up at them. They reflected like luminescent ornaments in his eyes. "I recall it every day."

"It is in shambles now because of the war."

Cassian frowned at the prospect of the countryside now a battleground. "It will rebuild. Mortal villages always do."

Finnian flashed his gaze, rich and green like juniper, onto Cassian. "I know you bargained with Mira to replenish the balance within the Land of the Dead and the Land of Entity. The balance that I disrupt with my necromancy."

Cassian's shoulders stiffened and he refocused on the magical fireflies, unable to look directly at him as he said, "I told you, I do not wish to curse you."

"Why?" His voice was almost a whisper.

Cassian reached for the words he did not know how to say. His tongue felt heavy with their weight. "Because I do not wish for you to suffer." It was a surface-level truth.

"Do you think I wish the same for you?" It came out rough, accusatory. A glare burrowed into Cassian's cheek. He could feel Finnian's frustration dissolving through his skin and bristling in his veins. "You asked why I called you here. It is because I wanted to make you a promise."

Cassian rotated, granting his full attention. "What do you mean?"

"Those in Hollow City will never perish." Finnian said, his tone full of resolution. "However, I will not revive those outside of my city. The rest of the world is yours, free of my tampering."

Cassian searched his face, astonished by his vow. Compromising in any way was the last thing he expected—for Finnian to show recognition of the burden his necromancy had placed on Cassian's shoulders. The situation of balance was temporarily resolved, and while Finnian's declaration was hardly perfect, it was *something*.

A smile broke apart his lips, carving adorable divots on both sides of his cheeks. "Is this what the High God of Death and Curses looks like when in shock?"

A flutter caught in Cassian's stomach.

No.

He shook his head as that flutter turned into warmth flooding his insides, threatening to drown him. "Do not make promises you won't keep."

Do not care about me.

Finnian reached out and grasped his hand. The chill of his rings startled Cassian's skin as he rearranged the hold to a shaking-hand position. "I vow on my title that I will not go back on my word."

Cassian's mouth went dry to the sensation of Finnian's skin, soft, like the velvet of a rose petal.

His eyes dropped to their joined hands, studying the tendons and veins along the back of Finnian's, over his knuckles and the various titanium rings on his fingers.

His delicate hold eroded Cassian's apprehensions. Within it was a preservation that his promise would uphold.

"Okay," Cassian murmured, bringing his eyes back up to Finnian's. "I will retract my list of souls from Malik. So long as you keep your vow."

"I apologize." Finnian brushed his thumb over Cassian's knuckles. "For stealing your souls."

His touch spread gooseflesh up Cassian's wrist. "I appreciate the repentance, Little Nightmare."

Better off as enemies.
Don't do this to him—to yourself.
Let go of his hand.

The command from his brain moved through his synapses but dissolved somewhere along the way. All sense of rationality and the harrowing reality of what awaited him seemed distant. So far away, he felt untouchable.

Tethered to Finnian, he finally felt grounded, like he'd been drifting for some time and failed to notice. It was just as it had been the night they sat along the stream in Augustus, talking, smiling, enjoying each other's company. He did not care, so long as Finnian was nearby.

"*Finny*," Finnian said with a playful note in his tone. "If you must call me by a nickname, I would prefer it to be that, rather than *Little Nightmare*."

Cassian smiled, a quiver rolling down in his chest. "Very well, *Finny*." He tested the name out on his tongue. The syllables balanced well and came out smooth. It felt personal and well-acquainted.

At the sound of it, Finnian's thumb ceased its movement along the back of Cassian's hand. Tingles danced up his tendons like currents of electric light. Finnian's gaze intensified around him.

He cleared his throat and lightly pulled his hand away, retreating it to the safety of his pocket, and shifted his stance, positioning himself sideways in the direction of the door—as if he planned on walking out rather than teleporting away. "I must go back. The war has brought in countless souls."

"Of course." Finnian crossed his arms, his eyes dark and holding onto Cassian's with growing fervor.

A wave of heat blew through his bloodstream and he tugged on the cravat tied around his neck.

Turning his head, he switched his attention back to the glowing specks floating around them.

It betrayed the foundation of which he stood on the past five years.

Each time that he yearned to seek Finnian out for no other reason than to see him, he'd withheld by reminding himself of Ruelle and all the ways she could hold him over Cassian's head. All the ways she could harm him.

The potential of Finnian's pain had always been greater than Cassian's own desire.

However, standing there now with Finnian, with the fireflies and his vow and apology, Cassian was not strong enough to walk away into that imaginary desert he'd trekked through for the last five years.

Without looking at Finnian, he asked, "When can I return to see you again?"

It was reckless and irresponsible. Stupid. So utterly stupid. But he didn't care.

A moment of silence passed, prompting Cassian to give in and look at him.

The magical fireflies drifted like fuzzy, golden stars around him. Their gleam illuminated the twinkle in Finnian's eyes and reflected off the whites of his teeth, displaying a hypnotizing smile.

"Whenever you wish."

SIXTEEN

THE HIGH GODDESS OF THE SEA

THE PRESENT
Finnian

INNIAN'S FEET TOUCHED down on familiar ground. The humid air hung around him, curling the ends of his short locks around his nape.

He breathed it in—the salt, the seaweed, the island flora. An ache split apart his chest as his eyes stretched down the cobblestone, winding alongside the palace and veering off through the garden entrance. Echoes of memories flooded Finnian's mind: Father leading him down the pathway by the hand, Naia not far behind, or walking shoulder to shoulder with her along the palace grounds, plucking honeysuckle and nursing them on their tongues.

He rotated and looked out at the greenery beyond the palace walls.

More memories blossomed—roaming in the village, listening to Naia talk with a mouth full of sourdough, their excursions in the jungle, ending each day at the water hole, making up excuses *not* to go back to the palace; of Father and their nights spent on the abandoned cove, gazing up at the hundreds of lanterns that filled the sea sky.

His throat constricted with grief.

He straightened to face the palace. The moonstone structure glistened under the sea-filtered rays of the sunlight like a pearl.

Not once had Finnian ever considered her a mother. She was truly a heinous excuse of one, and it didn't take him long during his childhood to abandon the hope of her expressing any form of affection.

He was in his fourth year the first time he'd snuck away from the servants. A feast for High Deities had distracted them.

He wandered into the palace garden, retracing his steps from earlier with his father during their afternoon stroll. Beneath a plantain tree, he'd noticed freshly sprouted lemongrass.

There was a curiosity within him. An indescribable knowing to carefully work the root up from the soil. He stuffed the herb in his pockets. They were overflowing when Mira found him, his face smudged and the lavish outfit the servants had dressed him in blotted with stains.

Her shadow loomed over where he sat, the evidence of his foraging in the holes dug with his dirty fingernails. She said nothing. And before he could hold up the herbs and display his proud smile, a strong force of water smashed into him.

It threw him back into a palm tree, his spine colliding with its trunk. The strong current filled his small lungs. The edges of his vision wilted. His skull throbbed with intense pressure. The impact surged against his limbs, on the verge of snapping his arms at the elbows.

The water relented. He slid down to the puddled ground. The rough surface of the bark scraped against his backside. He coughed and heaved to quench his burning thirst for air.

Mira's silhouette stood before him. He blinked to rid the burning of his eyes. She came into focus, her ghostly gaze aimed down at him.

Finnian held himself up on quivering arms and glared at her, so deep he could spot glimpses of the turquoise shine beneath the opaque color of her irises. His fury was bone-deep and filled his veins with dread.

She bent towards him, the motion pulling her long silver braid over her shoulder and swaying in the space beside her face. "Place your forehead to the ground. You have disobeyed your High Goddess. Now, you repent."

Finnian kept his eyes locked with hers, defiant. His fingertips curled in the soil, gathering globs of it in his palm to throw at her.

Too fast for his eyes to register, she cupped the back of his head and slammed it down.

His face struck the solid, muddied ground, crunching his nose. The sound reverberated in his skull and rattled through his teeth. Pain wept down his jaw and into his collarbones.

He wedged his palms into the wet terrain, straining against her hold.

In response, she crammed his face deeper into the cool dirt. Granules of sand coated his tongue, mixing with the metallic taste of his own blood.

"Know your place." The loud ringing in his ears distorted her words.

She released him.

The servants rushed to him.

"Get him changed," she ordered.

Resentment frothed in his mouth. The taste lingered on the back of his tongue during every insufferable feast he had to endure in her presence, when he introduced himself to others and they referred to him as *Mira's son.*

His childhood and the handful of moments involving her were like a caustic echo. He had been free of them, of her, for two centuries, and yet, as he approached the palace entrance, that same resentment coated his tongue.

Deities began to appear like pinpricks, dotting the courtyard in a kaleidoscope of colors.

"Tell me, Little Nightmare," Cassian started, casually stepping around him to stride along his left side instead of his right. "Are you eager for someone to one day challenge *you* to a duel?"

Finnian eyed him, warily, trying to make sense of his gesture that could easily be mistaken as *considerate.* They were about to enter a large room full of chattering deities. It was hardly the rowdy atmosphere of a pub, but the vast hall provided an echo, and his hearing would strain. However, Finnian refused to allow himself to believe the High God was expressing any generosity, because while they'd known each other for years, not once had Finnian ever shared the struggles of his impairment to him.

"I am the only one of my lineage," he replied flatly. Such trivial conversation topics were pointless to discuss.

"As of now, but that may change in the future."

Two guards held open the carved amethyst doors. Their attire was still the same—flowing white trousers, slick muscled chests embellished by foil-golden chains dangling from their biceps.

Time had apparently stood still beneath the sea.

"When that day comes, I suppose I will turn them into statues and use them as pillars around my city," Finnian said snidely as they crossed the threshold.

The High God gave a small shrug, unfazed. "When you've dueled as much as I, the task becomes a chore. Since I put those who opposed me on display, no one has challenged me in nearly two millennia."

Finnian ignored him and observed their surroundings instead.

The corridor was the same. Moonstone floors, sparkling walls, their edges and corners engraved with turquoise and gold.

The crowds in their path moved aside as they passed, recognition pulling their eyes round, enamored by Cassian, before quickly flitting them away.

Their awestruck looks faded as they noticed Finnian beside him. Noses wrinkled. Brows furrowed. Confusion muddled their eyes. Thin-lipped glares fixed on him, narrow and wary. Disgust. Contempt. Aversion.

Finnian had done well to avoid his own kind by isolating himself within the walls of his city, oblivious to the reputation he'd gained amongst them.

He was the first god born a witch. A stroke of luck. Perhaps a divine Fate by the High Goddess herself. Regardless, deities feared what they could not control, what they couldn't understand, and since the dawning of time, witches had been the one thing truly capable of evoking panic among the divine.

Such a hostile range of emotions did not affect him. If anything, it prided him to steal away the limelight from Mira. She lived for duels. For deities to stock her palace, enthusiastic to witness the High Goddess of the Sea win another battle for her title.

Cassian gave him a sidelong glance as they entered the vaulted great hall, as if he could hear the unrelenting pounding of Finnian's heart—uncontrollable, pumping in a frenetic, rushing rhythm.

He looked straight ahead, over the empty circle at the center of the hall, to the platform. Mira stood at the top, surrounded by her two attendants, the triplets, and Marina.

Cassian halted at the edge of the circle and stepped in front of Finnian, blocking off his line of sight to them.

He spun around, his face close to Finnian's. Too close. Mint and citrus and spice wafted from him as he leaned in. The fragrance, the vicinity of where he stood, it all felt oddly familiar, rousing a need in Finnian to reach out for him—pull him snug, or maybe tuck back that godsforsaken curl that consistently fell over his forehead.

Cassian's mouth stopped near the shell of his left ear. "Stay here."

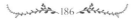

He swallowed and focused on maintaining his withdrawn expression, despite the flipping in his stomach. "Like I have a choice," he drawled.

Cassian glided back, his golden eyes bright and surreal and flashing with amusement before vanishing, leaving smoky, molten tresses to twist in the air where he once stood.

He reappeared next to the High God of Chaos and Ruin, at the end of the line of the Council members joined in the middle of the circle. The pointed ends of two horns spiraled up from the skull of whatever unfortunate animal carcass Acacius wore on his face.

The sensation of moths clawing down Finnian's esophagus haunted him.

A shudder ran down his spine.

He peered over the Council to his mother.

Her eyes wrapped around him and the blank expression she wore so well fractured, pinching her mouth into a scowl.

Finnian returned the visible trace of acrimony with a smirk, out of pure spite.

See, Mother, I can show emotion too. Fuck you.

Her frame seemed frailer, as if she'd lost a few inches of height and shed weight. The fat silver braid over her shoulder lacked shine. Coiling out from underneath the layers of her gown at the sternum was a blush-toned carnation, fully blossomed and lilting toward the hazy streaks of sunlight piercing through the skylights.

A touch from Father.

There was a twinge of something in her gaze, flitting away from Finnian and over those congregating in her hall, like a bolt which had come loose and trembled under stress.

It must've hit her hard when Naia broke her own curse. She could've easily employed witches and assassins to collect Naia, but the likelihood of their success was slim. Between Naia's title as a High Goddess, her husband and child with their Himura blood, and the Blood Heretics, Mira had enough common sense to know she didn't stand a chance.

Aware of the triplets glaring daggers at him, he shifted his focus onto each of them. A replica of the same face—cat-like eyes, button nose, round cheeks—framed by the same nickel-colored strands as Mira's.

The last time he saw them was in Alke Hall the night of his charity event, paralyzed and covered in Ronin's blood. Finnian had taken his time to repay them for when they'd ambushed him and his apprentices in the cemetery by allowing his ghouls to feast on them in their petrified state. Only after a few hours of the torment did he use Malik's cleaver to gut his insides, one organ at a time.

Once they regained control of their bodies, they were quick to flee.

Marina stood at Mira's other side, donning her black attire and sullen disposition. Her dark gaze leveled him, emotionless and intimidating as his own.

Out of all their siblings, Finnian's appearance favored hers the most—a fact he despised. They both shared the same indifferent nature and dark hair. Each held an appearance that favored Father. And while Finnian had only crossed paths with her a handful of times because of their nearly four-hundred-year age gap, his hatred for her lived deep in his core from the heartache she'd inflicted on Naia.

"Mira, High Goddess of the Sea." Iliana, the High Goddess of Life and Balance, addressed her formally.

She was positioned in the center of the line with her back to Finnian, luminescence feathering around the back of her long, black strands. The High Goddess hid her true identity with a chasm of white light over her face. Though, Finnian suspected all the Council members hid their true features with some sort of glamor.

"The Council stands before you today because Freya, a middle goddess of the sea, has called to challenge you for your title," she finished.

Finnian had watched interviews on the news of sailors claiming the middle goddess had guided them through a hurricane. A couple claimed it was she who answered their prayers when they became lost at sea, changing the current and washing their sailboat back to land.

"Do you accept this challenge?" The High Goddess of the Sun stood with a firm posture, her stature strong, expression steeled, emitting an aura that made her unapproachable.

There was a brief pause. A snag. It was quite unlike Mira to falter in a situation that would typically entice a disturbing excitement within her. "I accept."

She descended the platform, her heels clinking along the crystal. Her pace was unhurried, far from her typically ambitious strut.

Finnian barely recognized his mother.

Taking the final step, she scrutinized each of the Council members. Finnian had seen her stand before them many times with her pretentious ego on display—so condescendingly confident of her own power, obvious that she believed she could crush a deity of their caliber if they were to get in her way.

Now, though, Finnian could see it in the way she lifted her chin and shoved out her chest. The effort to appear more threatening than she actually was.

"Freya. Please come forth." The High Goddess of Fate rotated with an outstretched arm, the sequins of her dress reflecting with the movement, like the way light hit a seashell.

The flimsy material exposed the valleys of her shimmering hips and shapely breasts. Warm, buttery locks cascaded down her back. She'd always presented herself in entrancing ways, but how much of her appearance was nothing more than glamor? Finnian imagined her to be a bony hag underneath it.

Freya emerged from the crowd, a buoyant cheer to her step as she took her place in the circle across from Mira.

Under the current of freckles on her sun-kissed cheeks, Freya wore a lively smile that Finnian knew would only provoke Mira. If that failed, her chipper aura of what felt like an optimistic child definitely would.

"The victor of this duel shall go forth as the High Ruler of the Sea." The High God of Chaos and Ruin's deep voice resonated through the hall. "Whoever loses must accept their defeat."

Welcome to hell.

He suppressed another shudder.

"I accept the terms," Mira said.

Freya bowed her chin in acknowledgement. "It is an honor to be in your presence, Lady Mira. Allow me to formally introduce myself." She placed a hand on her chest. "I am Freya, daughter of a middle goddess of fertility and a middle god of wind. I, too, accept the terms. May you be blessed by the High Goddess of Luck today."

Mira's eyes hardened—two pools, bleached and chilled.

Finnian's lips quirked.

A tense silence fell upon them.

The heads of the Council swiveled to the end of the line, to Cassian.

"You may proceed." As the last word left his mouth, the Council vanished as a collective, their forms dispersing into silky ribbons across the hall.

Mira extended her arm; her sea whip formed in her grasp. A cylindrical shape of whirling water, slender and long, coiled along the floor like the tongue of a beast. Spiked teeth tore through its skin, ashen and covered in algae and bone.

Freya took two steps back, slow and calculated. Concentration parted her lips.

Do not let her push you into a defensive state.

Mira launched her whip, and it hissed through the air.

The muscles in Freya's legs clenched, grounding her heels. She threw her arm overhead and the snake-like end of the whip coiled around her wrist. The teeth elongated and pierced through her flesh.

Take her head on and shut down her attacks.

She enclosed her hand into a fist and grinned slightly. Trickles of blood seeped down her forearm. The churning water of the whip solidified and shattered. Shards of ice scattered like broken glass.

She lifted her other hand, and the pieces levitated, reformed into sharp ice, and shot towards Mira.

Swiftly, Mira folded both of her arms up into her chest and the icicles halted. She flipped her hands and pushed them outward. The icicles melted mid-air and the water gathered, forming a large channel. She reached for the end.

Freya closed the distance between them with graceful haste before the water could solidify back into Mira's whip.

Her weakness is close-combat.

Freya punched her fist through the spiraling chamber of water.

Mira dodged her hit and threw her foot out, landing a powerful kick in Freya's gut.

Finnian's heart pulsed in his throat. He kept his eyes on Freya's footwork. She regained her balance, jumped forward, bent her knees, and struck Mira's wrist. The water in her control fizzled and splashed across the crystal floor.

Draw in near and keep there.

Freya raised her hand right above her chin and her index and middle finger straightened together. The puddle at their feet assembled and sharpened into a spike. She thrust her fingers up and it skewered Mira's shoulder. The tearing of her meat and flesh carried through the hall.

She wobbled and her back hit a pillar. The crystal structure trembled. She gaped at the thick spike sticking out of her torso.

Finnian's lips curved. Such emotion was a beautiful sight to witness.

Puncture her confidence by taking hold of the sea.

Freya looked up and reached both arms towards the ceiling. The chandeliers hanging above shook. Tremors traveled through the soles of Finnian's feet and up his shins.

A large crack ran across the vaulted ceiling, and a surge of water burst through. Its rafters crumbled like rotted wood. Debris rained down across the crowd. Whirls of vaporous wisps filled the room as deities teleported out of the way.

Through the gaping hole of the ceiling, a vortex of the sea-sky violently churned overhead. It was like the sea itself reached down with an inexorable hand to devour Mira.

Mira rushed to evaporate the spike in her shoulder. She pushed her spine against the pillar and held up her palms.

The current slammed into her, its collision sounding a roar across the hall.

Mira remained upright against its force, her raised arms shaking against its powerful weight. An attempt to fight for its control.

Finnian's jaw clenched. Of course, it wouldn't be enough to knock his mother off her feet.

Hold your ground and do not let go.

Freya widened her stance and the muscles in her arms stiffened as she heaved her elbows up. The vortex of the sea screamed and writhed like a tornado planted between the two goddesses. Fish and kelp scurried against the push and pull, caught in the vortex's channel.

The languid force of water spun viciously, releasing Mira from its jaws. With fingers curled, the cords in her forearm flickered with tension. She pushed off her foot. The spinning body of water shifted in Freya's direction.

Freya screamed out and took an unsteady step, and another, closing in the distance. The water bowed to her command and moved forward, back to Mira.

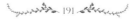

With the control of the jet stream tightly clutched in one hand, Freya tipped forward and threw her other arm out.

Mira jerked to dodge her hit, forgetting about the pillar against her back.

Freya locked her grasp around the stem of the carnation sprouted from Mira's sternum.

And lastly, to create your opportunity for the final blow, reach out and pluck the flower from her chest.

Freya tore out the blossom.

The muscles in Mira's arms rippled. Her chin fell in dumb shock.

Freya cried out and shot her hands outward. The swirling chasm opened its mouth and consumed Mira in a denouement.

A satisfying hum resonated in Finnian's chest as he watched Mira toss around in the belly of the current.

Freya's form relaxed as she spun in a languid motion, her muscles giving way to the flow of the sea dancing with her command.

It spit out Mira like a seed. She rolled across the moonstone and smashed into the bottom step of the platform.

And, like the tendril of a monster, the ravine withdrew back up through the ceiling and rejoined the sky.

The Council teleported back to their original formation, organized in a daunting line. They nodded their heads in agreement, understanding the brevity of this fall.

The Sea itself knew the winner of the duel. A cerulean current of water materialized over Mira's head, circling like a halo, before rushing across the arena to its new heir.

Freya looked up at the small, divine whirlpool above her head with a grand smile before it dissipated, fusing with her being. A new High Goddess had been chosen.

With the duel concluded, the Council dispersed once more.

When she falls, you will go to the highest point of the room and declare your new title.

Freya dropped her arms and moved in a valiant stride across the hall, stepping over Mira to ascend the platform.

Finnian stared at the folded body of his mother—unconscious.

Whispers sounded like a struck match across the vast room, quickly becoming a communal murmur.

The guards stationed along the walls gaped in shock.

Freya faced the mass of deities, shoulders tall, staring out and soaking in her victory with pride.

She extended her arms wide towards the audience. "On this day, Lady Mira's reign as the High Goddess of the Sea is no more." Her voice rang loudly throughout the hall, like assertive footfalls stomping across the earth. "Today, you shall know me as Freya, the High Goddess of the Sea."

An uncomfortable weight settled in the room, stiff and uncertain how to respond. Applaud? Cheer? Mira had reigned over the Kaimana Sea for more than three millennia. And she'd lost. Just like that.

And if you are there, Lord Finnian, may I thank you for the mentorship? I could never defeat Mira without your training, your knowledge of her frailties.

Back then, Finnian had worked for months with the goddess, sparring with her, guiding her towards his mother's defeat. Their plan had finally come to fruition.

Freya's eyes fell upon him.

Do what you wish, Freya.

The last of the memory played out vividly in his mind. He'd stood across from her, arms crossed, disinterested in her request.

Though, now, a euphoric triumph twirled in his stomach as he met her gaze with an acquainted ease.

"I want to express my utmost gratitude to Lord Finnian for his unyielding years of mentorship." She gestured to him with her arm, her affection soft and apparent as she regarded him. Heads snapped in his direction. "For without his guidance, I would not have come out the victor of this duel."

Eyes burned into his skin.

Off to the side of the circle, he caught the clipped twist of Marina's head in his periphery. The sharp motion slung her dark strands against her cheek.

Malik's glare carved as deeply as one of his scimitars. Finnian could feel it hacking down to his bones.

Vex and Astrid clung to one another, unable to tear their wide eyes from Mira.

Finnian acknowledged his student with the slight dip of his chin.

Another wrong made right.

His gaze jumped to Mira with a predatory intent. The memory of her looming over him in the garden as a child flared once again in his mind. The feeling of her sharp nails digging into his scalp. His hair wet and clinging to his neck. The harsh snap of his nose and the waves of bruising in his eye sockets.

Know your place.

A sinister anticipation tingled in his fingertips.

Footfalls broke the silence as a guard sauntered out from the crowd of deities into the circle, golden chains clinking against his oiled chest.

He bowed on one knee and lowered his head. "Long reign Freya, the High Goddess of the Sea."

SEVENTEEN

FAMILY REUNION

ORE GUARDS STEPPED forth and filled the circle, kneeling alongside one another, heads dropping.

"Long reign Freya, High Goddess of the Sea."

Their voices intertwined, forming a resounding crescendo that filled the great hall, amplifying the hushed whispers of the crowd.

"Mira has finally fallen."

With her chin held high and her hands joined behind her back, Freya stood on the platform and scanned the hall.

Finnian had dreamed of this day, swearing to relish in the feeling bursting in his chest when it manifested.

He'd met Freya five decades prior, long after he'd dropped the barrier spell warding off deities from his city.

She'd first wandered in, oblivious to its population of witches and their hostile nature towards her kind. Her sprightly spirit and vivacious outlook on life reminded him of Naia and his apprentices. Although her naiveté and cheerful demeanor irked his nerves, he felt compelled to teach her how to protect it from the world's cruelty.

It had been her to suggest taking over Mira's title, for the sake of ending the High Goddess's tyranny.

"Methodical as ever." Solaris appeared in the space next to Finnian's left side. "Bloody horrifying, but impressive. Though I expect nothing less from you."

Without sparing a glance at the High God of Fire, Finnian acknowledged his statement with a breathy scoff, keeping his eyes on the triplets as they shoved their way through the bowing guards to Mira.

"Mother!" Astrid fell to her knees and shook Mira by the shoulder. "Awake this once!"

Marina and Malik loomed over them.

"Mother, can you hear me?" Vex stooped down beside Astrid. "You must get up!"

Malik glowered down at Mira, lip curled in distaste. "Get up this instant. You look pathetic."

Marina's deadly gaze constricted around Finnian, her brow pinched, a deep scowl carved over her features. Any display of emotion was uncharacteristic for her.

"The mortals know of Naia's name." Solaris's scrutiny burned the side of his cheek. "Word of her title has spread amongst them—alongside the return of the Himura clan. It surprised her to learn the information came from the mouths of *your* former associations."

"Back when the Himura clan first exposed the power of their blood, humans shunned them," Finnian said. "Is that still the case with my sister's involvement?"

"No. For the most part, they have been accepting. Did you plan that as well?"

Finnian gave a silent reply.

"Of course you did." Solaris huffed out a sound, indicating he was not the least bit surprised. He followed Finnian's line of sight to Marina. "She hasn't left Mira's side since Naia broke her own curse."

Finnian smirked, the gesture sharp. "She is coming undone." He could see the fracture in her stonelike persona. An obsessive ire skulked in the black pits of her dark allure, hungry for retribution.

Marina grimaced and shadows draped across the hall, a smoky darkness smothering the midday light sneaking through the gaping hole in the ceiling.

Finnian unfolded his arms, letting them hang at his sides. "Is Naia well?"

"Yes." Solaris turned his head, studying the side of Finnian's profile for a beat. "May I tell her the same regarding you?"

A pinch throbbed in Finnian's chest. He longed to feel the familiar embrace of his sister, to meet his nephew and learn all the ways he favored his mother. The dream grew farther away by the passing second.

He recalled the stories of his uncle Xerxes and how it only took a matter of months for him to go completely mad from the Kiss of Delirium. It had been less than twenty-four hours since Cassian had cursed him. Then again, he wasn't sure, due to the unnatural way time moved in the Land.

His throat tightened.

He swallowed thickly. "I am well," he replied, knowing it would bring Naia happiness to hear he was doing okay. He hoped she was savoring her life, not wasting it away, burdened with guilt for allowing him to swap places with her. "Now leave. I have a family reunion to begin."

Solaris sighed. "I feel obligated to say something along the lines of *let your anger go*, knowing it is what Naia would wish of me."

The dusky shadows filtered around Finnian's ankles, drifting up from the moonstone like black fog. "Then I suppose it is a good thing Naia isn't here."

"I'll leave you to it then." Solaris vanished, throwing up a crackling gust in his wake. The night-black mist caught in its draft and swirled.

Finnian rubbed the tip of his finger and thumb together in hungry determination. His gaze flitted from Marina to Freya. His mentee gave a subtle nod.

He started across the circle between the guards. "I suggest you rise and get out of my way," Finnian said as he passed them.

Their heads bobbed up. Several went to lecture him for disturbing the moment. At the recognition of him, their tongues caught, tripping over their words, and they quickly rose and did as he ordered.

The last time Finnian stood in this hall, anger and a broken heart had blinded him. He had been volatile and desperate to impose suffering on Malik for the act he'd committed against Arran. Finnian had obsessively thought each day about his rash actions and how they resulted in his banishment. He regretted his impulsiveness back then, for it had made him break the promise he'd made to Father.

Take care of each other.

Indifference was not the only thing Finnian had inherited from Mira. Her pride and selfishness lived roots-deep within him, and in those disgraceful moments where he rotted away while reliving his past, he longed for nothing more than to reach down into the darkest parts of himself and rip them out.

He'd failed once, but he wouldn't a second time.

The shadows condensed and licked at his feet. They shrouded the floor like a crevasse and crawled up the walls of the hall. The room quickly emptied, vaporous puffs of fleeting gods whirling in the darkness.

Vex came at him first. Followed by Astrid. Always a duo.

With a swift and forceful rotation of his wrist, Finnian snapped their necks with a sickening *crack,* causing them to collapse.

A cleaver sailed over their bodies. The sharp metal of the blade stung Finnian's cheek. He continued forward. Before he could acknowledge the scratch, the wound sealed itself up.

Malik moved with a harsh velocity, latching onto Finnian's arm and hauling a blade straight into his gut. Liquid pulsed up Finnian's throat and clogged in his mouth. Jolts of agony lanced up his torso.

He smiled through blood-stained teeth and wrenched Malik by the forearm. *"Sangre hirviendo."*

Malik's skin sizzled and bubbled against the inside of Finnian's fingers. Between them, a sinuous trail of smoke curled in the air.

Malik's face twisted from the pain, and he recoiled.

Finnian tightened his grip around Malik's arm, ensuring both he and the dagger remained immobile. The lodged blade in his torso was a dull pain compared to the incessant years of Shivani's torture and being feasted on by executioners.

Malik hoisted his free fist back, knuckles wrapped in brass and aimed for Finnian's head.

Finnian caught him by the wrist, gripped tightly, and forced his arm up. The harsh *snap* of his elbow reverberated in Finnian's palm.

With a furious look in his eyes, Malik ripped his hand from the knife's hilt as his convulsing forearm crunched back into place with an unsettling *pop.* Flexing his fingers, he reached into his back pocket and pulled out a thick, fanged blade.

The shadows steadily rose to their waists like black mist.

Finnian's eyes clicked over to Mira. Marina no longer stood nearby.

Malik twirled the blade in his fingers before gripping it and firing it at Finnian's chest.

Finnian lifted his knee and threw out his foot. With a forceful kick to Malik's abdomen, he plummeted backwards. Finnian tore out the blade lodged into his stomach. A warm crimson fled down his pelvis.

The shadows surged up his spine and over his nape, consuming the room with a prickling, black chasm.

"*Belyse.*" The incantation lit his vision.

Nightrazers whirred and stepped out of the inky mass—phantasmal forms with swarthy faces and folds of needle-edged teeth. Their low growls rumbled throughout the room, a barrage surrounding him.

Finnian positioned his hand in front of his chest, extending his index and middle fingers under his chin. "You spent your whole life mocking Naia for hiding behind Wren when you are no different with your nightrazers."

Malik's blurred silhouette flashed in Finnian's periphery.

He spun and held out both arms. With magic crackling in his palms, he readied himself to unleash a fiery torrent.

The end of a blade pierced through his hand, driving him back on his heels.

His back slammed into the wall, the breath knocking from his lungs. Another blade punctured through his other wrist. The impact strained his shoulder.

With a sudden jolt, he tried to pull himself away, but Malik swiftly slammed him against the wall.

Malik's blood-curdling smirk shone wickedly through Finnian's brightened vision. "Brings up old memories." He cocked his head, driving another blade deep into his diaphragm. Finnian's nostrils flared against the echoes of pain shooting up his chest and into his throat. "I suppose it's my turn to get even now. After the bullshit you pulled back at your hall."

A fire eviscerated the nausea seething in Finnian's stomach. Fueled by pure spite, he summoned the energy to push against the blades that penetrated him. The slits in his flesh widened as he strained against the knives. Pain wept up and down his arms. He pressed his tongue against the backs of his teeth as the hilts carved through his meat.

With his arms free, he caught Malik by the hair and slammed his face into the crystal wall. Fissures cracked across the sheen surface. Ruby red filled their creases.

Malik grasped at the knife stuck in the wall and tore it free. Finnian bent backwards, the dagger's end swiping inches from the tip of his nose. He staggered as Malik rotated and swung the blade again. The tip scraped over Finnian's chin, the pain like a cat's scratch.

Malik's infuriating smirk was accentuated by the sight of his ripened sinew and cracked skull. A murderous thirst throbbed in Finnian's veins—to put Malik in his place once and for all.

Finnian snapped his arm out, palm pointed at Malik. "*Thoir do chridhe.*"

Malik halted mid-step and slapped a hand around his throat. A choke seized his breath. His eyes pulled back and went bloodshot. He gagged and hunched over. The blade in his hold clinked against the floor, lost in the pool of blackness.

Finnian curled his fingers like a claw, pulling at the control he had over Malik's internal system.

Blood soaked down Malik's torso. The pressure of bones splintering in his ribcage resonated; the sound of cartilage and muscle shredding followed. His heart bulged against the material of his shirt, like a magnet pulled to meet Finnian's command.

A set of teeth bit into the back of Finnian's right shoulder. He stumbled a little on his feet as claws impaled the base of his tailbone. Sharp talons ground over his spine. The nerves spasmed down his legs and his knees nearly buckled from the shock.

He growled.

Fucking nightrazers.

Their skeletal fingers roved over the side of his cheeks, dragging across his forehead.

With haste, Finnian formed a fist and yanked back his elbow. The muscled organ burst through Malik's chest and met Finnian's open hand.

Malik's body hit the ground.

Finnian gripped the blood-soaked heart and ripped his body around. With ground jaws, he plunged his knuckles through the core of one of the nightrazers. Violent-blue currents crackled in his palm, electrifying the whirring shadow masses nearby.

Their wails screeched against the glass walls of the hall.

The flashing rays of lightning dimmed, and the disengaging particles of the nightrazers drifted like smoke.

Two left. Finnian searched through the abyss, gauging its veil for movement.

Marina's powerful aura fabricated behind him, but before he could decide on how to diverge her attack, the slick tearing of flesh sounded. Pain ruptured between his shoulder blades. Liquid pushed up his throat, metal coating his tongue. He coughed, his circulation of breath suddenly cut off.

Tension squeezed behind his sternum. The beating of his pulse stuttered and his vision flickered.

Out of the corner of his eye, he could see Marina over his shoulder, feel her arm plunged into his ribcage, her fist wrapped around *his* heart. One sudden tug and he would pass out instantly, just as Malik did.

"I am *nothing* like Naia," she spat roughly next to his ear.

The muscles in his shoulders contracted.

He thrusted his arm overhead and siphoned the energy from within the walls of the moonstone crystal. Hundreds of glowing particles levitated in the air.

Like fireflies.

A moment flashed in his mind—clear yet unfamiliar. A man with a face he had no recollection of stood next to him, peering into the distance that Finnian was pointing to. The air filled with the dazzling specks in a haze of summer-budded trees and a tranquil, gliding stream.

Finnian blinked.

The memory dissolved as the magical particles built and mounted above him. A beaming sphere of light, celestial and blinding.

Its form expanded and devoured Marina's shadows, splitting apart the night.

Finnian pulled his arm down in a slicing motion and the bright, glaring orb dropped like a meteorite. The force pricked at his cheeks like a bitter frostbite. The glaring rays burned his retinas, but he refused to close his eyes.

Marina howled out in pain as she released the organ from her fingers. The scream was a sweet melody of what was to come.

But first, he needed to pluck the thorn out of his back that was currently her arm.

He pushed against the soles of his feet and drove himself forward. The release was instant, like the removal of a spear. Relief greeted him, followed by the throbbing of the wound. The stitching of skin and muscle was grounding.

An unrelenting anguish snarled and provoked his anger. That vibration of emotion echoed in his chest, up his neck, and into the tense muscles of his jaws.

How many years had he dreamed of this moment? To come face-to-face with his *family*. To revel in satisfaction with their blood coating his hands. Their bodies limp on the floor. Weak. Insignificant. Feelings he was all too familiar with. Feelings that seemed to follow him and Naia around and torment them every day of their immortal lives. These were feelings the triplets and Marina and Mira had never known the touch of.

It was an honor for Finnian to introduce them to such misery.

The incandescent light waned in its brilliance. The hall stretched out around them once again. Freya remained atop the platform, worry creasing her forehead as she frantically sought to find him through the dimming glow. Her look of concern caused his lips to twitch.

Marina's silhouette came into view a few paces from where he stood. Scarlet tears streaked down her cheeks as she shielded her eyes with her hands. A deity of night was, he figured, sensitive to light—a theory he was glad to confirm true.

Finnian mustered up some of his divine strength and sped soundlessly across the distance.

He reached out and clasped her wrists. The muscles in her arms flexed, but she was not quick enough. Finnian squeezed her bones and fractured them in his hold.

With a cry, she threw her head back in an attempt to collide her forehead with his. He caught her with both hands wrapped around her skull. She jerked back, but he fastened his grip and prodded his thumbs into each of her eyelids. "Do you think Mira loves you?"

Marina wailed as her eyeballs squished like kiwi underneath the pads of his thumbs. Streams of blood fled down the crevices of her nose.

"You are nothing to her." He lodged deeper until brain matter pushed underneath his fingernails. "Just like you were nothing to Father."

Finnian removed his thumbs from Marina's skull and threw her aside.

She collapsed onto the floor, unconscious.

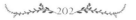

A greedy power pulsed between the rush of magic and blood against his bones. The high of it swelled in his chest, behind his eyes, with the urge to be ruinous. An urge to rip apart the entire fucking palace and every revolting memory it held of his childhood with Mira.

He snapped his head towards the dais. "One to go."

Mira was awake now, her drenched silver strands stuck to the sides of her cheeks and neck, the shine of her porcelain complexion faded to the shade of an egg's shell.

As Finnian advanced, Mira fumbled on her hands and knees up the steps.

The distress shadowing Freya's expression rearranged into amusement as she watched Mira scramble away. Only this time, Freya was no longer standing on the platform alone. Cassian was beside her, hands stowed away in the front pockets of his suit, a wolfish glint in his golden gaze as he watched Finnian.

The intensity of it didn't flare any discomfort or annoyance within him. Surprisingly, it sated a distant hunger in him he was unacquainted with. A starvation he did not know existed deep within him until this moment. There was a pride Cassian wore that he could not decode. He *enjoyed* the way Cassian observed him.

Finnian disregarded the feeling and rushed to the steps. He caught the hem of Mira's gown with the toe of his boot. She jarred backwards. The material ripped up her leg.

Finnian crouched down, eye level with her. "I do enjoy your fear, *Mother*." He elevated a hand and fabricated an icicle out of the droplets dampening the material of her gown, frosty air encircling it.

Mira did a double take at the water crystallizing in his grasp. The air around her flared with divine power, its gust rushing across Finnian's skin and coating his tongue like rotting fruit. With it came a bitter nostalgia of his time in Kaimana, with her divine power lurking in every living entity beneath the sea. He knew the repulsive taste of it well.

Finnian stabbed the spike through the back of her hand, pinning her to the step before she could teleport away.

The charge of her divine power fizzled out.

Her milky eyes flashed up at him, lethal and as sharp as needles. "It appears, after all these years, you are still unaware of your place. I am your mother."

He tipped his head back in a laugh. It was nonsense. Fucking ignorant words. "I have never considered you a mother. Naia and I deserved far better than *you*."

Mira flinched at the mention of Naia, as if he reached out and struck her.

She bared her teeth, her expression souring. "Do *not* speak of her to me."

Finnian ground the icicle in between the tendons of her knuckles. "Naia is the queen of my city now." He could feel the throbbing of his heart rate in his eyeballs; the tautness of his jaw muscles strained down the side of his neck. "She has a family, knows the warmth of love, the strength of power, and not a day goes by where she ever thinks of you."

That familiar, vibrational hum festered beneath his ears, crawled up the side of his cheek and into his temples. The dissonant thrum in his skull sent a quiver of panic down his chest.

"But *you* have." A smirk twisted on Mira's lips as she leaned forward, disregarding the spike pierced in the back of her hand. "*You* plotted my downfall. Tell me, how long did it take to come up with a plan? How much of your energy have I consumed when there has not been a day that I have spared my insolent son a single moment of thought? You are nothing but a foolish request from your father to have *one more child*."

The itch festered behind his eyes, prodding deeper, deeper, deeper. In response, dread infected his bloodstream and fired frantically through his veins.

Somehow, he'd activated the curse. Was it the image of the man and the fireflies from earlier, or the venomous impulse corrupting him as he broke his siblings like old toys?

There was a trembling beneath his skin as the pulsing amplified inside of his head.

This couldn't be happening. Not now. Not when Mira was before him—powerless.

He glared at her—a face with perfectly proportioned features, round eyes the color of her moonstone palace, pooling with spite. Even after losing her title, her kingdom, any hope to break her dreadful curse, none of

it had triggered a dose of self-reflection to admit how she'd ended up there. Her massive ego was still intact, and it disgusted Finnian.

Fury, resentment, it all muffled to the disturbing amusement rising in his throat. Silvery notes of laughter chimed out.

A flash of shock rippled through the vicious animosity of her expression.

"Look at you." He gestured to her with a wave of his hand. "The beloved island father created now worships *him*. Naia's name has spread among the mortals and she now has true power. You are stuck in a kingdom that is no longer yours, a prison you will never be free from." He let his head fall sideways, smiling at her mockingly. "*You* are nothing. A middle goddess of the sea who simply once was."

Her slap stung across his cheek. The sound sliced through the empty hall.

"You both are abominations! Disgraceful children who take after *him*!" She snarled, face contorted in an ugly rage. "One day, I will break out of this cage and force you to repent for what you have done!"

The taste of copper filled his mouth. He swiped his tongue across the cut on the inside of his lip.

Know your place.

The hum rang louder in his skull.

The edges of his vision frayed. Behind her stood the thirteen-year-old version of himself—ashen complexion, staring down at the back of his mother's head, a madness swirling in his black eyes.

Finnian blinked and the younger version of himself was no longer there.

Hallucinations.

He refocused on Mira and her hideous face, warped in anger.

You are not losing your mind. Not here.

He propped his elbow on his bent knee and shifted his attention onto his hand, curling his fingers into a loose fist. "Do you know what black hellebore does to a person?" He did well to keep his tone blank, pretending the icy fear in his veins was just another fabrication of the curse. "I would assume so, given Father was the High God of Nature."

Finnian conjured his magic and unfolded his fingers. In the center of his palm was a saucer-shaped blossom, its nodding petals velvet-black. "It makes a wonderful ingredient for potions and poisons for the myriad of symptoms it can cause—emesis, catharsis, bradycardia, anaphylaxis…" He cut his eyes over onto Mira. "Are you familiar with such terms?"

"Do not spout your witchcraft—"

Finnian snapped his arm out and rammed the pad of his thumb into the center of her forehead. "*Deglutire nigrum flore.*"

Mira gasped. A hex mark burned over her forehead, an onyx triangle with blossoms at each point, vines connecting them. A rune appeared in its center, slowly eating into her flesh like rot.

Her chest bellowed in uneven strides as she fought to breathe. She pawed at her neck, mouth split apart. The veins in her forehead protruded and her breath sputtered, like a stone caught in her throat.

Foam pushed out of the corners of her mouth—just as it had with Alke that day. Down his beak, over his feathers.

Mira fell over, the *thud* of her skull hitting the edge of the stair. He imagined it to split apart like a yolk, but it didn't. He watched her writhe and stare blankly up at the vaulted ceiling through bloodshot eyes. Frothy trails ran down her cheeks into her ears.

Her body convulsed one last time, and the awareness in her eyes wilted.

She lay on her back, chest no longer rising and falling. Not dead. Only treading the line that all deities could not cross.

"You will wake," he said, knowing she could hear him. "And suffer this same fate, over and over again with nothing but the silence of your own thoughts. Enjoy wasting away in your cage, Mother, for you will never lay a hand on Naia ever again."

Finny, don't do this!

The voice was Naia's, shrieking in the walls of his skull.

He swallowed the acid in his throat and rose up.

What have you done to our mother?

Finnian stepped over Mira and started up the stairs where Freya and Cassian awaited.

She will suffer.

She deserved to suffer, after all the hell she'd inflicted.

Nobody deserves to suffer.

Guilt fastened down on the tops of his shoulders.

She deserved it.

Mira deserved it.

Freya threw her arms around his neck. Her presence, her warmth, was like the sunlight casting its rays down on him. He clung to it through the sickness roiling in his gut. She was a cloud of hibiscus, a smile that was all teeth, giggling like a child.

"Are you well?" she whispered it into his unimpaired ear.

Something in him screamed for help, hoping she'd hear it.

He awkwardly patted her back. "Enjoy your new title."

"Visit anytime you wish." She gave him a squeeze. "Consider your banishment lifted."

He wanted to thank her. To tell her of all the nights he paced the square feet of his homes, longing to teleport back to Kaimana and check on Naia—to walk the cove, dip his legs in the water hole, be lulled to sleep by the clinking call of whales and the swarming jellyfish swaying through the moonlight glow. But the itch hewing his brain was growing louder, and the frantic edge was spreading in him like blood in water.

He released Freya and turned to Cassian.

The High God assessed him for a brief second before silently offering out his hand.

Finnian stared down at the smooth grooves of his palm, the slight curl of his long, pale fingers, with a frenzied desperation to grab onto him, a lifeline to pull him afloat from the dark waters submerging over his head.

He can fix this—fix me.

The voice was his own, hysterical and unhinged. A sound rattling in the inner depths of his skull that knotted his stomach.

Give him Ash's blood, it whispered.

The sight of Cassian weathered, like ink blotches spreading along the blankness of a page.

Finnian's heart rate jumped erratically.

He grabbed onto Cassian—solid, warm, familiar.

"Are you ready?" Cassian asked.

Are you afraid?

Finnian nodded.

Hardly.

The voice was one he did not recognize—deep, euphonious.

Cassian's fingers tightened gently around his hand, the surge of divine power cresting around them like a wave.

Take my hand and step where I step. We'll keep them as clean as we can.

The room around him, all his senses, slurred. He felt disoriented, as if he was trapped inside of a dream.

The memory was distant, nebulous, like he was looking at it through the bottom of a glass bottle. Though, it was a setting he'd been to before. In Augustus, walking the countryside and admiring the fireflies and nature, alone—until Cassian appeared and ravaged his peace.

Only, he wasn't alone. He was alongside a man with short, black hair and round, blue eyes. A man Finnian had no recollection of ever speaking to in his life—

Everett.

Delirium rattled in his bones, a resonance nuzzling marrow-deep.

EIGHTEEN

NOT STRONG ENOUGH

HE BEDSPREAD WAS black satin, its shine matching the sleek, onyx headboard that was an extension of the obsidian wall, glistening against the saffron glow of the fireplace across the room.

Finnian pressed his back against the stained oak door, grateful Cassian teleported him into a room and left.

Terror frayed at his nerves. He clenched his hands to control the trembling in his fingers.

A polyphonic stream of voices filled the vicinity of his skull.

You must right your wrongs.

Naia's name ran rampant amongst the mortals.

Mira had fallen.

Now, all he needed was to find Father.

You must.

How? Strapped to Cassian, how could he sneak off to Moros?

You have failed.

No, he still had time.

Father is already disappointed in you.

He could figure something out.

What makes you think he wishes to see you?

Naia is happier without you.

You ruin everything—

He gripped the sides of his head and squeezed his eyes shut. "I don't. I *don't* ruin everything."

The hum rang louder in his skull; a buzz rattled down his jaws and seized the nerves.

He slumped down on the door and tucked his head between his knees. Staring through the dark at the floor, he gripped his nape.

"I don't," he said again, hoping the words would slow his racing heart.

"You're pathetic."

The voice cut in the room and Finnian snapped his head up.

Someone stood in the corner, their frame short and dressed in a gray frock coat.

Finnian's stomach turned to stone as his thirteen-year-old self moved out of the flickering shadow of the firelight.

He stared down at Finnian, his expression steely and with a look of indifference. "Every second that passes, the curse sinks its teeth further into your mind. A few days' time and you won't have the wits to even find Father, much less save him."

Finnian's nostrils flared. "My plan will work. It will work. I *will* find him, and I *will* save him."

"And then what?" He tilted his head, the gesture patronizingly gutting. "How do you intend to escape, hm? You have already failed."

"No!" Finnian sprang forward and caught the lapels of his thirteen-year-old self's coat and jerked him forward. "I will make it all better."

A cruel smirk lifted one side of his mouth. "*How?*"

Sharp, hostile malice flared in Finnian. "I am not the helpless little boy you are. What makes you think I give a fuck about what you say?"

"Because I am always with you, aren't I?" His younger self spoke with an impassiveness that stiffened the muscles in Finnian's neck. "You cannot escape me. You *need* me to remind you of what it feels like to be helpless—forced to watch something you love break apart."

The glittering walls of the room suddenly felt as if they were closing in, like night itself was swallowing him down its throat.

Finnian released his younger self and stepped away, his hand shaking. "No."

Standing in Mira's great hall once more, frozen in horror, watching as she suffocated Alke; the fear burning in him as Father was led away by executioners; leaving Naia at the entrance of the palace, unknowing how long it would be until he saw her again—the memories engulfed him, and the same aches, the same heartbreak triggered in response.

"You are pathetic," his younger self repeated, spitting the syllables with disdain. "You have no idea where Father is, and your time is running out." His voice rose. "You will rot here with your shame."

Finnian's stomach pulsed with nausea. He ground his molars and leveled his thirteen-year-old self with a dangerous look. "I will burn down the entire Land of the Dead if I must."

His younger self huffed out a contemptuous laugh. "Nothing burns here without Cassian's permission."

"I will find a way!" Finnian shouted, his composure snapping.

The hum screeched louder, the sensation spasming the nerves inside of his brain. An itch he could not reach reverberated in his cheeks, down his neck.

He winced and let go of his younger self, throwing his hands over his ears. The ringing did not cease.

Desperate, he ripped the hearing aid out of his ear.

The resonance screamed louder.

Groaning against the tightness in his chest, he clenched his jaws. He wanted to raze his skin, dig through flesh, and pluck out the parasite eating away at his mind.

Come up with a plan.

Finnian turned away from his younger self, the sight of his smug grin only proving to further piss him off.

Get Father and leave this place.

His hands rested on his hips, fixating his attention up at nothing in particular, and sucked in a sharp breath to calm his nervous system.

I must.

The obsidian walls stared back at him. No windows, no form of expression—no paintings or decor of any kind. His own personal nightmare.

Perhaps this was just another cage meant to provoke the delirium within him.

"And what of Everett?" his younger self asked.

At the mention of Everett, Finnian rotated, pinning his younger self with a glare. "What of him?"

"You would burn the Land down, knowing he is here?" A cunning look twisted in his dark eyes.

It took every ounce of self-control for Finnian not to knock his young self's head clean off his body.

"He is already dead," he gritted out, slipping his hearing aid back into his ear.

"Because of you."

A chill froze down Finnian's spine. The breath hitched in his throat as he shook his head. "That's not true."

"How would you know?" His younger self took a step, eyeing him with malicious intent. "You can hardly remember him."

"It's the curse. I—" Finnian's palm came down on his chest where the mark throbbed. "He's—"

"A wrong that you will *never* make right." His younger self stopped with a breath's space between them, his voice grating against the buzzing in Finnian's head.

"I *will* make it right."

"You break everyone you love."

The words hacked through his chest. "*No,* I don't."

"Alke, Arran, Naia, Eleanor, Isla—"

"No." The lie burned his tongue.

Each one passed through his thoughts—every time he'd been on the receiving end of a painful look over something he'd said or done that had hurt them.

"Everett—"

"*Stop!*" Finnian shot out his arm and flames jumped from the fireplace and attacked his younger self. The blood-orange pyre devoured him, boiling skin and liquifying muscle down to the pearl-white bones of his face.

The gory hallucination dissipated and melted into vapor.

Finnian's breaths were shallow as the flames withered out, revealing the empty space before him.

You break everyone you love.

His heart palpitated.

"No, *no*—I don't." His hands lifted into his hair, squeezing clumps in his fists. "I don't break them. I *don't*—" He stumbled backwards, his weight too heavy on his unstable knees, and the backs of his shins smashed into the edge of the bed. He fell onto the cushion of the mattress.

Soft.

Eyelids stitched closed, he removed his hands from his hair and lowered them onto the satin material.

Cool to the touch.

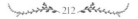

Similar to the satin bed sheets in his old home.

The sense of touch was an anchor, and he used it to guide him back down from the hallucination.

What would I be doing if I were in Hollow City right now?

Triple shot espresso. Down it in a heartbeat.

Gods, I miss coffee.

The frantic march of his pulse slowed the more he reminisced about his old routine and the comfort of his potion room. He imagined sitting at his workbench, surrounded by the pungent aroma of herbs, lost in his own headspace, preoccupied with crafting the perfect dose of hemlock to inflict paralysis rather than death. The potion's fame skyrocketed in the black market.

The unbearable hum of the curse had silenced. Relief rained throughout his brain. Through a deep breath, he peeled open his eyes and peered up at the ceiling.

Painted along the glossy black exterior were shimmering specks.

Was it a part of the obsidian crystalized into the wall?

Finnian lifted up on his elbows to inspect them more.

They brightened and then dulled, like a beacon of small lights in the distance coming in and out of sight.

Like fireflies.

Finnian's pulse flickered.

He recalled a memory: strolling along the bank of Augustus's river, marveling at the moonflowers while foraging valerian. It wasn't long when Cassian had ambushed him and they'd fought. It was the first time Finnian witnessed the High God relinquish all the souls within his ghouls. He'd chased Finnian around the forest, gutting the stream and tearing down the century-old oaks. A ruined paradise.

Finnian managed to escape, albeit with half of his flesh marred off from Cassian's dreadful divine power that caused decay. The High God had come alarmingly close to cursing him that day. It was by pure luck Finnian had teleported before Cassian could get his hands on him.

This is how he remembered the memory, but the images invading in his mind of who he assumed was Everett, strolling alongside him, were foreign. A completely different form of reality he had no reminiscence of.

Finnian refocused on the specks, still convinced they were mimicking fireflies.

Why were they plastered across Cassian's ceiling?

Do you see?

Finnian climbed to his feet on the mattress and stretched his arm towards them.

He siphoned the energy from the pinpricks, stripping away the magic shaping the shimmering particles. One by one, they vanished until it was an all-black, solid backdrop tenting over him.

Finnian's face paled as the energy flowed into his veins—energy attached to a spell.

They'd been created with magic. *His* magic. He recognized his energy, the droplets of water living within the river of his own body. He'd been in this room before.

Do you recall that night in Augustus?

Another memory flashed in the forefront of his mind: the late-1800s interior of his townhome; the smoky aroma of singed herbs and the chilled air of the basement that he'd turned into an alchemy station; hundreds of brilliant sparkles surrounding him and…

I recall it every day.

This voice was different, one he was well acquainted with—low-pitched, smooth, somber. A glimpse of ivory-blond strands and a broad smile stood beside him, encompassed by a sea of jewels.

Is his soul here in the Land?

Finnian's blood went frigid as a demand pinched in his gut. An insistence that dropped in his legs, begging him to move.

Yes.

Deities could shape-shift their appearances entirely. Why hadn't he thought about the possibility before?

Finnian dropped his chin to assess the bed he stood on, as if the satin would peel back its threads and show him the memories it held.

He was your lover.

Finnian lifted his sharp gaze to the door with what felt like venom prickling in his veins.

He hopped off the mattress **and started** across the room.

H<small>E</small> shut his mind off and followed the feel of the invisible thread binding him to Cassian—an intuitive pull in his gut leading him down empty corridors and a wide stairwell. His fingers brushed the engravings of the spindles along the railing with each step. The black stone walls of the hall were etched with small streaks of dancing gold. Black, gold, black, gold—Finnian's vexation grew from how plain and predictable Cassian's palace was.

He was your lover.

Finnian's eyes held onto the large glass door across the foyer.

Everett was your lover.

He swung the door open and stepped out into floral infused air. After twenty-four hours, nightfall had finally graced the Land.

He paced down a stone walkway through the dark botanical garden. Vines coiled around ruins.

He passed underneath an archway with dangling eucalyptus flourished with black roses. Eventually, it led him into a lemon tree orchard. Mint mingled in the air as he breezed by.

Who was Everett?

An iron gate came into view. The scent of fresh herbs stifled the citrus.

Finnian entered the threshold, his sights set on the back of Cassian's head, his light shade of hair reflecting in the moonlight.

He sat on a stone bench and peered across a bed of sage and rosemary to a winding stream. The silver streaks pierced through the canopy of branches above and glistened on its surface.

Finnian raised his hand, and a flame struck in his palm.

Push him.

He threw his arm out and the flame burst into an inferno, demolishing the greenery in its trajectory. Its hot gust stung Finnian's cheeks. A hellfire of violet and tangerine devoured the bench, obscuring his sight of Cassian.

What will he truly do?

Finnian clamped his fingers into his palm and the current of fire choked out.

Will he fight with me?

His heart hammered in the base of his throat. A thick veil of smoke rose from the charred remains of the garden.

Harm me?

As it swept away in the breeze, Finnian could see the bench was now empty.

The skin of his nape prickled with gooseflesh. A nefarious energy dropped behind him, and he whipped around, arm cast out.

Before he could activate any spells, Cassian grabbed a hold of his wrist and forced his hand down. "Enough of this."

"Unhand me!" Finnian fought against his grip, ripping his hand away.

Cassian allowed him to do so, frowning. His brow furrowed over his gaze, heavy and pained as it sifted all over Finnian's face.

He did what I said.

Finnian glanced around at the grove—the tranquil brook embedded in hawthorn trees, patches of hemlock, the vines of passion flowers ensnaring the iron fence. A peaceful sanctuary for Cassian to sneak off to and find solace.

Push him more.

Another flame flickered to life in Finnian's palm, and he sent its stream towards the flowers scouring over a row of basalt stone.

"No!" Cassian yelled.

Finnian blinked through the ripples of smoke as the flames torched the white blossoms gazing up at the moon.

Moonflowers.

Cassian strapped an arm around his waist from behind and tugged him off his feet.

The flames sputtered out. Finnian cocked his elbow back into Cassian's ribcage. The vibrations of his grunt rattled through Finnian's backside as he pushed off him, breaking through his arms.

Finnian drew up his hand. Energy materialized into the shape of a celestial dagger, tangible and solid in his grasp. He whirled around and his other palm came down on Cassian's chest, shoving him back.

Cassian's backside slammed against the iron fence as Finnian positioned the magical dagger's end to his throat. "Who was Everett?"

Cassian kept his chin lowered, the shadows of the night hiding his profile. A singular curl fell over his forehead.

"At first I thought it was the curse fucking with my mind, but I've been here before, haven't I?" Finnian inched closer, applying pressure on the dagger. "In your palace. In that room you stuck me in. The magic on the ceiling was *mine*!"

Cassian said nothing.

The breath grew heavy in Finnian's lungs, of smoke and impatience. He curled his fingers around the collar of Cassian's suit jacket, satisfied by the wrinkles it caused in the crisp material. "Or was it one of your sick illusions? The curse isn't acting fast enough and you need Ash's blood *now*. For what, revenge? We all know you and Ruelle despise one another. What could she have possibly done to someone like *you*—"

"Enough!" he snarled.

Finnian flinched, his hold slackening a little.

Cassian ripped his head up. Devastation marred his face as tears gushed down his cheeks, fat droplets catching in the creases of his nose, drenching his lips, dripping down his chin. The skin around his eyes brightened red and swelled. Such beautiful sorrow.

An ache splintered down Finnian's chest. His breath locked in his diaphragm, stunned by his own pain.

The dagger dissolved in his grip and he lowered his hand.

"I am not strong enough for this," Cassian said.

Finnian searched his broken gaze: two vibrant, golden hollows brimming with anguish.

He was overcome with a harrowing displeasure by the sight. Suddenly, he regretted everything. Storming out of the palace and provoking Cassian this way. Finnian wished to hug him, hold him, assure him everything was okay. He couldn't make sense of the feeling of grave concern awakening inside of him, of the innate need to dive deep within Cassian's waters and strangle the source of his pain.

"Who is Everett?" Finnian asked again, softening his voice.

He knew, but he needed to hear the words from Cassian.

"It was all a mistake. I shouldn't have…" Cassian shook his head, sniveling.

The cracking in his voice punctured Finnian's heart.

Lightly, he took a hold of Cassian's chin between his thumb and index finger, forcing their eyes to meet. "Shouldn't have *what*?"

Cassian delved deeply into his gaze. "I loathe you." He said it softly, like a poignant vow.

Fresh tears slipped down his face.

Finnian's jaw tightened, painfully confused by the contradiction.

"I loathe you just as much," Finnian said back, reaching for the resentment he knew to exist within, but it felt like cupping a fistful of fog. Centuries of it lived inside of him, disdain and contempt that bubbled up and caked his tongue each time he was forced to interact with the High God.

Though, by now, Finnian was well accustomed to the tartness of resentment. It was a taste he could not get out of his mouth each time he laid eyes upon Mira. True, discernable hatred that did not exist standing before Cassian now.

Cassian tipped forward and dropped his forehead on the top of Finnian's shoulder.

Finnian stiffened from the physical contact, surprised by the visceral reaction to put his arms around him, almost like a second nature.

"No," Cassian whispered. Tears dampened through the material of Finnian's shirt. "*I loathe you*, and I…"

"Long for you." The words pushed up his throat before he knew what he said.

A gasp caught in Cassian's throat.

It was like the unraveling of a stitch—the graveyard, the triplets, the mage, Malik threatening to carve Eleanor and Isla apart, Everett arriving and saving them, the fear blazing in his eyes as he tore the blades out of Finnian.

Cassian raised his head and pulled away. "What did you say?" His eyes flitted between Finnian's, ignited with a frantic hope.

You are mine to chase, to fight with.

"*You* are Everett." Finnian uncurled his fingers from Cassian's collar and stepped back.

Cassian reached out and caught him by the forearm. His fingers dug into his skin tightly, as if he may float away. "What is my name, Finnian? My *real* name."

The tender sound of his own name on Cassian's lips roused something within. He could feel whatever it was pushing out of the casket it was buried in.

His name was Cassian—or Everett, he was sure—but wasn't. Cassian hadn't clarified and Finnian didn't know what he was searching for in his memories. A moment hidden somewhere? Because of the curse? Or because of something Cassian did? He'd said he never should've done *what*?

Finnian's mind strained the more he pushed to reflect and remember, activating the buzz to resound at the crown of his skull.

No, no, no.

He yanked his arm free from Cassian. His touch, the sensation, his eyes reaching down and coaxing him—it was too much.

"I—" A stab prodded in the center of his brain, jarring down his spine.

He cringed and hunched over, his palm coming up to his forehead.

You break everyone you love.

Cassian supported him by the hold on his arm. "Finny," he blurted out, distressed.

If you must call me by a nickname, I would prefer it to be that, rather than Little Nightmare.

A cold sweat lined Finnian's brow. The smoke in the air lingered. It stuck to his cheeks, his neck. A queasiness rolled in his stomach.

When can I return to see you again?

The memory glitched in the back of his mind against the ringing.

Whenever you wish.

He could see it—laying in a bed of satin, their bodies intertwined, Cassian perched up on an elbow, gaze glittering down at him, the room dark, quiet, with flecks of shimmering particles suspended around them, Cassian's laughter fluttering his heart, the sound like the bow stroke of a viola. An insatiable longing, a tender devotion, an eternal affection embedded in Finnian's skin, dissolving into his blood, seeping down into his marrow until he was made of Cassian and Cassian alone.

I like the way it sounds on your lips.

"Cassius," Finnian whispered. "Your real name is Cassius."

The barrier encasing his mind fractured, and his memories burst forth like a raging ravine.

PART II

SUCH BEAUTIFUL SORROW

NINETEEN

LET ME SEE YOU

THE PAST
Cassian

RESH CASUALTIES OF the war crawled out of the River of Souls every day. Enough to provide a population decrease within the Mortal Land. Between the war and Finnian's vow to only revive souls within the territory of his new city, Cassian sent Mavros to halt Malik's killings.

Nathaira, alongside the Errai, greeted the souls emerging from the River. Other Errai guided souls from the mortal realm and distributed them in the Land. Cassian toggled between the two wherever he was needed most.

When executioners escorted in new deities assigned with punishments, Shivani would torture them for a certain length of time—as a welcome to Moros—and then call Cassian once they were settled into their designated sector of the prison. He would craft an illusion, a personalized nightmare, while deciding on their punishment.

After ushering two healed souls into the Paradise of Rest, he took the opportunity to sneak away.

He walked the path of his garden, his sights set on the entrance of Finnian's Grove. Its iron gate was flanked by blooming violets.

Halfway, his steps faltered.

Whenever you wish to see me again.

It had been nearly a month in the Mortal Land since he'd last seen Finnian. A short breath of time that felt like ages.

The yearning in Cassian consumed his thoughts, especially after their last encounter in Finnian's townhome with the sigil and pleasant conversation.

Cassian surfed his fingers through his hair, conflicted. Could he show up with no warning? Finnian had not summoned him since, and what of Ruelle? He knew she was watching him, waiting—

Stop overthinking it.

He dropped his hand, his shoulder slumped, and he sighed. The perpetual ache in his chest hadn't let up since he departed Finnian.

I miss him.

Letting that single thought steer his actions, he rearranged his appearance into Everett—of dark strands and vibrant blue eyes.

The gilded darkness of his divine power furled around him, and he disappeared.

THE earthy, floral scent of Finnian's home washed over him, braiding in his hair and sticking to the material of his tailcoat.

He stood in the center of the apothecary room they had been in last time.

The room was dark and cool. Various bundles of herbs hung upside down from the ceiling, drying. The workbench was cluttered with an open grimoire, gibberish scribbles on the page, crystals, bones tampered together with twine, and open vials.

Cassian smiled at the mess.

He didn't sense Finnian's presence nearby. It appeared Cassian was alone. A good excuse to leave.

Instead, he sauntered across the room to the wooden staircase leading up to an open door.

He stepped inside a small kitchen. A mortar and pestle sat on the round table in the corner. Beside it was a ceramic cup and a stainless steel percolator. No steam came from either, but Cassian could smell the remnants of coffee in the cup. They'd been sitting out for a while.

Finnian likes coffee. The detail was small, intimate; Cassian stored the information in his mind like a precious jewel.

Up against the brick wall was a wood stove with a cast iron pot and a teakettle on the unlit burners. Positioned on the other side near the window was a wooden cabinet and a washbasin on its surface. The look of a typical

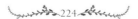

mortal home. It was far from the moonstone crystal palace Finnian had grown up in. It appeared the young god favored simplicity over lavishness.

Cassian shifted his weight to glance around the threshold. The old wooden planks creaked beneath his feet.

The short corridor led into a sitting room. Mahogany-threaded couches faced a small hearth where embers in its pit faintly glowed. He could see Finnian sitting with his two apprentices, begrudgingly teaching them how to spark a flame with their magic.

A twinge of jealousy struck Cassian's chest.

He strolled over to the kitchen table to take a seat. Halfway through the room, the energy in the air shifted and a warped gust ruffled behind him.

"I was starting to believe you had forgotten about me." Finnian's voice traveled through him, a silvery ring of chimes.

He pursed his lips to control the width of his smile before turning around. "Impossible. The war keeps me busy is all."

"Well then, I am glad you found the time to drop by." Finnian started unfastening the buttons of his billowy, long-sleeved shirt, one by one. The flash of his rings mesmerized Cassian. "I had business to sort out. I am glad I did not miss your visit."

"Business that required you to button your shirt, I see," Cassian mumbled.

Though, he couldn't pull his eyes away from Finnian's collar hanging open, exposing the arches of his clavicles and the defined cuts of his torso, his bare skin the shade of maple syrup. His black strands were down and perched over his shoulders, a stark contrast to the beige linen.

"For the sake of avoiding Eleanor's nagging." Finnian continued undoing the buttons, making it to his navel.

Several necklaces dangled around his neck—a dark gemstone with blood-red spots, another that was metallic and adorned with golden-brown blotches, and a teal pendant that looked as if it had been dug up from deep within the sea. They rested between the smooth contours of his pecs.

Finnian's look was disheveled, but in an arousing way Cassian had never found appealing before.

Cassian noted how Finnian's arms were now relaxed down at his sides. Silence had settled between them, prompting him to lift his eyes, meeting Finnian's twinkling green gaze, alight with happiness. The slyness of his smirk and the flicker of his dimples caught in Cassian's stomach.

A flush rose on his cheeks and he cleared his throat, averting his gaze to the cast iron pot on the wood stove. "Your home. It is comforting. *Eclectic.*"

"Is that a sophisticated way of saying *too cluttered for my taste*?" Finnian strolled past him, untucking his shirt from his waistline. There was a playfulness caressing his tone, a comfort in his character that Cassian had only caught glimpses of in the past. It was the complete opposite of the pragmatic, hardheaded version he normally presented.

Cassian pocketed his hands, a light smile tugging on his lips. "Perhaps a little too cluttered, but I find the quality endearing."

"What other qualities of mine do you find joy in?" Finnian glanced over his shoulder as he gathered the cup and the percolator.

Cassian watched him place them in the washbasin. "That you are a mage and choose to hand wash your dishes."

Finnian spun around, scratching at his nape with a sheepish look. "I used to help Naia in the kitchen when I was younger. Because I didn't want Mira to know about my magic, I refrained from using it. The act is nostalgic, I suppose."

The mention of Naia wrung Cassian's gut. It was a reminder of the future to come—the mark he would leave on her in the upcoming years. She'd be cursed to live in a land with Mira. The cruelty of it outweighed the bigger picture, something Cassian had to keep in the back of his mind. In the end, Naia would bear a demigod child of the Himura bloodline, and he would use it to end Ruelle once and for all.

"Ah." He kept his response short, countering the nagging need to confess everything to Finnian.

They stared at each other for a moment.

Finnian regarded him with soft eyes and a curve to his mouth. It made Cassian's skin kindle and his eyes flit around, fidgeting with his fingers inside of his pockets. If Finnian kept looking at him that way, he wasn't sure what he'd end up doing.

"I hear the mortals are erecting altars and temples across the western lands in honor of the High Goddess of War and the High Goddess of Peace," Finnian said, regarding the conflict.

"Mortals tend to show their devotion when they are in need of something."

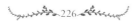

"I don't believe that only applies to mortals." Finnian crossed his arms. "Deities and mages can be quite vexing as well."

"You seem to speak from experience." Cassian raised his eyebrows, pinpointing the tension in Finnian's shoulders.

"It appears the occupation of a leader is accompanied by a never-ending to-do list. It *is* rather annoying." He scowled.

Cassian cracked a genuine grin. "Do tell."

"I'll make tea. Have a seat." Finnian pointed to the kitchen table before moving across the kitchen to the wood stove. "What kind do you prefer?" He crouched beside it and opened the side door.

With the snap of his fingers, a flame sparked on his fingertip. He reached inside the box and lit the logs.

He'd grown stronger since the last time they were together. Cassian distinctly recalled Finnian speaking an incantation to perform the same spell. Now, he could do it without uttering anything.

Cassian glided to one of the wooden chairs, unbuttoned his tailcoat, and gently sat, hoping the fragile legs of the furniture wouldn't snap. "I enjoy lavender or lemon."

Finnian held a hand up and one of the glass jars on the shelf above the washbasin floated into his palm. "Lemon balm?"

"Yes, please." Cassian twisted his head to survey the rows of jars crammed full of dried herbs. "Do you enjoy tea?"

With a slow swivel of his wrist, the teakettle filled with water. He positioned it over the flame on the stove. "I prefer coffee, but Eleanor is an avid tea drinker. I keep a stock on hand for her."

He spoke of the apprentice as if she were a close friend. Was that all there was to it?

"It sounds like you care for her," Cassian murmured, and then held his breath.

Finnian pulled out the chair across from him and took a seat. Lounging back, he extended his legs, and his shin brushed the side of Cassian's ankle. A spark of heat climbed up Cassian's inner thigh. "I care for many people."

Do not ask.

"Isla, Naia…" Cassian listed off, internally cringing at himself. He joined his hands on the surface of the table, resting his weight on his elbows.

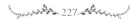

"Eleanor and Isla are close friends. They help me more than I help them now. Did you know they created a city council and organizations to perform various other duties? Because of this, I am able to deal with more pressing matters—like the two mages who attacked each other this morning and destroyed a building in the business district. Apparently, their family history is riddled with feuds and violence." He rolled his eyes.

Cassian's grin broadened, amused by Finnian's complaining. "Sounds like an eventful morning."

Not lovers then. The relief unclenched the ball in his chest.

Finnian grew quiet. He rested his forearm on the table, his fingers flexing and flickering tendons across the back of his hand. "You never asked me why I decided to create a city."

"You were teaching Eleanor and Isla how to use a sigil." Cassian glanced at Finnian's rings, secretly measuring the infinitesimal gap between their hands.

"Do you recall every little thing I say?"

"Of course."

The hushed hiss of the fire and the quiet boil of the water filled the silence.

Finnian's eyes cast downwards as he drew circles on the surface of the table with his finger. "Ask me why."

Cassian moved his full attention from the ring on Finnian's index finger to his face. Something about his bashful tone and the way he was no longer looking at Cassian piqued a grave interest in him. "Why?"

"The day Naia leaves Kaimana, I want her to have a home to go to. Shacks and graveyards were places she told me *not* to settle down in."

"I believe a house would have sufficed if you didn't want to go through the hassle of running a city."

"Primarily, I created it as a boundary for myself." Finnian's circles widened closer to Cassian's hand. A subtle brush to his knuckles, leaving tingles where he touched. "After I learned of the deal you had struck with Mira, I desired to compromise."

Cassian's heart struck the walls inside of his chest and his lips parted, baffled by what he'd just said.

Finnian lifted his gaze onto Cassian then. The discomfort was easy to read in the slight flush creeping across his cheeks.

He was being vulnerable, truthful, sharing his feelings. It was an openness Cassian couldn't quite wrap his mind around. He'd dreamed of peeling Finnian's layers back to behold what was inside—something unfathomable, given their rocky relationship.

Cassian wanted to reciprocate in some meaningful way, express to Finnian how grateful he was, knowing the levels of unease it probably made him feel to share. And yet, all Cassian could think was how utterly reckless it was, how much Finnian had gone through for his sake. *A city.* The idea was astonishing, and beautiful proof that Cassian did not stand alone in his feelings.

The capacities of his actions were limitless when it came to Finnian, and it appeared Finnian, too, felt the same.

The sound of boiling water grew louder.

Cassian studied the somberness across Finnian's features, conflicting feelings warring in his tight chest, a paralyzing panic he did not expect to feel.

Suddenly, his limbs felt jittery.

He removed his arms from the table and raked a hand through his hair. "Why? To appease your guilt for the length I'd gone through not to curse you?" It wasn't meant to come out accusatory, but a genuine question. One Cassian hoped the outcome would be a disappointing truth—that Finnian did not care for him, but instead he simply had a wish to make things right.

"The same reason you came to see me." Finnian's tone was rational, his expression stoic, so absolute and sure of his feelings. It immediately enhanced the fright in Cassian.

Finnian sat up in his chair and leaned over to grab Cassian's hand.

His skin warmed, ensnared by Finnian's touch. The threads of his self-control threatened to snap against the sensation.

It was validation. The only kind he needed to snatch the edge of Finnian's chair and yank him closer. To bring their mouths together and taste him, swallow his words. But before he could do so, Ruelle's face flashed in the front of his mind, freezing the warmth coasting his veins.

Whoever yearns in your soul will be just in reach, but never able to fully grasp.

His heart stuttered, and he abruptly ripped his hand from Finnian and stood.

With his back to him, he rubbed a hand over his face, gaping down at the dark-stained wooden floor. "I took your father away from you, chased you around with the threat of a curse. Do you honestly expect me to believe you created a city for my benefit?"

Finnian's chair scooted back, making a *scratch* sound against the wood.

Cassian could feel him moving in, his body heat drifting against his backside, like a blanket of comfort he desperately wanted to lean into.

One day, when you know the kiss of love, all you will have left is regret.

An ache cracked his ribcage. He couldn't do it. If he ever came to regret his actions involving Finnian, he wasn't sure he could live with himself.

Cassian removed his hand from his hair, fingers coiling into a fist.

I should have stayed away.

I have no choice here.

He whipped around, eyes blazing. "We loathe each other. You raise the dead and I despise you for it."

Finnian's nostrils flared. "You also cannot curse me. You've chased me, yes, but you always help me. You sent your god of death to check up on me regularly, prior to creating my city. Say whatever you wish out of your conflicted feelings, but you came here today for the same reason I crafted a spell to keep every deity out of my home but you."

Cassian's eyes slightly widened.

He hadn't even considered such a thing. A mage's power was endless with their knowledge, and Finnian mentioned it previously. Hollow City was protected by magic from the war, from other deities even locating it. Of course he had enough sense to protect his home.

Only Cassian was an exception.

A peace filled the hollow patches within his chest.

Finnian's trust meant something to him, and he held it in the palm of his hand like a gift.

This is what Ruelle is waiting for.

He scoured Finnian's face, brow crumbling in defeat.

She will use him. Just like she used Saoirse.

He did not know what to do.

And it will destroy me this time.

The water screamed in its pot.

"I should not have come, but I ache when I am not in your presence," Cassian's voice strained.

The tension melted from Finnian's features.

His eyes fell to Cassian's lips, and he inhaled deeply. "And do you think I do not share the same feeling?"

Gods, Cassian craved him. The desire swelled outside of his skin and consumed him whole.

I am not strong enough for this.

Cassian's mouth went dry, the breath in his lungs swiftly draining the longer he held Finnian's gaze. "You cannot care about me."

Finnian took a daring step closer. "Oh, it is far too late for that."

Cassian's pulse flickered, and he backed away, his tailbone meeting the edge of the cabinet.

"I will hurt you if I let you in," he said, breathless against his own desire.

"I do not break as easily as you'd think." Finnian closed in and propped his hands up on the surface of the counter behind Cassian, pinning both arms around him. The tips of their noses grazed.

Cassian's jaw set. He turned his head away, internally scolding his willpower.

"Cassian." His name left Finnian's lips, a whisper, pleading. The sound of it slowly spread through him like spilled honey, weakening his resolve.

His breath trembled as he reached for his good sense. To turn away and leave. But yearning was all he could find—spilling out of the chambers of his heart, overflowing, warping his better judgment.

Fate be damned.

He snapped his arms up, cupped Finnian's cheeks, and whisked him into a kiss.

The undying thoughts of Ruelle silenced.

His mind stilled.

The kiss was depraved breaths huffing into mouths, fingers tangling in hair and in clothes. Cassian had not realized how starved of Finnian he'd become until the taste of him touched his tongue.

Finnian's teeth sunk into Cassian's bottom lip.

Pain ruptured in his nerves and a quiver zapped down his middle as Finnian's hands slid up his back. One tangled in his hair and gripped the

side of his head, while the other clung to the back of his shoulder, finger-nails clutching the material of his tailcoat.

He used the grip to deepen their kiss, reaching down inside of Cassian and making a mess of him.

"I loathe you," Cassian said against his lips. He ran his hands down the sides of Finnian's neck, over his shoulders, around his waist, and grazed underneath the back of his shirt. "I long for you." He traced his fingertips over Finnian's spine, memorizing every divot of bone, the lush terrain of his skin.

Finnian tightened his grasp in the back of Cassian's strands and lightly tugged, breaking apart their kiss and pulling away with hooded eyes, dark and full of lust. "Let me see *you*."

It took a second to process Finnian's request through the state of his arousal. "Is Everett's appearance not to your liking?"

Finnian dipped beneath his chin, leaving a trail of wet kisses down the bulb of his throat. "If I am going to kiss you…" He smoothed his palms over the plain of Cassian's pecs to the starched knot at his collar. "…run my hands over you…" He unraveled the knot with one hand, working the buttons of Cassian's waistcoat with his other. "…then I'd prefer it to be the real you."

Heat unfurled in Cassian's abdomen at the request.

He inhaled a breath of humid air from the boiling teapot and rear-ranged his appearance into his true form.

Finnian's movements turned sluggish as he slipped the waistcoat down Cassian's arms, fixing his attention on the transformation.

Cassian felt his jaw jut out and square, the rigid slice of his cheeks sharpen, and the swirling hue of blue irises brighten into two golden diamonds. "Happy now?"

Something primal crossed Finnian's features.

He chucked the waistcoat over his shoulder and devoured Cassian with another kiss—a feral rush of swollen lips and twirling tongues; hands tangling in clothes and fingers knotting in hair; bodies curving into one another; a desperate frenzy to drink the other in.

Tension twined through Cassian's insides. He held Finnian's cheek and kissed down the line of his jaw. He wanted to taste every inch of him.

Explore the scape of his skin with his tongue, over the contours of his collarbones, down his chest.

He gathered Finnian's shirt over his head, careful not to let it catch on his hearing aid, and tossed it somewhere across the room—having only a brief thought to pause, neatly fold it, and place it somewhere more appropriate than a ball on the floor.

As if Finnian could sense his thoughts, he tightened his grip on the loose knot of his collar. "Don't even think about it."

Cassian chuckled as Finnian yanked him off the edge of the cabinet, their bodies hard and pressed against each other.

Finnian's divine energy pricked the air. A cloud of crimson fabricated around them.

Cassian was nudged back as his feet left the floor. He stumbled on his footing, landing on a satin-covered mattress.

"I take it this is your room," Cassian said, breathless, glancing around at the cluttered bedside table and cloth strewn in an unmade state.

Finnian climbed on top of him and pulled the hem of Cassian's tucked shirt out of his waistband. His movement ground his arousal against Cassian's pelvis, creating a friction of pleasure that rose into his lower belly.

"Do you have someone iron your clothes for you?" Finnian asked.

A laugh burst from Cassian, the harmonic sound echoing in the room.

"You do." The chilled air hit his chest as Finnian worked his shirt over his head, disheveling his hair. "Your deities of Death iron your clothes for you."

Cassian propped himself up on his elbows, bare-chested, grinning. "Not all of us are mages who can use our magic to do the task for us."

"Do you see me performing magic to undress you?" Finnian traced the pads of his fingers down the lines of Cassian's abdomen, his pupils dilating and swallowing up the playful glimmer in his gaze.

Cassian's heart rate accelerated. The desire to become one with Finnian was as maddening as his own curses. He reached forward to undo the fly of buttons on Finnian's trousers, but Finnian lightly pushed against him.

Cassian sank down flat on the mattress, allowing Finnian to explore every bend of muscle along his torso with his lips. Slow, wandering kisses explored his stomach, teasing above his waistband.

Cassian's muscles quivered and his head fell back on the pillow.

Finnian's fingers worked to undo the buttons of Cassian's trousers.

"I want to watch you fall apart," Finnian said, voice gruff.

Cassian twitched against the material, eager.

"I want to make a mess of you." Finnian worked Cassian's trousers off and crawled back up, settling his head between the crook of Cassian's neck.

The crystals of Finnian's necklaces were cool against the skin of his shoulder. Gooseflesh spread like water down Cassian's nape.

"Hear you say my name."

Finnian gently took him into his hand, swallowing Cassian's hitched breath with a kiss.

A zealous heat burned in his bloodstream.

"I loathe you." Finnian stroked, slow and languid.

A shiver blew through Cassian and his hips jerked.

Finnian nipped at his earlobe, the side of his neck, his clavicle. "And I long for you."

Tension coiled further and further up Cassian's midriff, a pleasure climbing against the swift beat of his pulse. It wasn't enough.

He clutched Finnian's shoulder, teeth gritted, hips moving to the pace Finnian set. "I yearn for more."

Finnian's thumb swirled at his tip. "More of what?"

Cassian trembled as he slid his hand into Finnian's hair, letting the tendrils fall in between his fingers.

Dazed, he met Finnian's eyes. "More of you."

Finnian sat up then, straddling Cassian's lap as he unfastened the buttons on his own trousers.

A thrilling tremor struck in Cassian's chest as Finnian's eyes drifted and darkened with intense hunger. He was a sight to behold with his tan cheeks tinted red, strands of his black hair stuck to his face. The pieces near his temples were curled.

A miniscule detail that spurred Cassian to say, "Remove your glamor."

After all the changes he'd noticed over the years in Finnian's hairstyles, he was sure of it.

Finnian paused on his buttons, head cocking with a wolfish smirk, his dimples cutting in his cheeks. "My, aren't you observant?"

"You are rather *overt* with your glamor," Cassian teased.

Finnian's chuckle rumbled as his onyx-black strands lightened to the shade of coffee. Their ends crawled up his chest and met his shoulders. Curls coiled throughout, creating a bed of waves in its bone-straight texture.

Cassian stared at these small changes, captivated.

Finnian freed himself from his trousers. The muscles danced beneath the skin of his torso as he sank down. He held himself up on his hands at each side of Cassian, dragging his length against the inside of Cassian's thigh, over his hip bone, and against his own arousal.

A tremble shook through Cassian, followed by a wrought tension gathering in his stomach.

Finnian cupped both of them and squeezed.

A mind-numbing pleasure swept over Cassian.

Finnian's mouth parted and his chin fell, exhaling a shaky breath.

Greed swelled within Cassian as he chased the feel of Finnian against him, moving in sync with his rhythm. It still wasn't enough.

He reached down and grabbed Finnian's wrist. "Give me more, Finny."

Finnian halted and stared at him intently for a moment. "Are you sure?"

"Implicitly." Cassian widened his knees, inviting.

Finnian continued to hang over him, their faces inches apart. A subtle excitement lit in his eyes. "I presume this is not your first time with a man?"

Cassian rolled his hips in a lazy motion, enjoying the bursts of nerves shooting up his abdomen from the friction.

Finnian bit back his bottom lip in response.

Satisfied with his reaction, Cassian gave a lousy smirk. "I am over five thousand. What do you think?"

Sexuality confinements within the mortal society were nonexistent to deities. They lived far too long and grew bored far too easily.

"A *you are correct* would have sufficed," Finnian grumbled, stretching over to his bedside table to dig inside a drawer.

Cassian chuckled.

Finnian pulled out a vial filled with yellow-tinted oil and doused his hand with it. The fragrance of olives touched Cassian's nose as he lifted his arms and gathered Finnian's long strands out of his face. He neatly tucked them behind his shoulders.

Centuries of sound and static had plagued Cassian's mind. He'd walked each day unknowing of peace, secretly envious of the souls he led into the

Paradise of Rest. It was an eternal landscape of respite he'd carved within his own realm. Cassian always longed for the day he would be granted such serenity.

Finnian was his stillness in the storm; silence in the screaming; peace in the chaos.

The evening sunlight trickled through the window, reflecting the various shades of green in his eyes. Glittering particles of dust shimmered in the rays. It was all a dream. It had to be. Laying on his bed, the feel of his fingers drawing circles of pleasure, slipping deep, flexing, curling.

Cassian's ragged breaths filled the room.

Finnian caught each one and gulped it down in a kiss.

"Long for me." He sat up on his knees and hooked both arms underneath the crooks of Cassian's legs, lifting his hips.

He entered with a careful thrust.

Tingles shot down Cassian's spine and a moan spewed from his lips, arching into him.

Cassian felt possessed by a longing to tear out of his own skin and claw through Finnian's until they were one. It was unhinged and delusional, a delirium he'd never craved before in his life.

The ecstasy of Cassian's desire surged like a river in his blood.

"Always long for me." Finnian gripped both hands around Cassian's waist and buried himself deeper.

Cassian rolled the back of his head into the pillow. The sensation of building pleasure coiled like a vine, slowly wrapping around him, consuming him.

"Always."

TWENTY

MY REAL NAME

THEIR DAYS ENDED and began with one another.

After the exasperation of running a city and a realm, Cassian would appear in Finnian's home. Some nights, Finnian was waiting for him. Others, Cassian would mindlessly sort through the clutter of his house and find places for the objects, or he would attempt to make coffee in the percolator—a mortal task he wasn't familiar with.

Finnian had a stock of roasted beans stored away in his cabinet. With the mortar and pestle, Cassian ground them to powder. The tricky part, though, was figuring out how to light the stove without the assistance of magic. It appeared Finnian did not have any matches lying around.

"I cannot make your coffee if you do not supply me with a way to create a flame," Cassian chided him one night.

They were lying side by side in Finnian's bed, the sheets tangled around their bare legs.

"You do not have to make me coffee," he said with a crooked smile

"After a long day of work seems to be the most appropriate time *to* drink it. That is when I enjoy my beverages the most."

Finnian turned over on his side, propping an elbow up and resting his head on his hand. The muscles in his bicep flickered beneath the skin, and his long hair brushed over his chest. "All I can think about throughout my day is you in my bed. If you think I am going to stop and drink coffee before kissing you, you've gone mad."

A blush heated Cassian's cheeks. He hid it by staring up at the ceiling, disapproving of the somersaulting in his stomach.

The next day, he brought his own matches.

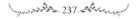

When Finnian appeared in the middle of his kitchen, he smiled at the steaming cup on the table, and then devoured Cassian in a mess of wet kisses down his jaw, his neck, over the length of his torso to his waistband.

Cassian's mind slipped into a fog. He barely registered the sly swivel of Finnian's wrist magically unfastening the buttons of his trousers, or Finnian dropping to his knees.

"Neat trick, Little—"

Finnian ceaselessly praised him with his tongue.

The back of Cassian's head hit the wall. Huffy moans sprang from his throat. His fingers weaved in Finnian's strands, tugging them at the scalp. Waves of pleasure liquified his insides. He moved his hips, chasing the gathering of nerves and need.

"*Finny.*" His name left Cassian's mouth in a scant breath. He fought through the trembling of his limbs and tried to pull out of Finnian's mouth. "I am—"

Finnian dug his grip firmer into the back of Cassian's waist, holding him in place, swallowing even deeper.

A moan fled out of Cassian and the tension gripping his abdomen released.

He shuddered, bliss floating through him.

Finnian licked his lips, smirking as he rose to his feet. He strolled across the kitchen, grabbed the cup, and twisted to look over at Cassian as he took a sip.

"You're right," he said. "I feel refreshed."

Cassian relaxed his weight against the wall and let out a breathy laugh, his stomach dipping at the sight of Finnian's dimpled smile over the rim of the cup.

At the end of each week, Finnian would spend his nights at a tavern with Eleanor and Isla—a social outing Cassian would join in as Everett. The setting was often loud and rambunctious.

Finnian mostly sat quietly with his drink, the corners of his mouth pulled up subtly as he watched Eleanor and Isla ramble on. Though, Cassian did not miss the way Finnian's eyes tracked their lips as they spoke, or how he occasionally misunderstood their words and replied to them with something out of context.

Eleanor and Isla simply repeated what they'd said, but Cassian could see the flush of awkwardness under the tan complexion of Finnian's cheeks.

He easily recalled what Finnian had told him about overcrowded settings with loud noises, and how his brain had to work harder to listen.

It made sense, when they'd arrive home, and Finnian would peel the hearing aid from his right ear with a relieving sigh. After, he would retreat down to the basement and revel in the silence of his potions, while Cassian plucked a book from his shelf and entertained himself with a mortal story, granting Finnian the quiet he needed to soothe his overstimulated brain.

"You do not have to go," Cassian said to him from the bed one evening. "Surely your apprentices would understand."

Finnian stood beside the bed, dressing. "I know I do not, but I enjoy the time with Eleanor and Isla, as well as the tavern's atmosphere." His arms paused from buttoning his shirt, and he glanced back at Cassian. "I will not let Mira take that away from me."

There it was, that fierceness of his that Cassian loved so.

And the truth was, he enjoyed the nights out as much as Finnian did. The distance from the Land and the souls and the constant decision-making was nice.

One night, they sat across from each other, with Finnian casually sipping on his pint and playing with the teal gemstone strapped around his neck. The tavern was mostly empty, and the voices were a tolerant murmur. Cassian could tell from the attentive light in Finnian's eyes that he was unbothered by the noise level.

Eleanor and Isla had dispersed to get refills or chat with friends, leaving Cassian alone with Finnian all to himself.

"That gemstone," Cassian said, pointing to it. "It's where you store the souls of your ghouls, yes?"

"It's a chrysocolla." Finnian gave the chain a forceful tug and it snapped off his neck. "A pendant, actually. A family heirloom passed down to Mira." He held it across the table for Cassian to inspect.

Cassian leaned forward with his pint in hand. "She gave it to you?"

"No." Finnian laughed lightly. "I stole it."

Cassian passed him a flat look, secretly enjoying the glimpse of his dimples. "Of course you did."

"Since it's been passed down through the generations, an abundance of divine energy resides within it," he explained, that disturbing light twinkling in his gaze any time he talked about witchcraft or sorcery. "It is not so different from a relic. Items with intense divine power are limitless pools of energy to siphon from."

A hard look passed over his face as he stared at the crystal. "The first time I used it was on Alke, after Mira murdered him. I lacked knowledge and control over my magic back then, but with the pendant and the magical properties in the water hole Naia and I used to sneak off to, I managed to revive him."

Finnian had only told him of the memory once. It came up when Alke's undead form appeared in his house, perched atop the stove, watching quietly as Cassian boiled water in the kettle to make himself a cup of tea. Apparently, the bird felt a semblance of trust now to show itself to Cassian, confident he would not relinquish its soul to the Land.

Cassian had thought about it, but *boydens* were loyal creatures. Even if he did cast its soul back into the Land, it had the capability of traveling between realms. Their devotion to their masters triumphed over the laws of the Universe.

"That must've been difficult for you to endure at such an early age." Cassian wished to reach over and grab Finnian's hand to comfort him, but he was hesitant. They were in a tavern full of mortals, and Cassian had to remind himself, in their society, two men touching in any intimate sense could potentially attract negative attention.

Finnian ran his thumb over the pendant, lost in the memory. "It's a myth that *boydens* obey High Gods over their masters. I was convinced that was the only reason Alke answered Mira's call that day, but then, years later, I learned I was the first of my lineage, a High God, and it didn't make sense."

"A *boyden*, first and foremost, will do whatever is necessary to protect their master," Cassian said.

"Precisely. Alke landed on Mira's arm that day to keep her from abusing me." Finnian looked up at him then, the melancholy visible in his eyes. "I have wrongs that I wish to make right—with Naia and Father. And one day, I will see to it that Mira falls as a High Goddess."

Cassian felt a determination rise steadily in him. If setting out to make things right would bring Finnian happiness, he was willing to do everything in his power to make sure all of Finnian's plans came to fruition.

Cassian stretched his leg out underneath the table, caressing Finnian's ankle with his own. "I swear, the day that happens, I will ensure you are present to witness it."

Finnian gave a weak smile and drew his attention back to the pendant. "She never attempted to find this again. I believe she was too distraught by the events that night." The teasing lilt of his tone reappeared as he clasped the chain around his neck. The pendant rested on his sternum.

"Do you have to use the gemstone each time you revive someone?" Cassian asked. "I watched you use it the night in Augustus, when you revived the dog, but not at the cemetery…"

He realized his error when Finnian tilted his head, lips curving. "You *were* following me."

A blush nipped at Cassian's cheeks, dismissing his previous stalkerish behavior with a wave. "That's besides the point."

Finnian chuckled.

"No." He took a sip of his stein and said, "As I grew to learn more about myself as a mage, I was able to craft an incantation. Back when I was constantly running from you and your endeavors to relinquish all my souls, I'd hide them in the pendant." Finnian took another gulp.

"*Vivifica* is how I pull the souls straight from your Land and place them inside their physical bodies. *Excitare ex somno* is how I summon them from my pendant to assist me, if I am not near a graveyard or corpse. The pendant's power helps me partially restore their physicality, giving them husks to fight in."

Cassian ran a hand through his hair. The texture and length were not his own. Sometimes, he forgot he was under the appearance of another.

He dropped his hand and let out a breath, unsure *how* to ask the unnerving question prodding at him. "The temples resurrected across the city by your followers, do they also perform these spells?"

If they did, they hadn't been successful. Cassian was meticulously aware of the souls in his Land, and since Finnian had made his vow, only those who were citizens of his city had not arrived.

Finnian inclined his head, mischief glittering in his gaze as he rested back in his chair. "If they were, how would you respond?"

The challenge provoked the High God in him to be taken seriously.

Cassian swiped his thumb over his bottom lip, eyeing him in a warning. "I may not have it in me to curse you, Little Nightmare, but the same cannot be said for others."

"*Finny*," he corrected in a snide manner that irked Cassian.

"At the moment, you are acting like a *Little Nightmare*."

Finnian huffed out a smug laugh. "I am actually quite curious to see what hides behind this tamed facade you present to the rest of the world." Under the table, Finnian grazed his foot up the side of Cassian's shin. "The day you unleashed a bit of your true power onto the triplets, I could see a glimpse of it then."

Tendrils of heat crawled up Cassian's thigh. He raised an eyebrow, pausing the rim of his pint at his lips. "Shall I head to one of your temples now and put on a show?"

Finnian's eyes darkened. "As much as I would find that arousing to witness, necromancy is not a teachable art. It is a talent you are born with. You do not have to fret about reckless mages mimicking my ghouls."

Cassian had to swim past *I would find that arousing* and the ravenous way Finnian was watching him to comprehend what all he'd said.

"I suppose I have nothing to worry about then." He downed the rest of his stein in a gulp and licked his lips, aware of Finnian's eyes tracking his movements.

Silence settled between them for a beat, thick and rising with a tension tingling across Cassian's skin.

"The night is still young," Finnian finally said, his voice sultry and glazed like molasses.

Blood rushed to Cassian's groin, and he pushed his empty glass away. "I am ready to depart when you are."

CASSIAN lay on his stomach, one arm stretched underneath the pillows, eyes closed. The sunrise of another day bled through his lids. Another morning tangled in the satin cloth of Finnian's bed.

Finnian's fingertip stroked feather-light drawings along the scope of Cassian's back. He wasn't sure how long he'd been out, but the sensation of Finnian's finger brushing along the middle of his back had not ceased.

A flutter caught in his stomach and he smiled into the pillow. It had been centuries since he'd *slept.*

He blinked the sleep away from his eyes and kept still. If he shuffled, Finnian would know he was awake. He wanted to savor the moment for a bit longer, before he sat up with nothing left but to return to his Land.

The War of Sons had ceaselessly spread through the Mortal Land. Two sons from the same country—Julian and Silas.

In his childhood, Silas had been shunned and banished. He rose to monarchy in the neighboring country and reigned—just to overrule the family who tossed him aside. It was not about gaining territory. It was about revenge. A battle that had infected the nations, forcing other nearby countries to become involved.

The death count had grown significantly. With it, a choir of prayers sang to deities. Specifically, the High Goddess of Peace and the High Goddess of War.

All deities had mortals they favored. It was how they inevitably concerned themselves among mortal disputes. Which then turned them into deity disputes. It was the Council's job to shut down any opposition between deities to avoid wars amongst their kind.

Cassian had already heard rumors of the High Goddess of Peace and the High Goddess of War at each other's throats. It was only a matter of time until Cassian would be forced to step in and threaten one of them with a curse, simply to rein their personal feelings towards their favored mortals back in.

"What are you thinking so hard about?" Finnian's fingertip stroked up the knolls of his spine to his nape.

Cassian smiled into his pillow. It was impossible to hide from him. Beneath Finnian's aloof demeanor, he was always watching, observing, noticing every subtle shift of skin, muscle, and tone. This was one detail Cassian had quickly discovered in the few weeks of their relationship.

He rolled over, knowing Finnian did not have his hearing aid in. He'd recently started removing it in Cassian's presence, when they were in the safety of his home, or during sex. It was a quality Cassian took pride in.

"The war," he replied.

Finnian was propped up on his elbow, expression sated, looking intently at him. "The casualties?"

Cassian reached up and twirled one of his wavy strands. "Yes. Mothers, fathers, children. All civilians. Separated from one another."

"Such constant despair must be strenuous for you." Finnian frowned, and Cassian could detect the line of tension under his tone.

"War is ruthless and often over issues that can easily be resolved with words. I despise when the edges of it touch those who are innocent. To be quite honest, I am relieved when souls enter my Land, because pain and suffering can no longer touch them. But when they first arrive, they are afraid and their emotions are often taxing. I cannot make another understand what I already know, and yet, at the same time, I feel sympathy for them."

Cassian wasn't sure when he'd stopped talking about his truths, his thoughts. He gave Mavros, Nathaira, and Shivani a portion of these things, but only what grazed at the surface level. He'd never had the desire to scrape up the muck that had collected deep beneath and hand it over to another, as most tended to avoid dirtying their hands with someone else's turmoil.

Although, after he'd said everything, it didn't occur to him that Finnian might grow agitated by his ideology of death. It was a topic they both saw with very different perspectives.

To Cassian's surprise, though, Finnian grabbed his hand and gently unraveled his fingers from the wavy strand.

"I want to believe the things you say." He brought Cassian's knuckles to his lips. "But I simply cannot make sense of death in my head."

Cassian could see the hardness in his eyes at the mention of death and separation. Swirling in the midst of that hardness was a primal fear, and it drowned in his gaze.

Cassian's expression softened, and he said, "Ask me whatever you wish, and I will tell you anything."

"Do you…" Finnian shifted and lay on his back. He positioned Cassian's palm over his chest. The tip of his index finger ran in circles over the tendons on the back of Cassian's hand as he stared up at the ceiling. "Naia, do you know if she is well?"

Shame gripped Cassian's chest. The question was a blatant reminder of the deal he'd struck with Mira. "I hear she has taken a friendship with her servant, Gianna."

"May I inquire how you know?" Finnian asked, his voice low, quiet.

Cassian flipped his hand over and idly played with Finnian's fingers, stroking up and down each one. "Your father calls for me every once in a while."

Finnian glanced over at him, eyes bright with interest. "Calls for you?"

Cassian smiled, his fingertips exploring up the contours of Finnian's chest. "Usually through a vine snaking up my ankle, or sometimes, he ravishes in the dramatic and sends tremors through the terrain of my Land. He tells me of what goes on in Kaimana, as he still has a deep connection with its flora."

Finnian chuckled, his dimples flickering on each cheek. "Of course he does."

Gooseflesh dotted over the skin of his chest as Cassian's fingers ran down his abdomen. "If you wish to visit your father, I will arrange it."

Something flitted across Finnian's face, signs of hesitation, reservation, sorrow. Cassian's hand stopped moving, his fingers resting on Finnian's navel. He studied him for a beat.

"I do not think I am the person I need to be in order to make him proud," Finnian confessed, the burden of remorse pulling at his features.

"He talks of you all the time. And Naia. Relives years of memories he has with you both. When he runs out of those stories, he bores me with his grand adventures, turning insects into relics and such."

A bittersweet gleam appeared in his eyes as he continued to stare up at the ceiling, his fingers lazily coasting back and forth down Cassian's forearm. "He made me and Naia promise to take care of each other before he was escorted away. I have failed him."

Cassian's heart squeezed, despising the visible shadows of pain warping over Finnian. He ran his palm over Finnian's chest, up his neck, and cupped his jaw, guiding his eyes to look at him. "There is nothing you could do that would make Vale love you any less. You are a fool if you believe so."

Finnian gave a frail smile. "And you are a fool if you trust me enough to take me to your Land and not attempt to free him."

Cassian scoffed, giving his chin a playful squeeze before letting go. "It's impossible, but you are welcome to try." He shifted onto his back, stretching out his legs and curling his toes underneath Finnian's feet.

"That is it? No threats of curses?" His eyebrows raised. "I know how much you relish in handing those out."

Cassian laughed, running a hand through his hair. "I am not a monster who *enjoys* cursing."

"To most, you are." Finnian flicked away the curly strand that relentlessly dangled in his face. "You are Cassian, *the High God of Death and Curses.*" He recited it in an evangelistic tone, overexaggerating the fear of his title.

"Cassius." The truth escaped him before he could overthink on whether or not to share it.

Finnian sat up and looked down at him. "Hm?"

It had been several millennia since Cassian had experienced the adrenaline-laced thrill pumping through his veins—the way a mortal described standing over a ledge or a rooftop.

He swallowed and slightly rotated his head to face Finnian. "My real name is Cassius," he said. "I was named after my father. When I became the High God of Death and Curses, I knew my title would supply me with a list of enemies. The less they knew about me, the better. So, I introduced myself among deities as *Cassian.* Only my siblings know of my real name. And now you."

"*Cass-i-us.*" Finnian said each syllable slowly, like balancing a precious gemstone on his tongue.

The notes of it sent pulses through Cassian's stomach. "I like the way it sounds on your lips."

"You must trust me to reveal something so personal."

Cassian held his eyes for a long moment. His adoration for Finnian filled every crevice of his soul, like magma solidifying in a stone's cracks. The stronger his adoration grew, the more he was plagued by haunting images of what their future could become.

"You are someone who cares deeply for those close to your heart. I do not question your character, Finnian. Never have. I am enamored by you. Every day. But I fear my desire for you will only hurt you."

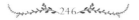

That infuriating boldness sparked to life in his gaze and his expression pinched. "If it is your enemies you fear, they do not stand a chance."

"Long ago, Ruelle and I had a disagreement. Since, she has longed to see me happy just to take her revenge."

At the mention of the High Goddess, Finnian's jaw set. "How much control does she have over your Fate?"

"Ruelle weaves the threads of mortals' Fates from the moment they enter the womb. She can send them to riches, or she can send them to ruin. However, she has less power over us deities, though she can still see the course of our threads. That alone gives her great power over our lives. She will use you to get to me, Finnian. If that frightens you, I understand. I can leave now and never—"

"Whatever she throws at us, we will face. *Together*." Finnian said, full of resolve. "I am not afraid of Ruelle."

Together.

A guttural instinct rose in Cassian, sharp and fierce. No matter how steep, how brutal the path became, he would do everything in his power to protect Finnian. Though, the selfless part of him knew the best way to protect Finnian was to leave him be. Keep their individual threads from entangling further than they already had.

"I do not think you understand. I tried to forget about you, to stay away from you. I've walked this long purposely avoiding growing close to another, knowing it was what Ruelle waited for."

Finnian lay on his side, pulling his body flush against Cassian. His brow wrinkled in disapproval. "That is no way to live."

Cassian sighed, tucking Finnian's wavy strands behind his ear to ensure he could hear, exposing the scar on the base of his jaw. "She's done it before."

"To one of your prior lovers?"

"Saoirse, the High Goddess of Light. We were together for nearly a decade before Ruelle intervened." Cassian brushed his thumb over the harsh patch of skin under Finnian's earlobe. Movement to avoid the twisting in his gut. "She manipulated the fates of those who crossed with Saoirse's, making her life a perpetual existence of hellish bad luck. Mortals banded together and raided her temples, her followers fell ill to disease, and a mage murdered her demigod daughter."

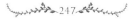

Cassian paused, the pad of his thumb following the scar down Finnian's jawline.

Finnian stared at him with an unnerving intensity.

He wasn't sure if it was Finnian coming to terms with the severity of the situation, or if it was merely because he spoke of a past lover.

Cassian grazed the back of his fingers up the scar to Finnian's ear. "Eventually, Saoirse could no longer handle the torment, and we went our separate ways. Ruelle continued to weave obstacles in between us to keep our threads from intertwining again."

Finnian remained quiet, eyes sharp and intently tracking Cassian's face.

Cassian lowered his hand and met Finnian's eyes, a silent plea to share his thoughts.

"Do you still long for her?" he asked.

Buttery warmth spread throughout Cassian's chest, flattered by the rigid jealousy in Finnian's tone.

A small smile pulled at his lips. "I do not. It is why Ruelle no longer meddles in affairs between us. They hold no leverage. The last I saw of Saoirse was a year ago during my niece's birthday celebration, and I can assure you there were no lingering feelings."

Finnian let out a terse breath through his nose, bringing his hand up to hold the side of Cassian's face. "Sounds like Saoirse did not care for you the way I do."

"It is easy for you to say such things, but what of your city, your apprentices, your followers, your title? Ruelle could ruin it all—"

Finnian pulled him into a kiss.

His lips spread, inviting in and caressing Finnian's tongue. The earthy, sweet taste of licorice, Finnian's favorite snack, filled his mouth. His thoughts, his worries, they snuffed out like a candle's flame.

Finnian gently broke away, fusing his forehead to Cassian's. "There is nothing to fear. Ruelle could strip away all that I have, but I would never leave you behind to her destruction," he whispered.

The vow branded deeply within Cassian. An assurance he never knew he craved.

"*When* she comes for us," Finnian continued, "we will handle it. Until then, savor the moment. You are here, with me, in my home, and there is nothing that threatens us. We have time to figure it out."

He rested his head down on the pillow. "Now, tell me stories—how you became a deity, your journey in the Land. Tell me of all your past lovers. I long to know everything about your life, Cassius."

Cassian lifted his hand once more and grazed the back of his fingers down the side of Finnian's neck, reveling in the frisson that rippled across the skin in his wake, mentally reciting what Finnian had said to him back in Augustus.

Be in the moment. No matter how much his mind leapt into the future, eager to plot out and prepare all the ways Ruelle could come between them.

He desired to keep this peace, to focus on Finnian's presence at his side, regardless of what their future held.

"Whatever you wish."

TWENTY-ONE

I AM YOURS TO RAVAGE

ROTHY PINTS OF beer floated across the tavern, a roadway of glasses traveling in the air to their designated tables. Chatter of voices and high-pitched laughter filled the room.

"I don't mean to pry, Everett," Eleanor, the mage with ginger locks, said from across the table, "but you've been hanging around a lot these days."

Her appearance had evolved from the look of a young adult to a woman. Her round features had thinned, and the loose skin of her freckled arms had toned.

Cassian sat his pint down and licked his lips. "What can I say? Hollow City has grown on me."

Isla, sitting beside him, looked over. She was a mess of untamable curls and vivid-brown eyes. "And I suppose that includes our city's founder as well?"

Her coy smile and raised eyebrows warmed Cassian's cheeks.

He averted his gaze down to the ale dripping down the sides of his stein.

It had been a year in the Mortal Land since Cassian started making regular appearances as Everett in Hollow City. He'd gotten to know Finnian's apprentices well, the layout of the city, the residents, and their businesses.

Eleanor was the more extroverted one, often speaking what was on her mind, regardless if it was an appropriate time to or not. In the last year, she'd developed a city council made up of humans and mages, and she took the liberty of supplying a staff to help with mayoral duties.

Isla was more introverted, and her down-to-earth demeanor did well to hide her fierce nature. She ran the organizations loyal to Finnian with assertiveness. As his name and title continued to spread, mages from all over flocked to Hollow City and devoted themselves to him.

"I suppose we have you to thank," Eleanor said, propping her elbows up on the table. "Before you came along, we couldn't convince Finny to wear the attire fitting for a city founder. Those horrid linen shirts with half of his chest exposed." She rolled her eyes. "He presented himself as an angsty adolescent that had just rolled out of bed."

Isla chuckled lightly, twirling her finger in one of her long curls. "He appears more official—and *intimidating*. The members of the organizations are terrified every time he pops in for a visit."

"The waistcoat is a sophisticated look. If only he'd wear a tailcoat as well," Cassian mumbled.

Eleanor barked out a laugh, smacking her hand down on the table in unison. "I think I would die of shock if that were ever to happen. Isla tried to buy him a pair of regal top-boots once, but he refused to part with the old ones he had."

"He's a creature of habit. And values comfort above all else," Isla said before taking a sip of her brown, malty beer.

Cassian had grown accustomed to his days in Hollow City. Disguised as Everett, he'd often roam the streets and explore the businesses—the pastry shop that served delightful lavender tea, banks, printing presses, and grocers. His favorite, though, was a tailor shop where he purchased a fitting pair of trousers, a white muslin shirt, and a single-breasted waistcoat in Finnian's size. Measurements memorized on the tips of his fingers.

The outfit was intended to be worn during official business, and when Finnian had tried it on, he groaned and tugged at the high collar.

"It's befitting for the founder of the city," Cassian had told him.

"Not a damn chance," he'd muttered, face scrunched in discomfort.

Cassian smiled the next morning when Finnian teleported away, wearing the outfit.

"Finny didn't intend to be caught up all night at work," Isla said, plucking a few peanuts from the bowl at the center of the table, "but three new organizations arrived to present their products to him. I imagine he won't dally around if he knows you are waiting for him."

Finnian kept busy with the underbelly of the city. Humans stuck to one side, mages to the other. The Bogart Strip was hidden in the magical side where Finnian had created his black market, safeguarded by a portal only mages could step through.

Cassian would lie next to Finnian in bed and listen to him gush about all the arcane trinkets and potions in its ominous alley. Despite his innocent excitement, the market attracted attention from all sorts of dodgy visitors. However, it was a huge contributor to the revenue of the city, while simultaneously the biggest cause of conflict.

As covens of mages congregated and settled, competition arose, rivaling began, and it seemed like each day, more and more were requesting to meet with Finnian—for he had to approve items before they could be sold in his market.

"Tell us about yourself, Everett." Eleanor cracked open a peanut shell and popped the contents inside of her mouth. Her eyes were cloudy from the alcohol. "What do you do?"

Cassian rested back in his chair and took another swig. "I am an undertaker," he said, the first occupation correlating with death to pop in his head.

"*Oh.*" Isla stifled a laugh in her palm, exchanging a look with Eleanor.

Laughter spewed out of her. Bits of peanut spit across the table as she doubled over. "You were probably thrilled to arrive, only to find it's ruled by a necromancer!" She banged on the surface of the table, wheezing in between her giggles.

"I think you picked the wrong city to find employment in." Isla playfully nudged his arm, smiling wide.

Cassian cleared his throat and crossed his arms as Eleanor's laughter echoed over the clatter of voices. He bit back his smile, watching her freckled cheeks turn bright red.

Nobody in Finnian's city perished. Ghouls were stationed all over the crevices and dark alleyways along the magical side. They were his eyes, his ears, his civil guards.

Cassian's fingers twitched each time he strolled past one of the undead creatures, itching to relinquish its soul. A habit ingrained within him that he learned to counteract by reminding himself how much the ghouls and necromancy meant to Finnian.

"I work outside the city," he explained. "It is why I am gone for weeks at a time. The war has, unfortunately, kept me busy."

Eleanor wiped the corner of her eyes, coming down from her cackling. "I must say, Everett, I did not believe opposites attract until now. You give rest to the dead bodies while Finny revives them."

Isla shook her head at Eleanor, amused.

"That sounds like a brutal line of work." She turned her head towards Cassian. "It seems the war has no end in sight."

"I guarantee Everett has no desire to talk about the war," Eleanor said pointedly, in response to Isla. "Let's talk about other matters far less depressing, shall we?"

Isla gave her a playful look and stuck out her tongue. "In that case, we need refills." She stood from the table.

Eleanor gulped down the rest of her beer and then said, "It is your turn to cast a charm on the barkeeper."

Women were socially *not allowed* to order drinks in bars. A preposterous concept that Cassian could not wrap his mind around, but nevertheless, he found it amusing to watch the two mages cast their charms and get their well-deserved way.

"Everett?" Isla gestured to his half-full pint with her eyes.

"Yes, if you don't mind."

They both started across the tavern to the bar.

When they returned, they didn't ask any follow-up questions about Everett.

As the night carried on, Cassian sipped on his beer and listened to them tell stories of the past—all revolving around Finnian.

Once, he'd used his sorcery to mark a large, runic sigil above the entire city just to make it snow for a child. Once, he'd disguised a simple pear as a heart-shaped mound of gold and donated the profit back to his mages. There were many *onces*, and Cassian couldn't determine if all were true, but he smiled at the thought of Finnian's kindness. Although, the stories only made Cassian miss him more.

Eleanor became louder and more animated the more she drank. Isla's laughter transitioned into hiccups.

Cassian's gaze flitted from them to the door. It had been a few weeks since he'd seen Finnian. Duties in the Land and Council business had kept him busy.

Acting as a warden to souls had taken a toll on his mental energy. Just in the past week, he'd approved over two thousand to be reincarnated, punished seventy-eight rotten souls and tossed them into the Serpentine Forest, and dealt with the twenty-two souls who had attempted to escape and were caught by the Errai near the gates of his Land.

Tension was growing among deities because of the war. Division was slowly forming. They were choosing sides between the High Goddess of Peace and the High Goddess of War. Iliana had called five Council meetings in the last month to discuss the matter. All of which, Cassian had avoided Ruelle's presence and vanished the second their meeting was adjourned.

Silas, the mortal who was shunned from his home country as a child, was the catalyst for the violence. It was no surprise that the High Goddess of War backed him.

Julian, the mortal on the opposing side, gave several failed attempts to cease the war against his brother. The High Goddess of Peace was doing all she could to answer his prayers.

Soon enough, someone would act out of line and the Council would be forced to intervene. In turn, Cassian would have another divine being to punish in his prison.

He envied those with no responsibilities. In the last year, he'd grown greedy with his time and how much of it he spent with Finnian. They went through lulls where their schedules kept them from seeing one another, and Cassian often daydreamed of a time where that wouldn't be the case.

The night creeped into the early morning hours. Isla and Eleanor abandoned hope that Finnian would arrive before the sunrise and left Cassian at the tavern alone.

He switched from beer to bourbon and moved to a table in the far corner. The tavern was quieter now, dim lights like rays gleaming through honey.

He was hidden from the women circling the tables of men like vultures. Propped up on laps, whispering lustful promises in their ears until they couldn't handle it any longer and stood up with the woman in hand, venturing out the back door of the tavern into the shadow-littered alleyway.

Cassian swirled the bourbon in his glass.

One year of time with Finnian. Three hundred and sixty-five days with him that seemed to have sped by like a falling star. How long would Ruelle give them?

Cassian stared at his reflection in the bourbon.

Sickness clotted his stomach at the thought. Ruelle was infuriatingly patient. She would wait. Let Cassian's thread tangle with Finnian's until he'd forgotten what life was like before him. It would be the best way to inflict more suffering when she finally decided to meddle.

Fear welled up in him each time he envisioned Finnian's absence in his life. Crippling, paralyzing fear he did not know how to solve.

In time, he would curse Naia, make a bargain with her, and then curse her again. The Himura demigod's blood would be his and he could do away with Ruelle. However, that was years away. He needed a solution at the ready—*just in case.*

Only, coming up with one felt like digging for a needle in a haystack, as the possibilities of Ruelle's hand were limitless.

He let out an exhale and centered his focus back onto his surroundings—the calm setting of the tavern, the cool glass in his hand, the smell of peanuts and smoke in the atmosphere.

It had been hours. Finnian was probably held up with more tasks. That's how to-do lists worked. Cross one thing off just for another to be added.

I should wait for him at home.

A *click* of heels sounded along the wooden floor.

Cassian lifted his chin.

"You look like you are in need of company," a woman purred.

She did not wait for permission before sliding into the chair beside him. The strong fragrance of her perfume burned his nostrils.

She crossed her legs under the table, and her heel brushed up Cassian's shin.

He moved his foot, breaking their connection.

She leaned in and rested her arm along the back of his chair. The tight dress she wore hugged her hourglass physique like a glove. It sported a daring neckline, and the position she sat in gave Cassian a clean view of her cleavage.

"I am in no need of company." He sat his bourbon on the table, ignoring her close proximity to his space. She'd arrived earlier in the night with three other women. They'd gone their separate ways and made several rounds amongst the men.

She brushed her lips along the side of his neck, and a pang shot up into his skull.

His stomach knotted and he recoiled. Blood rushed to his head and his heart accelerated. His vision swam and swayed a bit.

He gripped the edge of the table to stabilize his balance. The teeth of his divine energy cut into his veins and latched onto the magic infecting his blood.

She came closer, nuzzling her breasts against his arm. "You don't look so good." Her voice wrapped around his ears like a song.

A surge of heat flushed in his abdomen. Tension pulled his muscles taut. *What is happening?*

Cassian shot up from the table. His legs wobbled as he put distance between them.

He had never been one to have lustful urges towards a pretty face alone. If feelings weren't involved in the matter, he rarely gave them the time of day. He barely knew this woman. Logically, she was attractive, but he couldn't make sense of the burning ball of need in his chest. The intensity beating in his blood, hot and pulsing up the sides of his neck—

He lowered his hand to the spot she'd kissed. Raised, puffy skin met the tip of his fingers.

Nausea churned in his gut.

A spell.

"It seems you've had too much to drink." She rose from the chair and trotted towards him.

He stumbled back until he hit the wall. His breath hitched. The cold surface overwhelmed his heated skin through the material of his waistcoat.

"I am fine," he gritted out.

"Let me assist you." Her hands came down on his chest and smoothed across his abdomen, an instant trigger of arousal he did not approve of.

"It is more pleasurable if you give into it." She wedged her knee in between Cassian's legs, gaining access to press her hips into his. The friction she created against his length filled his mind with a smog. It was like trudging through tar without escape.

He couldn't teleport and risk revealing his identity to a mortal, and if he tried to cast an illusion in this state, he could potentially hurt her.

She nuzzled into the crook of his neck and drew circles along his skin with her tongue.

Cassian shuddered, the sensation rolling a sickness in his stomach. The blood beat thickly in his ears as he attempted to push himself off the wall and—

The woman was thrown back.

A body forced itself between them. Its presence swift and sudden, blowing a sweet earthy gust up Cassian's nose.

She staggered, tripping over her heels, and caught herself clumsily on the edge of a nearby table. Tendrils of her dark hair flapped in front of her mouth from her rapid breath.

She hooked her head up and her small features contorted with indignation, stained red lips curling up in a snarl. "Don't you dare lay a hand on me—"

Recognition stole the words from her mouth and melted the anger from her face.

"I suggest you find another man to cast your trickery on, lest you enjoy losing your tongue," Finnian warned, his tone tight and impatient.

The woman dropped her chin in a frazzled apology and rushed past them towards the exit.

Cassian let his head fall back against the wall. A cold sweat broke out over his body. He pulled at the crisp collar of his waistcoat.

A gentle set of hands clutched his shoulders. The straining in his muscles eased momentarily.

"Are you alright?" Finnian asked, his voice soft, concerned.

He loved the way Finnian spoke to him, tender and slow. A constant silencing of the fluxing thoughts in his mind.

But it also made him become all too aware of the strong stream of warmth spreading down into his groin. The pinpricks of magic trapped in his bloodstream throbbed in response to his overwhelming desire.

Perverse fantasies flowered in the front of his mind—taking Finnian up against the wall, on the table, the bar, the floor.

He squeezed his hands into fists, as if he held onto the fraying thread of his self-control. "I need you to let go of me."

Finnian studied him for a long second, eyes narrowing. He lifted his fingertips to the side of Cassian's neck.

Tremors wracked down into his stomach. His breath rushed out but didn't return.

In the past, Cassian had loathed the blank expression Finnian wore so well. All his emotions hidden, Cassian found it extremely frustrating how he could not read him. As they grew closer, those blank expressions became fewer and far between. Mostly when they were around others. Never when it was just the two of them, though.

Only now, the blank expression remained set in stone on his face, and Cassian felt an old sense of resentment rise in his chest with the question on his tongue: *can you undo the spell?*

Finnian inclined his head, exposing the curvature of his throat in a delicious angle. Quietly, he gauged Cassian's demeanor and the feverish tint to his pale skin. His lips twitched.

"Finnian," Cassian growled.

His smile grew as he took a step, pressing his chest snug against Cassian's shoulder. "It appears you've been bewitched."

Cassian's hips trembled. He arched into Finnian's pelvis, creating a pleasureful pressure against his own arousal.

Shame burned through him. The same lust aching inside of him to devour Finnian was what he'd felt for a stranger less than a few seconds ago.

He pressed his head back against the wall. "Remove it," he rasped, slinking the crook of his elbow over his eyes. His forehead was hot and damp.

Finnian hooked Cassian's chin with his thumb and index finger. Slowly, he rotated Cassian's head sideways, jutting out the part of his neck infected with the mark.

Finnian's mouth came down over his skin. A gentle, languid stroke with his tongue.

Cassian shuddered from the sensation as Finnian dragged his teeth across the mark and broke away.

"Come on." He lifted Cassian's arm from his face and guided it over his shoulders, supporting most of Cassian's weight. "Let us go home."

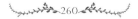

His lust had evolved into a frenzied, manic need by the time they stepped into the entrance of Finnian's house.

"Cassian, High God of Death and Curses, bewitched by a lowly wench." Finnian teased, slumping down to lower Cassian onto the edge of the mattress. "They are known to bed men and then steal their belongings. Quite the conniving seductresses, if you ask me."

"Shut… Up." Cassian clawed at the buttons of his waistcoat. "Fix it. Undo the spell."

Finnian kneeled in between his legs and assisted him with the buttons. The feathering of his fingers against the fabric zipped heat straight down between his legs. "Who says I can?"

"You raise my souls from the dead, but you cannot do something as simple as this?" Cassian scraped the back of his hand over his damp brow.

"I missed you," Finnian said, guiding his arms out of his waistcoat. "I apologize for being so late. You didn't have to wait there. You should've come home."

Cassian's pulse vibrated in his ears. He hung his head to his chest. Every inch of him felt like it was on fire. He squeezed his eyes closed. "Why can I not fight through this?"

Finnian lightly worked the tunic over Cassian's head. "It will pass. You will just have to endure the lustful rage for a few hours."

Cassian's eyes popped open, and he straightened up. "I think I shall go then."

"Whatever for?"

The mattress dipped behind Cassian.

He looked over his shoulder to find Finnian removing his hearing aid. He placed it on the bedside table beside his necklaces and lay back on the bed, smirking. He'd already shed his own waistcoat and unfastened the buttons of his shirt. The opening hung low and exposed the chiseled cut of his chest, honey-tan skin, flawless, a canvas inviting him to mark it up with his teeth.

Cassian's eyes widened, comprehending Finnian's coy response. "Absolutely not. Not—not like this."

Finnian sat up and lifted onto his knees. "You want to, though." He crawled towards Cassian. "I see the way you look at me, the way you wish to devour me. So why not take advantage of the spell and do your worst?"

Cassian looked straight ahead at the wall, his jaw pulsing, warring with himself to remain firm in his moral decision. "Lust and adoration are two different things."

Finnian's finger skimmed up his spine, the warmth of his breath moistening the side of Cassian's neck as he leaned in. "Oh, but they go wonderfully well together, don't you agree?"

His shoulders went rigid. "Finnian, I have no desire to show you anything but gentleness, and if we do this, I will ravage you until there is nothing left."

"I am yours to ravage." Finnian punctuated his statement by sinking his teeth down on Cassian's shoulder.

Cassian groaned and snapped around. His hand cupped Finnian's cheek, and he hooked his thumb underneath his jaw, using the grip to pull him into a starved kiss.

Finnian slumped back, allowing Cassian to climb onto his lap.

His hands moved in a rush, stripping Finnian's shirt. Desire thrummed like a bursting ravine in his veins. Gods, he'd missed him. The way Finnian playfully nipped at his bottom lip, the small noises he trapped in the back of his throat in moments of pleasure. Each intimate and raw detail they shared felt sacred.

Finnian stretched out Cassian's bottom lip with his teeth as he broke away and lowered onto the mattress. His hair spread out around his face across the satin, and he stared up at Cassian through hooded eyes.

Cassian remained propped up on his knees straddling Finnian, breathing hard with bruised lips.

He shucked his shirt off and bent down, kissing along Finnian's ribcage, sinking his teeth into the skin.

A light gasp escaped Finnian, followed by a shiver that wracked his body.

Cassian's tongue stopped, and he lifted his lips to look up.

Finnian stared down at him, his gaze dark from the swelling of his pupils. "Do that once more, and I don't think I will last much longer."

Cassian smiled. The urge in him was carnal, animalistic, to hear him make the sound again.

He sank his lips back down over Finnian's skin, leaving drowsy kisses between each crevice of his ribcage. As he did so, he worked to unfasten the buttons of Finnian's trousers.

Finnian writhed, his hips jerking up and his hands burying into Cassian's hair.

There was a satisfaction in seeing the crazed need for release on his face, trembling in his limbs.

Cassian pushed the waistband of Finnian's trousers down. Before he could descend his kisses further, Finnian grabbed a fistful of his hair and tugged.

Cassian sat up on his knees. "Let me have my way," he said through a breath, restless with the need to tease him a bit more.

"Oh, I intend to." Finnian reached up into his drawer, grinding their lengths against each other as he did so, and pulled out a vial of oil.

A quiver of nerves bolted up Cassian's spine as he rushed to unfasten the buttons of his own trousers, never realizing the effort it took to remove an article of clothing. A pang of frustration clenched in his chest as he threw the pants onto the floor.

He went to lift his leg over Finnian to trade positions.

Finnian snatched a hold of his wrist, stopping him.

Impatience gritted in his molars as he stiffened to hold himself up on his knees. "What—"

"Stay as you are." Finnian handed him the vial of oil and lounged back on the pillow, thoroughly enjoying the baffled look on Cassian's face. With a bastard smirk, he said, "Ravage *me*."

The desire buzzing through his bloodstream was excruciating. But now this?

A deranged laugh shook out of Cassian. He rubbed a hand over his face, sitting back on his heels.

For a brief moment, he wondered if *this* was Ruelle's revenge. A fate that led to being bewitched, pumped full of lust, and plagued with an unclear head just to be tempted in the cruelest, most agonizing way he certainly could not resist.

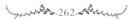

"Finny." His voice cracked, and he brought his fingers into his hair, curling and pulling at the roots. "I cannot—*will not*—do *this* for the first time under a bewitchment—"

"I removed it back at the tavern," he said.

Cassian blinked at him, dumbfounded. "You did?"

"Yes." He lifted up on his elbows, a cocky gleam in his eyes. "I also plan on finding that mage and burning her lips for placing them on you."

But how—

That infuriating kiss on his neck.

Cassian slowly unraveled his fingers from his hair and let his arms float back down to his sides. He couldn't tell if he was more aroused or furious by his cunningness. It was amazing how easily one deity could push him to the point of insanity.

"What you are feeling is not a lie." The mischief in Finnian's expression rearranged and a tenderness took its place. He dipped his chin to grab ahold of Cassian's gaze. "The side effects of the spell still linger in your blood, but it only heightens your desire. It no longer makes you lustful for anything with a pulse. How you feel, what you crave right now, is not a lie. You love me as I love you. Now, would you please just—"

"You are going to drive me to madness." Cassian doused his length in the oil.

Finnian barked out a laugh, flipping over onto his stomach. "Consider me your curse, then."

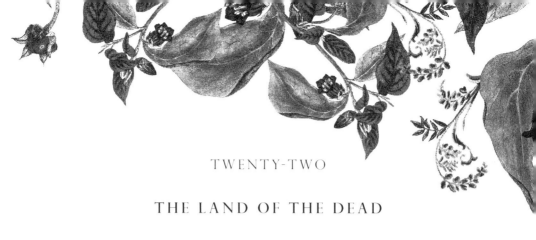

TWENTY-TWO

THE LAND OF THE DEAD

REMORS RUMBLED FROM the Mortal Land. Sorrow seeped beneath the soil of the earth and bled into the Land of the Dead. Cassian could feel it. A twinge of despair, a cresting storm preparing to uproar.

His stomach twisted with each passing second, anticipating the call of his name through a summons.

He stood on the bridge overlooking the glittering lilac water of the River of Souls. Their wraith-like forms crawled onto the bank and took form. Nathaira greeted them with white butterflies adorning the air around her.

The Errai guided the souls on their journey to the Lavender Fields of Healing. While their personas could not match the cheeriness of Nathaira's, their layers of silver chiffon and marble masks were far less daunting than the executioners' attire.

Mavros appeared at Cassian's side, the sound of his presence like water being sucked between teeth. "My lord, it is done. The executioners are on their way with Tamesis."

A middle goddess of slaughter. Also the daughter of the High Goddess of War. They both favored Silas, the mortal, with bloodlust and a vengeance against his family for banishing him years prior.

Cassian balled his hands in his pockets as Julian Vincent stepped onto the bank. Silas's brother, the one who longed for peace.

It appeared there was finally a victor in the War of Sons.

"Take him to the Grove of Mourning," Cassian ordered. "His death was gruesome, and he will need time to heal."

The situation was tiresome. Tamesis had stepped out of line and murdered the mortal that the High Goddess of Peace favored. She would be punished for interfering. Not on behalf of the mortal she'd slaughtered in a vile, repulsing way, but because if she went without punishment, the High Goddess of Peace and the deities who had sided with Julian would retaliate.

Cassian despised politics, but it was the Council's duty to maintain the order and law of their world.

"Right away, my lord." Mavros said, bowing his chin.

As the attendant backed away, preparing to teleport, Cassian lifted his hand to stop him. "Mavros, one more thing."

Mavros paused and slightly angled his head towards him. "Yes?"

"Please go to Finnian and inform him that I am dealing with a matter." Once Tamesis arrived, he would be responsible for her punishment. "I will come to him when I am able, or he may come to me, if he wishes."

"Of course." Mavros vanished.

In the three years they'd been together, it became a norm for Finnian to ask about Vale or the way the Land operated, but when Cassian offered to bring him to his home, the idea never sat well. Whether it was facing the reality of his father or simply being surrounded by a permanent end, it was clear that Finnian had no interest in stepping foot inside the Land of the Dead.

While Cassian respected his feelings, he longed to share it with Finnian; to show him death wasn't as grim and hopeless as he believed it to be. That, and there was the simplicity of how much he missed Finnian. Two weeks in the Mortal Land had waned by since Cassian had visited, and it felt like his own personal prison sentence.

Cassian let out an exhale. The ripples of his divine energy encased around him in dark tendrils as **he prepared** to teleport to Moros.

THE iron door to Tamesis's chamber swung open and Cassian strode out. Her wails echoed down the corridor as the door fell shut behind him.

Her punishment had been decided among the Council. Cassian was to do to her what she had done to Julian, and then she would suffer her sentence in isolation, under an illusion of eternal starvation.

Cassian's performance of torture smeared specks of dried rust down the front of his waistcoat. The urgency to clean it was sharp, but he settled for pulling his handkerchief from his pocket to wipe away the blood drizzled across his cheek.

After finishing the most macabre part of his job, the scenery distorted and Cassian's foot touched down on the stone pathway, surrounded by the sage and freshly budded rosemary of Finnian's Grove.

He needed somewhere tranquil to come down at, for the dissociation to fade—the void that overtook him each time he was forced to inflict pain on another. Contrary to his title and reputation, he never took much pleasure in his divine power or the strength that came with it in his seasoned age.

Loosening the cravat knot at the base of his throat, he made his way around the overgrown hemlock to his favorite bench.

Only, it was not empty.

Cassian skid to a stop, admiring the back of Finnian's inky-black strands tied behind his relaxed shoulders.

The heaviness in Cassian's chest gave way to the sight of him.

He'd dreamed about this moment. To have Finnian sitting in the grove he had crafted for him. To spend mornings sitting on that same bench and watch Finnian foraging the herbs for whichever potion or spell he was currently working on.

Cassian walked lightly, his limbs feeling weightless as he drew closer.

"Finny," he said as a greeting. A gentle way to announce his presence, knowing since he approached from the right that Finnian's hearing aid may not pick up on his footfalls right away. "You are here."

Finnian angled his head sideways to regard him. "I am," he said, smiling warmly. "Though I think your attendant is paranoid that I am going to steal the souls. He has checked up on me every ten minutes."

Cassian chuckled and claimed the seat beside him. "I have no doubt that he recited a lengthy set of rules to you."

"The Ruler of Death's job is endless, it seems." He swiped his thumb over the blood smudge on Cassian's cheek. Magic prickled in his pores.

"I guess my handkerchief didn't suffice."

Finnian wiped another spot along his brow and surveyed his face for any missed spots. "I know how you loathe the feeling of blood on you."

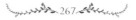

Cassian's heart warmed, and he gave Finnian's hand a light squeeze. "I appreciate the gesture."

It had been over five thousand years since the day he and his siblings were murdered, and how he'd been forced to lay and bleed every last drop of mortal blood from his body in the Serpentine Forest. Memories weathered and stripped from the time that had passed by.

Though, no matter the years, a speck of blood on his skin still made his pulse jump and his vision tunnel.

"What is this place?" Finnian lounged back on the bench and peered through the garden. "Mavros was vague when I asked."

Cassian stretched out his leg and rested it against Finnian's. "It is called Finnian's Grove."

Finnian turned his head to look at him, eyebrows raised, eyes widened slightly.

"I do enjoy evoking new expressions on your face." He grinned, reaching up and playfully pinching at Finnian's cheek.

"*My* grove?" He straightened on the bench and peered out at the blossoms, the hawthorn trees budded with berries, the calm current of the stream.

Cassian joined his hands together in his lap. "Yes, it has all the magical herbs and plants a mage could desire. It was after I left you at the cemetery. Five years went by and each day was insufferable. To cope with the ache, I would come sit here in my free time and daydream about what to fill the empty space with. All the ingredients you needed for your witchcraft, a place to wander when you desired to clear your head."

Finnian grew quiet, his eyes drifting in thought. "To waste the day away in bed together," he murmured. "Spend my days foraging and crafting potions, uninterrupted. Never burdened by the stretches of time we are forced to endure now without seeing one another." He turned to Cassian with a sad slant to his lips. "Sounds like a dream."

A long strand of hair escaped his tie and fluttered in the breeze. Cassian reached up and pushed it behind his shoulder. "Anything you want, Finny, and I will make sure it's yours."

"And if I said I want forever?" he asked with a sense of deliberation, searching Cassian's gaze.

It was a loaded question.

A somberness hardened Cassian's expression.

Thinking too far into their future twisted his gut. Ruelle had cast a toxic shadow of her presence everywhere in their relationship. Through each moment of tenderness and happiness, Cassian had to wonder when such joy would be taken away from him.

He had not spoken to Finnian of Ruelle in years, and Finnian had not brought her up once. It was a topic neither wished to face the reality of.

Although Finnian did not know the details, he was smart enough to assume Ruelle was a thorn in Cassian's side. She had become an item on their to-do list that they both willingly kept overlooking.

Then there was the secret that had its teeth in Cassian's throat, biting deeper each day.

How was he supposed to tell Finnian of his plan to curse Naia? Not once, but twice? Chain her to Kaimana and then take her child. Finnian loved his sister dearly and would put her happiness over his own. And if Cassian had to choose between the two, he would *always* choose Finnian.

No matter how grim the road would be, Cassian would possess the Himura demigod blood and inject Ruelle's heart with it.

His jaws pulsed, and he lowered his hand to his lap. His stomach soured with the secret burning on his tongue. "I will do everything in my power to grant it to you."

A moment of silence passed between them.

"You once told me long ago how you were tired of life." Finnian's eyes pressed with intensity into his, touching the deepest parts of him. "Is that still the case?"

Cassian recalled the moment he referred to. In Augustus, on the bank of the stream, sitting next to him while he twirled a moonflower in between his fingers. It was the first time in a long while he'd felt a semblance of contentment.

He reached over and lightly squeezed Finnian's hand. "Life is never tiring when I am with you."

Finnian held his eyes for a moment longer, pleased by his answer, before he straightened and looked out past the entrance of the iron gates towards the rows of lemon trees.

"You really do enjoy the taste of lemon." A lightness fell back into his tone.

Cassian rested his arm along the back of the bench, enjoying the tickle of Finnian's strands. "It is nostalgic. Iliana used to squeeze the fruit and garnish the beverage with mint during hot summer days when Acacius and I were children."

"During your mortal days?"

"Yes. Our mother died shortly after Acacius was born, so Iliana filled that motherly role for us."

Finnian rotated his head and Cassian noted the subtle interest in his expression. "Do you ever see her? Your mother, I mean."

"She chose to move on to the Paradise of Rest. A place souls can reside peacefully and—"

"*Rest?*" Finnian teased.

Cassian rolled his eyes, amused. "I see her every once in a while, but only when she calls for me. I try to avoid disturbing those in their eternal peace."

"It is nice." Finnian stared out at nothing in particular, a frown pulling the corners of his mouth. "That you can see her whenever you desire."

Cassian sensed the anguish drowning him. He saw it in his eyes when he spoke of Vale. Each time he had told Cassian a story of his childhood with his father and Naia. His voice lowered almost into a whisper, and he always averted his gaze.

"If you wish to see him—"

"I don't wish to."

"But if you did, all you need to do is call out his name."

Finnian turned his head towards him with a touch of bemusement. "Simply call out his name?"

Cassian shifted in his seat, running his tongue over the back of his teeth. He rarely said the next part aloud. "Vale is in Moros, yes, but I do not confine him to his prison. He is wise and knows if he were to try to escape, he would not benefit from it. From time to time, when Acacius is not in the Land, he will visit Nathaira in her meadow, but he rarely does so. The Council believes he is wasting away in an illusion of eternal thirst."

"If I call for him in your Land, he will come to me?" Finnian asked, dubiously, brow knitted. "His name alone, or can I call him by *father*?"

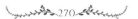

A small smile formed on Cassian's lips. He loved how thorough his Little Nightmare was. "Either. Vale would recognize one of his children by their breath alone."

Finnian nodded slowly in agreement, eyes gleaming and drifting away from Cassian. He leaned over and propped his elbows on his knees, running a hand over his face and gripping at his chin. "I suppose he would."

"Your father would love to see you—"

"Show me your Land." Finnian abruptly stood and looked down at Cassian. The trace of his frown, the moisture pricking at his eyes, the sadness pulling at his features, all of it was gone.

The belief that his father would be disappointed in him was a burden he would continue to carry. Cassian could tell him hundreds of times how Vale didn't feel that way at all, but those were words Finnian needed to hear directly from his father.

The fact was, he was there, showing interest in Cassian's Land, and that was more than enough. Death was something he vehemently disagreed with, and yet, he'd come, despite the discomfort it brought. Cassian would take the opportunity to show him around, hoping to change his perception of death—even if just by a little.

He let out a breath as rose to his feet and held out his hand for Finnian to grab onto. "How do you feel about pomegranates?"

"Let me guess." Finnian intertwined their fingers together. "It's called the *Pomegranate Orchard*?"

Cassian laughed, leading him to the hawthorn coppice. "Let us start there."

TWENTY-THREE

ACHES OF TIME

THE PAST
Finnian

 HERE IS SOMETHING he isn't telling me.

A guttural feeling flared in him each time he graced the subject of Ruelle.

They did not have the type of relationship where they kept things from each other. They spoke of their troubles, counseled one another, granted advice if need be. And when they disagreed, they always met each other with guards lowered.

Life with Cassian was coming home after a long, mind-numbing day to find him on the sofa, cravat untied and hanging around his neck, all his buttons undone, dozing off to the sweet silence Finnian's home provided. He'd peek one eye open and give a genuine smile as Finnian sauntered over to lie with him. They'd rest in the quiet of each other's company for a minute, and then talk throughout the night, sharing details of their days, until it transitioned to hours of kissing and hands pulling at each other's clothes. Some nights were sensual and slow, and others were sultry and starved.

It became a ritual. Whether they were in Finnian's home in Hollow City or Cassian's palace in the Land of the Dead, they had integrated into each other's lives. Something about that unsettled Finnian the more he turned over Ruelle and her need for revenge in his mind.

He laid in bed with Cassian stretched out beside him. The soft intakes of his breath indicated he'd finally drifted to sleep. Not that deities needed it, but Finnian had learned over the years that when he lulled Cassian into it, he would wake feeling refreshed after the temporary halt to his overworked brain.

The crackle of the fire from the hearth filled the dark room.

Finnian tucked his hand under his head and stared at the ceiling. The obsidian glinted against the glow, and the time they strolled down the countryside in Augustus played in the front of his thoughts.

Darkness only scares those afraid of the unknown.

It had been over a decade since he'd sat on the bank surrounded by moonflowers, listening to Cassian say those words.

He'd felt the walls of his chest heave then, just as they did now.

Darkness. The unknown. All of it petrified him to his core. To stumble in its jaws, unprepared and helpless.

The fireflies had always been something he envied. They had the power to carry the light with them everywhere they went.

He extended his arm upward and a trail of magic glistened like a stream dipped in the cosmos, swirling and grasping at the ceiling.

"Movere lucem."

The twinkling specks spread across it. A swarm of dazzling fireflies embedded in the crystal, the luminescence permanently fusing with the obsidian.

Finnian stared at them, his heart brimming as he reminisced—the cushioned seats of the theater hall, how engrossed he had been in the music when Everett quietly sat in the chair beside him, the scent of freshly plowed grass and petrichor as they strolled down the dirt path into the trees. All the efforts on Finnian's part to entice Everett. He was attractive and Finnian had full intentions of seducing him.

The hand on his throat and the appearance of Cassian looking back at him had genuinely taken him off guard. The shock had frozen through him like a creek during winter.

Now, though, their past as enemies made him smile with nostalgia. He'd always enjoyed pressing Cassian's buttons and tousling his flawless composure, intrigued to see what lay beneath the surface. His darker side had always appealed to Finnian.

He quietly sat up and snuck out of the bed.

With a swivel of his wrist, his trousers appeared around his waist. He slipped into his linen shirt, not bothering to button it up, and headed towards the door.

He gave a final peek behind him to ensure Cassian's eyes were still shut before sliding out of the room.

DUSK filled the sky, spilling silhouettes across the Pomegranate Orchard. Slick, inky-black serpents slithered and coiled around the base of the trees. They hissed as Finnian strolled by.

Their jobs were to chase away the souls who did not have permission to enter. Only Cassian could grant a soul the right to eat from his fruit.

The serpents remained idle in Finnian's presence, and he grinned half-heartedly to himself. He felt like a king as they glided across his path out of his way, prideful of his place alongside Cassian.

Three years was the rush of a breath to a deity, and yet, Finnian caught himself hanging onto every second, committing each of his moments with Cassian to memory. Something he'd been too young and foolish to ever think of doing with Father or Naia, back when he was too self-righteous to believe that time did not yield to deities.

Finnian tucked his hands in his pockets, the gesture creating an odd sense of closeness to Cassian, as if he were there walking alongside him. Cassian retreated his hands into his pockets when he was anxious, or to combat the tension gripping in his shoulders. These little things about him had made themselves a home in Finnian's mind.

He knew if he asked Cassian to tell him about his past with Ruelle, he would oblige without hesitation. Yet, Finnian had avoided doing so, because a part of him didn't wish to know. He wished to remain suspended in the blissful existence of life with Cassian.

The twinge in his gut told him they were on borrowed time. He could sense the dark clouds of a storm swelling over their heads. A shortness of breath that felt perpetually caught in his lungs, like he could hyperventilate at a hair trigger's mercy.

He knew two things: something conspired between Ruelle and Cassian long ago, and Ruelle sought revenge on Cassian because of it.

She'd targeted Saoirse and meddled with the fates of those who directly impacted her and her title. Finnian knew little of the High Goddess, but evidently, Ruelle had hit Saoirse where it hurt.

Finnian thought of everything and everyone he loved. Ruelle could take it all away so easily, but it wouldn't be enough to push Finnian to break things off with Cassian. Nothing would. So then, what?

If I were the High Goddess of Fate, what would I do to hurt Cassian?

Something squished underneath Finnian's boot, pulling him from his thoughts.

He stopped and lifted his foot. Sticky globs of the rotted arils stuck to the sole of his shoe. The pomegranate was split and smashed into the soil, oozing bright red and gleaming underneath the arching sunrise that exploded over the jagged peaks of Moros in the distance. A scape of periwinkle, rosewood streaks smeared across what remained of the twilight sky.

Finnian crouched down and examined the shiny red skin and the blackened heart of the fruit.

A savage smile split his lips as he plucked one of the withered arils up and crushed it between his fingertips.

Ruelle could take everything from Finnian, but he would never let go of Cassian.

However, Cassian was more selfless than he was. Cassian was *good*. He did not have the heart to stand by and allow Finnian's life to crumble, all because of him.

Ruelle was well aware of this.

I would make him bleed.

TWENTY-FOUR

UNRAVEL

THE PAST
Cassian

S THE RULER of death, it was a peculiar thing to celebrate the life of another. A refreshing change of color in the monotonous landscape of his days.

He'd spent hours in a crowded waiting room with Finnian, pacing the lengths of its walls. Members of Finnian's organizations filled the space.

Eleanor, for once in her life, sat next to Cassian, quietly biting on her nails. It made him rather anxious and drove him to attempt conversation with her about the new cat she'd recently adopted or the foiled stitching along her trousers that she'd done herself. By hand, not with a spell—a fact that had caught Cassian by surprise. After five years in a city full of mages, he'd learned to assume they did everything with magic.

The wails of a newborn child reached past the door that everyone circled and paced around, freezing them in their tracks.

Cassian had never witnessed such a bewildered look on Finnian's face as when he held Isla's child for the first time. Breaking from his indifferent character, tears glistened in his eyes as he cradled the tiny mortal bundled in blankets.

It brought a smile to Cassian, seeing Finnian experience something new that evoked such emotion.

The smile lasted only a few seconds before dread sank into his stomach.

Their future crept in the back of his thoughts, obsessing over the fact that Finnian would one day have a nephew. A nephew Cassian planned on stealing to use for his own gain.

With the moment equivocally ruined, he bid his farewell to Finnian for the day and teleported back to the Land.

He strolled into his sitting room, straight for the bar cart, poured a glass of bourbon, tipped it back, and reveled in the burn numbing his esophagus.

A tumultuous energy pressed at his backside.

His shoulders stiffened, and he cut his eyes to the fluttering insect at his left.

Divine power pricked in his veins as he summoned a serpent to appear around his nape. It struck through the air, catching the death's-head hawk-moth in its mouth.

It appeared his day was only destined to grow worse.

A low rumble of laughter came from the furniture behind Cassian.

He steeled in a breath and spun to greet his brother. "Acacius."

The High God of Chaos and Ruin was lounged back on the sofa, propping his feet up on the accent table. His pale strands were tied back off his shoulders, and he wore a normal set of trousers and a fitted shirt. It was uncharacteristic of him to be in anything but his ominous robe and an animal carcass mask.

He tilted his head along the back of the cushion to look at Cassian. "And wherever are you coming home from?"

Cassian refilled his glass, swung it back, and gritted his teeth. "Remove your feet from my table."

Acacius ignored his demand. "Could it be the young god's city?"

It had been a decade since they'd had a conversation regarding Finnian in the graveyard, when Cassian had arrived to intervene with the triplets and Acacius had followed him. In those ten years, Cassian had not reached out to Acacius, and Acacius had kept his distance. There was a wedge between them, and it was Ruelle's doing.

"Why are you here?" Cassian turned his attention to the window, the sour taste in the back of his throat growing thicker. He washed it down with another drink.

Acacius teleported from the sofa, materializing in front of him. He smoothed out the lapels of Cassian's tailcoat. "I am here because I seem to have found myself between a rock and a hard place."

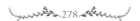

Cassian's heart stuttered as he analyzed his brother. There was a weight in him. A resignation in his eyes, a sag to his features one could easily mistake for exhaustion.

Acacius let out a dejected sigh and met Cassian's gaze. "I have avoided the quarrel between you and Ruelle for as long as time would allow, but it seems now that time has come to an end."

Cassian gripped his glass tighter. "And you choose her side."

Acacius frowned, crossing his arms. "Is that what you really expect of me?"

"You have always had a tendency to fall quickly and walk blindly until you spiral off a cliff."

His jaw set. "I assure you, I am not the one walking blindly here."

Cassian dismissed his stupidity with a lousy wave and moved around him. "Do what you wish with your unrequited love, Acacius."

"Ruelle truly loves me. Must I really attempt to convince you of our relationship?"

The brevity of his foolishness crawled all over Cassian. It was dosed with the guilt and resentment burdening him that had stolen away precious moments with Finnian. More and more each day, it was growing difficult to remain present.

Rage clipped in his vision, blotching the edges, and he whipped around. "If that is so, tell me why your darling Ruelle is so determined to torment me for something that took place between us thousands of years ago? If she were truly infatuated with you, Acacius, don't you believe she would've let go of her vendetta by now? Do not fool yourself into believing what she feels for you is real when you are nothing more to her than a puppet."

Acacius smiled, the cut across his face vicious. "And you truly believe that you mean anything more to Finnian? If his love was true, he wouldn't have hesitated to give up his necromancy, but that hasn't come to pass yet, has it? Because he never will. He will continue to steal your souls and you will stand by and allow it. You and I, we are no different, Brother."

Cassian crushed his drink in his fist. Fractures of glass pierced through his skin and flesh. He stormed forward and snatched Acacius by the collar of his shirt. Ebony whorls of divine power swelled around Cassian's backside, streaked with tendrils of golden lace, meeting the violent midnight storm of Acacius's power in a head-on collision. "You and I are *not* the same!"

"Are we not?" Acacius roared back. "You love Finnian, despite his faults and selfishness! As do I with Ruelle!"

"Why are you here?" Cassian snarled.

Acacius slumped in Cassian's hold, and the tension filling the space between them snuffed out. The ripples of their divine power disbanded into smoky ribbons drifting in the air, like cirrus clouds separating in a sky.

The longer Acacius went without replying, the more Cassian's pulse jumped in fear.

Cassian shook his brother. "What is it? Tell me!"

Acacius lifted his head, brow crumbling in a dreadfully devastating way that filled Cassian's stomach with nausea.

He held his brother's eyes, desperately trying to decipher the source of their angst. Though, deep down, he knew.

"I came here to warn you," Acacius said. "Ruelle is about to begin the process of unraveling yours and Finnian's threads of Fate."

The breath died in Cassian's lungs.

What did you expect?

Five years seemed too short in the grand scheme of their immortality. Not now. *Not yet.* He refused to believe it.

"No." He tightened his hold on Acacius's shirt.

"You cannot resist this."

Cassian shook his head. "Even if it comes to pass, whatever she throws at us, it will not make a difference. We will not let go of one another."

Acacius's eyes fell shut. "Brother, I know you. You will loathe yourself when mortals scorn Finnian for his necromancy and deities raid his city, when it is nothing but rubble and the lives of those he loves are underneath its ruin. When all he adores has been destroyed and there is nothing left but you. You will blame yourself, and, with time, he will come to loathe you. Just as Saoirse did. Walk away from him, so Ruelle does not have a way to meddle."

The reality split like steel through his chest.

His mind chased every which way, all the possibilities Ruelle could inflict, their outcomes, and how—*if*—he could prevent such tragedies.

Once again, Cassian was at a loss.

It was just as he'd been back then with Saoirse, with no choice but to watch as her love for him withered. He'd nearly lost all sense and cursed

Ruelle out of anger, unable to prove to the Council she'd meddled in the fates surrounding Saoirse's.

He forced his curled fingers to let go of Acacius's shirt and backed away. His wide eyes set on the large window behind Acacius, watching the dawn's rose-gold light slowly seep into the room.

Acacius was right. He couldn't do it—stand by and watch Ruelle take everything away from Finnian, at the cost of being with him.

A blaring white noise invaded his ears, and a rush of disorientation spun his head. He took a step back, and another. There was an unrelenting pain aching in his heart.

He'd been naïve with Saoirse, to believe his feelings for her had been love. Perhaps to some degree, but not like this—not attached to his soul. An extension of himself. A love rooted so deeply, the thought of losing it sent Cassian into a paralyzing panic.

He could imagine the tedious road stretching out before him—a path filled with loneliness and endless despair. How could he ever continue on without Finnian?

Acacius gripped him by the shoulders. "Brother. Look at me."

Cassian flinched at the sudden touch.

His eyes flitted onto Acacius, his tongue lead-soaked and his face prickling with numbness. "I cannot give Ruelle what she wants." He brought a shaky hand up into his hair, a scream clawing up his throat. "I cannot give her what she wants!"

"I know!" Acacius squeezed both of his shoulders. "She will give up on you in time. I promise. Once she releases her obsession to seek revenge, she will fall into my love. It will heal all her wounds, and you will be free to love him again. I will make sure of it."

Hopeful words of ignorance, unwilling to believe the truth. It was all a lie. Ruelle would never love him, just as she would never get over the belief that Cassian had taken her happiness away from her.

"You must give it time, Cassius."

His heartbeat slurred as he dropped his hand back down to his side. "What am I to do? I cannot let go of him."

"You have no other choice." Acacius gave his shoulder a final squeeze before retracting his hand. "I can buy you one more hour with him. Go say your goodbye."

HE thought of Finnian and the detrimental feeling he'd described when he watched a person succumb to their death. The separation of breath, of light in their eyes. The end. The goodbye. For whatever reason, he could not understand. What was the purpose of life when it led to death?

Cassian had listened to Finnian rant hundreds of times over the matter, and yet, he never quite knew the words to say to help him understand.

NIGHT had fallen in the Mortal Land when Cassian appeared outside of Finnian's home, frantic and trying to process everything Acacius had said. Too occupied to think clearly, he hadn't realized he'd shown up in his divine form—not as Everett. The thought followed him as he raced down the alleyway and through the backdoor of the townhouse, hoping no mortals had spotted him.

Finnian was hunched over his workbench when Cassian swung the door open. The gust rustled the flickering candlelight scattered around the room. The knob hit the brick, alarming Finnian to snap around.

"Wh—" His words fell short as he took in Cassian's frazzled demeanor. He quickly rose from his stool and crossed the room to get to him. "What's wrong?"

"I do not know where to begin." Cassian was surprised to hear the quaking in his voice. He ran an anxious hand through his hair, his breath quick and shallow. "I must tell you everything."

Finnian swiped his hand up and the door behind them shut. "Okay." He studied Cassian carefully, worry pulling at the corners of his eyes.

"A long time ago, Ruelle fell in love with a mortal." Cassian gripped his strands at the roots, attempting to steady the pace of his words against the invisible clock of his mind.

Why hadn't he told Finnian of his past with Ruelle sooner?

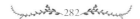

"His name was Klaus, and he was murdered by a group of bandits," he continued. "He was at the wrong place at the wrong time—a fate Ruelle could not change because she was merely a middle goddess."

Finnian listened quietly, his expression unreadable. It sparked a jolt of uneasiness through Cassian's already knotting insides.

"She came to me and begged that I bring Klaus back to life, but I refused. To do such a thing would be a steep price that I would have to pay for allowing the laws of the Universe to bend." Cassian shook his head, rubbing his hand down his face. He dug his grip into the sides of his cheeks, peering down at the floor as he relived the ancient memory.

"That day she told me: *Heed my warning. Whoever yearns in your soul will be just in reach, but never able to fully grasp. One day, when you know the kiss of love, all you will have left is regret.*"

He'd stood over her back then, watching her tear-stained face twist in rage. Once she finished her threat, he told her to leave his Land. She would not be getting through his gates. Looking back, he expressed such an apathetic disposition towards her grief, but he sensed that if he had given her an inch, she would've clung to it with false hope.

Tension pulled at Finnian's features. "Did Klaus not choose to re-incarnate?"

Cassian let his hand fall back down to his side. "He chose to enter the Paradise of Rest."

He reached for Finnian, desperate to hang onto him, as if that alone was enough to turn their threads of Fate into granite. "Acacius came to warn me." A lump swelled in his throat. "Ruelle is going to begin unraveling the threads of our Fate. She will go after your city, after everyone within it, anything she can do to separate us from one another. And she will not stop until your thread no longer desires to reach out for mine."

Finnian's face paled. He shifted his body, pulling his hand away from Cassian as he looked down, eyes flitting around the floor. The tendons in his neck went rigid, and his pulse flickered visibly underneath the skin of his throat.

"Finny," Cassian said. "Talk to me."

"You should have told me the situation's entirety long ago." Finnian's voice rose as he snapped around to Cassian, his expression hard.

"I know." Cassian's voice cracked. He grabbed Finnian's hand again.

"Weaving mortals' fates for her own gain must go against the Council." Finnian seemed lost in thought as he spoke.

Cassian shook his head. "I do not have proof, and my word against hers would only create division among the Council. Ruelle is meticulous and others do not know the side of her that I do."

His demeanor shifted sharply, withering the shock in his gaze and setting it ablaze. "I told you once before. She can do her worst, but it will not make a difference."

"You do not understand what she will bring upon you. Do you honestly think I can stand back and allow your life to fall apart because of me?"

Finnian studied Cassian for a beat before letting out a clipped breath. "What is your plan, then? I assume you accounted for a worst-case scenario, and I know you. You wouldn't have let time go on without crafting up something."

Cassian frowned and looked down at Finnian's hand in his own. "It is something you would not approve of."

"Tell me anyway."

MINUTES had passed since Cassian had told him everything—how he intended to curse Naia, take her child, and kill Ruelle with its blood—and not a word had left him. Afterwards, he'd grimaced, turned away, and stalked over to his workbench, palms on its surface, shoulders taut, staring down at the clutter.

Cassian took a step towards him. "Finny, it was the only way I knew to—"

"If our threads of Fate are to be unbound…" His voice was set, trembling with chilled fury. "I will be the one to do it. Not Ruelle. It will be done *our* way."

Needle-like pinpricks spread throughout Cassian's chest. It was the opposite of what he wanted to hear. He needed Finnian to be stubborn and refuse to let things end this way. He needed Finnian to tell him there was another way to beat her. To hell with Ruelle and Fate.

"What are you saying?" It took everything in Cassian to keep his voice above a whisper. Finnian's impairment was always in the back of his mind that way.

Finnian faced him, pain cracking over his stone-set expression. "I am saying in the next century, you will carry through with your plan. You will curse Naia twice. I will remain here and set my sights on the Himura clan and draw Ronin to Hollow City. I will antagonize him. Make him hate me. In return, he will grow into a strong mage and attempt to overpower my rule in the city. When the time comes for Naia to hand over her child to you, she will offer herself in exchange and break her own curse. I know my sister. I will steal some of my nephew's blood then and trade places with her. Hollow City will belong to her. Ronin will already have a place here. Their child will grow up safe. I will ensure it."

The note of dread in his words accelerated Cassian's heart. "And what of *us* during the next century and a half?"

Finnian went to the bookshelf at the back wall and waved his hand in the air. The structure of the books in the center melted away and a metal vault attached to the brick appeared.

He twisted open the handle and pulled out a vial filled with glittering cherry liquid. "I made this potion from one of the pomegranates in your orchard."

The hysterical beat of Cassian's blood surged up his neck and his head went light. "You assumed this would happen?"

"I asked myself: what would be the worst Ruelle could do to someone like you? We've been with each other for five years, and in that span, she hasn't done a thing. If I were her, I would want you to grow attached just to rip it all away." He paused, eyes locked with Cassian's. "She will not touch our threads of Fate, because we will let go of each other before she can."

And if one of them did not care for the other, their threads would unravel on their own. Leaving Ruelle powerless to interfere.

"No," Cassian said with brutal finality, eyeing the potion in his grasp. Despite the twinge in his gut that agreed it was the right thing to do. "Absolutely not."

Finnian glared at him. "I refuse to let her touch our threads, have that power over us. If we cannot beat her until Naia's child is born, we have no other choice."

"*No*," Cassian said again, this time harder. "Whatever the potion does—*no*. We'll find another way."

He knew what it would do, how precious one's memories were of those they cherished. He'd witnessed it time and time again. Souls pleading and

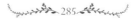

crying for permission to eat from the fruit. Their memories of loved ones too heavy on their souls. Wandering in the Grove of Mourning was a process that would eventually soak up the pain, but forgetting was easier than sitting in the hollow shell of time, at its mercy, while waiting for the throes of love to separate from the memories of those they left behind.

Finnian started towards him. "It removes my memories of us. If I do not care for you, Ruelle loses all leverage, and you have time to execute your plan."

Crippling dread shook in his legs. "No."

He hated the thought of Finnian scouring his orchard late in the night, wracking his mind on ways to fight back in a battle that was never his to begin with. Remorse flooded Cassian for never telling Finnian the truth.

"When I trade places with Naia, you will have the blood of a Himura demigod, and you can use it to kill Ruelle. The pomegranate is directly linked to you and your divine power. When the time comes for me to regain my memories, you must make me drink from your blood."

"*No!*" Cassian shouted, bothered by how calmly Finnian spoke, how quickly his plan was forming. It was becoming too real, too overwhelming for Cassian to process.

Finnian reached out and cupped his cheek. A weak smile slid over his mouth as he pulled Cassian in, fusing their foreheads together. "We must do this, Cassius."

Cassian squeezed his eyes shut, inhaling a deep breath to steady himself. "You are much stronger than I am. Let me drink it."

"You know that will not work. The orchard sprouted from your divine power." Finnian's fingertips hooked along his jawbone and buried their noses against each other's cheeks. "You promised me forever."

His vision blurred to the moisture collecting in his eyes. He ground his teeth, his hands enveloping the sides of Finnian's neck. "And if your memories fail to return?"

"Then you must find a way to help me remember us."

Cassian's chest caved in. "*Finnian.*" His voice crumbled.

Finnian held onto him tighter. "Once I drink this, every memory I have of us will be altered. There will be no warmth, no hesitation for you. You will be the High God who has attempted to curse me relentlessly, and I will feel nothing for you but hatred."

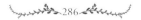

Cassian pulled away, tears soaking down his cheeks, shaking his head. "I—I cannot do this." He bent over and hung his head, hands coming up to squeeze his nape.

Finnian disappeared and reappeared with another vial. "I will embed my desires in the potion through a spell, so everything goes according to plan, but just in case, here. This is a binding potion."

He shoved it in the front pocket of Cassian's trousers.

"*If* something goes wrong, by chance, and I don't regain my memories, you must force me to take it. It will keep me bound to you. I know myself. I will find a way to break out of Moros and go after my father to free him and escape. You cannot allow me to do something the Council will demand my punishment on."

Such punishment that would be catastrophic and forced by the Council's hand that Cassian would not be able to sway.

His body shook, and he squeezed his nape harder. "I do not wish to do this, Finnian! You will go on without a remembrance of me, while I" — he slapped a hand over his chest — "will be forced to carry on my days with our memories without you. *I will not make it…*" A sob scraped up his throat.

Finnian threw his arms around Cassian's neck, and their chests collided.

Cassian clung to him with broken wishes and no gods to pray to, crying into his partner's skin.

They could beat Fate. Their love was strong enough to hold on. They didn't need to do this. A century apart felt like a life sentence. Cassian couldn't do it—stand from afar and watch Finnian live a life he wasn't a part of, to face him and receive nothing but contempt.

"You *can* do this," Finnian whispered, caressing the back of his head. "I promise you, *when* we come out of this, our Fate will be *ours*. Untouched."

"I am not strong enough to face you when you despise me. Even if it is only temporary."

"You have before."

"Not after knowing what it is like to love you."

Finnian pulled back and dipped his chin, connecting their lips.

He tasted of licorice and salt, of coffee and early mornings with the sun dawning the city buildings. Notes of burning sage wafted from his hair. The remnants of crushed hyacinths lingered on the pads of his fingers. Cassian

held onto it all. The soft, plush touch of his lips, and how Finnian kissed him fiercely, with passion.

One day.

He held the sides of Finnian's face, crushing their lips together—prolonging the inevitable.

Something coiled underneath his arms. His heartbeat flickered in his throat as he looked down at the vines constricting around his arms and legs. It forced them apart and anchored Cassian backwards.

"No, not yet!" His pulse felt as if it had stopped. Tendrils of his divine power snaked out and cut away at the vines.

They grew back tenfold, sprouting thorns and protruding Cassian's skin. He could feel the venom injected into his bloodstream as the muscles in his limbs went slack.

"You must leave." Finnian popped the cork from the potion. "I cannot see you here."

Cassian refused to give in. He fought against the vines. His hair slung in his eyes, sticking to his damp cheeks.

Crimson, glittering smoke rose from Finnian's feet and slowly drifted up, encasing around Cassian. He could feel the charge of power, the blood-red abyss climbing over him and preparing to cast him into another scene. Panic lit his chest and dropped into his stomach.

His teeth gnashed as he pried an arm free from the strangling vines around him. "No, Finny! Wait—"

"I loathe you," Finnian gave him a final smile, his eyes pooling with tears.

"Finnian!" Cassian bellowed.

He lifted the vial to his lips and threw back his head.

The world heaved and swallowed Cassian into darkness.

And I long for you.

THE words came to Cassian then. If he had one more chance to explain it to Finnian, he would.

Death was love, and love was death again.

TEARS OF A HIGH GOD

ASSIAN STOOD OUTSIDE the city limits, face-to-face with its familiar outskirts, his presence concealed in a black cloak. Woodland creatures scurried across the ground cover. Crickets and cicadas sang. The sounds had once brought him peace, but they now scraped at his ears.

He pulled at his hood as he peered through the night, as far through the thicket of trees as he could see. Just beyond it, out of reach.

It has been only two days since he'd departed from Finnian, and the stones in his chest had crumbled into a numbness. Like a disease, it spread down his limbs, taking everything in him to raise his arm and reach forward.

He extended his forefinger and the invisible barrier encasing the city flared, a solid, glass-like, glowing blue wall. Rippling rings bounced across it from his touch.

It felt like acid had coated the back of his throat as he curled his fingers into a fist. Discomfort knotted in his stomach, and his breath went light. The reality of what they'd done crashed down on him and he backed away on shaking legs.

He was not welcome.

THE absence of Finnian haunted his thoughts. What was he doing? Was he okay? Now that he loathed Cassian, would he find another lover?

He could not shake loose the image of Finnian laying with another.

Finnian hated him now. He had no reason to wait.

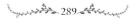

The ache in Cassian's chest was like a scalpel, wedged deep beneath the skin.

Trembling from the thought, he sought solitude in the Serpentine Forest. Dropping in the mangled depths of its belly, he threw his arms over his head and cried out. The furious, gut-wrenching roar shook the cypress trees. The Achlys dispersed like field mice. He collapsed to his knees and wailed until he could no longer.

The Land fell to silence in mourning.

A century and a half.

A century and a half he would have to walk with this pain.

THE news of Naia's escape came to him through Mavros.

"My lord," he said, his brow pinched with concern, as it had been several weeks since Cassian had fallen back into the Land after Finnian had sent him away. "It won't be long now."

His words brought no reprieve to the strangling ball caught inside Cassian's lungs.

As if Mavros could sense this, he added, "The sooner your plan begins, the sooner you will be reunited with the young god."

It was a flicker of hope lit in the strangling abyss, one Cassian fixated all his energy into keeping alight.

However, weeks and months spanned in the Mortal Land without Naia being found.

"Perhaps she is being cloaked by the young god," Nathaira suggested.

Cassian paced the space of the bridge overlooking the River of Souls, jaws pulsing. "Impossible. When I looked through the Fate of the obsessively reincarnating soul, he was murdered by Marina on Nohealani Island, in an inn. If they can't locate her, it means she is being cloaked by the island's protector—her father."

Nathaira rested back on the railing of the bridge, her calm demeanor only further irritating Cassian's nerves. "You know that you cannot interfere in this, no matter how much you wish for your plan to speed ahead. If that is the soul's Fate, we must be patient."

Cassian spun around and glared across the distance of his Land, a fire bristling in his blood as he set his sights on the jagged mountaintops behind the Serpentine Forest.

"Tell Mavros to clear my schedule for the hour." His demand came out in a harsh tone. "I have an old friend I must pay a visit to."

Nathaira lifted off the railing and appeared at his side. "Lord Cassian, I plead you to come down from your anger before you go see him."

She'd always had a soft spot for Vale. He was her High God, and she glorified him. From the day he was escorted into the Land, she'd taken it upon herself to keep him company. Cassian had found Nathaira on numerous occasions outside of her cottage alongside Vale, who taught her the ways of nature. It was how her meadow came to be.

Cassian cut his eyes onto her, a warning. "Save your wisdom for another time, Nathaira." He placed his fist inside his pocket. "Nothing will keep me from seeing mine and Finnian's plan through. Not even my dearest friend. He's concealing her on his island, and until Naia is found, I cannot move forward. For all we know, my interference is all the soul's Fate has been waiting on."

He heard the words leaving his mouth, the threat and severity in his tone. As if he would burst into Vale's confinement, resorting to violence first before a conversation. He couldn't blame Nathaira for her assumptions. Lately, he'd been anything but his usual level-headed self.

Nathaira's stare burned the side of his cheek, her tranquil features rigid with disapproval. "Listen to yourself. Vale is protecting his daughter. All I am saying is do not leave here furious and say or do something to your *oldest friend* that you will later regret."

Cassian pressed his tongue against the roof of his mouth.

There was a voice of reason that existed within him who'd heard her, agreed with her, even. But that voice of reason dwindled more and more as the days passed, forced to walk alone on the road he and Finnian had carved together.

Nathaira frowned and placed a hand on the top of Cassian's shoulder. "I know you are hurting, Cassian, but do not let Ruelle turn you into her—obsessed with vengeance and hurting others to get it."

The mention of Ruelle's name filled his mouth with a bitter taste.

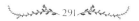

"I appreciate the effort, Nathaira, but I will do whatever I must to ensure Vale reveals Naia's presence on his island." He gently lifted her hand from his shoulder and took a step. "And when this is all said and done, Ruelle will be nothing but bone caught between my teeth."

CASSIAN held onto the flickers of light shining across his ceiling.

One day, he told himself.

The muscles in his chest spasmed with grief as he lay in bed, its other side an empty satin pit.

Finnian was in the gleam of the fireflies painting his ceiling; the lingering earthy scent and floral fragrance were still embedded in the pillow; the bundle of dried lavender hung above the headboard.

One day, Cassian recited over and over in his mind. *We will have our one day.*

It did nothing to relieve the ache clawing apart his entrails.

He left the bed and did not return to it, as the comfort, the sleep, did not come as easily to him anymore.

CASSIAN waited on the dais of his throne, his hands confined to his pockets, too on edge to sit. It took a grave amount of effort to remain still on his feet.

Mavros stood at his side, hands joined in front of him, in a somber quiet.

Four Errai emerged alongside the soul, a wall cloud of bodies draped in slate robes and pale-plated masks.

Cassian's heart pounded, the beat of blood thick in his ears.

The familiar soul stopped before Cassian, the flare of its energy dripping crimson. It pulsed like a heart, harboring lifetimes of pain and sorrow and resilience.

"Let me go back," they said.

"Not yet." Cassian's eyes jumped to the deity on the right. "Take them to the Lavender Fields of Healing."

"I must go back to her," the soul protested.

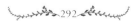

The feeling of splinters lodged in Cassian's heart. He resonated with those words, but his empathy could not sway his decision. "You will. *Soon.* One day."

The soul's energy festered, an intense flare of vivid red. "I must—"

A heavy shadow of divine power rose from behind Cassian, clawing over his shoulders and around his head—a terrifying, umbral backdrop. "You will obey me, as I am your master in the afterlife. You are to rest, heal. When the time comes, I will allow you to return." He flashed his eyes onto the deity to the right again. "Now, take them away."

Before the soul could dispute, they disappeared amongst a tailspin of swirling blackness.

Cassian pinched the bridge of his nose, his lungs constricting his breath.

Mavros cleared his throat. "My lord, I—"

"High God of Death and Curses."

Cassian's pulse jarred. He held up a hand to silence Mavros.

"I summon you."

Spurts of adrenaline pumped through his system at the sound of Mira's summoning.

Finally.

That flicker of hope within him burned brighter.

"Continue your thought when I return." He straightened his shoulders and inhaled. Turning to regard his attendant, he said, "I have a little goddess to curse."

And without a second to waste, he vanished.

CASSIAN opened his kitchen cabinet, the lemon juice on his fingertips leaving sticky prints along the wood. He clenched his jaw at the mess as he reached inside for a glass.

A percolator stared back at him.

Memories flooded in: mornings in Finnian's townhome, the crackling of the fire in the stove, the boiling of the water, the bitter aroma of the coffee filling the kitchen, Cassian resting against the edge of the counter, an arm slunk around Finnian's waist, tucking strands behind his ear.

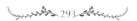

An ache thrummed in Cassian's hands, echoing up his arms and into his heart.

The muscles in his chest pulled taut, and he slammed the cabinet door shut.

CASSIAN slumped against the bench in Finnian's Grove.

The sunrise spilled over the mountaintops of Moros. Its rays dripped across the tops of the wisteria and the hawthorn, bleeding over the scene in streaks of terra cotta mauve.

He stared vacantly at the patch of white trumpet blossoms.

They are my favorite.

His pulse slowed to the memory. The trickle of the stream, the beam of fireflies, the familiar energy of Finnian's presence at his side.

They flourish in darkness and I find something poetic about that.

He recalled the twirling moonflower between his long fingers, and how his eyes filled with meaning as he'd said it.

Cassian longed to hear him say it again.

One day.

"*LORD Cassian, High God of Death and Curses.*" The words left Naia's mouth in a clumsy, nervous jumble. "*Come to me.*"

Cassian fastened the button at the center of his suit jacket, unsure of what would be left of him when *one day* arrived.

He materialized in a shadow-lit library, the scent of aged books and seaweed-infused air triggering memories of Finnian. The century-old, stained pages of his grimoire, and how he secretly enjoyed snacking on dried seaweed because it reminded him of home.

Cassian rested his back against one of the shelves, arms crossed.

"I appreciate your time, Lord Cassian." Naia stood across the room in a blue velvet gown, keeping a safe distance from him.

He could sense her hesitation in her unnerved demeanor. She'd always been that way, timid and too afraid for her own good. The stark opposite of Finnian.

Cassian stared out the window and up at the moon, distorted from the wavelengths of the sea. "Aren't you supposed to be preparing for your wedding, Little Goddess?"

"That is why I have summoned you."

He'd been waiting years to hear Naia say these words, expecting that flame of hope to double its size when the time came. But that wasn't the case.

All he had left within him was a bleak, hollow space filled with a singular desire.

Cassian wanted to call Finnian and tell him their plan was on track. He wanted to hear about Finnian's side and how things were going—preferably draped in sheets and hidden away from the world. Finnian could tell him about the black market and all its success; how he'd pretended to be after Himura blood for a make-believe revenge scheme against Malik for killing Arran; the plots he had in store to right his wrongs. Cassian wanted to hold him, tell him how much he wished he could've been there to comfort him after Eleanor and Isla's deaths, that they were in his Land and had found peace.

They had over a century of time to catch up on. Cassian just needed to hang on. They were almost at the end.

Then, finally, the weariness **in his soul** could drain away.

CRIMSON rained down all around him. The ground beneath his feet shuddered. He swerved the shards of ice and jagged briars of blood, the child secure in his arms. Trapped on the godsforsaken island.

"This is pointless, Little Goddess," he hummed. "Look around you. Do you see what is happening?"

Naia, a beautiful mess of silver damp locks and fierce emerald eyes, lunged for him.

The heel of his palm lodged into her collarbone and she tumbled back.

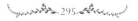

Cassian's breath hitched as the syringe fumbled from her grasp. A force of life blew through him and he rushed forward. If he could get his hands on it, they would be one step ahead in their plan—

A set of fingers wrapped around the syringe. Fingers he could recognize mixed in with a hundred others—honey-tanned, long and lithe, soft and tender, decorated in titanium rings.

Finnian swirled the syringe triumphantly with a vicious smile. "Too slow, Cassie."

A lump swelled in Cassian's throat. The nickname was atrocious and used purely out of spite, but he didn't care. It was probably an amusing detail Finnian had intentionally added when crafting the potion to alter his memories.

Over a hundred years had passed since he'd stood before Finnian. He looked the same, and yet so painstakingly different. His shoulders had filled out beneath his dress vest. The tie stuffed under the collar was crooked. His strands curled at the ends in reaction to the rain.

He fixed a superior look at Cassian, eyebrows piqued and paired with a smug smirk.

Cassian clenched his teeth to keep from grinning. Gods, he missed him.

It is almost done.

"Finny, no!" Naia yelled.

Keep going.

Cassian growled and dove for him.

A cloud of ruby swirled around Cassian's fist.

His soul let out a long breath and smiled.

"I HAVE come to you with a proposition." Finnian stood angelically in front of the Land's gates, looking right through Cassian. "As my sister has already broken her curse by handing over her freedom, I am here to exchange my freedom for hers."

Cassian didn't allow himself to dwell in the resentful way Finnian regarded him. The plunging of what felt like daggers through rosewood. Instead, he focused on the forward momentum of their plan.

He is here; we are almost finished.

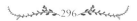

Cassian cocked his head like an intrigued predator, playing the part. He pulled a hand from his pocket and swiped a finger over his bottom lip. "You have my attention."

CASSIAN strolled down one of the many dark corridors on the lower levels of Moros. The hollowness that had taken root in his heart filled with each step.

I promise you, when we survive this, our Fate will be ours alone.

Cassian entered the room. The two executioners gave a bow as he passed through.

He joined at Shivani's side as she stared down at Finnian, body slack and arms suspended up by the chains mounted in the ceiling. His head hung, chin buried in his chest. Blood and soot smudged his cheeks.

The Chains of Confinement blocked the majority of a deity's divine power, leaving enough for them to regenerate at a tedious speed. Though, not enough to feed power perpetually into holding up a glamor.

Without it, Finnian's coffee-stained strands were waves rolling over his shoulders, down his back, and exposing the puffy-white skin on the base of his jaw, angry patches that marked his lobe and the conch of his ear.

It felt as if Cassian had swallowed Shivani's blades and they'd gotten stuck in his heart. The pain nearly stole the breath from his lungs seeing Finnian this way—battered and broken because of him.

I will beg for forgiveness when he wakes. However long it takes.

Shivani handed him a small plastic bag. Inside of it was Finnian's necklaces and rings.

Cassian placed them safely in the inside pocket of his suit jacket, alongside where he'd stored Finnian's hearing aid.

Arms crossed, Shivani glanced over at Cassian. "He's out cold."

"I put him under an illusion." Cassian began rolling his sleeve up to his elbow. "May I use one of your knives?"

She reached into one of the pockets of her cargo pants and pulled out a switchblade. It danced around her fingers as she handed it to Cassian.

Cassian crouched in front of Finnian, took him in one more time, and tucked a frizzed piece of hair behind his ear.

Come back to me.

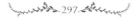

Cassian made a clean cut across his own wrist and held the scarlet, oozing incision to Finnian's lips.

He tipped Finnian's head back to ensure every drop made it down his throat.

The cut on Cassian's wrist stitched up. His jaws set as he stood and retracted his divine power that was currently holding his lover under an illusion. It had to work.

Cassian's heart sped up as he waited.

It will work. Finnian said it would.

Finnian's eyes snapped open and the muscles in his arms tensed, jarring the chains keeping him in place.

Teeth bared and stained red, he ripped his head up, eyes burning with a wrath that should've dissipated by now. "Is this part of my torture? Throw me in illusions until I go mad?"

Cassian took a step back, the sting of Finnian's glare traveling like bile over his skin. He tightly gripped the handle of the blade in his palm.

No.

With a snide twitch of Finnian's lips, he huffed out a laugh. "Feed me whatever fucking illusion you wish, but Ash's blood will never be yours—"

Cassian jerked his hand up and recast the illusion.

Finnian's body went slack again.

A sense of vertigo tilted Cassian's world.

He blinked once, twice down at the god in front of him.

Spots invaded his vision.

His whole body went weak, a feeling of bones collapsing and skin sinking.

Cassian felt the cool grip of Shivani's hands around his forearm. "My lord," she said, but her voice sounded muffled, traveling through layers to get to him.

He pulled at the tie around his neck. "He—he doesn't—"

"My lord." One of Shivani's hands pressed against the middle of his back. "It will be okay. We will find a way to make him remember."

"No." He slit his wrist again.

"Come on."

And again.

His teeth chattered, letting the wound drain into Finnian's mouth.

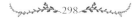

Only to retract his illusion and for Finnian to react in the same venomous way.

"You will not break me."

Cold, spiteful, and regarding Cassian with an unfiltered disdain.

It will never end.

Cassian rubbed at his chest.

This is my hell.

His heart palpitated, the chambers and muscles of the organ constricting in sorrowful beats.

He knew it. Their plan was shit. Everything he'd endured up to this moment had been for nothing. Forget Ruelle and his desire to kill her. What good would her death be if he didn't have a life with Finnian to look forward to afterwards?

Cassian fell to his knees. The blade in his grasp clanked against the floor. His hands trembled as he lifted them to Finnian's sleeping face. Tears stung his eyes.

"I need you." His lips quivered. "Please. I can't go on without you any longer."

Cassian bound their foreheads, praying to whatever god that would listen. "Come back to me."

TWENTY-SIX

DROWNING

ASSIAN TOPPED HIS glass off with bourbon. The muscles in his arms flexed before he downed it in a single gulp. The fiery liquid enhanced the emotion thrumming throughout his system.

He will never remember me.

We will never get back what we had.

Why did I agree to do it?

I should have never let him drink the potion.

We could've figured out another way.

He would be forever forced to meet the look of resentment on Finnian's face. All because of their altered memories in Finnian's mind that Cassian knew nothing of.

He would've painted me as a monster.

No hesitation, he'd said.

Cassian's chest caved. He inhaled, but it felt impossible to fill his lungs.

His grip tightened around the glass, and he squeezed, shattering the drinkware. Broken shards sliced the skin of his palm, the insides of his fingers.

It was supposed to end. Finnian's memories were supposed to return. Cassian hadn't thought about what he would do if they failed to come back. The thought had been too devastating to consider.

How could I be so naïve?

Because it would have drowned you.

He shouted and grabbed the bottle of bourbon and sent it flying across the room. It crashed into the wall. Liquor and broken glass made an amber mess on the floor.

He grabbed another bottle and slung it as well. And another, screaming, spit flying out of his mouth. Memories of the past burned behind his eyes—flickers of Finnian's smile, the dimples in his cheeks, the tender recognition in his gaze as it fell onto Cassian.

His fists came down on the bar cart, breath heavy, pieces of hair falling into his eyes.

"I must say, it pleases me to see you so distraught."

Cassian's spine stiffened at the alluring melody of her voice.

Through his ardor, he felt the distinct plush of her divine energy seeping into the room.

He pushed a hand through his hair, taking a moment to relax the corded muscles bulging in his neck before spinning around. "What do you want?"

Ruelle sat with one leg crossed over the other, the slit of her rose-lace dress riding up her thigh and over her hip. She was settled back in the chair with her elbow propped on the arm, gripping her chin. "I hear you have taken the young god into custody."

Cassian glowered at her, longing to choke the life out of her sparkling gemstone gaze.

When he did not reply, she continued. "It appears he is in possession of the Himura demigod's blood."

Cassian had watched her carefully over the past century and a half. With Finnian's memories altered and with him despising Cassian, their threads had been separated by their own volition. She could not meddle if there was nothing to meddle in. However, it seemed now that Finnian was back in Cassian's realm, she was suspicious.

He obsessively turned over the fact in his mind as he stared at her.

His mouth went dry, and he swallowed, casually placing his hands inside his pockets. "It is a dangerous item for someone like him to possess."

Ruelle tilted her head in a sanctimonious manner. "What is your plan once you have located it?"

"That will be something for the Council to decide as a whole."

They were already nervous. Naia's new title as a High Goddess of Eternity was one thing. The power to turn mortals into immortal beings was another. It would cause an uproar of prayers among the Mortal Land. Her power would only grow. And then there was the matter that she'd blessed eternal life to Ronin, a Himura witch, and then together, they had a demigod child whose blood could kill a deity. Gods were already conspiring against her. If she were to make Ash immortal, Cassian was sure there would be another deity war.

Ruelle gave a breathy laugh. "You have never been one to tell a lie and do it well, Cassian."

"You can see the Fate of the child," he said. "Why are you here pretending to play the fool?"

"You've thought it out. I am not like you or your siblings. I do not have a realm to uphold, and much like you and your deities of Death, I work with my own lineage as a collective. One of them could easily take my place."

"Do you have a point in sight?" Cassian gritted out with forced restraint.

"You want me dead." She stared at him for a moment, silently challenging him to tell another lie. "Isn't that so?"

Despite the palpitating of his heart, Cassian's expression remained cavalier. "Desiring your death should not come as a surprise, Ruelle. Truly, after how long you have tormented me."

He'd known it was only a matter of time until she figured out their plan once Finnian came back to him. Ruelle was many things, but she was no fool.

Ruelle raised off the chair and strutted towards him, her auburn strands gleaming like silk waves down her shoulders. "Did you not think I found it odd when yours and Finnian's threads miraculously untethered?" She rounded behind him. "There is only one way this plays out, Cassian."

His pulse throbbed in his skull.

He tightened his hands into fists inside of his pockets, reining in the monster within him that urged to devour her. "Do tell."

Her small hands smoothed up his back and onto the tops of his shoulders. "Rest assured, while I cannot weave the threads of a deity, I have other ways of making one suffer. Why do you think I have involved Acacius in my scheme?" She lifted on her toes, her breath scratching Cassian's nape. "You will find where Finnian is hiding the blood, and you will hand it over to me, or your precious beloved will know the true depths of torment and Ruin."

The muscles in Cassian's shoulders went taut under her palms.

Cassian did not miss the way she spoke of Ruin, insinuating his brother's involvement. Whether Acacius knew her true intentions or not, he would do anything for Ruelle. Cassian did not doubt his brother's love for him, but he did doubt his judgement. Ruelle had Acacius wrapped around her petite, smooth fingers. Manipulating his gullibility and desire for love would be Acacius's downfall.

Cassian slowly turned and towered over her, the buzzing of his fury reverberating in his ears. "Am I to believe you would not use the blood on Finnian in the end? That is what this is about, Ruelle. What it's always been about. You long to see me suffer for the heartache I caused you when I refused to resurrect Klaus."

At the mention of Klaus, the cunning look in her eyes formed into malice. "I wish to inflict far worse upon you." Her voice twisted. "To show you what it is like to experience true loss." She smirked viciously, a backdrop of teeth behind red-stained lips. "In Death, you will lose your title as ruler, forced to spend eternal separation from your beloved—as I have."

True misery.

He could see it. Nothing but a yearning soul in his own realm, drowning in reveries. Forever separated from Finnian.

A calm spread apart the tide of his anger, settling everything inside of him.

He had walked a little over a century with a bone-deep despair, just to one day be on the other side of Finnian's eyes with their past reawakened in his mind. He could still revive Finnian's memory. There was time. Find the blood and kill her before she could touch him.

But Finnian's life was never something Cassian was willing to bet on.

One thing Cassian knew to be true after his five thousand years: he loved Finnian. The young god was in his blood, in the shivers of his soul, and if death was Cassian's fate, then he was willing to accept it if it meant Finnian lived.

Finnian did not remember him, anyway. He would carry on with his days, and Cassian could hold on to their memories—in death.

"I will get the blood," he told her. "However, you will not trifle with Finnian's thread. You will leave him be." Whirling masses of his divine power surged over his shoulders like a monster in the shadows, sucking the air out of the room. "I have nothing to lose, Ruelle. Set your sights on him, and your beloved Klaus will share his pain, tenfold. My title be damned."

She lifted her chin, eyes narrowed. "Get me the blood, and I vow to leave Finnian's Fate untouched."

CASSIAN paced down the throne room as Mavros took long strides beside him to keep up. The crowd of deities parted for him before he fabricated onto the stairs of the dais.

"There is the soul of a *boyden* in the Land. It goes by Alke." Cassian stared out at the Errai before him. He could feel the tranquil presence of Nathaira to his right, the comfort of Mavros to his left. Aligning the back wall with three executioners stood Shivani. "*Boydens* are loyal to their masters, even in death. Alke is somewhere in the Land, but he will remain hidden unless he hears the specific call from Finnian. You will search for him, and you will not stop until he is found."

As the ruler of the Land, Cassian could sense every footprint, every breath within his realm. This damn *boyden* seemed to be the one exception to this. Its devotion and power ran deep and had followed it into the afterlife.

Memories surfaced: Cassian cleaning up the small kitchen of Finnian's townhome, the bird perched on the top of the stove, scurrying down the short hall, disappearing up the chimney. Cassian *knew* Finnian. Right now, Finnian believed his goal was to find Vale and free him. He wouldn't hide the blood somewhere far away. He'd keep it nearby, in case he needed to use it as a last resort.

Alke was the perfect hiding spot. A place nobody else would think to find.

THE chains held Finnian's arms up, his body limp against their weight.

An illusion of darkness currently suffocated his consciousness. It smothered any sense of awareness and kept his mind calm. Cassian did not

wish to bring any suffering upon him, but he would have to figure out how to revive the lost memories soon.

Moros was connected to Acacius's realm. He often made rounds in the prison. If he saw Finnian was unharmed, it would look as if Cassian was doing nothing to get the information out of Finnian. Something Acacius would report back to Ruelle.

Cassian knelt and used his handkerchief to wipe the sweat and soot of the Moros air from his brow. Frizzy waves of his hair clung to his neck, his cheeks.

Pain speared through Cassian's chest as he gently peeled the strands back. *I miss you.*

He longed to say the words, to tell this version of Finnian everything of their plan and their relationship. But he knew it wouldn't work. This Finnian believed the worst in Cassian. He would trust his own false memories over Cassian, regardless of his truth.

Then you must find a way to help me remember us.

Once upon a time, they had truly despised one another. A resentment hid lapses of curiosity, tender twitches of the heart, slowly wearing one another down until that hatred evolved into a maddening love.

That is where their story began.

"I loathe you." He infused the phrase into his illusion, stitched it into every thought, every spare space of Finnian's mind. "How much do you loathe me?"

AFTER a year's time of scouring every inch of the Land, Alke was nowhere to be found.

"He dropped by today," Shivani informed Cassian.

Cassian paced the pathway in front of the ivy-covered ruins, his throat tight. "Acacius will go back and tell Ruelle I am doing nothing."

The possibilities of how Ruelle could make Finnian suffer were limitless.

Sweat coated his underarms as he pulled at the tie around his neck.

Being the ruler of Death, he knew what needed to be done.

A sickness roiled in his stomach.

He rotated to face Shivani.

She wore a black robe, the front unzipped and showing her stocky cargo pants and brown top, rusty blood crusted all over the fabric. Specks of it marked her bronze cheeks and the hairline of her tight ponytail. She held the look of a true goddess of slaughter, one who took manic joy in carving skin from bone.

"Do it," he ordered her. The words burned like acid on his tongue.

Her brow furrowed, studying him with hesitation, the way someone gauged the insane. "My lord, are you certain? We can figure out another way."

He'd never seen her *hesitate,* much less dispute over the idea of torturing someone.

Cassian refused to think too hard about what he was commanding her to do. The moment he did, something vital in him would collapse and he couldn't fall apart. He couldn't. Not yet.

"Do it," he repeated, irritation wringing his insides.

Shivani placed a hand over her forehead, distressed. "The young god is resilient, my lord. To do what you are asking, I will have to—"

"I know what you will have to do!" Cassian snarled, his entire body going rigid.

She flinched, taking a step away from him.

In all the years they'd known one another, he'd never lost his temper on her.

Regret burrowed in the hollow remains of his chest.

I don't know what to do.

No longer able to stand the look of her wary body language, he turned away, raising his arms and gripping the sides of his head.

I need you. I need you, Finny.

"I apologize, Shivani." Tears burned his eyes. "You must do this. I do not wish to curse him—" His voice quavered at the thought.

It was what he would do if Finnian were anyone else; what Ruelle had been waiting for him to do.

Shivani crouched beside him and wrapped her arms around his neck, the stench of copper filling his nose. "I will do what I can to get the information out of him, my lord. You have my word."

FINNIAN'S wails echoed throughout the mountain and shuddered across the soft fields of lavender.

Cassian sat on the edge of his bed, hands pinned over his ears, rocking steadily back and forth.

As the ruler of the Land, he was connected to the terrain, and because of this, the cries played relentlessly, like a banshee caged in his ears. He'd grown accustomed to them. It was like a switch he learned to activate when needed. Only now, it was impossible to turn it off.

After giving Shivani the order, he confined himself to the walls of his chamber. No matter what, he had to resist doing something irrevocably stupid—like teleporting to Moros and interfering, or worse, unshackling Finnian and setting him free.

Another excruciating cry mauled at Cassian's ears.

He ripped up from his bed, his muscles straining. His divine power flared in his veins, chipping away at his self-control.

You cannot interfere.

He dug his hands into his hair, staring down at the onyx-crystal floor. The shape of his feet blurred. He blinked away the moisture collecting in his eyes as images of Finnian, bloody and writhing in agony, assaulted his mind.

Finnian's gut-wrenching scream reverberated through him again and again, tattering his heart.

I can't do this.

He stormed for the door, gripped the handle—and froze.

A curse would be worse.

You must not let it get to that point.

Cassian teleported, forgetting to put his suit jacket back on.

The tart breeze brushed through his hair as he dropped in between rows of pomegranate trees. Serpents scattered at his presence, coiling up the bark and slithering into the shadows.

Cassian's eyes flitted around the silhouettes of the branches. Sitting around and doing nothing would only make him go insane.

Find the bird.

Find the bird and this can all end.

Lifting his fingers to his lips, he did his best to mimic Finnian's call to summon Alke. It hadn't worked yet, but Cassian didn't know what else to do.

The whistle traveled across the orchard.

Cassian waited, concentrating on the dark sky for any signs of movement.

Nothing.

Finnian's scream went on and on, trapped, as if it were stuck in a vase.

Cassian slumped down into a crouch. His hands scraped through his hair and over his ears as a sob broke in his throat.

He folded in on himself, weeping.

Perhaps this is my own curse.

COME BACK TO ME

ASSIAN'S STOMACH TURNED to the strong stench of heat and metal coating the air.

He stood before Finnian, slumped in the chains, watching the pink of his organs mend back together. Blood streaked his skin; it puddled at his feet; a current of it flowed across the floor and dripped into the flaming vortex at the room's center.

The inferno came from Acacius's realm. It split through Moros and raged Chaos.

"He's a stubborn little shit," Shivani said from beside Cassian. She mindlessly twirled one of her knives between her fingers. "I torture him and then let the executioners have their way with him. He still refuses to talk."

Cassian's jaw pulsed at the visual. He clenched his hands into fists inside his pockets.

How did he tell someone the weakness of the one he loved, knowing full well they would exploit those weaknesses to hurt them? Those treasured pearls were guarded in his hand. From the moment Finnian opened up to him, he vowed to never do anything to abuse Finnian's vulnerability. His trust and comfortability meant everything to Cassian.

I cannot afford to hold back any longer.

Alke had not been found, and the longer time went without the blood, Cassian feared Ruelle would do something to proclaim her threat. He had no way of protecting Finnian from her.

A sickness clumped in Cassian's throat. "When you torture him, target his left ear. Any injury to it will make him anxious. He cannot hear out of his right one due to an injury he received during a fight with his mother."

Cassian swallowed thickly. "Cut his hair off. It will trigger him, as he values being autonomous."

Shivani glanced at him. Not once had she pulled for information from Cassian. He knew she was doing everything she could to learn the things that would set Finnian off herself, rather than involve him anymore than he already was.

Time was running out, though.

A paralysis pricked in his chest and down his arms as he turned to leave. *Make this work. You have to get through to him.*

He stopped at the door and added, "His biggest fear is to be powerless against another. Put him in a situation that reminds him of how helpless he is."

Shivani remained quiet for a moment, as if she were giving Cassian a respectable second to hold himself together.

"I understand, my lord."

An hour had passed.

Cassian stood over him, stomach shriveling at the sight. Tears filled his eyes and dripped down his cheeks at the vicious garnet puddle seeping across the floor, collecting around his shoes.

Finnian hung limp from his chains with a knife buried in his sternum, another lodged in the side of his neck, in his left ear canal. Slowly, agonizingly bleeding out. A permission granted by Cassian. What was he thinking?

I cannot do this.

The ends of his fingertips numbed as he brought his hand up to clutch his chest. A sharp twinge prodded within.

Through his divine power, Cassian could hear the oozing of blood from arteries, filling the floor like sap, the slow thudding of Finnian's heartbeat like a weakening whisper, the wheezing of lungs as they collected with blood.

Cassian attempted to breathe through the closing of his throat. The taste of copper coated his tongue. The sharp twinge in his chest grew worse, spearing straight through his chest cavity and coming out on the other side. He felt the pain lance between his shoulder blades.

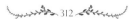

What have I done?

He stepped back. The blood squished underneath the sole of his shoe. A shudder ran up his leg and over his spine. His stomach twisted and a sickness climbed up his esophagus.

I cannot do this—

He pulled at his tie, his breaths shallow and broken. Spots pricked in his vision. He hunched over. His hands came down on his knees. A sob broke through his hyperventilating.

He lifted a shaky hand up to his forehead, sticky with a cold sweat.

I cannot—

He squeezed his eyes shut.

If he remembers, it will all be over.

The torture will end.

Divine power thrummed in Cassian's veins, pouring out like inky ribbons blotched in water. They swam around Finnian and enclosed him in an illusion.

You are not here. You are home. In the comfort of your apothecary room, scribbling notes within your grimoire, a piece of licorice in between your teeth, the soft bubbling of a potion in your cauldron. As you work, you think about who you loathe most in this world.

Cassian felt the illusion weave in the depths of Finnian's mind, and he stood. Shoulders stiff and eyes bleary with tears, he headed for the door. If he didn't leave now, he would give in and unchain Finnian. Beg for forgiveness. Let him go free.

Cassian went to grip the knob, but his hand traveled straight through the iron handle—as if he were in an illusion himself.

He felt the color drain from his face. Nausea burned in his gut as he reached through it again and again.

Needle-thin thread snagged around his fingers and ripped them back. The bones in his knuckles snapped like twigs.

Ruelle.

He ground his teeth, glowering through the moisture in his eyes at the gilded twine slackening around his reconstructing fingers.

She is going to trap me in here—

Make me watch while he—

Then he saw it: Ruelle orchestrating her razor-sharp threads to rain down all around her, ethereal and slicing through Finnian like he was made of paper. Severed and split apart, legs unattached from his body, like a soul in the Serpentine Forest after an Achlys freshly feasted on it.

He gasped for air as his whole body tremored.

Another image forced into his mind: Finnian lying on the ground, wheezing, blood soaked down his face, eyes steady on Cassian, a smile curling across his stained lips. *Dying.*

Panic ignited in Cassian's chest.

A warning.

He squeezed his fingers into a fist and ripped his hand from Ruelle's threads. They split and dissolved, littering the air like sparkling dust.

Cassian pressed his fist against his forehead, his chest sprinting in uneven breaths.

He was running out of time.

THE luminous scape of the Land of Entity bled through the open window overlooking the round table. Each Council member sat at the respective places in their thrones.

Cassian leaned his weight into his elbow on the arm of his own throne, chin propped in his hand, covering a portion of his mouth as he listened to the conversation.

"News of the High Goddess of Eternity has spread across the Mortal Land," Azara said, her feelings on the matter ambiguous as she spoke in her usual curt tone. She flicked her sharp gaze around the table, her posture straight and her vibrant orange strands braided and pulled back from her face, emphasizing the sharp angle of her cheekbones. "Temples and churches are being erected all over in her name. Mortals who did not believe in us are converting. All because of her."

"Chaos is brewing," Acacius said, his expression grim. The skin around his eyes was pulled tense, and he wore a straight line on his lips. Though Cassian did not miss the way he wrung his hands in his lap. A tic he only expressed when he was anxious. "Deities are unnerved by the Himura demigod, and the immortal Himura witch."

"Deities are unnerved by Naia because she has not made her feelings known," Ruelle defended. "They see her as Mira's daughter and are fearful of what they do not know."

The knot in Cassian's stomach constricted at the sound of her voice.

"It is only a matter of time until praises ascend Naia onto the Council." Iliana rested back on her throne, the exhaustion palpable in her golden gaze.

"Preposterous." Acacius formed fists in his lap. "She is married to a Himura."

"It appears you have unresolved prejudice against the Himura bloodline," Ruelle snapped, eyes twisting around him.

Acacius whipped his head in her direction, glowering, "When they have the blood to kill us, why yes, I do."

"*They* do not," she corrected coolly. "Only their demigod offspring."

"And what happens if Naia bears another child?"

"She has free will to do as she desires."

"And the children?"

"*Enough*," Iliana's voice raised.

Ruelle pursed her lips, cutting her eyes away.

Acacius continued to glare at her.

"Word of her title is all over the mortal news stations. They are beginning to idolize her," Iliana said matter-of-factly. "As her story and title continue to make headlines, the mortals will only come to adore her more. Because of her presence alone, they no longer shun the Himura clan."

"What of the deities?" Azara asked. "There is division among them. Those on the opposing side will eventually go after the child."

"*If* Naia ascends onto the Council," Iliana said, "it will calm the gods. We represent order and law, and if she is a part of us, they will trust that she, nor her family, carries no ill intent. Those who go after the child will be reprimanded."

Acacius scoffed grudgingly, directing his disapproval to Iliana. "Protect her god-killer offspring? Mark my words, Sister, the Himura demigod will use its blood to end us all."

Iliana eyed him, composed and regal, not the least bit riled by his outburst. "It would be best for you to remember the reason the Himura bloodline exists, Brother. All things must have a balance. It has been five years since Naia returned to Hollow City, and the peace has not been disrupted. The Himura witch, nor the child, have stepped out of line."

"If they do?" Azara asked Iliana. "Their punishment?"

Iliana twisted to look at Azara, her long blonde hair brushing over her shoulder. Both held each other's intense gazes. "We will treat them as if they are gods, and they will be punished as one."

The muscles in Cassian's jaws flexed.

If Ronin or Ash stepped out of line, it would be *his* responsibility to punish them. A curse, time in Moros, whatever it may be—normal protocol he was typically unfazed by.

However, Finnian had worked too hard, sacrificed too much, to lure Ronin to Hollow City and hand it over. Not only that, but Naia was of grave importance to Finnian, and the idea of inflicting torture onto Finnian's brother-in-law or nephew rolled his stomach.

"This all started because word got out of her title." Acacius scowled. "By the fucking mouths of Finnian's organizations that he left behind."

I will right my wrongs.

Finnian's methodical plots amazed Cassian. Though the dread swelling inside of him left no room for pride. It appeared Finnian was accomplishing everything he set out to do.

"Brother," Iliana called, snapping Cassian out of his introspection. All heads pointed in his direction. "You have been awfully quiet. Tell us your opinion on the situation."

Cassian flitted his gaze over each deity sitting before him. There was a reason he and his siblings created the Council thousands of years ago. If they so desired, they could destroy the universe. The Council was law, yes, but for those sitting around the table, it was order, balance. One could not act without others' permission. A power without freedom.

Cassian fixed his attention onto his sister, ignoring the scrutiny of Ruelle's gaze, like a hand trapped around his throat. "Naia becomes a member of the Council. We can keep her power under control, as well as the actions of the Himura bloodline. The uproar and uneasiness among the deities will settle, and those with opposition can be met with retribution."

Iliana passed him a small smile of gratitude. He recognized the relief set in her tense shoulders beneath her tailored, button-up blouse. "Then it is settled." She rose from her throne and smoothed out her blush, knee-length chiffon skirt. "Meeting adjourned."

Azara disappeared like a breath, the sound of her departure punctuated by the sparks of fire cracking in the empty space of where she sat.

"I suppose time is ticking then." Ruelle twisted her head at Cassian with a demeaning smile playing on her lips. "Wouldn't you agree, Lord Cassian?"

A spiraling pang shot through his chest.

There was a distinct manner in her voice only he could decipher.

Your time is up.

THE wails of Moros intertwined in a single, haunting ensemble, filling the corridor and swarming Cassian. The oppressive warmth coated his skin, forming beads of sweat across his forehead.

He wasn't sure how long he'd stood there, face pale, staring at the silhouettes from the flickering sconces bouncing off the stone door.

On the other side, he could hear the ragged breath Finnian drew, the groans slipping out in between. The stench of flayed flesh coated Cassian's nostrils and down the back of his throat.

Shivani had briefed him before she'd left. Finnian's fortitude was slowly wavering. She'd managed to slice through his mental barrier by severing his hair. Each lock cut by her precious knives had chipped away some of his fight.

Cassian was not foolish enough to think Finnian would give in, though. That he would enter the room and somehow get Finnian to confess where Alke hid. He was much too stubborn to make things easy. If anything, Shivani had only pissed him off and provoked his sense of spite.

Cassian was at a loss.

Which curse will you choose?

He had many in his arsenal. Less severe ones that mimicked mortal diseases, to ones that attacked and festered the mind.

The tightness in Cassian's chest reached up to his throat, squeezing the breath out of him.

He knew which one to go with. The stronger mental stamina the deity possessed, the more brutal of a curse they would need to be under in order for Cassian to get results. It was his protocol—weighing his victims' personal limitations.

Cassian's heart raced, his pulse spiking with indecision. Tension ached in the muscles down his neck, his shoulders, his back—his body begging him not to step inside the room.

It will work out in the end, he reassured himself. *It must.*

The curse would only speed up the process. Gnaw away at Finnian's mind, and, while doing so, perhaps uproot the memories of their past.

Cassian couldn't stop envisioning how it would go—Finnian with venom in his eyes, the pain branding his face as Cassian dealt the blow.

Panic quivered his insides like a turbulent flight.

He pressed the heels of his hands into his eye sockets, desiring to release the scream trapped in his throat.

I don't want to do this.

He dropped his hands and blew out a shaky breath. Adjusted the cufflinks of his sleeves.

You are Cassian, the High God of Death and Curses.

Straightened the tie at his neck. Smoothed the lapels of his suit.

You took his father, cursed his sister, and tried to steal his nephew.

Slicked back the incessant piece of hair that perpetually fell in his eyes, and pushed back his shoulders.

Just as he did in the past, Finnian loathes you for everything you are, everything you have done to him.

He blinked away the tears stinging in his eyes, focusing on the smooth granite of the door.

For a fleeting moment, he was back in that crowded mortal street standing outside the apothecary, its windowsills cluttered with pathos and ivy and various-sized bottles, advertising medicinal remedies.

Just like you loathed each other before.

A light in the darkness.

Cassian held the memory close as he readied his divine power in an ominous cloud, and teleported inside the room.

INKY mist drifted over the Serpentine Forest like a grim curtain. A chill nipped at Cassian's cheeks as he stood at the mouth of its entrance.

Finnian had broken out of his cell in Moros by learning the mechanics of the serpentine bars. A feat Cassian had expected, hoped for, even.

He held up the vial, its silver substance incandescent under the midday sunlight of the Land.

There was no reason to keep Finnian locked up in Moros now. With the curse nibbling away the barriers of his mind, he would either crack and give up the blood, or, if the Universe decided to be kind, it would eat away at the magic altering their memories. Either way, Finnian had given him the binding potion, and he intended to use it.

Regardless of Finnian's resentment, it was enough to have him near Cassian. His presence, the sound of his voice, to staunch the wound oozing in Cassian's heart.

A hiss of air and divine power sounded behind him.

He casually tucked the potion inside his pocket as Acacius came to stand beside him.

"I hear he did a number on my executioners," Cassian said.

"Any idea how to reverse a hex?" Acacius gave him a sidelong glance, the ends of his mouth curling in a smirk. "Better to go assist him now, lest the Achlys have their way with him."

"They know not to touch him."

A beat of silence.

The playfulness in Acacius's demeanor shifted, and he turned his head, revealing the somberness across his face. "I presume you are doing everything you can to get the demigod's blood."

Cassian's nerves cringed at the mention of the blood—of Ruelle. He was sick of it all.

He leveled Acacius with a dangerous look. "Do you think I would've cursed him otherwise?"

A melancholic shadow passed over Acacius's features. It gleamed in his golden gaze, steadfast on Cassian, pained and remorseful. "Cassius, I will not stand by and let you kill her."

Acacius's loyalty to Ruelle burned furiously through Cassian. He stepped up into his brother's space. "But you will stand by and let her kill me?"

Acacius's eyes widened. "I—that's not—" He shook his head, searching Cassian's face in stupid bewilderment. "She has no intentions of doing such a thing."

Cassian scoffed, smiling harshly. "Explain why else she's gone to such lengths for me to locate the demigod's blood."

"She intends to confiscate it. Nothing more, nothing less."

Cassian shook his head, truly dumbfounded by his brother's ignorance.

Acacius latched onto his arm. "Brother, she is uneasy at the moment, because she knows you wish her dead. That is all. I swear to you, I will not let her end your life. Nor will I let you end hers. There is a middle ground here."

Cassian barked out a laugh, scrubbing a hand down his face. He was at a loss for words. The effort it required to convince Acacius was too taxing. A mental effort Cassian did not have.

He yanked his arm free from his brother and turned his back on him. "Think what you must, Acacius. Ruelle is lying, and it is not me who she is lying to."

THE village of souls were in celebration. Dogs crowded at Cassian's feet. The rays of sunlight soaked through his pores. The anguish deteriorating in his heart lightened.

Finnian was at his side, mocking the names of his Land, smiling.

It was not a dream.

"Can you tell me who Everett is?"

I can tell you for as long as you wish.

THE night smothered the Land.

Cassian collapsed against the bench in Finnian's Grove, heart squeezing with a pain that made it difficult to breathe through. The curse was hurting Finnian. Something Cassian had inflicted upon him. A pain brought on by his own hand.

He stared vacantly at the patch of white trumpet blossoms.

They are my favorite.

The back of his nose stung at the memory.

They flourish in the darkness and I find something poetic about that.

Cassian longed to hear him say it again, with their *one day* nowhere in sight.

The bleakness of their reality bruised his chest. An agony that felt like it had sunk straight into his marrow, anchoring him further down. He was growing weary from the weight of it.

Footfalls thudded down the pathway behind him.

Before he had a chance to turn around, a gust of heat roared against his nape. The vibrant blood-orange glow of the fire caught in his periphery, and he teleported out of the way.

The grove burned. Embers dusted the air. Hints of rosemary and sage infused in the smoke. The hawthorn leaves withered, their branches crumbling. The moonflowers shriveled on their stems and fell to the charred ground.

Finnian's silhouette shone through the inferno, his arm extended, fueling the destruction of his own precious grove.

Hysteria seized Cassian's chest like a windstorm.

No. This is all I have left of him.

The moments they'd shared, the love, all of it seemed to be in another lifetime. Perhaps an illusion Cassian had conjured up to trick himself into a delusional state of happiness.

Nothing they had seemed destined to last.

The heat of the flames rippled across his face and stung his eyes, already filling with tears.

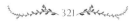

As he watched their love burn, he thought of Ruelle, and how this was all she desired from the start. Everything he and Finnian had was smoldering before his eyes, becoming **nothing** but wisps of what once was.

"You are Everett." Finnian's grip released from Cassian's collar, his tan complexion paling at the realization.

That cruel spark of hope relit inside Cassian's chest.

He caught Finnian by the forearm, clasping his fingers deeply into skin. "What is my name, Finnian? My *real* name."

Come back to me.

His heart split like thin paper as Finnian wrenched away and curled over, gripping at his head. A pained sound tore from his lips.

Cassian held onto him, his pulse jumping. "Finny?"

Fear, shame, guilt, they prodded him, knowing the source of Finnian's pain came from the curse.

Come back to me.

Frenzy trembled in Cassian's limbs.

His breath held as he studied every motion, every shift of muscle and skin on Finnian's face.

He wanted to get down on his knees, beg, plead, tell him everything about their past. They were almost there. *Almost.* If he could just remember.

Come back to me.

"Cassius," Finnian whispered. "Your real name is Cassius."

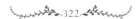

PART III

A SIGN OF LOVE'S PRESENCE

TWENTY-EIGHT

I LONG FOR YOU

THE PRESENT
Finnian

THE MAGIC OF the potion lifted, and the blood rushed into his head. The seconds came screaming back to him before it had happened—the vial to his lips, Cassian's form being swallowed by divine power, the devastation mangled on his face, destroying all the resolve Finnian had to go through with it.

The image had spiked through his heart. *I cannot do this either,* he had wanted to tell Cassian, but he knew that would only be a catalyst to convince them not to continue.

He hadn't been able to breathe through the tears as he tipped the potion back.

The empty vial had slipped from his hand, and he fell to the floor and waited. Clutching at his chest and gasping for air, his whole body wracked with tremors.

With what breath he had left, he squeezed out the final words to seal his fate: "*Glöm sanningarna. Tro lögnerna.*"

Every memory of Cassian would be altered. He would not feel treacherous affection in their arguments, his eyes would not wander over Cassian's lips. He was the High God who imprisoned his father, who tried time and time again to curse Finnian, mercilessly.

Now that it was over, it was as if he'd woken up from a slumber, dissociated, as his mind raced to process the last five years since he'd handed himself over to Cassian.

Five years. In Moros, tortured and cursed.

Something had gone wrong.

"Cassius," Finnian said, like an answered prayer. He ripped his head up, latching onto Cassian's gaze, bronze-gold under the pool of his tears.

Finnian's heart fractured. Five years since they'd been reunited. Five years since their plan was supposed to have reached fruition. What torment that must've been for him.

Cassian lurched Finnian into a tight embrace. "I missed you."

Finnian threw his arms around Cassian's neck, burying his face in his shoulder. "I am so sorry." Tears trembled in his voice, dampening his cheeks. "I don't know why the potion's effects didn't break. I am so sorry it took me so long to come back to you."

"You have nothing to apologize for. You were tortured and cursed by my hands. I—"

Finnian ripped away, heart pounding. He studied Cassian, searching to locate the wears and tears of the past nearly two centuries, to acknowledge all the changes.

Finnian wanted to know when Cassian had started wearing his hair shorter on the sides, who had given him the watch on his wrist—because he knew Cassian would never take time out of his day to purchase something for himself—or when the sunlight had faded from his gaze. He looked barely alive. A husk, like one of Finnian's ghouls, forced to walk the earth with their soul tethered to their flesh, hollow and vacant.

Oh gods. Finnian tightened his grip on the tops of Cassian's shoulders to stop himself from kissing him, to breathe life back into his soul. He could feel the haste of time clipping at their heels. Years had passed. What was the situation with Ruelle now? What had driven Cassian to curse him?

"The blood," Finnian said. "We must finish this. You cursed me, which means Ruelle—"

Cassian hauled him back into a hug. "We will."

Finnian fell silent, momentarily relishing in Cassian's warmth, the firm beat of his heart. "I have a feeling we are strapped for time. *Please.*" His whole body was on edge, fueled with an urgency that stemmed from the tightening in his gut to get a move on.

"I never should've let you do it," Cassian murmured.

He didn't like this. The way Cassian held him, as if it was the last time, or the way he spoke, airing a grievance he'd carried around for far too long.

Finnian pushed off his chest and took a step back. His limbs quivered, but he squared his jaw and said, "I'll call for Alke. We have to end this."

Cassian lightly held onto the tips of his fingers, staring down at them, wistful and terrifyingly melancholic.

"Finnian," he said, lifting his gaze, "let me have this moment."

Their eyes met and the sides of Finnian's throat constricted. There it was again. A note of finality, drawing near.

"Why?" Finnian lashed out, tearing his hand from Cassian. He wiped at his tear-stained cheeks.

A pathetic smile formed on Cassian's lips. "Because I do not know what the future holds, and I would like to savor this moment with you. It is the only thing that has kept me going for the last century and a half."

Finnian's heart plunged into his stomach. "Stop talking as if this is our final moment together. We have walked this far. I will not let anything stop us."

At the flare of his frustration, the ringing sounded in his head. A distant, haunting buzz snagged down his jaw, rattled in his teeth.

He ground his molars.

"Finnian." Cassian's weary plea tightened his chest.

The breath went light in his lungs. "No." His voice wobbled.

Rotating towards the grove, he ignored the thrumming in his skull and put his fingers to his mouth. He inhaled deeply, but as he went to whistle, the breath stuttered out at the view of the ruined garden.

Ember-lit remains of charred stems and dust blackened the ground.

You ruin everything—everyone you love.

A lump swelled in his throat.

The itch burrowed like a corkscrew, and he cringed.

He rolled his neck against the writhing nerves under his skin and blew against his pinched fingers.

The high-pitch call rang through the darkened sky.

"Stop." All emotion drained from Cassian's voice and filled with alert. "Something is off."

Alke emerged down from the charcoal-soaked clouds and into the stream of moonlight, his cobalt feathers glistening like raindrops.

"No!" Cassian thrusted out his arm. Bands from his gilded abyss shot forth.

The movement was subtle, and had Finnian not learned to be wary of the night, he would've overlooked the whirling mass snaking through the darkness like a specter straight for his bird.

"Alke, stop!" He slung out his hand and a stream of fire expelled from his palm, roaring up into the sky. The fiery glow lit up the silhouette of a shadowy monster widening its jaws and catching the bird in its mouth.

Alke cried out.

For fuck's sake.

Finnian jolted towards Cassian, but the ground trembled and a force knocked them backwards.

Finnian felt the dense divine power against his skin as his back collided into the ashy remains of the grove.

Nightrazers flocked around him, a collection of black holes all pointed down at his face.

He pushed against the skeletal grip locked around each of his biceps, lifting his back from the ground. The restriction around his arms tightened, and he was shoved back down.

He let out a grunt as needle-fine teeth tore into his arm. Another set took a chunk out of his side. Waves of pain seized up into his neck, rippled in his ribcage, burned down his leg.

Fucking nightrazers.

Nostrils flared, he channeled his magic into his right hand, his pain sublimating into unadulterated rage.

An explosion of brassy tangerine fire spilled from his palm. The spout heaved like magma from a volcano. Screeches filled the air. The nightrazers scattered like vultures, giving Finnian enough time to hop up to his feet.

Quickly, he stuck out his hand and spun in a circle, barricading himself with the flames. The heat smothered his breath, but he didn't care. They would keep the nightrazers at bay until he got a grasp on what was—

"Finnian!"

He snapped his head in the direction of Cassian's voice to find him thrashing against the iron bars of the fence, bound in place by the Chains of Confinement.

Finnian clenched his jaws as a figure stepped into his line of sight, obscuring his view of Cassian. An animal's skull with horns twisting out of the skull hid his face.

In Finnian's periphery, another stepped into the firelight, her fingers clasped around Alke's neck.

Marina pried apart his beak, allowing access for a shadow the size of a worm to slink down his esophagus.

Old memories flashed in Finnian's mind of that day—Mira looking down at him, holding Alke by the neck.

Know your place.

Rage beat in his blood, the intensity of it harmonizing with the steady ring trapped like a fly in his head.

The shadow slithered out from Alke's mouth, its body curled around a syringe. A viscous vermillion shining in the fire's gleam.

His nephew's blood.

TWENTY-NINE

EVEN IN DEATH

 INNIAN ROLLED HIS head to sate the quaking in his jaw.

She is just like Mira.

The voice was unhinged, an overlapping of whispers.

She deserves to suffer.

"Is this your revenge for what I have done to our mother?" Finnian asked, his tone belittling, as if she were a bratty child having a tantrum over her favorite toy. That's all Marina had ever been, spoiled and pampered by Mira, taught to look down on Father, Naia, and himself. He could hardly stand the sight of her.

"Lord Acacius was kind enough to aid me in my goal," Marina said, smiling in the same patronizing way Finnian had spoken to her.

Gods, he regretted not inflicting more torment on her back in the great hall.

Alke's body dissolved into particles and melted away in her grasp. The small orb of his soul fluttered away like a firefly.

"Acacius!" Cassian snarled, jerking against the chains holding him against the fence. "Release me at once!"

Acacius twisted to look back at Cassian. "I do this for your own good, Brother."

Finnian kept his eyes locked on Marina. She held the syringe up against the silver glow of the full moon, inspecting its contents. "And what do you plan to do with it?"

Acacius's disturbing mask faced Finnian. "She plans on handing it over to me—"

"You are a fool," she muttered.

A monstrous shadow hoisted from the ground and devoured Acacius before he could respond.

This nightrazer was colossal compared to the others. It stood meters tall, its form a writhing void, entrapping Acacius against the fence with another set of the Chains of Confinement. If he wasn't alongside Cassian, Finnian would've found it amusing.

"Marina!" Acacius shouted out, enraged. His mask had fallen off during the collision. Pinned near Cassian, the resemblance of their appearances was uncanny. Two High Gods rendered powerless by the daunting creatures of the Night.

Kill her, the voice lulled.

A tremor vibrated down Finnian's nape.

The muscles in his shoulders spasmed from it as the black gloom thickened around him, obscuring Cassian and Acacius from his periphery across the grove. Nightrazers morphed from the darkness, like ghosts dripping in oil, baring their rows of teeth in the folds of their faces.

They surrounded Finnian, advancing slowly like a pack of wolves.

One corner of his mouth pulled into a cruel smirk as he cut his eyes back onto Marina, quirking his head. "Kill me and you will avenge Mother? How cliché."

She twirled the syringe into a more secure grip, like the way one held a gun when preparing to aim. "Death frightens you. It is why you bring souls back from this realm. You cannot fathom endings."

Finnian's gaze fell to the blood. Fear pricked his skin like hoarfrost. A foreign feeling.

Death could never touch him, and now it was right in front of him. One wrong move and he would become a permanent resident of the Land.

He glowered at her. "And you cannot fathom being a failure. Yet, here you are, trying to make sense of it. Because you know, deep down, Mother does not love you. She loves your power, what you can do for her. Nothing more."

The monsters stalked closer, pulling at the space that remained.

Marina's lip curled, and she disappeared as one with her shadows.

Finnian inhaled a sharp breath.

A nightrazer lunged from his left. Another from behind him.

Violet-blue lightning sparked to life in the sphere of his hand. He drove his arm out and sliced it through their cores, electrifying them from the inside. Their spectral touch chilled his bones, as if he'd reached inside a corpse.

Ear-piercing wails sounded over the hissing of the electric popping and sizzling in his palm. One by one, their forms lifted like a dreary fog.

Finnian matched their pace, cutting them down before they had a chance to lay a finger on him. He could sense the movement of Marina's divine power mixed in, hidden amongst them, waiting to strike.

His heartbeat hammered against his sternum. Between the beating of blood and the unyielding ringing of the curse caught in his skull, his hearing went uneven, cutting out the sound waves funneling into his left ear.

The veil of nightrazers was endless, and the more energy he wasted on them, the more it gave Marina a chance to attack.

"Enough of this!" Finnian squeezed his hands and the pulses of electricity sparked like a match. The lightning transformed into an angelic, ivory light, wisping around his knuckles.

He punched both fists together, and it erupted in a beam of milky radiance. The shadows around him flailed together, screeching—a horrid sound that reverberated in his bones.

Marina's pronounced aura materialized behind him.

He spun around, already anticipating her attack, jutting out his palm and catching the needle in between his index and middle finger. He shoved the syringe back against Marina's enclosed hand.

She locked her stance and hooked her leg around the crook of his knee. With a forceful jolt, his knee folded, and he crumpled down like a puddle at her feet.

His back hit the ground with her heel above his face. He rolled before it could stab through his skull.

Up to his knees, he slung his arm towards her. The crescent scythe of white magic threw her backwards.

In mid-air, she vanished in a blurred plume.

Finnian heaved himself upright. Magic crystalized in his palms. He sent two dagger-like gleams sailing through the air, following the ripples in the blackness.

She fabricated in front of him and thrusted the syringe again.

He swerved the needle by a hair's breadth and threw out his arm. The heel of his palm made contact with her clavicle. "*Sanguis ardeat.*"

She stumbled backwards, crying out.

Finnian watched the skin of her arms, the patches exposed in her neckline, her cheeks, all bubble like plastic in a bonfire. The spell boiled the blood of the victim.

He took the opportunity to lunge for the syringe.

She was swallowed up by her divine power again, leaving him to fight the wispy spirals.

The muscles in his neck went rigid. "Marina!"

The itch in his brain prodded deeper, deeper, deeper.

He rolled his shoulders, clenching his jaws against the clamor of urges filling his thoughts.

Kill her.

Use the blood on her.

She deserves it.

Finnian slapped a hand over his chest where the curse mark throbbed on his pec.

No, you must use it on Ruelle.

Bloodlust surged in his veins and pulsed in his eyes.

Marina killed Kaleo.

He could taste the chemical of the curse like a film on his tongue.

But think about how satisfying it will feel to watch the light leave Marina's eyes—

A small, black mass latched its teeth into the flesh of his arm.

He growled and slung his arm to knock it off, but the creature burrowed its fangs in even deeper.

Another bit into his calf. He stomped his leg. It clung to him.

Hundreds of contorting shadows, the size of ravens, swarmed and stuck to him.

"*Mortifer—*" One crammed inside of his mouth, its cotton-like body dry on his tongue.

He channeled his magic through his pores. Fire doused across his skin as a shield, burning them off. They smothered the flames, purged down his neck, arms, legs.

His divine power flared, an instinct to teleport. However, the action clamped against the demand of the binding potion, linking him to Cassian.

As far as he could go, Marina had her dark army.

He jerked and flailed his limbs, smashed his teeth together and ground the shadow in his mouth to a pulp. The acrylic taste gagged him, but he strained the muscles in his throat to swallow it. It stuck to his tonsils, heaving up back into his mouth. His eyes watered.

The shadows on his arms and legs hung like sap, forcing his hands behind his back and coiling them together at the wrist.

Before him, the night rippled like a parted sea, and Marina stalked towards him.

Finnian's pulse spiked as he eyed the syringe in her grasp.

"Finnian!" Cassian roared, his voice booming and loud—an assurance Finnian would hear him, in the case his brain had not fully adjusted to having his hearing aid back in yet.

The thought pricked in Finnian's chest.

He didn't bother looking away from Marina. In the veil of her night, he knew he would not be able to see Cassian from where they stood.

He wished he had let Cassian hold him a bit longer earlier. Savored his warm embrace. Finnian should've kissed him. It had been so long since he'd felt Cassian's lips on his own.

He regretted not telling Cassian that he loved him, that he was sorry for the suffering his plan had caused.

"Time's up." Marina was only a few strides away. Her dark eyes narrowed on him, depraved and hollow. A barren wasteland. "Not even Father can save you now."

The breath froze in Finnian's lungs as he remembered Cassian's words. *All you need to do is call out his name.*

"No!" It came out as an indecipherable shout due to the shadow residing in his mouth.

Marina cocked her arm back and plunged the needle toward his heart.

Finnian flinched.

A gentle gust swept through his hair.

Everything silenced.

Finnian's frantic pulse echoed in his ear.

A lovely floral fragrance touched his nose—and it felt as if his heart had stopped completely.

"Hello, my darling."

Gooseflesh spread down Finnian's arms at the sound of his father's mellow voice.

Chest rising and falling sharply, Finnian peeled his eyes open to see his father's backside, cloaked in a velvet green robe, staring back at him, the same one he could recall fidgeting with the hem of as a child.

Marina choked out a sound, a horrid gasp and sob. "F-father?"

She staggered backwards, blinking up at their father in a rapid procession. Mouth agape, tears welling in her eyes. Her arm sat inclined with the syringe pasted in her grip—half-empty.

A heavy chill froze over Finnian's core.

No, no, no.

The realization shattered in his chest.

No, no, no, no, no.

The shadowy leeches clinging to his limbs dissolved. Along with them, the suffocating abyss of night lifted. Beyond its cloak, the Land blossomed in radiant hues of plum and tangerine. A brightness that felt inherently wrong.

Numbness spread in Finnian's limbs, as if his body had disconnected from his head.

Cassian and Acacius came into view across the grove. Their furious shouts muddled against the shrieking in Finnian's head.

This can't be happening.

Marina fell to her knees before Father. The syringe rolled across the ground. "I-I didn't mean—I—you were—" she cried, her entire body quaking in tremors.

Father bent over and cupped her tear-stricken face. "My darling, I forgive you."

A gut-wrenching sound tore from her, and she grabbed his hand, clinging onto him. "Please don't leave me. Please stay. You mustn't leave me yet. *Please.*"

The static in Finnian's mind shook his vision. A quiver that would not silence. The sensation jittered and trembled like ice in his veins.

How could I ever love a son like you?

Father tenderly pried Marina's wet fingers from his hand. He flipped his palm up and a white, bowl-shaped flower unfurled in his grasp. Delicately, he tucked the magnolia blossom behind her ear.

She threw a hand over her mouth and folded in on herself, wailing.

You ruin everyone.

He kissed the top of her hair before turning around.

Streams of blood oozed from the corners of his eyes, down the crevices of his mouth, that were somehow pulled up in a content smile. The sunrise climbing over the peaks of Moros feathered around him, the finest brush strokes encasing him like a heavenly casket.

You failed.

"My boy." Father curled his hand around Finnian's nape and pulled him to his forehead.

The glitching voice in his brain stilled, granting reprieve, and his posture crumbled into Father's embrace. The walls of his chest caved. His mouth opened and closed. He had so much to say, so much he'd *longed* to say. Centuries of reciting the perfect words.

I am sorry for breaking my promise.

I am sorry for not seeing you sooner.

What have I done?

Forgive me, Father.

He'd spent years in the Land, dismissing Cassian each time he suggested visiting. All to avoid facing the disappointment he assumed Father would have in him, believing it would be too grave to handle. Time he could've spent making amends. Now it was all lost. *Gone.*

"You've done well," Father said.

The words fractured in Finnian's heart.

He tangled his fingers in the front of Father's robe, his shoulders shaking from the sob stuck in his chest. "I am sorry. I am so sorry. I never meant—I wanted to come see you—I-I just—my promise—"

"I know." Father's weight gradually slackened against Finnian's forehead.

Finnian recalled this: his back wedged in the sand, hundreds of bull sharks swarming the sky, the sunlight warming his cheeks as he peeked over at Father, who laid on his back with his hands perched under his head, eyes closed. A smile tugged on his lips, as if he could sense Finnian staring.

Finnian wanted to go back to that moment and lay on that cove with him again in comfortable silence. He wouldn't have taken it for granted like he had then.

Father gave one final squeeze around Finnian's nape. "You have nothing… to apologize for… Finny."

The parting in his words strangled Finnian's breath. "Father?" He went to pull back, but Father's hand fell from his nape. His body went limp and slumped against Finnian.

"No! Father!" Finnian strapped his arms around him, the weight of his body buckling Finnian's knees. They fell to the ground. Finnian held him snug. "Father!"

The Land shuddered. Vines emerged from the dirt and snaked across the air for Father. The green stems coiled around his limbs.

"No!" Finnian cut through them with his hands. More and more sprouted and glided up Father's torso, around his neck, into his hair, across his face.

A blazing panic burned through Finnian.

Do not take him from me.

He dug his heels into the dirt and scraped back with Father in his hold. They fought against his pull, winning. He extended an unsteady arm and flames struck from his palm, igniting the vines.

They endured the fire, but did not wither, continuing to confiscate Father in their blackened state.

Finnian's breath stuck in his throat, his lungs constricting for air.

What should I do?

I don't know what to do—

"Finny," Cassian said from the other side of the grove, loud enough to be heard but still with softness. A melody in all the noise. In it, Finnian could hear what he said. Father belonged to the Land now. It would take him outside the gates, where he would be properly escorted inside. Not as a prisoner, but a welcomed soul.

The resistance gave way in Finnian then. His back bowed as he cried into his father's robe.

The vines slowly slid him from his lap.

His grip on Father's robe cut off the circulation in his fingers.

This is it.

He is leaving.

Forever.

Snot and tears fled down Finnian's lips. The vines pulled against his hold.

You have to let go.

He released his fingers, and the vines extracted Father from his lap.

The soil crumbled and swallowed Father down under.

Deeper than the earth.

Finnian gaped down at his lap, at his palms—empty. His chest moved in large gulps, his breath shallow against the painful pounding of his heart.

He stared at the seam in the dirt, his brain attempting to comprehend the last few seconds.

The ringing jarred in his skull, vibrating down his spine.

This is all your fault.

If you could've gotten to him sooner—

I told you, you are pathetic—

You failed.

Finnian squeezed the sides of his head, rocking back and forth. "No, no. I—"

You ruin everything and everyone and so does she.

His chin lifted to Marina across from him. She was a puddle on the ground, weeping into her hands. The syringe laid beside her, still half full.

He'd always taken comfort in knowing Father was alive, regardless of the distance between them. His beating heart meant there were possibilities. A day Finnian could dream about. One day, Father would be free, and they could see each other whenever they wished.

A dream stolen from him.

Deranged fury erupted like tiny bombs in his chest. The intense breath of it fanned the jittery insanity detonating underneath his skin.

Kill her.

He jumped up and charged forward.

"Finnian!" Cassian roared.

Thin, silk-like threads snagged around his body, trapping his arms at his sides and sealing his legs together. His shoulder buried into the ashen remains of his grove, and his cheek ricocheted off the ground. Clouds of the

dead cinders coated the air, sticking to the inside of his mouth. It swirled in the wake of Marina teleporting away.

"No! Ruelle!" Cassian bellowed across the grove.

The High Goddess of Fate stepped through the dust, the particles crystallizing and falling like droplets of ice. They stuck like gemstones in her auburn hair. She held out a bent arm, her fingers curling into a fist.

The threads around Finnian squeezed taut, slicing like barbs through his skin. His nostrils flared to the warm feel of blood seeping down flesh.

With a flick of her finger, a thread coiled around the syringe and delivered it to her palm. "Close to madness, yet, Finnian?"

He jerked in the threads and their grip seized around him, slicing deeper. Baring his teeth, he said, "Come closer, Ruelle, and I will show you just how mad I am."

A hard look pierced in her eyes, and she moved her hand slightly to the left. The thread followed her command and penetrated through the meat of Finnian's arm, rubbing against the shell of bone.

He ground his teeth against the agonizing bursts ricocheting up into his jaw.

The curse fed on the pain, amplifying the itch in the center of his mind so deep it burned.

Suddenly, it all made sense. Cassian's odd demeanor from earlier. The way he'd held Finnian close, as if it was the last time. Ruelle had threatened Finnian. It was the only reasonable explanation as to why Cassian had cursed him, and the murderous edge to her features told Finnian she was there to make Cassian pay for refusing to return her beloved back to life.

Finnian scraped his chin across the ground to rotate his head.

Cassian thrashed at the chains keeping him contained like a trapped animal. The tendrils of his divine power slammed like stones within the bindings.

Somehow, as if he could sense Finnian watching him, he paused in his violent motions, his attention falling onto his partner, face struck with pure terror.

Finnian connected with his gaze, giving him a look of inquiry, like a child asking for permission.

Recognition crumbled his brow, and he nodded solemnly. *Do what must be done*, Finnian could hear him say.

His eyes flashed back to Ruelle, glaring down at him.

The source of it all.

"*Animabus suscitate et venite ad me.*" The incantation buzzed on his tongue.

The ground rumbled beneath them.

Ruelle's eyes darted around.

"*Animabus suscitate et venite ad me.*" His solar plexus filled with a warm pool of magic.

"What are you doing?" Ruelle glowered at him, taking a step. Her knuckles went white as she constricted her grip. The threads cut further into Finnian's flesh.

"*Animabus suscitate et venite ad me*!" He chanted it louder.

Ruelle lifted her head towards the beings flooding in behind him. Souls of men, women, children, jungle cats, dogs, birds. Finnian recognized their energies. His magic never forgot the touch of a soul. Each one, he'd lulled back from the dead in his city.

Two came around him and stood on either side of his head. A woman with untamable curls and another with ginger locks, their sights set fearlessly on Ruelle.

Tears stung Finnian's eyes as he said, "Help me. One last time."

"Even in death," Isla murmured without looking down at him.

Eleanor slapped her hand on her chest, over her heart. "Even in death."

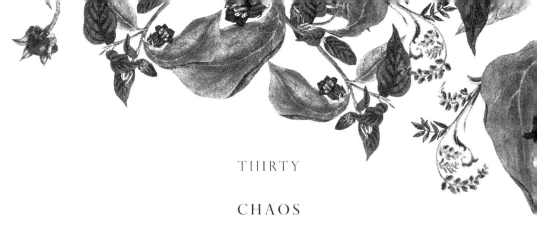

THIRTY

CHAOS

Cassian

 ASSIAN FRANTICALLY FOUGHT against the chains constricting him to the fence, his heartbeat wildly surging in his chest.

She is going to kill him with what's left of the blood.

He shouted through clenched teeth as he strained his muscles and pushed against the chains.

The battle razed over the rubble and embers of Finnian's Grove.

It played out quickly.

The souls charged Ruelle.

Isla crouched at Finnian's side and murmured an incantation. The thread bound around him set ablaze in bright green fire.

Ruelle secured the syringe around her waist with a thread and thrusted both of her arms out. Gilded webs sprung from her palms and entrapped several souls at once. She was a goddess seasoned in her divine power, ensnaring soul after soul, barely flinching.

Eleanor prepped her middle finger and thumb before striking a quick snap towards the enemy. Starlight purple sparks shot from her fingertips, nailing Ruelle on her shoulder. The force skidded the High Goddess back on her feet.

Ruelle twisted her head in Eleanor's direction, her glare lethal.

Cassian's attention shifted to the two souls appearing before him—young women who had once been citizens of Hollow City. Both rushed to unbind the chains from Cassian's limbs.

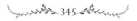

"Ruelle!" Acacius roared from Cassian's side. His mask had been cast aside during the harsh hit he took against the fence. The cords of his neck bulged, the muscles in his arms straining against his own set of chains.

Ruelle spared him a glance as she spun and swerved around Eleanor's bright, explosive attacks zipping across the air.

Cassian's pulse spiked as he eyed the souls working quickly to untangle him.

Ruelle threw out one of her arms in Acacius's direction. A silk-like stitch traveled from her palm. The end coiled around Acacius's chains and pulled. They released their grip and fell to a pile near his feet.

The two souls removed the last of the chains from Cassian's legs.

He pushed off the fence with his sights set on Ruelle, but his shoulder collided into a sturdy form that matched his own strength.

"Cassius, stop this!" Acacius shouted.

The soles of Cassian's feet dug into the terrain, solidifying his stance against his brother.

The jade flames scorching the web around Finnian fizzled out, and he crawled up onto his knees, his form blurring as he sped halfway across the grove.

Cassian stepped back and swerved to bypass Acacius.

"No!" Acacius caught him by the lapel of his suit and yanked him backwards.

The prickle of Acacius's divine magic rose the hairs on Cassian's nape as the scenery around them distorted.

A charcoal cloud swallowed them and spat them out. Pale trunks of banded cypress trees surrounded them. Fog drifted up from the bubbling hot spring, its bank mangled with deadly nightshade.

Acacius had teleported them across the realm to the Serpentine Forest.

"She is going to kill him!" Cassian snarled at his brother.

"You have it all wrong—"

In a quick, harsh motion, Cassian swiped his right arm between him and Acacius. The bare branches of the forest began to bend and spiral together at the order of their master. The trees around the two gods bowed and twisted their limbs around Acacius's body, swallowing him whole.

As the arboreal prison gripped Acacius, constricting his limbs, he flicked his index finger upwards at the hot spring. It began to cyclone,

opening the portal to the High God's own realm. Liquid magma spit out from the center of the whorl, forming a stream that Acacius pulled towards the trees entrapping his body.

Both brothers locked eyes for a brief moment before Cassian turned to make his escape back to Finnian.

Acacius's face contorted, and he bellowed out a feral, primordial sound.

Shells of pure ruin bombarded the trees and dirt and left craters in their wake the size of small homes. Branches splintered. Soil flew in clumps towards the sky. It was as if Acacius had called down an invisible air raid on the forest around them.

Cassian winced. The noise of the magical onslaught amplified in his brain like a never-ending ring. A temporary sense of paralysis swept through him. The world spun and his eyes throbbed from the sensation.

True chaos.

Channeling all his energy into his palm, Cassian extended an arm towards Acacius in a clumsy, panicked motion. A translucent, black helix of divine power shot out and hit Acacius in the thigh, soaking through his pants and into his flesh. Blackening, his skin peeled back and decayed, melting the sinew from his bone.

Acacius's limbs quickly turned from brown to pink to red as the virulent power ate through him.

His brother was immortal, immune to pain in the same sense Cassian was. Yet, even knowing these things, a pang of remorse clenched in Cassian's chest. Acacius would always be the rosy-cheeked, blathering little brother who used to follow him around in their mortal days.

Cassian wrapped his power around himself and teleported, seeing only the white blur of Acacius's bare eye socket before landing back at the battleground.

He gritted his teeth and hung on to a singular thought: *Get to Finnian.*

Cassian's feet instantly came out from underneath him and his chest hit the ground. Gasping, the air left his lungs.

He lay in the pathway of his garden, in front of ruins covered in ivy, with Acacius's boot planted firmly in the center of his shoulder blades. His brother looked more corpse than god, but he still had enough power to twist Cassian's arms around his backside.

"Stop this—"

Acacius was violently knocked backwards into a bed of rose bushes and vines.

Cassian's palms touched the ground, and he lifted to his knees.

Nathaira rushed to his side as he spat up a thick splatter of red. "My lord, are you okay?"

In front of him stood Mavros in the path, blocking Acacius.

Cassian's two unshakeable pillars, always ready to fight with him to the bitter end.

He hoisted himself up to his feet, watching his brother do the same.

Acacius's flesh bubbled across bone as it healed. He rolled his shoulders, glowering dangerously at Cassian, disregarding Mavros as if he were invisible.

Acacius was the sort to wear his heart on his sleeve, devoted to his greatest weakness: love. Cassian could hear the words spoken through the look he gave. *You will not lay a hand on her.*

He would choose her time and time again, regardless of her true intentions. Acacius was not stupid. Deep down, he knew Ruelle had lied. But the truth was too much for him to stomach.

"Never better." Cassian said to Nathaira. He swirled his tongue inside his mouth, cleaning the blood from his teeth. "Now let us end this."

THIRTY-ONE

COME TO ME

Finnian

INNIAN RACED TOWARDS Ruelle, swerving and sidestepping her threads.

Herons hailed from above. Wolves leapt with teeth bared. Soldiers with pikes, mages with tomes, commoners with just fists—they all raged forward to protect Finnian. Though, the High Goddess moved as if she were made of water, dodging the attacks flawlessly, beautifully, eyes crisp and ready for the souls. Her threads tangled around them like nets around thrashing prey.

"We'll create an opportunity for you!" Eleanor called out behind him. "*Ignis!*"

Sparks of fire blazed over his head and rained down over Ruelle.

Eleanor thrust her palms out and moved them side to side in quick, distinct motions. The scattering of fireworks rose from the ground and formed a line in front of her; with each strike of her palm through the air, a blaze of sparkling flame homed in on Ruelle.

The High Goddess danced between the blasts, though a few singed her dress, bubbling her sheen skin beneath. Eleanor's flaming ammunition sputtered out, giving Ruelle the opportunity to grasp her by the hand and seize the mage in a web of threads, gagging her mouth before she could cast another incantation.

In a sharp cut, Ruelle's head twisted towards Finnian and the corner of her mouth lifted into a smirk. She thrusted her open palm in his direction.

Finnian instinctively slung his arm out in defense, his fingers flexed.

A bright sigil flared on the back of his hand.

Ruelle's elbow bent in a deformed angle and snapped, proving she was still breakable.

The words burst from Isla's mouth without hesitation: "¡*Cae al vacío*!"

The ground beneath Ruelle's feet began to swirl, break away, and fall into a spiraling vacuum of nothingness. Before she could get sucked into the black ether, she snapped her arm back into place and quickly shot off two tangles of threads, one from each hand, and wrapped them around posts of the nearby fence.

She hung over the abyss for a moment before hoisting herself to safety, using the threads as leverage.

With the same two spools of golden power, Ruelle shot her hands out towards Isla, the gatherings of tendrils swarming both of the mage's legs and crawling up her like hungry roots.

"Finny, now!" Isla shouted before they reached her mouth.

Finnian fixed his magic on one of the spindles of the iron gate. His fingers curled into a claw and the metal screeched as it tore apart. He flipped his hand upright and sliced his arm to the right, the motion commanding the iron spear to aim for the thread holding the syringe at her waist.

She spun, her auburn strands lifting off her back, and the iron pierced straight through her abdomen. Blood blotched the fine fabric of her dress.

She bared her gritted teeth, unfazed by the pain, as she ripped the iron spindle from her torso. In a singular motion, she cut the metal into pieces with a bundle of threads and sent them sailing through the air like grapeshot for Finnian.

Before they could penetrate his skin, Finnian calmly swirled his left hand in front of his torso, stopping the shrapnel in its path and transmuting each piece of iron into a pointed, crystalline dagger.

With a circle of his index and middle fingers, the cloud of glinting needles whirled.

Finnian gave a quick, forceful push forward with the same fingers and the deadly gale started towards the High Goddess—a small, iridescent cyclone.

Ruelle's hands came up in front of her and she crossed them over her chest, as if she were laying in a casket. Her eyes shut.

Finnian watched the thin, celestial threads weave through the empty spaces of the souls storming towards her. Golden light emanated from them, braiding together and flattening to form a thick, sharp blade, looping around the entire battle. The halo circled them, faster and faster.

Ruelle opened her eyes and smiled with all the force held within her being. She clenched her fists and sliced her arms in a rapid movement in front of her.

Finnian blinked, and the large, glowing ring of thread pulled inward and back to Ruelle, bisecting everything it touched.

He was forced off his feet. The souls caught in it were thrown back. His storm of crystals slowed and fell.

The ground cradled the back of his head. His vision flickered. The crystal lodged in the canal of his right ear came loose, and the transition was sharp, cutting off all sounds as it fell out.

He swallowed, and something tightened around his throat.

"Finnian!" Cassian bellowed.

The call was not audible in his impaired ear.

He coughed, choking for breath.

My hearing aid.

Fright burned through him. He went to lift on his elbows and quickly search for it.

Something tugged against his nape.

He cringed and settled for looking over his cheekbones.

The blurred silhouette of Ruelle's heart-shaped face and auburn strands came into focus.

She strutted across the field towards him, the syringe secure in her grasp, a thread in her other hand, balled into a tight fist.

The thread glinted in the sunlight and Finnian followed it, his fingers tracing over his Adam's apple to feel the thread burrowed deeply in his skin, mangled and severing through flesh and cartilage.

One harsh pull from Ruelle and he would be decapitated.

She slightly raised her arm. The thread carved deeper into his throat. Pain wailed down in his shoulders and into his chest, crushing cells and atoms like they were arils.

He cried out, but the sound got lost in the blood filling his esophagus, dripping copper into his lungs.

His eyes flitted up to the Land's vast sky gazing down at him.

You deserve this.

The itch screeched in the depths of his skull, aching behind his eyes.

You ruin everything—everyone.

He blinked, and a face appeared, hanging their head over him.

"Father is dead because of you," his thirteen-year-old self said, sickly pale and with shadowed eyes.

Finnian's heart accelerated at the thought of death.

A life-force blazed in him to move, get up, fight. He could feel his bottom half already beginning to reattach.

His muscles spasmed as he attempted to rise again. Agony rippled up into his skull. Blood clotted in his throat. He choked on the taste of salt and iron filling his mouth.

"You are weak." His younger self glared down at him. "Always have been."

The thrumming rang louder in his mind, the vibrations of it splitting through his system. He clenched his teeth against it, but a whimper escaped him.

Ruelle came for him in a slow and maleficent stroll, knowing she'd already won.

"You cannot win this," his younger self said. "Give up."

Images of Cassian, woeful and heartbroken, invaded his thoughts. After the misery he'd gone through at Finnian's own hand, forced to watch from a distance holding their memories, their love, inside. All for the sake of their plan. It would not be for nothing. It couldn't be. Finnian couldn't let it end like this—

Something tickled the tip of his index finger.

Finnian's eyes dragged over to the right.

A peony unfolded, a rich layer of velvet petals.

Father.

His arm extended fully, planting the pad of his middle finger on the stem, and siphoning its energy into his veins.

He saw it in flashes. Time stamps stained like the pages of an old book.

Father, a young boy, buoyant and cheerful, ankle-deep in soil, caressing stems from the earth; a young god on his travels, befriending birds and deer, sprouting oaks and maples, turning barrenness into lands rich with soil for harvest, molding mountains like sculptors carved clay; a woman with long, dark hair and a broad smile, eyes alight and swimming with

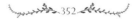

adoration as Father kissed her forehead and dipped down to rest his cheek against her swollen belly.

"Any day now," she said.

His sea of happiness drenched Finnian's chest, so vast, so consuming.

Father stood out amongst the ruin of his island, the ache bruising his heart.

He wept, the sound gut-wrenching as he held the woman in his arms. Rain pelted down from the sky, mirroring his sorrows.

She took his cheek, smearing blood across his jaw. "You will be a wonderful father, Vale."

Her last words.

He cried against her chest, the silence of her heartbeat, of his unborn child, deafening.

The memories skipped ahead of themselves to Mira pacing the width of their bedchamber, hurt rupturing across her delicate features.

"You do not love me, Vale!" she shouted, the depth of emotion present in her tone. "Not like you loved her!"

Father whipped around, expression enraged. "You stole her from me!"

"I did not know the island was occupied by mortals!"

Father's eyes filled with tears. He turned away from her, shaking his head. "I apologize, Mira, but I cannot love you the way you long for me to. Not when you are the reason I—"

"You are separated from your *true* beloved."

Father looked back at her then, taking in the thin set of her lips, the droplets falling from her porcelain eyes.

"Yes," he said.

The memory evaporated. A brilliant white shined. Behind it, Finnian could hear the wailing of a child.

"Naia," his father said, a smile in his voice. "Your name is Naia, darling."

Naia's childhood stretched out before him. The birth of each of his siblings. Father growing magnolias and gifting them to a young Marina; twirling a young Astrid on the dance floor; teaching a bright-eyed Vex how to skip stones without angering Ziven, a river god who resided in the River of Souls; sitting on a large stone with Malik at his side, pointing out butterflies.

And then: Finnian in his sixth year, cradling a fish Malik had killed. The gills on the side of its slimy, silver scales open and frozen in place.

Finnian looked up through fat tears at his father. "You must return it to life."

"Finny, my boy." Father kneeled and cupped his hands underneath Finnian's, helping hold the fish. "That is not something I can do."

Finnian scowled through his tears in disbelief. "You are the High God of Nature. There is nothing you cannot do! Bring it back. It did not deserve to meet its end at Malik's cruel blade. What if it has a family? Someone who misses it?"

Father smiled softly, wiping Finnian's wet cheeks with the back of his finger. "My dear boy, death is a part of life. Do not pity those who step into its Land, nor the ones they leave behind."

"But—but death is separation," Finnian sobbed, hugging the fish to his chest. "Separation is pain. It is how I feel when we are not together."

Father stared at him, eyes glistening. "Death is peace, Finnian, and pain is simply a sign of love's presence."

The memory melted away.

In its place, an ethereal cloud, a white cosmos, wrapped around him. He was standing now, surrounded by the bright, plush landscape.

He glanced down at his hands, his legs, and ran his fingers through his short hair to confirm he was his present self.

When he looked up, Father was before him.

His eyes widened and something shattered in his chest. A lump swelled in his throat. He snapped forward, throwing his arms around Father's neck.

"I am so sorry." He cried into the shoulder of his father's robe, hanging on to him. "I always mess up. It seems impossible for me to do the right thing. In the end, all I ever do is hurt those closest to me. You, Naia, Cassian. Everything I did to right my wrongs was for nothing. Ruelle is going to kill me."

Father broke away, wrapping one hand around his nape. With a genuine smile, he studied Finnian. "Do you know why I gave Wren to your sister?"

"To aid her in time of need," he sniveled.

Father gave a breathy laugh, bringing both hands up to cradle Finnian's face. "She assumed it was because I believed her to be weak. I assured her that nobody, not even High Deities, can do everything alone."

He pulled Finnian into a hug. "My boy, you are strong and have made up for your wrongs. I was never disappointed in you. Forgive yourself. Stop trying to do everything on your own."

Finnian rested his weight on him, sobbing into his shoulder. He could feel the magic around them coming undone. The solid figure of Father under his arms softened and began disappearing like mist. "Please. Don't go. Not yet."

"I am always with you." Father turned his head and kissed Finnian on the side of his hair. "Eternally."

His father's voice carried like a leaf caught in a breeze, swirling, dancing, fading.

Finnian gradually drifted from the moment, like stepping out of a dream.

"Finnian!"

The Land's sky stretched out before him, its lavender-soaked clouds hazy and quickly covered by Ruelle as she came to loom over his side.

Tears slipped from the corners of his eyes, trailing down his temples. An ache stretched into what felt like a crater taking shape in his chest.

He wanted to go back. So much so, that for a fraction of a second, the thought crossed his mind to give up, let Ruelle kill him. Because then, he could return to Father.

"Finnian!" Cassian yelled from somewhere afar.

His sonorous voice split through the ache, through the desolate thought of death.

Finnian sucked in a breath to respond, but the thread constricted around his throat, assaulting his tendons.

Ruelle did not acknowledge Cassian's shouting as she held up the syringe, readied in her grip. "I sincerely apologize for this."

Bullshit.

He narrowed his eyes on her, his heart thudding in his chest.

Stop trying to do everything on your own.

After a lifetime of stubbornness and isolation, Finnian finally understood his father's words.

A smirk slit across his mouth, baring blood-stained teeth.

"Naia, High Goddess of Eternity." Each word felt like flesh grinding against a hacksaw as he spoke, but it was worth it as a baffled look morphed over Ruelle's beautiful face. "Come to me."

THIRTY-TWO

THE HIGH GODDESS OF ETERNITY

BRIGHT STARLIGHT POURED out at the edge of the grove, and Naia stepped through it.

Gracefully, she lifted her arm to free Wren from her silver strands, rippling in the gust of her divine power. The golden hairpin emerged to life and slashed the threads banded around Finnian's throat.

The pressure released and he gasped in a breath.

Naia pushed off her legs and collided into Ruelle. They skid across the ash-dusted grove. The syringe toppled across the ground.

Finnian saw them then, the twinkling of the threads in the sunlight, raining down as Wren sliced through them, weightless. A cage, disbanded.

In less than a breath's second, Cassian appeared at Finnian's side, rushing to unravel the thread from around his neck.

The knot in Finnian's chest eased at the sight of him unharmed, though his hair was a disheveled mess, and blood stained the corner of his mouth.

He grabbed onto his forearm and slowly hauled himself up to track Naia and Ruelle.

Cassian hissed a demand at him that he did not catch.

He regarded him with a look of confusion before wincing from the stabbing pang in his abdomen—a reaction to the stretching of muscles as he sat up all the way.

Cassian's eyes snapped up to his right ear, then the ground around them, searching, while simultaneously continuing to unweave the string from around his neck.

Ruelle's backside was smashed up against the only hawthorn trunk still upright.

Azara and Iliana stood behind Naia like two torchbearers.

Naia's palm was firmly planted on Ruelle's sternum, her other hand drawn up and a thumb pressed to Ruelle's forehead.

Snowy starlight crested around Naia like waves. "Ruelle, High Goddess of Fate." Her voice was thunderous, almighty. "The Council is gathered to see to it that you are punished for your digressions. In the order of our name, you have manipulated your power of Fate for selfish and impure intent."

Our name.

"No!" Acacius fabricated in the center of the grove, his robe only ribbons and his bone visibly jutting out of his forearm and ribcage. His pale skin slowly stitched across newly formed muscle and tissue.

Iliana whisked around, her gilded eyes shining like heated crystals, and she raised her palm to silence him.

Acacius collapsed to his knees, slamming his eyes shut in some sort of pain. "Sister, no!"

The brilliant rays of white rippled in large rings around Naia as she continued. "Ruelle, from this moment forward, you will no longer bear the gift of immortality."

A thin, metallic ring screamed out as the incandescence beamed hotter, brighter, like a burning star.

Finnian squinted against its power, tears welling in his eyes.

Stunning.

It seemed that not only could she grant immortal life, but she could also take it away.

Pride swelled in his chest. She was elegant and so much like Father that it hurt.

His stomach dipped at the reminder of Father.

Finnian tightened his fingers around Cassian's forearm, a lifeline to keep him afloat.

The frozen opalescence dimmed and the sharp shrill fell flat, revealing Naia and Ruelle in its draining light.

Finnian glanced over at Cassian. His chest was still, with bated breath, as he peered at the two goddesses. Blood smudges stained his fair cheeks.

His hands were covered in it, but the threads were completely untangled from Finnian.

As if he could sense Finnian's staring, Cassian turned his head to look at him, offering his hand in between them. He opened his enclosed fingers to reveal the *bidziil* crystal in his palm.

Finnian glanced up from his hearing aid onto Cassian's weak smile. Guilt and sorrow and an outpouring of so much damn love flooded Finnian. Even after all the years that had passed between them, Cassian still had his well-being in the forefront of his mind.

He accepted his hearing aid, quickly inserting it as he fixated back onto Naia and Ruelle.

Ruelle slid down the bark of the tree, her auburn strands matte under the sunlight. The sheen of her divinity was stripped, and it showed in the pallid hue of her complexion, the muted brown in what once was a bronze, glittering gaze.

Naia took a step back and bowed her head. Always the respectful one. "I apologize for what has transpired here today, Lady Ruelle, but it was the will of the Council." She lifted her chin then, looking straight at Ruelle. "And the will of my heart, for the pain you have brought upon my younger brother."

Strangely, Ruelle regarded Naia with a wistful smile, crinkling the skin at the corners of her tear-filled eyes. "No need to apologize, Lady Naia. You have my gratitude."

Finnian exchanged a look of apprehension with Cassian.

Why would Ruelle be grateful? Especially after everything she'd put them through to seek her revenge.

Naia held Ruelle's stare for a long moment.

Acacius crossed the grove in a trail of charcoal-blue smoke to Ruelle's side.

Naia made no move to back away at his close presence. She acknowledged him with a small dip of her chin that he did not return as he rushed to scoop up Ruelle.

Together, they vanished.

Cassian let out a frail sigh, shifting his attention to the souls surrounding them in the grove.

Finnian took one last look at each of them, memorizing their distinct energies, the faces, saying his peace to them one last time.

You could keep them all.

The voice came in a distant whisper, under the muffled shrill scratching in his mind, prodding at the nerves in his jaws, down his spine. He was growing so used to the curse's chronic itch and manic murmuring that it did not immediately trigger an unfurling fear throughout his insides.

Mind it no attention.

His eyes found Eleanor and Isla, their arms hooked, waving and smiling at him. "We love you, Finny."

Cassian snapped his fingers, and the souls disfigured and took flight in the air as luminous orbs.

Fireflies.

A blissful grin broke apart Finnian's blood-crusted lips. "I love you too," he whispered.

Iliana rotated to Cassian, her expression somber, disheartened.

Cassian held her gaze, silently exchanging grief-stricken feelings.

Acacius had chosen Ruelle over the Council, over his siblings. How would they recover from that?

Iliana gave a single nod of mutual understanding before teleporting away. Milky wisps curled in the air where she had stood.

Azara passed Cassian a brief look before her form dispersed into crackling embers shortly after.

Finnian looked at his sister, her deep green eyes shining and squished in a broad smile directed at him. *Truly her.* Not an illusion or a hallucination.

Warmth seeped like spilled wine in Finnian's chest, and he smiled, stretching his arms wide.

She leapt forward on her feet and materialized in a white-jasmine wisp, crashing into him. "I made it to you, Finny!"

He laughed as tears snuck down the crevices of his nose, embracing her with the strength of a god and straining her bones.

She was a cloud of espresso and white sage and a floral garden; of city air and frequent visits to the local bakery on 10th Street; fruity and pungent like the inside of Ronin's brewery.

"I missed you so much," she sniveled into his shoulder.

Finnian held her between his knees, her hair sticking to his damp face. "I missed you so much more."

THIRTY-THREE

DEATH IS LOVE

"Are you okay?" Naia pulled away and ran her fingers over the dried blood of his neck to inspect for any wounds that hadn't healed. "Gods, Finny, I missed you. I have much to tell you."

An effusion of warmth consumed him from the sound of her voice. "I am fine," he assured her. "How did you know to bring the Council?"

"Alke. He journeyed to Hollow City and informed me of the situation. I ascended onto the Council a few hours ago—thanks to all the efforts of *your* organizations…" She gave him a pointed look. "When I arrived, I told Iliana everything. She was baffled that you did not shed a breath of it to her," she said to Cassian.

Finnian pursed his lips, grateful for his bird's undying devotion.

He shook his head, giving Cassian an inquisitive look. "How did Ruelle not foresee the Council's involvement then?"

"I considered involving Iliana and the Council many times, but Ruelle had both of our threads under a microscope. Any case I tried to make against her, she always foresaw it, and was able to falsely prove me wrong," Cassian explained, his hand never leaving Finnian's back. "However, I doubt she would've been keeping a close eye on Naia's Fate, with her being a High Goddess now."

Naia's brow fell as her fingertips glided along the inky swirl of the curse mark over Finnian's Adam's apple.

She blinked through the tears gathering in her eyes. "You fool," she whispered.

Cassian frowned, watching the places her fingers traced.

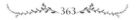

Finnian didn't wish to think about the curse right now. He would deal with it later—figure out a spell to cast on himself to slow its tendrils, but for now, he wanted to enjoy the moment. Ruelle had been defeated, and Naia was there, right in front of him.

Finnian lightly took her hand and lowered it from his neck. He dipped his chin to latch onto her gaze. "I see the winter god has taught you quite a bit since I've been away."

The color of her wisps was radiant, like a pearl cut from the finest stone, beautiful and bright just like her.

"Theon is an excellent teacher." She gave a lousy smile as she wiped at the fat droplets rolling down her cheeks. "I was teleporting around Hollow City in less than a month after your departure."

Finnian grinned at the image. "And what of my nephew?"

A small, pitiful laugh slipped out through her sniffles. She placed her other hand over the back of his and squeezed. "He is absolutely dying to meet his uncle."

Finnian had envisioned the moment many times. Prior to regaining his memories, he'd often imagined it while he was in his cell, trapped in Moros—after he'd rescued Father and escaped. He would daydream of escorting Father to Hollow City, standing on the roof of his favorite skyscraper with Naia, Ronin, and Ash. Some semblance of being a family, a true one, without Mira's bullshit and the triplets and Marina.

Father will never get to see Hollow City.

Finnian's heart grew heavy, like a stone caught in his chest.

"Naia." He averted his eyes down to their joined hands. His throat tightened. "Father is—"

An itch thrummed like an insect buzzing in his brain.

Father will never meet Ronin.

Cassian's hand smoothed up his back and lightly gripped his shoulder. "Vale has passed," he finished.

Father will never meet Ash.

Naia's breath hitched.

Finnian grimaced at the sound. He didn't want to see her reaction, because it would make the situation too visceral.

Father will never get to live again.

"He awaits at the gate." Cassian turned to look at Finnian. "If you'd like, you both may join me as the Errai escort him into the Land."

All because of you.

"Of course." Naia's voice wobbled. "Thank you, Lord Cassian."

Finnian focused on the warm sensation of Naia's hand over his; the nerves awakening in his toes after his torso had been severed into two; the imprints of Cassian's fingertips on his shoulder; the distant fragrance of lavender infused in the light breeze. Anything but the reality of the topic they spoke of, anything but the burning itch and the haunting chorus of voices harassing his mind.

He could feel Cassian's prismatic gaze studying the side of his face.

Finnian wanted to assure him everything was fine, but he could not lie. Not only that, but it would be useless. Cassian knew him better than that by now—with every tic and shift of expression Finnian intentionally gave, Cassian could see beneath his surface.

Finnian ground his teeth to halt the quivering of his jaw and managed a stiff nod.

Cassian moved his hand up Finnian's nape and into his hair, cradling the back of his head.

Like second nature, Finnian eased into his palm.

Trickles of Cassian's divine power sank through his scalp and dissolved into his bloodstream. The thrumming in his brain silenced, and his muscles relaxed in relief.

Cassian held out his other hand in the center of them and said, "Let us go see him off."

Naia hesitated, making no move to do as he said.

The corner of Cassian's mouth lifted as he looked at her. "I have no intention of cursing you again, Little Goddess. Two was enough."

She blew air into her cheeks, her face scrunching.

Finnian chuckled as he guided both of their hands into Cassian's.

WISTERIA blossoms stuck in Finnian's hair as they strolled towards the colossal iron doors at the center of the obsidian wall. In its stone held the carvings of deities Cassian had triumphed over during the Great Deity War for his title.

The first time Finnian had seen the engravings was five years ago, when he came to exchange his freedom for Naia's. Prior, he'd only ever teleported directly into the Land. He'd stared up at them, naming them fools for their losses. Now, all he felt was a sense of pride. The Land and everything within it, they were pieces of Cassian, pieces of home.

Finnian held onto Naia's hand as they traveled through the winding path in the enchanted wisteria. There was a wise energy among their roots. If Finnian were to siphon it, he was sure he could mold it and use it to gravely injure Marina.

The thought grew more and more enticing as they approached her.

She sat on her knees, her legs sprawled out at her sides, face buried in her hands, crying beside Father's body. A magnolia blossom rested in her lap.

Finnian had never seen such emotion on Marina. It was odd and only hardened his animosity towards her.

A figure stood over her, tall and broad and wearing a velvet, evergreen robe. Crowning his head was a constellation of olive and orchid—soft, muted tones, just like his persona.

Ever the gentle, loving father.

An ache split down Finnian's middle.

Naia passed him a look, squeezing his hand.

Finnian directed his attention down onto Marina—the source of his pain.

She should've killed me, not him.

Rage skewered sharply through him, like a spiked mace running up his gut and into his ribcage.

He ripped his hand from Naia and charged forward, bypassing Cassian.

Father's soul spun and glided like he was made of water, acting as a barrier.

He stuck his hand out, pressing his palm against Finnian's shoulder. "No more fighting."

Finnian glared over him at Marina. "She murdered you! She murdered Kaleo! She has tormented Naia for far too long!"

"I will take responsibility for her actions." Despite Finnian's raised voice, Father spoke softly.

Finnian's eyes jumped back to him, incredulous. "Father."

"Finnian, you are each a product of your environment. The blame is mine and Mira's to carry. You have *all* suffered because of our mistakes. There are two sides to each coin. As you and Naia received animosity from Mira, Marina received the same from me."

Finnian's jaw set. He couldn't fathom Father being anything but kind, but the twinge in his gut reminded him nothing was ever as it seemed.

He glared down at Marina, watching her shoulders shake from her sobs. For the first time since he'd known her, she resembled a broken child.

"Promise me" — Father settled both hands on each of Finnian's shoulders — "that you will let your hostility go. The life of a god may be eternal, but that is no reason to carry on without granting forgiveness. Forever is wasted if you spend it in anger."

Finnian turned his head away, jaw flexing. He wanted to refuse, to make Marina bleed by his own volition, but it was Father's request. How could he say no?

"Fine," he forced out.

Father slid his hand off his shoulders and stepped around him to Naia.

A smiling sob sprang out of her. "Father."

Father matched her tearful smile and held out his arms.

She jumped into his embrace. "I cannot believe you are here," she whimpered.

He lifted her feet off the ground. "You have mesmerized me, darling. I am so proud of you."

"You were right. All along. I apologize for how long it took me to believe in myself."

Father chuckled. "You move at your own pace. Never at the speed anyone else urges you to. It is one of the many qualities I admire about you."

Naia craned her head back and turned slightly, gesturing to the gilded hairpin in her silver strands. "Wren refuses freedom. No matter how many times I try."

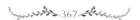

"That comes as no surprise." Father brushed the hairpin along its wings. The solid gold shed to a colorful butterfly, and he smiled. "Do take care of those I cherish, Wren."

The relic fluttered its wing before solidifying back into gold.

Naia squeezed Father's neck, sniffling into his shoulder.

Father lowered her feet back to the ground and brought his hands to her cheeks, smiling down at her. "Please tell my grandson how much I love him."

"I do. I do every day," she hiccupped between her tears. "He's brilliant and infatuated with flowers. Says he can feel you within their properties. He's beautiful. He has my silver hair and Ronin's eyes and Finnian's scowl."

Cassian and Father shared breathy laughs.

Finnian wanted to roll his eyes, savor the last moment of humor, but the brevity of the situation rang in his core. How could he laugh, or even smile, when they were approaching the end?

I shouldn't have dismissed seeing him all those years ago.

"Enjoy your life, Naia." Father tucked one of her sliver strands behind her ear. A bud sprouted and yawned open into a deep-red dahlia in place of his finger. "Every day of it."

Naia clasped ahold of his wrist, her chin quivering. "I promise," she squeaked out.

Father wiped away her falling tears and kissed her on her forehead.

He gently slid his wrist out of her hold and rotated towards his son.

Finnian's racing heart palpitated, and he crossed his arms, looking away. "Don't." The word came out sharp.

"Finny."

A lump swelled in his throat.

He stared down, the long ends of wisteria grazing the ground. "I will never see you again."

"You will."

Lies.

Heat flared up his neck and behind his eyes. He snapped his head up at Father. "No, I won't." He slapped his hand on his chest. "I am immortal."

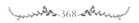

Father placed his hand over the back of Finnian's. His tender touch reached through Finnian's stubborn will and straight down into his soul. "Wherever you go, I am with you. *Always*."

Finnian's eyes burned. "In my heart, in my thoughts, it's hardly enough." A ragged, broken sound punctuated his words. He inhaled. "You and I will be parted for eternity, and I will carry our love with me *alone*."

"Finnian." Cassian frowned at his side.

Naia's fingertips brushed his arm. "Finny—"

"No." Finnian ripped his hand away. Nerves spasmed through his system and caught in his stomach. He staggered back from them. "I—"

A quivering in his bones felt like static trapped in his skin.

Pressure constricted his chest.

He pushed the heel of his hand against his sternum as his lungs wheezed to grab onto air.

He couldn't let go. Not yet. He needed to fix this. A spell. He could use a spell. Keep him here forever and—

Cassian grabbed him by the wrist and yanked him forward. Their chests collided as Cassian's long arms strapped around him.

"Finny," he whispered.

Finnian dug his face into Cassian's shoulder to muffle his own sob.

"I can't—" he hyperventilated. "I can't say goodbye."

"You don't have to," Cassian murmured, holding him snug with a hand on the back of his head, the other around his waist. "Death is much more than a collection of endings. Will you allow me to prove this to you?"

Finnian curled and uncurled his fingers at his sides. His limbs felt heavy, numbing. "I fear it won't make a difference."

A part of him knew Cassian was right. Life was far too complex for death to be so plainly bleak. But on the other hand, no matter how necessary death was, Finnian could not bring himself to comprehend it. Eternity was all he knew. No ends, no separation. He couldn't make sense of the ephemeral.

And no amount of explaining would change the fact that Father's time was up. Death was cruel that way. It did not give warning. It blew in when it so desired and left devastation proudly in its path, uncaring of those caught in its wake.

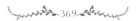

"You do not have to understand it," Cassian said. "You just have to find a way to make peace with it."

Trust him. Like you always have.

Back when they were enemies and Cassian first told him death was not a terrible thing, Finnian had despised how easily he'd believed him. He had refused to acknowledge the twinge in his chest each time he thought about the possibility. Though, he couldn't help but do so.

Despair had existed all around him. As a boy, he could recall its presence in Father's eyes; through his travels in the Mortal Land, in women and children and men taking refuge in dark corners of alleyways as shelter; every person that sought him out and begged him to revive their child, their lover, their friend.

There has to be more than this, Finnian always thought to himself. *A place with no hurt, no anguish.*

Cassian lightly pulled away, hands still in Finnian's hair and on his waist. He met his gaze, brow slightly lifted, looking at him in a way that asked, *are you ready?*

Finnian gave a weak nod.

Cassian returned his attention to Father.

Finnian did not. He could feel Father watching, the adoration pouring out and infusing in the air and dissolving deep into his pores. A love that sank into his marrow. He wanted to reach out and freeze it right there.

Father wrapped an arm around Finnian's side, reaching out his other hand to scrub through Cassian's hair. "It has been a nice life, old friend."

Cassian scoffed through a small smile, smoothing his strands back. "I am happy to rid you and your moss from my prison."

Father laughed. "I will find a way to grow it in the afterlife, I promise you that. I've taught my successor well."

Cassian rolled his eyes. "I have no doubt."

Father let out a breath, his smile shrinking into a more wistful one.

A solemn look shadowed Cassian's features as he held Father's eyes. "Are you ready, Vale?"

Father stared at him for a long moment, squeezing Finnian's side one last time before stepping away. "Yes."

Finnian's pulse beat frantically in his throat.

Cassian slipped his fingers through Finnian's as he looked at Naia and then down to Marina. "Both of you, follow."

Marina made no move to get up. She shook and wept like a fragile, broken thing.

Finnian's nostrils flared, the sight clotting a sickness in his gut.

Naia breezed past them and kneeled beside Marina. "Come on, Sister." She gently took hold of Marina's forearm and hauled her up. "I will hold on to you."

Surprisingly, Marina did not dispute.

Together, they rose to their feet.

With one hand, she clung to Naia's arm, and in her other, she clasped the magnolia against her stomach. Her porcelain complexion was splotchy and hideous from her tears.

Finnian's eyes flickered to Father. He watched them with small pride—a fulfillment of some dying wish. Finnian was glad Naia could be the one to grant that to him.

The iron gates rumbled the ground as they split apart. A trail wound through the forest of wisteria.

Lustrous, fiery globes drifted under the wispy branches like small stars. They skipped and dashed across the air, a fading giggle echoing behind them.

Two Errai cloaked in bone-gray attire met them at the trail, their faces hidden behind their marble masks.

They both bowed in greeting and then gestured to Vale to stand in the empty space between them.

He did and they started forward.

Cassian strolled behind them with Finnian in hand.

Naia walked at Finnian's other side, her arm interlocked with Marina's. Both of their heads were lifted, their eyes chasing the glowing spirits.

"They are souls," Finnian whispered to Naia.

"Amazing," Naia breathed out, captivated.

Beyond the swaying tendrils of wisteria, Finnian could make out the knolls at the entrance of the Lavender Fields of Healing. The sight spiked his heart rate, compressing his breath.

This is it. This is truly it.

His chest tightened.

I can't do this. I can't watch him leave me—again.

Resistance burned the muscles in his legs. He went to pull his hand from Cassian, but Cassian's grip constricted.

Finnian cut his eyes over at him.

Cassian gave him a comforting look that said, *you are okay.*

Finnian let out an unsteady exhale as they emerged from the tree line.

The delicate breeze of the Field ruffled through his hair, fluttering his shirt against his torso.

Naia's breath hitched at the view of the rustling lavender. "Beautiful."

They came to a stop and the Errai both turned sideways and stretched an arm out, gesturing to the vast, lavender locks. "Lord Vale, High God of Nature, it is an honor to welcome you into the Land of the Dead. In the Lavender Field, you will find healing. Your troubles, your pain, it will all fade. May you find peace in Death."

Father's body shifted to take a step.

"Wait!" Finnian lurched forward, catching the velvet material of his robe in between his fingers. "I am not ready for this!"

Father twisted to face him. It was strange to not see the baby's breath gracing his dark strands; his scruffy cheeks devoid of color; eyes that were as crisp as the earth's soil, now the same pastel lilac sparkle as the energy shining over his head. Proof that what had happened in the grove was real.

He was dead and everything screamed in Finnian to find a way to reverse it.

Father lifted Finnian's hand up between them and turned his palm upright.

"I create blossoms knowing only a few will survive a day." He swiveled his own wrist in a familiar motion and a large trumpet-shaped flower blossomed in Finnian's open hand. "But there is no such thing as finality. The cycle continues, time and time again. You must let it."

Tears welled in Finnian's eyes, pricking at the back of his nose. The flower petals tickled against his skin. He'd never had the chance to tell Father what his favorite flower was as a boy, and yet, somehow, he knew.

Father leaned in and kissed his forehead. "Even in death, Finnian. Love is the only thing truly immortal."

Finnian's vision blurred Father into a silhouette. He pursed his lips to smother another sob.

Father stepped back and gave him, Naia, and Marina a final look.

Finnian blinked away the moisture collecting in his eyes, desperate to memorize this moment. One last time. To float in Father's presence, like the calmest sea, feeling as it began to drain away.

Eyes glistening, Father said, "I love each of you. Deeper than the earth."

Finnian's eyes fell shut.

Naia curled her other arm around his waist and pulled him into her side. Footfalls shuffled through the stalks of lavender.

He is leaving me.

His legs shook against his own weight. Naia held him closer to her side, as if she could feel his trembling.

He is leaving me.

The hard pounding of his heart echoed in his skull.

He is leaving me.

"Finny," Naia gasped through her weeping. "Look."

Finnian opened his eyes.

Father waded through the waist-high lavender. A woman with long black hair raced for him with a small child in her arms. They soared across the Field, flickering from human form to radiant orbs shooting over the blossomed ends of the lavender.

At the sight of them, Father stopped and his shoulders melted, as if all the weight of his sorrows had drifted away. The centuries of pain and misery that life had brought. All stones he'd done well to carry.

This is peace.

"Daddy!" the child called out, giggling. He had Father's smile, a contagious warmth in his eyes.

"Vale! We've been waiting." The woman's beaming face drew closer, almost there.

A happy laugh left Father, and he threw his arms wide. "I am here. *Finally.*" The words left him like a breath of relief.

The woman and child leapt into his open embrace, and he held them like he had held Finnian and Naia many times.

"I am here," he said. "And I am not going anywhere."

A cracked sound scraped up the back of Finnian's throat. He slapped a hand over his mouth to hold it down.

Marina clung to Naia, a loud, violent cry pouring out of her.

Naia soothed her with a hand in her hair as her own sobs shook through her. She buried her face into Finnian's arm, her breath erratic and her posture slumping on him.

He lifted his arm to support her, but it prickled, like the nerves were short-circuiting. Emotions he'd ran from his entire life flooded in, threatening to capsize him.

Cassian's hand slid over his nape and into his hair. His lips lightly met the side of Finnian's temple.

In his touch, the pillars in Finnian's heart crumbled, and a mangled cry broke free. He folded inward and wailed.

"Love is death," Cassian whispered, holding him close. "But death is love again."

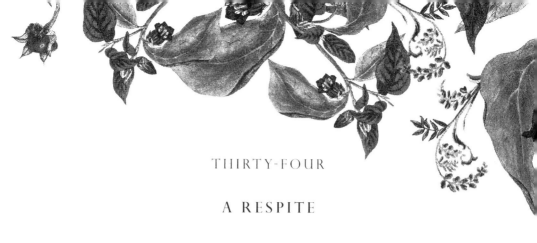

THIRTY-FOUR

A RESPITE

Cassian

HE WIND STIRRED the powdered remains of the grove. Fine particles of dust floated in the air, glistening like star dew. Cassian watched them drift and twirl.

It seemed fitting, after all these years, for their love to burn, preserving the ashes in the crevices of his Land.

Cassian stuffed his hands in his pockets and inhaled deeply—the stale, crisp scent of the grove, citrus and mint, tangled in a honeyed botanic fragrance wafting from his own garden.

He lifted his head and appreciated the buttery, soft pink dawn spilling over the peaks of Moros.

His heart ached for the friend he'd lost, for the brother who betrayed him, and for what was to come. A bittersweet ache he gladly welcomed.

Finnian's footfalls sounded behind him—a light step, barely audible, except for the slight twist of his heel as he pushed off his foot. A sound Cassian had memorized long ago. A sound that shot an instant dose of euphoria through his system each time he heard it.

Only this time, that euphoria was muddled with melancholy.

Finnian stopped at his side and followed his gaze out to the grove. He frowned and rolled his neck. Cassian observed closely out of the side of his eye. The twitchy, uncomfortable motion was a product of the curse.

Finnian lifted his arm, hand upright, and slightly curled his fingers.

Bright green stems protruded up from the ash-covered soil. Their ends budded and sprouted white, trumpet-shaped blossoms.

"I apologize for destroying the grove," he said quietly, shamefully.

"You were confused and simply trying to figure out what was real."

"I will regrow it all. The passion flowers, the hawthorn, the rosemary. All of it."

Cassian rotated his body towards Finnian.

Finnian stared at him, brow pinched. "What is it?"

He raised his hands from his pockets and slipped them over Finnian's cheeks, slowly bridging the space between them until he met Finnian's lips.

Cassian's insides liquified. A quiver trembled through him and his knees nearly buckled from its delightful sensation. *So long.* It had been so long since he'd kissed Finnian.

His thumbs hooked at the base of Finnian's jawline to deepen the kiss, injecting more of him into his bloodstream.

Finnian inhaled a breath through his nose and clasped both sides of Cassian's waist, digging his fingertips into the material of his waistband.

The world, the shit, the last century and a half of their lives. It was all behind them.

In Cassian's mind, he was back in Augustus with Finnian, walking the trail underneath old oaks, the dabbling of the stream like a calming lullaby, with Finnian at his side, pointing at the fireflies.

That was his peace—Finnian and their lips on each other's with nothing between them. No busy schedules, no conflicts, no warring. Just the two of them.

He held onto this as he glided a hand down the side of Finnian's neck, settling his palm over Finnian's pec. Divine power rushed through his blood into his fingertips.

Finnian's eyes snapped open, and he shoved away from Cassian—too quickly for Cassian to snatch ahold of him.

A wild look of disapproval warped his features. "I will not let you do it." He stepped back until there was a suitable length separating them, glaring with that beautiful scowl of his. "Not like this, Cassius. Give me time. I will craft a potion and break the curse myself."

A sad smile curved over Cassian's mouth, knowing that was precisely what Finnian would say. "You do not have that kind of time. The curse will only grow worse as the days pass. I am finished waiting for us to be whole again."

"Not like this!" Finnian snarled, his eyes twisting furiously. "You absolve the curse, *you* will pay the price. I refuse to let that happen."

Cassian couldn't help but think back on the many arguments of their past. Standing face-to-face this way, and all the times that Cassian thought he would explode from the aggravation Finnian riled within him. They had come so far. Their words had finally reached one another after years of opposition. And as Cassian reflected, he realized how none of the things they'd disagreed on really mattered in the grand scheme of it all.

What mattered was this: Finnian stood before him, bold and terrified, unsettled by the idea of his partner experiencing any more loss or heartache. Everything in between, their journey to get to this moment, Cassian would do it all over again in a heartbeat.

"I love you too much," Cassian said, "to allow my curse to weather your beautiful mind."

Pain etched Finnian's expression. It revealed itself in the tight line of his mouth, the fallen corners of his eyes. As quickly as it appeared, it flitted away.

He inclined his head, defiant, a challenge. "Then you will have to catch me first."

Cassian expected nothing less from him. "You are bound to me through the potion that still entangles us, and from the moment you traded places with Naia, your soul belongs to me. There is nowhere you can run to."

Finnian's nostrils flared, and he clenched his hand into a fist in front of his stomach. "I will fight you then. I will not let you give up everything for me."

Cassian drew in a breath and let it out in a ragged exhale. "You *are* everything. I am tired, Finny. I want a life with you. An uninterrupted life. I want to waste away in bed with you, live somewhere in the countryside, have a garden, take midnight strolls, and do whatever else we wish to do."

"You adore your Land, the souls."

"I do," Cassian said. "But my time as its ruler has come to an end."

The defiance fell from Finnian's face. "If you do this, you will be giving up your title as a High God."

Cassian stared at him for a long moment, taking in the creases along his forehead and the frown weighing down his lips. "I want our *one day*, Finnian." His voice crackled, and he clamped his shaking lips.

Peering up, he ran a hand through his hair and blinked away the tears stinging in his eyes. "I've waited for over a century. It was the thing I clung to when the darkness engulfed me—when I couldn't step foot back into Hollow City, when you faced me with such disdain, when I had to sit back and let Shivani torture you…" A sputtered cry broke through his words and he paused, gripping his hair tighter in his fist.

Finnian crossed the distance.

Without a word, he lightly unraveled Cassian's fingers from his hair. He guided Cassian's hand underneath the collar of his shirt and spliced his palm over the curse mark. Cassian could feel the edges of it raised on his skin.

"I won't stop you," he said, somber. "So long as this is what you truly desire."

Cassian brought his other hand to Finnian's nape and anchored him forward, connecting their foreheads. "Close your eyes."

Finnian sucked in a breath and did as he requested.

Cassian lowered his hand along Finnian's spine and rested it in the middle of his back, pulling their bodies snug. His divine power hummed in his fingertips. "Where do you wish to go?"

"You cannot distract me."

"Tell me anyway."

"Augustus," he said.

Cassian closed his eyes. "What else?"

"I'll grow a garden. Teach you how to dry herbs to make your teas."

"I will cook us breakfast each morning. And perhaps we can get a dog," Cassian replied, smiling.

"A live one, you mean?"

Cassian chuckled. "Yes, a *live* one."

Finnian nudged his nose against Cassian's cheek. "And we will live happily—with no end."

Cassian curled his fingers, pressing the tips into the skin of Finnian's chest. He inhaled. "Forever."

Like ink being spilled in reverse, the dark coils of cursed magic began to untangle from Finnian and back into Cassian's palm.

He exhaled, relishing in the pinch of agony within his arteries. A wrong of his own made right.

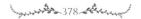

"Let us share a final set of **goodbyes**," he said, "before our life begins."

THE atmosphere stilled. A gray-slate wall encompassed the sky, casting a monochromatic hue across the Land. In its backdrop, hundreds of dazzling specks flourished in its darkness. Rain wept down, mourning the fall of its ruler.

Atop the knoll flourished in lavender, souls gathered outside their village. They sang and danced around him. Crowns of black pansies and hemlock adorned their heads. Garlands of wisteria bounced around their necks.

The rain pelted the tops of Cassian's shoulders, drenching his hair and clothes.

He smiled and watched his souls praise him one last time.

Nathaira twirled amongst them, her sodden brunette strands flying in the air. She had always glowed in Cassian's eyes, but as a High Goddess after Vale's passing, she was marvelous. Laurel braided down her arms and over the corset of her gown, and she swayed with her eyes closed, content and with true peace.

Shivani chanted and jumped in the spot behind her. She wore a pair of jeans and a linen blouse, her complexion unmarred of rust and her hands empty of knives. It was a strange sight.

Finnian stood across from Cassian, his curls soaked against his forehead. Droplets gathered in his eyelashes and trickled down his face. He stared at Cassian with a glistening gaze, his neck free from the curse mark.

As the celebration quietened, the rain ceased, and strips of bronze tangerine streaked across the dreary sky.

"Mavros," Cassian called out.

The crowd of souls parted, making way for his attendant.

Cassian held his arm out and formed his divine energy into a gleaming globe within the palm of his hand. The outside looked as if it were made of glass, but its center pulsed in milky black waves.

Mavros approached, clasping his hands together. He stopped in front of Cassian and closed his eyes, pointing his head down towards his mentor's feet.

In a gentle motion, Cassian grasped his fingers around the orb and squeezed until it shattered, releasing the vaporous energy inside. The onyx smoke swirled like ribbons and spun around Mavros's head twice before entering through the skin between his eyes.

"It is done," Cassian murmured, sharing a small moment between them.

Mavros bowed his chin, acknowledging Cassian with more respect than he'd ever deserved.

He was proud of the Land, everything he had created, and he knew Mavros held a heart inside him built just like his own. The souls of the world would continue to find their rest.

"All hail, Mavros, High God of Death and Curses."

The souls applauded and began chanting the song of the Land.

Mavros kept his head lowered. "I will not let you down, my lord."

Cassian patted him on the shoulder. "I am not your lord anymore, Mavros. In fact, you are technically mine."

He raised up and said, "You will always be my lord. My guidance."

Cassian gave his shoulder a small squeeze and smiled. "If you need anything, I am only a summons away."

"Go enjoy your long-awaited vacation, Cassian. You've earned it."

Cassian turned to meet his lover's gaze and extended his arm.

Finnian's fingers glided over Cassian's, hooking his grip around the heel of his palm.

Golden light poured over the land, and its rays spilled across Finnian, refracting off his olive-tan skin like gilded string. His eyes had not shined so brightly in a long, long time.

Go, the Land said. *Be free.*

THIRTY-FIVE

ONE DAY

Finnian

RMS CROSSED, FINNIAN shook his head at the absurd monstrosity. A statue of himself eclipsed the midday sunlight in the center of Alke Square, the heart of Hollow City.

Cassian pointed at the divots on either side of the statue's cheeks, his watch reflecting glints of passing vehicles and pedestrians. "Adorable," he said. "You managed to get his dimples."

Under glamor, his ivory strands were a warmer blond, the irises of his eyes were copper, and the angles of his features were less pronounced. Even as a middle god, Cassian was still known to all mortals and needed disguise.

Finnian sighed and looked over at his sister. "Are you going to raise statues of us all?"

Naia gave a shrug, giving him a sidelong glance, full of playfulness. "Only of those I love." Her waist-length silver waves were the same onyx-black as Ronin's, her height shorter, and she'd added small imperfections to her divine features—a longer nose, thinner lips. Apparently, the mortals flocked to her when she revealed herself outside of certain sectors of the city. It was an attention Finnian could tell she was still not used to yet.

Wearing glamor came like second nature to him. It was why the moment he dropped into the city with Cassian, his hair shifted to the same silver shade as Naia's, and his features took on a more approachable cut, rather than a permanent scowl.

Finnian smiled and ran his fingers over the bronze plate at the foot of the statue that read:

Finnian, High God of Witchcraft and Sorcery,
founder of Hollow City.

His heart squeezed. The city around them was not built by his hands alone.

He swiped his thumb over the empty space beneath his name, a plume of magic etching letters into the metal.

Co-Founders: Isla Harper And Eleanor Jenkins.

Naia leaned over, grabbing Finnian's arm. "Runa will be delighted! Perhaps we can add statues of them as well. What do you think?" She twisted her head to her husband.

Ronin stood on her other side, expression casual. "Whatever you want, babe." The leader of the Blood Heretics looked the same: messy dark strands tied partially back, doing nothing to rid the curtain of bangs in his eyes, dressed in baggy black clothes that swallowed his physique.

Naia clicked her tongue with a smile.

Finnian rolled his eyes. "You add a statue of Ronin, and I will personally destroy it myself."

Naia giggled as Ronin scoffed in the backdrop.

"Dad said you would say something like that," Ash said.

Finnian looked down at his five-year-old nephew and met his deep-set gaze with a smirk. "Your father is a smart man, at times."

Ash traced the engraving of Isla and Eleanor's name on the plate, as if he could feel the magic particles webbed in its bronze.

"Your uncle is all talk." Cassian tilted forward to wink at Ash. "He would only vandalize it a bit."

Ash cocked his head up at him with raised eyebrows. "Dad also said to give you crap for trying to steal me as a baby."

The amusement on Cassian's face faltered, and he cleared his throat, straightening up. "Yes, well…"

Finnian barked out a laugh as Naia rolled her lips to downgrade her grin.

Ronin did no such thing. "That's my boy."

Ash peered up at Finnian intently, intrigued.

Finnian stared back at him, marveled by the little boy. He had traces of Naia with his wavy shoulder-length silver strands and kind aura; of Ronin with his eyes, as rich as the earth, and his witty remarks; of Father with his angular features and gentle disposition.

"Were they your friends?" Ash gestured to the names on the plate.

An ache in his chest throbbed, and he nodded. "They were my best friends."

"Iris's mom tells her stories of her great-great-great grandma Isla all the time. Says she was *badass*."

"Ashy darling, that is a curse word." Naia scrubbed her fingers through his hair.

"I don't say it unless it's what someone else said first," Ash mumbled to his mother, fixing his ruffled strands.

She huffed through a growing smile.

How can she quarrel with that?

Finnian gave a breathy laugh. "I, once, watched her shoot an arrow made of magic straight through a man's skull."

"Finny!" Naia scolded, lightly smacking him on the arm. "That's horrible!"

Ash's eyes grew wide with fascination. "Magical weapons, like my dad's briars?"

Finnian couldn't help the flat look that dawned over his expression. "Yes, but *much* cooler."

"They sure used to scare you shitless back in the day," Ronin drawled under his breath.

Cassian chuckled at Finnian's side.

Finnian shot Ronin a look of annoyance, and Ronin returned it with a clever smirk.

"Dad cursed," Ash said to his mother. "Are you going to scold *him*?"

Naia reached her arm out and flicked Ronin's chest with her full strength, knocking him back. "No, sir!"

Ash cackled at his father's dramatic reaction of recoiling and rubbing the spot on his pec.

A small laugh rumbled from Cassian as he watched.

This was Finnian's dream—to see his sister happy and loved, to be standing beside Cassian with nothing between them. A dream he'd held onto for years. Always at the end of the hardships.

Now that he'd arrived, he wasn't sure how to feel, or what to do with himself. A part of him itched to get lost in a potion recipe to soothe the voice in the back of his mind that said, *this will all end one day too.*

The other part of him had made peace with such truth. Nothing lasted forever, and while he disagreed and loathed that fact, he was slowly starting to accept it as a greater truth than himself.

Finnian rotated and took in the bustling of his city, the steady flow of traffic, travelers passing by on the sidewalks, those sitting at the outdoor tables of nearby restaurants and cafés.

He'd built something he was proud of—a home for Isla and Eleanor, for Naia and her family.

If only Father could've seen it—just once.

A sense of sorrow flooded his chest, and he exhaled.

Cassian shifted at his side and faced the city, hands tucked away in his pockets, resting his arm against Finnian's. Notes of lemon peel and the spice from his cologne drifted in the space between them.

Finnian glanced over at him. It was surreal, seeing him in broad daylight in a modern suit in the city they'd called home during the start of their relationship. A testament of how much time had passed.

"Your father knew of your city," Cassian said, peering straight ahead.

Finnian shouldn't have found it surprising how Cassian knew what he was thinking. "Through some divine connection of nature?"

"No, I showed him pictures. Online. We looked it up."

Finnian nodded slowly, processing. He gradually straightened his head to stare out at the city, his lips curving. "I wasn't aware you could get internet access in the Land of the Dead."

Cassian snorted. "I had to keep up with you somehow."

Warmth drenched his ribcage like syrup. "You looked me up."

"The mortals are fond of you. It appears they find you charming, despite your insufferable indifference."

Finnian's smile deepened at the sound of his light-hearted sarcasm. "I can be charming when I wish to be."

"Oh, I am aware." Cassian flashed his gaze to him.

Heat prickled in Finnian's cheeks.

He gave Cassian a sly smirk, knowing the effect it had.

Cassian's pupils flared in response to the look, swallowing the fiery rings of his irises.

Finnian winked at him as Naia hooked her arm around his elbow and rested her cheek on his shoulder.

"Could you imagine Father scouring the sidewalk with city-folk?" She chuckled.

"Like you have room to talk," Ronin piped in. "You gawked at *every-thing* your first year here."

Finnian puffed out a quiet laugh as Naia pinned Ronin with a look. "Says the man who *gawks* anytime I use my divine strength."

"I think that sort of thing warrants it."

Something tickled the inside of Finnian's hand.

He dropped his chin to see Ash staring eye-level at his relaxed palm, his arm slightly raised and his small fingers hovering inches from Finnian's, unsure if he should hold his hand or not.

The hesitation, the urge for affection—such childlike innocence, wonder that Finnian could recall once feeling.

Death is not about separation.

Finnian smiled to himself.

Death is about peace.

He finally understood it as he grabbed his nephew's tiny hand.

*A promise to find those we **are intertwined** with in life.*

TOGETHER, they teleported.

The salty, humid air stuck to Finnian's skin. Old, dusty memories of his childhood sprung to mind—dangling his legs in the water hole at Naia's side, his back in the sand at Father's favorite abandoned cove, weaving breadfruit leaves with his magic.

Outstretched before them was the tropical greenery of Nohealani Island. The sea-breeze slapped at their backs, tossing their hair haphazardly in all directions.

Naia held the porcelain jar to her chest, tears already cresting in her eyes.

Ronin gently tapped on Ash's shoulder, beckoning him to stand back a few paces alongside him and Cassian. "Remember what we talked about last night?" He placed his index finger over his lips, a silent request to keep quiet.

Ash nodded obediently up at his father and stood respectfully still, watching Finnian and Naia.

They had agreed on this days ago, after Mavros delivered the jar of their father's ashes. They were to spread them on the island, the last place in the Mortal Land he called home.

Naia stepped up to the headstone jutting out of the sand. Along its granite read: *The High God of Nature, Vale*. Wreaths and garlands of tropical flowers decorated its corners and the ground around it. The islanders, no doubt.

Finnian told his legs to move, to follow Naia, but his body felt frozen.

Ash appeared at his side and looked up at him, somberly so. He gave Finnian's hand a reassuring squeeze before releasing it.

The act was almost enough to break Finnian.

He let out a breath and joined Naia's side.

"Father would pinch my cheeks during dinner feasts to cheer me up, after Mira scolded me for my table manners," he said. "I refused to smile for him, therefore he'd give up and sit his hands back down in his lap. Only, a few minutes later, I would nearly bite down on my spoon, startled by the vine tickling up my pant leg."

A teary giggle slipped out of Naia. "Or the time he summoned bees to infiltrate the great hall during breakfast when the triplets were antagonizing you."

It was Finnian's seventh year. While he hardly recalled the topic that he and Malik had gotten into it over, he had been close to losing control of his magic and sending the silverware spiking through his skull. Father must've sensed such, because seconds before Finnian reacted, a swarm of bees randomly burst into the hall.

Finnian smiled widely. "Or the time he grew bouquets for the kitchen maids to thank them for their hard work, and they all became infatuated with him and kept baking him ginger loaves."

A cackle burst from Naia. "He never knew!"

"He would set the loaves aside and just drink his tea."

"And they kept baking them for him!"

"He must've had hundreds of them!"

They both shook with laughter, hanging onto each other, imagining Father, oblivious, as batting-eyed maids circled around him.

Finnian wiped the tears at the corners of his eyes, releasing a long, sated exhale.

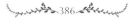

They both grew quiet as the weight sank in. That those amusing moments were ones of the past. Memories were all they had left of him, and they overflowed.

The back of Finnian's nose stung. He straightened his shoulders and held onto Naia's arm, reminding his trembling limbs that he had support.

Fixing his gaze out among the dense thicket of tropical ferns and palms, he let out a shaky breath. "He would want to be one with the sand."

Naia looked up at him, her round eyes pooling. "Sand travels the waters," she recited with a sad smile, "it crests in the waves and delivers onto the shore with the tide. It remains for as long as it needs, and then it is pulled back and continues the cycle over again."

"It is the way of nature; the way of life," Finnian's voice coated thick with tears, the words embedded in the deepest waters of his mind from all the times Father explained it to them.

Naia removed the lid to the jar and grabbed a fistful of Father's ashes.

She drew in a breath. "I suppose there are a million sentiments I could express to you, but I believe you already know just how much you meant to me. Therefore, I will leave you with this: your love is everything to me. Words would never be enough for me to express how grateful I am to be your daughter. Thank you for teaching me how to be vulnerable, to observe and show kindness to others, for always being my light in the darkness." As the words left her mouth, she sprinkled the remains in the sand around her feet.

She handed off the jar to Finnian, and it felt as if it held basalt.

His stomach knotted and his limbs locked up, despite his brain's orders to *do as she did.*

The comforting touch of Cassian's hands settled on top of his shoulders as he moved up behind him, providing an instant release to the ache drilling in his chest. It gave Finnian enough courage to dip his hand into the jar.

He expected the ashes to feel different, divine somehow, but they didn't. They were light—lighter than the granules of sand beneath him. They squished in between his closed fingers. Proof of his father's existence; of the long life he lived. It seemed unfair, somehow.

"There is impact," Cassian whispered in his ear. "Impact on those who touch our lives. You came into mine and I haven't been the same since. The time we were apart, you remained etched deep in my soul, Finny. That is what it means to live, to love. There is purpose in that. Vale touched the lives of more souls than you could ever imagine."

He was right. From a young age, Finnian recognized that about his father. It was impossible not to smile when he came into a room. When he spoke to a person, he granted them his full attention. He was considerate and always going out of his way to help others—the kitchen maids and their bouquets, sneaking stationed guards sweet treats from the feast, calling the staff of the palace by name and inquiring about their children.

Finnian lifted his fist from the jar and held it out. A memory of his boyhood lit behind his eyes, as a child, gazing up at Father, the stream of morning light feathering around him in rays of cornflower through the layers of the sea; Father looking down at him, smiling softly.

His ashes were the last tangible thing Finnian had left of him.

"I don't want to let go."

I am scared to let go.

Ash squealed, the sound of his feet squeaked in the sand. "He's here!"

Finnian, Naia, and Cassian both turned to look.

Ash hopped around, and his footprints in the sand quickly filled with an assortment of blossoms—dahlias, peonies, moonflowers, baby's breath, poppies, hibiscus.

I am always with you.

A sob caught in Finnian's throat.

Naia threw her hand over her mouth as a cry sprang loose.

"Grandpa Vale must not be that far away if he can grow us flowers!" Ash trailed around Ronin, his footprints becoming beautiful floral arrangements. "Do you see? Mama, look!" He beamed, pointing down at them. "Uncle Finny!"

"Yeah," Ronin said, his voice tottering with tears of his own as he glanced up at Naia. "He's not far away."

Cassian smiled broadly at Finnian, all-knowing.

The only truly eternal thing in life was not the life of a god or a goddess, but the love that gathered in one's soul, transcending flesh and scouring the edge of the dawn to reunite us in small moments. Perhaps that was the entire meaning of life, to always find each other again.

Naia buried into Finnian's side, her tears dampening the material of his shirt and sticking to his chest.

Finnian held her tightly with one arm, the ashes sprinkling from the crevices of his enclosed fingers in his other hand.

"I love you, Father." Releasing one finger at a time, he slowly let go.

NESTLED in a forest off the outskirts of Augustus, their stone cottage sat isolated from the world.

A faint trail of smoke curled from the chimney. Frost coated the branches of nearby evergreens, each tendril of grass, and the glittering stalks of rosemary, sage, and mint in the garden.

The morning had never appealed to Finnian. He preferred nighttime, when the world and the mortals silenced. Though, in his new life, he was beginning to prefer the dawn—a scratch at their front door from their puppy whimpering, a sound he could not hear without his hearing aid, but knew when it occurred from Cassian jumping out of bed in nothing but a flattering pair of velvety boxers to scoop up Juniper and rush her out onto the front lawn.

Finnian loved leaning on the doorframe and watching Cassian cheer the pup on as they both drew shapes in the icy grass.

A bird house rested underneath the nearby lemon tree, a resident inside, its cobalt feathers marked with dripping caramel. Alke never strayed far, and it had become too vexing for Mavros to try and contain him in the Land—an entertaining struggle that Finnian couldn't resist smirking at.

The aroma of espresso, paprika, and freshly baked sourdough wafted throughout the house. The dance of a string quartet sang from a spinning vinyl record. All worries were forgotten as Finnian snuck up behind Cassian at the stove and whispered kisses down his neck. Clothes were shucked, and they found themselves under the satin sheets of their bed, lost in each other's skin.

Soft and tender top-lip kisses, dragging and hazy. Slow hands, grazing, exploring, as if it was the first time they'd touched. He loved the way Cassian trembled beneath him, the way his eyes glowed with pleasure.

Once was never enough to sate Finnian. He was greedy and his thirst was unquenchable. He wanted to lose himself in Cassian's breath, sink deeply beneath his skin, and burn there forever.

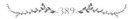

Life with Cassian was chilled nights snuggled up by the fireplace, with Juniper burrowed in the mountain of blankets strewn over their sofa; 2AM baking extravaganzas after Cassian found *another* new recipe; Finnian casting a spell on the pastries in the oven when Cassian wasn't looking to correct their flattening posture; long strolls through Augustus's countryside during the summer, the stream trickling in the background alongside the crickets and frog calls, fireflies glowing like stars between the trees, dandelions and other herbs stuffed in Finnian's pockets; Naia pulling up in their driveway, and Ash spilling out of the backseat and up the front porch steps, excited to spend the weekend with his uncles; days hunched over a workbench, the spiced aroma of cinnamon, and a bubbling cauldron with an eagerness in Finnian's fingertips as he scribbled notes in his grimoire; Cassian plucking mint leaves and squeezing lemons by hand for a delicious, summer ambrosia; sunset lounges on the patio, a book in Cassian's hand as he stole peeks over the top of the page at Finnian, drawing sigils on the boards and growing sagebrush from the runes.

"What would you like to do today?" Cassian lowered his book to his chest and pet soft strokes over Juniper's head, snuggled in his lap.

Finnian sipped on his iced cold brew, peering out at the blush and ginger strokes across the sapphire horizon. They had no summons, no one waiting for their orders or guidance. They had each other and all the time in the world.

Finnian turned his head and met Cassian's content gaze, eyes like small galaxies, and smiled softly. "Whatever you wish."

EPILOGUE

THE FIRST TIME Acacius saw her, the need to destroy everything in his path ceased.

He'd never longed for stillness—the kind mortals sought from overlooking a lake at dawn, or the hush at dusk when the world softened. Not until Ruelle. The engrained need constantly stirring within him to leave chaos in his path had quieted. If only for a second.

Ruelle glittered like frost, turning everything she touched to beauty.

As he stared at her now, absent of her divine complexion, her auburn waves no longer glistening like velour, he still thought the same of her.

She stood across the room from him in a gust of moths, their wings fluttering over the soft skin of her rosy-shaded cheeks. Clutched in the grip of her small fingers dangled a gold thread. She held a dagger in her other hand, an ancient relic only the High Goddess of Fate could use. Its silver blade was double pronged with a citrine gemstone pommel. The dagger's aura pulsed with rich, divine power.

Acacius's insides twisted.

He started towards her, but she shook her head. "Stay where you are."

"Put away the dagger," he commanded, the muscles in his shoulders tensing. "And I will."

"You know that is not how this works." As she spoke the words, Acacius's moths crystalized and fell like hail. Their frozen bodies shattered across the floor of his home.

When she is gone, these remnants are all I will have left of her.

The thought burned his throat. Panic welled up in his chest, and he stormed across the room for her.

She inclined her head and threads clawed from her forearms and tangled around his limbs. They bound tightly and his knees buckled. He shouted as he strained his arms against their grip.

"Ruelle!" he snarled, his heart tattering at the sight of her calmness. Peace was already softening her features, and she held a look of knowing in her gaze, almost as if she pitied him.

A sickness turned in his stomach as his eyes flashed from her face to the gold thread hanging in between her fingers. It was unlike the others that he'd glimpsed throughout the years. A part of him knew whose it was, but the other part of him wasn't willing to accept it.

This was the last thing he'd expected when he'd teleported her from the Land of the Dead and into his realm. He was prepared to console her, to vow that the Council would grant her immortality back. He'd ensure it.

But the moment they landed within the walls of his home, she'd forced them apart with her threads and drew out the dagger. She had it with her all along.

He knew. Dammit, he knew what she was doing. He knew, but he didn't want to stare down the truth.

Ruelle wanted the Himura demigod's blood to ensure it did not get used on herself or anyone else. She told him so.

Ruelle is lying, and it is not me who she is lying to.

Cassian's words returned to him, sharp and painful.

Acacius fought against the threads bound around him. It was no use. He couldn't free himself through physical strength to stop her.

His whole body slackened, and he looked up at her. "I know I am not the one you want." His voice cracked. "I know you do not love me as I love you, but I will do anything. *Anything* for you. Please, let that be enough. Let *me* be enough for you."

She was all he could think about. The sheets of her bed tousled, the early rose-gold sunlight slipping through her window, her strands spread across his arm, her lips on his, her presence beside him, her words filling him.

Ruelle slowly approached him. A sign that his words had reached her.

She leaned down and kissed his forehead. "I love you, Acacius, I do. There is no question of that. But I must do this, for me."

His eyes fell shut, her decisiveness stabbing through his heart. The pain stole his breath, and a lump swelled in his throat. "I love you. *I love you, Ruelle*. We can have a happy life together. Please, allow me to show you."

"It is not enough." She guided his chin up with her fingers, meeting his eyes. "You are not the one I long for, Acacius."

Her words tattered like razors mixed in the blood of his heart, shredding every chamber, every artery, every valve, to slivers.

He wanted to believe their story had never been a placeholder for her. A pawn until she reunited with Klaus. He had gazed into her eyes hundreds of times, but he'd never looked past the surface, never truly delved deeply within them, too terrified of what he'd find.

"You planned it all." Tears slipped down his cheeks, blurring the shape of her in front of him. "It is why you continuously watched over Naia's Fate, why you broke apart Cassian and Saoirse, why you threatened to unravel his and Finnian's threads. You could see it all intertwined and how your life would end."

"I did."

Her confession was another cut.

"Then why not use the blood on yourself? You had it in your hands." His tone was thick with disapproval, of a gut-wrenching rage. He knew the answer, having been with Ruelle long enough to know the complexities of Fate, but he needed to hear the words directly from her.

"It would've caused ripples in others' Fates. Vale was meant to die. Naia was meant to take away my immortality. Just as I was meant to cut my own thread."

He lowered his head.

One finger at a time, she lifted her hand from his face. "You deserve someone who truly loves you, Acacius. I cannot be that. When I am gone, please do not think of me. Find your own happiness, as I am."

Acacius stared down at the floor, her bare feet caught in his periphery. Her light skin was dirt-stained and speckled with dried blood. The imperfections were a horrid reminder of her mortality, of the past few hours and how none of it was only a nightmare. The finality of her words was real, and there was nothing he could do.

The tears were endless, dripping like rain from his eyes. This was the end, and he knew it. If she would stay, he would gladly be second-best for the rest of their days, even knowing that he could never fill her heart the way Klaus had.

The idea of her disappearing from his life made it difficult to draw in a breath. Inky splotches painted the edges of his visions. The blood of his pulse throbbed in his ears.

"You have my gratitude for everything, Acacius," she said, her voice wobbly with her own tears. "Please take care of yourself."

He sobbed, unable to watch. Everything in him screamed to fight through the threads holding him captive, but a distant part of him wished to respect her desires. The destiny she'd meticulously tracked to arrive on this day.

The slice of the dagger, the tearing of her thread—it was deafening. It echoed in his ears, again and again.

He lifted his chin and watched it play out, slow, unmerciful. The crumble of her knees, the fall of her body, the way her eyelids fluttered closed right before her head hit the floor. Her long hair fanned around her face. She held the dagger in her uncurling grasp, one half of her thread in the other.

No.

Acacius's body shook with disbelief.

No. She can't be—

The threads around him crumbled and turned to dust.

She isn't—

His trembling hands slid over the sides of his head, tangling in his strands.

Dead.

He blinked through his fuzzy vision down at her, analyzing the emptiness in the room. The plush, sweet, cloud-like presence of her aura that filled every space she was in—it was gone. He felt the absence of it the moment she'd cut the thread.

Pain stabbed through his chest, and he felt overwhelmingly dizzy. Time slurred around him. He remained stuck in the moment, gaping at her corpse, drowning in the marrow-deep ache of his splintering heart.

"Ruelle?" he croaked, crawling to grab her hand. "Ruelle!"

He hauled her up in his arms and hugged his head into her chest as he wept.

WIND ruffled the tops of the lavender stalks. Their purple tips filled the atmosphere with a sweet, earthy fragrance.

Acacius stood atop the knoll under a wisteria, its plum blossoms adorning the tree like an umbrella. The wispy branches swayed around him as he peered into the distance.

Ruelle hung around a man's neck, a vibrant smile lit over her face. She held him with fervor, a passion she'd never shared with Acacius before. Laughter spilled from her lips before she pressed them into the man's.

That true, pure happiness—she could've one day found it in him. If only she'd had more time to let go of Klaus, she would've seen Acacius and the wellspring of love pouring out of him.

The chasm of emptiness mined deeper into his core.

The loss. The pain. Ruelle's fate could've been different.

He obsessively turned the past around in his mind.

Everything had gone wrong the moment he entrusted Marina to help him find the Himura demigod's blood. If she would've handed it over to him, he could've gotten rid of it and brought peace between her and Cassian. Naia would've never appeared and Ruelle would still be at his side.

Marina was to blame for his sorrows.

The High Goddess of Night had not known true Chaos; had never felt the wrath of insatiable Ruin. Wherever she was, he would find her and destroy her for what she'd taken from him.

Without Ruelle, his devotion withered and burned and turned into a violent, vengeful smoke.

ACKNOWLEDGEMENTS

THIS was my first time writing a sequel. I went into it with more nerves and fears than I care to admit. Naia's story was within the realms of my comfort zone, while Finnian's story presented many challenges. I was terrified I would not be able to execute the vision I had in mind.

Finnian is calculated, petty at times, and stubborn to a fault. However, beneath his complex nature, he's got a heart of gold. And as much as I found myself struggling to mold his story, I've never had something come so naturally, creativity-wise.

This book is where I found my stride, my voice. I was proud of the story I'd told in *The Goddess Of*, and I am equally proud of *Even in Death*. It carries an ambition I was afraid I would not reach.

This book wouldn't have breath without the help of many.

First and foremost, to Sleep Token, who will probably never read this, but who I owe all my gratitude to. If it wasn't for your music, I'd probably still be banging my head against my desk with a bad case of writer's block. If you ever do read this: thank you for existing and creating.

To Ariel, my amazing critique partner, for always reading through my terrible first drafts and gushing about them. I am so happy that I found you.

To Kar, a reader that quickly turned into a friend. You have no idea how big I smiled the first time you tagged me in a post, raving about *The Goddess Of*. Readers like you are the reason I keep going. Thank you for every post, every share, every little thing you do to support me and my stories, and for beta reading *Even in Death*.

To Persephone, for taking time out of your busy schedule to beta read *Even in Death* for me. When I first stumbled across your Instagram page years ago, I fell in love with your moody/gothic vibe and all your playlists, and I thought, *I want to know her!* And now here we are. You have become such a sweet friend to me.

To Holly, for acting as a sensitivity reader to Finnian's impairment. Your detailed notes and feedback helped me shape Finnian's character, and for that I am so grateful. Please know that *your* story moved me, and I hope to do the same for those who read Finnian's.

To Tessa, my shepherd in the darkness. Thank you for always guiding me to my full potential.

To Rena, for your dedication in creating such divine art for my books. When we started the cover for book two, we quickly realized that we were going to have to step it up if we wanted to create something as good as (or better than) book one. You understood the assignment and completely outdid yourself with *Even in Death*. I can't wait to see what we come up with on the next book! I am so incredibly grateful to have you in my corner.

To Brit, my editor. Thank you for continuing to help me grow, and for all your kind comments. I would not be the writer that I am right now without your guidance.

To Tara, for making my audiobook dreams come true. When I received the email from you to turn *The Fragile Divine* into a set of audiobooks, I was convinced it was a scam. A signed contract later, and book one is out on all audiobook platforms with book two not far behind it. Whatever potential you saw in me and my work, thank you for giving me a chance.

Also, to Dreamscape Media and the whole team, thank you for making the process of turning my books into audiobooks so seamless. You make me, as a creator, feel seen and heard, and I appreciate that so much.

To Karina, for always creating beautiful masterpieces for my stories, and for putting so much passion into Finnian and Cassian's commission. It was such an honor to be able to include it in the book. You are such a lovely human, and I am so happy to know you.

To all the lovely artists who have created other stunning commissions for Finnian and Cassian's story: @lulybot, @luxurybanshee, @dar.a_art, @ladyeruart, and @avendell.

To Mia, Sunday, and Aki, my furry companions that never leave my side—through the late nights and the days where I am glued to my computer. I've always said we don't deserve dogs, but damn it, I am so happy we live in a world where they exist.

To Paris, because I think of you every time I sit down and write, especially when I am snuggled under an electric blanket. It's not the same without you.

To Mom and Sis, my two biggest cheerleaders, for your incessant questions and for begging me to constantly tell you what is going to happen in the next book. (Spoiler: I have no idea.) Your passion and adoration for this world and these characters that I've created are what keep me going. I love you both so much.

To Dad, Brandon, Ariel, my grandparents—for all the times you proudly tell people of my book and urge them to go buy it. Just know that I am honored, and your support means everything to me.

To Leo and Ema. Always dream big.

To Chase. My life partner, my lover, my friend, my companion, my everything. There are so many things I could list off, but we both know that'd be the length of another novel. Just know that I couldn't do or *be* any of this without you. I love you, today, and every day beyond.

And to the readers:

This was my journey of how to make sense of endings, of death, and of separation. They are inevitable. The things we cannot avoid, and as we become older, they greet us more frequently. As someone who is sensitive and loves wholly, these topics are a constant anxiety that I face. So of course, I was like, "Let's write a book where the main theme is death, and the protagonist falls in love with the embodiment of it!"

The level of vulnerability it took to write this book was terrifying, but I think the world needs more of that. We all search for something real, even if we don't realize it or not. In relationships, jobs, daily life. So, I hope that through my vulnerability, you were able to resonate with it, that you came out of this book and felt something, *anything*. Because that's how you know it was real.

Thank you for being here, for showing up and giving my book a chance. To those who signed up for the cover reveal, for ARCs, who sent me DMs, posted about my books, left reviews, hyped it up through word of mouth, and everything in between—you've made this year so special and surreal.

I say this all the time, but don't think for a moment that it's just empty words: your support means *everything* to me. I get to do the thing I love every single day because of you.

I promise to continue to grow as a storyteller and become better in my craft. I can't wait to write more stories in this world. I hope you will continue to follow along through this journey.

RANDI is a lover of evocative words. She aspires to create characters that live on with her readers. When she's not daydreaming about her next story, you can find her staying up too late, immersed in a book or webtoon with coffee in hand, or enjoying the company of her husband and their three dogs.

You can find her on Instagram (@randimgarner) where you can sign up for her newsletter and stay up to date with her upcoming releases.

Made in the USA
Monee, IL
21 March 2025

c08ec3ec-623a-49a7-ba5d-41accb08f0b5R01